TO THE DEATH

Books by
PATRICK ROBINSON:

NOVELS

Ghost Force

Hunter Killer

Scimitar SL2

Barracuda 945

Slider

The Shark Mutiny

U.S.S. Seawolf

H.M.S. Unseen

Kilo Class

Nimitz Class

NON-FICTION

Lone Survivor (written with Marcus Luttrell)

Horsetrader: Robert Sangster and the Rise and Fall of the Sport of Kings (written with Nick Robinson)

One Hundred Days: The Memoirs of the Falklands Battle Group Commander (written with Admiral Sir John Woodward)

True Blue (written with Daniel Topolski)

Born to Win (written with John Bertrand)

The Golden Post (written with Richard S. Reeves)

Decade of Champions: The Greatest Years in the History of Thoroughbred Racing, 1970–1980 (written with Richard S. Reeves)

Classic Lines: A Gallery of the Great Thoroughbreds (written with Richard S. Reeves)

TO THE DEATH

A new novel by

PATRICK
ROBINSON

Vanguard Press
A Member of the Perseus Books Group

Published by Vanguard Press
A Member of the Perseus Books Group

Vanguard Press books are available at special discounts for bulk
purchases in the U.S. by corporations, institutions, and other organizations.
For more information, please contact the Special Markets Department
at the Perseus Books Group, 2300 Chestnut Street, Suite 200,
Philadelphia, PA 19103, or call (800) 810-4145, ext. 5000, or e-mail
special.markets@perseusbooks.com.

Designed by Trish Wilkinson
Set in 11 point Minion

Library of Congress Cataloging-in-Publication Data

Robinson, Patrick, 1939–
    To the death : a new novel by / Patrick Robinson.
        p.   cm.
    ISBN 978-1-59315-476-9
    1. Presidents—United States—Staff—Fiction. 2. Terrorism—Fiction.
3. Terrorists—Fiction. I. Title.
PR6068.O1959T6 2007
823'.914—dc22   2008007401

10 9 8 7 6 5 4 3 2 1

CAST OF PRINCIPAL CHARACTERS

United States Senior Command
Paul Bedford (President of the United States)
Professor Alan Brett (National Security Adviser)
Admiral Arnold Morgan (Personal Adviser to the President)
Rear Admiral George Morris (Director, National Security Agency)
Lt. Commander Jimmy Ramshawe (Assistant Director, NSA)
Vice Admiral John Bergstrom (C-in-C, SPECWARCOM)

United States Navy
Commander Rick Hunter (SEAL team leader) (recalled)
Commander Bob Wallace (USS *Grabber*)
CPO Mark Coulson (SEAL dive chief)
LPO Ray Flamini (SEAL diver)
Commander Hank Redford (USS *Cheyenne*)
CPO Skip Gowans (Sonar, USS *Cheyenne*)

U.S. Police Officers
Pete Mackay (Boston Police Department)
Danny Kearns (Boston Police Department)
Mike Carman (NYPD)
Joe Pallizi (NYPD)

American Travelers

Donald Martin (Boston financier)

Elliott Gardner (President, Boston corporation)

Middle East Jihadists

General Ravi Rashood (C-in-C, Hamas)

Mrs. Shakira Rashood (Hamas field agent)

Ramon Salman (Boston-based Hamas chief)

Reza Aghani (Boston terrorist)

Mohammed Rahman (Palm Beach insurgent)

Commodore Tariq Fahd (First Minister, Hamas)

Major Faisal Sabah (2/IC, Hamas, Gaza)

Colonel Hassad Abdullah (Hamas field officer)

Fausi (Jordanian attaché/chauffeur)

Ahmed (Jordanian embassy cultural attaché/spy)

Captain Mohammed Abad (CO, Iranian submarine)

Lieutenant Rudi Alaam (Navigation Officer, Iranian submarine)

National Air Traffic Control

Steve Farrell (Radar Operator)

Northeastern Air Defense

Colonel Rick Morry

Major Scott Freeman

Washington Writers

Anthony Hyman (White House Presidential Staff)

Henry Brady (*Washington Post*)

Israeli Personnel

Ambassador David Gavron

Colonel Ben Joel (Mossad team leader)

Lt. Colonel John Rabin (Explosives Chief)

Major Itzaak Sherman (Israeli patriot)

Abraham (Bodyguard and hitman)

Brockhurst, Virginia

> Emily Gallagher (Mother of Mrs. Arnold Morgan)
> Jim Caborn (Manager, Estuary Hotel)
> Detective Joe Segel (Murder inquiry)
> Matt Barker (garage owner) (dec.)
> Fred Mitchell (Doorman, Chesapeake Heights)

Ireland

> Detective Superintendent Ray McDwyer (Skibbereen Police)
> Officer Joe Carey
> Jerry O'Connell (West Cork farmer) (dec.)
> Patrick O'Driscoll (Central Milk Corporation)
> Mick Barton (Shamrock Café, Skibbereen)
> Bill Stannard (Captain, *Yonder,* Crookhaven)

London

> Reggie Milton (Dover Street doorman)
> George Kallan (Admiral Morgan's bodyguard) (dec.)
> Al Thompson (Chief bodyguard)

Scotland

> Admiral Sir Iain and Lady MacLean

CHAPTER 1

Logan International Airport, which sits atop a zillion-ton concrete promontory, hemmed in by runways, tunnels, and the harbor, was heaving with travelers. Thousands of them, packed into lines for tickets, lines for check-in, lines for security, lines for coffee, coke, donuts. They even had lines for cheeseburgers, and it was not yet 8 A.M. on a gloomy, freezing January morning.

South. South. The demand was always south. South to Florida. South to Antigua, Barbuda, St. Barts, south to the islands, any island, anywhere to get the hell out of this cold, snow, sleet, and ice. It was the peak of the season. High fares. Ruinous hotel bills. Nobody cared. This was the icebound airport of the winter-grim northeastern city of Boston, Massachusetts. Beyond the departure terminals, a bitter easterly wind howled straight off the slate-gray waters of Massachusetts Bay. A mile to the west stood the frozen granite towers of the downtown area.

All this had once been home to a battle-hardened race of New Englanders who accepted the cold, fought it, and shrugged it off. Not any more. Modern prosperity, air travel, and a sense of indignation and entitlement pervaded. *Goddammit, I don't need this tundra crap. Get me out of here.*

Thus the eager vacationers collided in a tidal surge with the already-irritated business crowd, which was, *en masse*, fed up with late takeoffs. As Monday mornings go, this one was up and running.

"This is totally fucking crazy," muttered Officer Pete Mackay, adjusting his gloved hands on his light machine gun as he moved through the crowd.

"Tell me about it," said his teammate, Officer Danny Kearns. "Osama bin Asshole could vanish without a trace in the freakin' donut queue."

Mackay and Kearns were buddies beyond the confines of the Boston Police Department. Each of them brought a missionary zeal to the fan base of the New England Patriots. For almost eleven months of every year, and sometimes for twelve, they believed to the depths of their souls that this year was theirs, that the glorious years of Super Bowl victories would stand before them again.

They lived football. They ate and slept football. Each of them would awake in the night, leading the blitz as the Patriots surged forward; the big, bullnecked Pete Mackay, in his dreams the greatest defensive lineman who ever lived; Danny, more modestly, the fastest running back on earth. Whenever they could, they went to the games together, taking turns bringing the kids, Pete's Patrick and Sean, Danny's Mikey and Ray.

Both cops were fifth-generation Boston Irish; they both lived on the south side of the city, across the water from the airport. And their great-great-grandparents had emigrated from Ireland around the same time, right after the famine. No one could remember when the Mackays and the Kearnses did not know each other. Both Pete's and Danny's fathers had been Boston cops.

The whole lot of them had attended the same grade school in Southie, played football together, played baseball together in the streets, got in fights with their neighbors, and endured a cheerful scrappy childhood. Pete and Danny both made it to Boston University, and both played football—though not at the highest level, however much effort they put in.

Subsequently, both men viewed the Patriots with a kind of stricken pride, a complicated self-irony that burst into an unreasoning, inflamed passion when the Barbarians were at the gate—that is, when any other team from any other city in the United States challenged the boys from Foxborough.

As a cop, the 34-year-old Pete Mackay was scheduled to go right to the top. He was ambitious, tough, and cynical, though not unreasonably. In action, he was still fast on his feet and a master at dealing with the occasional outbreak of inner-city violence. Like Danny, he was an expert marksman. Also, he packed a right hook like a jackhammer, should anyone be foolish enough to attack him.

Officer Kearns, the resident comedian of the precinct, was not quite so dedicated to the police department. He had a very beautiful Italian wife, Louise, and by the end of most days he was about ready to call it quits and get home to the family. His straight man, Pete, also had a pretty wife, Marie, but he was always looking around for crimes to investigate, chatting with the detectives, moving steadily toward the day when he would become Detective Sergeant Mackay.

They were a popular team, Mackay and Kearns, and they both spent a lot of extra hours raising funds for the families of police officers killed or injured in action.

This morning, in the jostling hub of the airport's Terminal C, they were on high alert for anything that looked even remotely suspicious. Normally they patrolled slowly, moving from one end of the terminal to the other but never straying too far from the sightline of the security staff.

This morning it was more difficult, owing to the sheer volume of passengers. The shouts of the airline staff rose above the throng—*This way, sir . . . I'm sorry, sir—right to the end of that queue right there . . . We're moving it along, sir, just as fast as we can . . . just keep moving along . . . keep moving right along.*

"Jesus, Pete," said Danny. "I was in Greece one time, and they treated herds of fucking billygoats better'n this."

Pete Mackay laughed, like always at Danny's humor. But then the innate Boston cop on terrorist alert took over. "Yeah, but this is serious. We couldn't hardly move if anything happened. I been trying to calculate, maybe a full half-minute from here to get to the security guys—unless we knock down a coupla dozen passengers."

"You mean like Ryman against the Steelers last month—that time he took three defensive linemen with him—hell! That was some play."

"I guess that's the kind of thing—a head-down rush. But seriously, these are tough operating conditions, and we have to stay in view of the passengers and staff."

"Sure as hell be better if we could move a coupla feet without crashing into someone."

The two police officers tried to move along toward the head of the queue, but turned back. "Just don't want to get out of sight of security, that's all," said Mackay.

Donald Martin was the junior vice president of a Boston brokerage house, and he was doing his level best to clear the new passport control system and get on a flight to Atlanta. He had no baggage and expected to be back home in Newton, west of Boston, by midnight.

He was traveling with the president of his corporation, a silver-haired financier, a Boston Brahmin named Elliott Gardner, thirty years his senior. Donald was quietly reading the *Globe;* his boss was staring somewhat aimlessly into the distance, bored sideways by the airport procedures, unamused that their first-class tickets did not allow them to bypass this unattractive closeness to the rank and file. Particularly as the queue had come to a tiresome halt.

Behind them stood one passenger, apparently alone, and behind him was a family, two very young children presumably with mom and dad. They had a lot of baggage piled on a cart. One child was screaming. Elliott Gardner hoped to god that the family was not traveling first-class on Delta to Atlanta.

"WA-HAAAAAH!" wailed the child. "Jesus Christ," muttered Elliott Gardner. And then he felt a mild tap on the shoulder. The passenger behind him was making contact. He turned around and came face-to-face with a youngish man, well dressed, no more than thirty, of decidedly Middle Eastern appearance. He could have been Turkish or Arabian, but not Jewish or even Israeli. This was a face born and bred in desert or casbah.

The man smiled broadly. "Excuse me, sir," he said. "I have two quite heavy briefcases here, and I'm just going over there to Starbucks for some coffee. Would you mind keeping an eye on one of them for me—kick it along if the queue moves?"

Elliott glanced down at the brown leather briefcase on the floor. A well-mannered man, unaccustomed to rudeness, he replied, "No problem. Leave it right there."

Donald Martin absent-mindedly looked up from his newspaper and asked, "What did he want?"

"Oh, just to watch his briefcase while he went for coffee—he's over there, heading for Starbucks. Guess I should have had him get some for us, since the goddamned queue has stalled."

"Where is he?" said Martin, suddenly alert.

"Just over there at the Starbucks counter."

"What's he wearing?"

"Some kind of tan-colored jacket, I guess."

Martin swung around and pointed, "You mean him, that guy moving down the hallway, against the crowd?"

"Yeah, dark hair, that's him. What's up, Don?"

"Well, he just walked straight past Starbucks, for a start."

"Probably going to take a leak," replied Elliott.

"Well, he just broke every rule in the book, about leaving luggage unattended. And so did you. You have no idea what's in that briefcase. AND the guy looks like a fucking Arab."

Elliott Gardner looked startled at this apparent brush with a dangerous corner of the outside world. And his very junior vice president threw his right arm in the air and looked straight across the crowd to the patrolling Pete Mackay and Danny Kearns.

"*OFFICER!*" he yelled, loudly. Very loudly. "*RIGHT HERE—OVER HERE, PLEASE!*"

Officer Mackay spun around. He could see Don Martin's raised arm, and he dodged and ducked thirty yards through the crowd. Danny Kearns was right behind him.

When they arrived, Donald Martin was herding people back, away from the briefcase, which now stood in solitude like a couple of roosters in a cockfight, hemmed in by the spectators.

"Officer," said Martin, "a guy who looked like some kind of an Arab left that case right there and said he was going to Starbucks for coffee. But he didn't. He went right past Starbucks, and he's on his way out of the building right down that corridor."

Pete Mackay grabbed a small state-of-the-art stethoscope from his belt and stuck one end into each ear, the long tube onto the briefcase. "Jesus Christ!" he breathed. "Danny, there's a slight ticking sound. Get the detector."

Danny Kearns pulled a wire contraption from his belt and held it against the case. It immediately bleeped. "That's metal inside, Pete, and possibly explosive. This is a fucking live one."

"What's he wearing?" yelled Pete. "What the hell's he wearing?"

"Tan-colored jacket," replied Elliott Gardner. "Black T-shirt. He's not tall, short black hair. Looks obviously Arabian."

"GO GET HIM, PETE! LET ME TAKE CARE OF THIS."

Danny Kearns had patrolled for a lot of hours in Boston's airport. And he knew the real estate. Out through the wide glass doors, there was a four-lane throughway for dropoffs, cars, limos, and buses. Officer Kearns was accustomed to making split-second decisions, but had not previously been confronted by anything quite so urgent. Whether to evacuate the terminal as fast as possible? Or to take the death-or-glory route, grab the briefcase and get it out of here, hoping to Christ the sonofabitch didn't blow?

The latter course held another diabolical question—what to do with the damn thing once it was outside? The terminal on the departures level was surrounded by concrete parking lots, and Danny Kearns sure as hell didn't want to be holding the goddamned time bomb for longer than necessary.

His mind raced. If he flung the briefcase into the concrete ramparts of the parking garage, he'd wreck a few cars and maybe knock down a couple of floors, maybe injure or even kill a dozen people. If he left it in the terminal while he ordered people out, it would surely kill a thousand.

No contest. Danny Kearns, Patriots fan, husband of the beautiful Louise, father of Mikey and Ray, grabbed the briefcase. He held it in the classic grip of the running back, tucked against his body, his right hand securing its underside. Instincts, honed from watching thousands of hours of NFL football, caused him to run with a slightly lower gait than normal.

He looked ahead at the glass doors, and he set off, legs pumping, running hard for the first objective, brushing aside passengers, hitting anyone in the way with a crunching shoulder charge. Ahead of him was a group of maybe six people blocking the doors—*the goddamned defensive secondary, too many of 'em.* Danny rammed into the first astounded air passenger, then spun away, coming back in, hard on the left, grimly hanging on to the briefcase.

The doors were open; a redcap with a luggage cart blocked his way. But Danny Kearns saw only the free safety, a deep defensive backfield man, ready to hammer the tackle home. He rammed out his left hand and caught the luggage guy right under the chin. Then he cleared the empty cart and charged out into the airport dropoff zone.

A bus braked and was hit in the rear by a taxi. Two cops on duty heard Danny yell, "*CLEAR THE PARKING LOT RIGHT NOW! I'M HOLDING A FUCKING BOMB!*"

The two cops saw him running for the center of the roadway and charged out into the traffic. A limo driver hit a truck. An SUV mounted the sidewalk. And Danny Kearns kept running, dodging, sidestepping, and now he was shouting, yelling over and over, "*GET OUT OF THE PARKING GARAGE—VACATE THE AREA!*"

In front of him was the low concrete wall of the garage's first floor, and Danny prepared for the greatest throw of his life. He could see that the area he wanted was empty, like a yawning end zone. In Danny's mind, Tom Brady, the Patriots' legendary quarterback who was still going strong at age thirty-five, was urging him on. The massed ranks of the Patriot fans were roaring him home.

He adjusted his grip on the briefcase, fumbling for the handle. Then he straightened up, swiveled, spun around, and leaned back, a lot more like a javelin thrower than a quarterback. And then he let fly, hurling the briefcase into the garage, hurling it as near to the center as he could.

He watched it fly, whipping over the roof of a Cadillac and then tumbling to the concrete floor. Danny, still shouting, still imploring everyone to get the hell out of the garage, hit the deck, right under the low wall that separated the garage from the roadway. He covered his head with his arms, suspecting correctly that if the terrorist had any clue what he was doing, the timing device would be overridden by any major impact on the briefcase.

Thirty-two seconds later, the case detonated with a stupendous blast. It sent four cars into the air, blew twelve more sideways up to ten yards from their parking spaces, and knocked down four concrete- and steel-reinforced support pillars. The second floor of the parking garage collapsed onto the first. The third floor was punctured by a 25-foot-wide crater, and possibly forty cars were effectively totaled. However, only twelve people had been in the direct line of the blast and were quite badly injured by flying debris. No one was dead.

The entire area was enveloped by smoke and flames from burning gasoline, and the unmistakable smell of cordite hung on the air. Logan International Airport had been transformed into a battle zone, and Officer Pete Mackay was right in the thick of it.

While Danny Kearns had been removing the bomb, Pete Mackay had pounded through the terminal after the man in the tan-colored jacket. At the second emergency door, Pete had busted through to the sidewalk and kept running, praying that his quarry would make an exit at the next automatic door, and knowing that he, Pete, could run a hell of a lot faster outside than anyone could inside the packed terminal.

He reached the doors before the blast. And as he did so, the man who had left his briefcase in the care of Elliott Gardner came running out. It was, perhaps, the moment for which Pete Mackay had waited all of his life. He slammed that terrorist with a block that would have made a grizzly bear gasp.

The man cannoned back into the door and crashed to the ground. Pete Mackay had his hands around the man's throat before he hit the ground, his head crashing into the sidewalk. But that was when the briefcase detonated, and as it did so a third man entered the fray, another Middle Eastern–looking character who burst out of a black limo on the sidewalk and delivered a vicious kick to Mackay's ribs.

Pete fell back, temporarily winded, grabbing for the man's ankle. But by now the first terrorist was up and running, heading for the black car. Pete was still on the ground when the second man tore himself away and rushed for the driver's-side door. He piled in, revved, and accelerated. The light tan jacket could be seen right beside him.

Pete Mackay climbed to his feet, ran into the road, and leveled his machine gun. The car drove straight at him, but Pete held his ground, pumping bullets through the windshield until the last second, when he dived clear. The car veered out into the stalled traffic. The driver was dead, but he slumped forward and rammed down the accelerator. The vehicle lurched diagonally, hit the rear end of a Hertz bus, and flipped over, exploding in a fireball.

Danny Kearns was now up and heading across the traffic to help his partner. But the left-hand side of the car was an inferno. Danny kicked out the passenger window, and together they hauled clear the terrorist in the partially burned tan-colored jacket and dragged him away.

Within minutes, police cruisers from all over the city were headed out to Logan to assist with the total evacuation of the terminals. Incoming flights were diverted to Providence, Rhode Island, and only outgoing flights that had already left the gate were permitted to taxi out to the runway and take off.

Officers Mackay and Kearns assumed a loose command in Terminal C, and in effect they just turned the long passport lines and security lines toward the main doors and told everyone to leave the airport with all speed. Plainly the police department had no idea whether this was another 9/11, and the airport blast might be the harbinger of a whole series of attacks. No one was taking any chances. Logan International was history as far as this day was concerned, and according to security forces there was no possibility of its opening again for at least forty-eight hours.

The intense bush telegraph that hits local media newsrooms when something this big happens was instantly into gear, and by 8:45 A.M. the entire city knew there had been a big bang at the airport. Terrorist-related. Right now, the police were denying access to television crews, which traditionally managed to get in everyone's way during emergency operations, as this now was.

The media on these occasions are apt to assume an air of slightly irate self-importance on the basis that they are a great deal more significant than the firemen trying to extinguish the ferocious blaze in the parking garage and the army of cops trying to stop anyone else from getting blown up, or perhaps even killed.

But how could this have been allowed to happen? How the hell could the security forces have been so incompetent? Do you expect heads to roll? The public has a right to know . . . what's the status out here?

At this moment, the police decided to dispense with all that and allowed no broadcasting crews into the airport. Nonetheless, news of the terrorist bomb at Logan International had hit the airwaves in every corner of the country—and, within a few minutes, every corner of the world, regardless of time zones.

National security went to the highest level. The National Security Agency at Fort George G. Meade, Maryland, was vibrating with communications, and at five minutes before 10 A.M. the president's national security adviser was in the Oval Office to brief the boss on this latest outrage—an estimated thousand lives saved by the heroic actions of a couple of Boston cops.

Al Qaeda, however, had unquestionably struck again, even if it had turned out to be in the parking garage. Every police officer in the entire country was on heightened bomb alert.

Paul Bedford, the Democratic Party's right-of-center president, was an ex–U.S. Navy lieutenant. As commander in chief of the United States armed forces, he still found it more comfortable to consult with the high-ranking generals and admirals of his younger days than he ever did with professional politicians.

There was a myriad of reasons for this: possibly the unquestioning patriotism of the military, perhaps their impeccable good manners and respect for high office, or maybe their clarity of thought, the military's instant grasp of what *can* be done, what *could* be done, and what *must* be done. Paul Bedford admired the way the admirals and generals did not confuse the three.

Today he was due to have a private lunch in the White House with Admiral Arnold Morgan, the former head of the National Security Agency and former national security adviser to the president. Admiral Morgan had effectively put President Bedford into power a couple of years previously. And Bedford still, in unguarded moments, called the admiral "sir"—because, in the president's mind, it was still young navigation officer to nuclear submarine commander. And it always would be. *Yessir.*

Admiral Morgan would arrive at noon, which was not, by the way, to be confused with thirty seconds past the hour, nor indeed with one minute before the hour. *Noon was noon, goddammit.* And Paul Bedford always looked forward to the moment his desktop digital clock snapped over to 1200 from 1159. The door would fly open as the admiral let himself in, unannounced, called the end of the forenoon watch, and snapped "Permission to come aboard, sir?"

The president loved it. Because it not only brought back distant memories of nights spent at the helm of a U.S. Navy guided missile frigate, racing through the Atlantic dark, but it heralded the arrival of the man he trusted most in all the world.

This morning, however, events were crowding in upon him. These half-crazed al Qaeda fanatics had apparently had a serious shot at blowing up one of the busiest airport terminals in the country, and according to the CIA this latest Islamic offensive might not be over yet.

His new national security adviser was the dark, angular Professor Alan Brett, former lecturer at both Princeton and West Point, former colonel in the United States Army, and a firm believer that in the past thirty years only George W. Bush had had the slightest idea about showing the proper iron fist to Middle Eastern terrorists.

Paul Bedford did not believe that Alan Brett considered him to be soft, but he always sensed that the former infantry colonel erred on the side of a hard, ruthless response to any actions taken against the United States. President Bedford had no problem with that. Besides, Alan Brett's motives were unfailingly high.

A half hour ago, the professor had briefed him fully on the explosion at Logan. He had also produced a preliminary CIA report, which recommended no one drop their guard, that al Qaeda might not be finished on this day.

A nationwide security clampdown was in effect. All East Coast airports were either closed or closing, once the incoming passenger jets from the western side of the Atlantic had safely landed. Every aircraft coming from the eastern side of the ocean had been turned back to Europe. They had already shut down JFK in New York, Philadelphia, Washington Reagan and Dulles, Atlanta, Jacksonville, and Miami. Only the smaller airports were allowing transatlantic flights to land, mostly stranding thousands of passengers hundreds of miles from their destinations.

If the al Qaeda operatives had been bent on causing death and chaos, they had achieved the latter in spades. Large-scale death had been averted thanks to the actions of Pete Mackay and Danny Kearns, whose photographs were currently in the hands of President Bedford.

The president was anxious to speak to Admiral Morgan, but right now he could only listen to the incoming intelligence, and the news was not all bad. The passenger wearing the tan-colored jacket, dragged from the wreckage by Officer Kearns, had been shot in the upper arm and suffered burns on his left hand. He was alive and conscious under heavy guard in Mass General Hospital. According to the name on the Egyptian passport he was carrying, he was Reza Aghani. His cohort, the driver of the getaway vehicle, was dead.

The CIA, however, was in permanent communication with the National Security Agency over at Fort Meade, and according to Professor Brett they had a lead—one that he believed made the plot more complicated and a lot more dangerous.

0955 Friday 14 January 2012
National Security Agency
Fort George G. Meade, Maryland

Lieutenant Commander Jimmy Ramshawe, assistant to the director, was, by any standard, on the case. It was usually possible to ascertain his degree of interest in any given case, or surveillance report, by the general condition of his office. Traditionally it looked like a mildly dangerous minefield with small(ish) piles of documents placed strategically around the floor, the more pertinent ones in closer proximity to the desk. Today it looked like a medium-range guided missile had just come in.

The Ramshawe floor contained more detail on the activities of al Qaeda terrorists than you'd find in the seething cauldrons of Islamic fervor in Baghdad. That pile of data was close to the desk. Real close. The lieutenant commander had been in the building since 0500, after a heightened alert had been issued on the strength of reports from the Surveillance Office phone-monitoring section.

Ever since 9/11, the agency had insisted on strict intelligence phone observation on every single call made from any of the bin Laden family's former residences in the city of Boston.

This stringent policy was forged in private consultations with the former NSA director, the president's closest confidant, Admiral Arnold Morgan, who wanted it enforced—*regardless of who the hell now lived there, regardless of laws about rights of privacy, human rights, last rites, or any other goddamned rights, including the pursuit of happiness.*

There was one residence in particular, in the Back Bay area, that had constantly given cause for concern. The Surveillance Office had picked up so many cell phone calls that appeared to emanate from Baghdad, Tehran, or the Gaza Strip, they'd given up being startled. None of them made any sense, none of them had ever proved alarming, and none of them had ever amounted to a hill of beans.

But today's message, received on a cell in the very small hours of the morning, seemed more specific than anything recently transmitted. The recipient was unknown to the Boston Police Department, but he was of Middle Eastern appearance, a man called Ramon Salman, who had been photographed but never interviewed. And that cell phone call had been transmitted to Syria from a block of apartments on Boston's Commonwealth Avenue, from a suite of rooms formerly occupied by Osama bin Laden's cousin.

This small sequence of coincidences was inflamed by the wording of the one-way transmission. Mr. Salman was the only voice. There was no acknowledgment from the other end of the line. However, that was kids' stuff for the National Surveillance Office, which had, at the turn of the century, routinely tapped into Osama's phone calls from his cave in the Hindu Kush, direct to his mother in Saudi Arabia.

They pinpointed this morning's call to a position near the center of Damascus. The translation from Arabic to English read:

"*D-hour Charlie Hall 0800 (local). Reza in line—exit with Ari regroup HQ Houston. Flight 62 affirmative.*"

Lt. Commander Ramshawe had every code-breaking operator in the agency hitting the computer keys; fingers were flashing downward like shafts of light. The huge glassed bulletproof building quivered with activity. But, after eight hours, no one had cracked the clandestine communiqué directed, almost certainly, at one of the al Qaeda or Hamas strongholds in the Syrian capital.

Worse yet, Ramon Salman had vanished. Really vanished, that is. When Boston police had smashed their way into his apartment at 7 A.M., they had been greeted by empty cupboards, a couple of bathrooms stripped even of toothpaste, and a kitchen bereft of any form of nourishment. The phone was cut off, the television cable input was dead, and even the answering machine was disconnected. *Sayonara,* Salman.

As Lt. Commander Ramshawe put it on the phone to his boss at 7:30 A.M., "Beats the living shit out of me, Chief. But I don't bloody like it. And who the hell's Charlie Hall when he's up and running?"

At approximately 0809, Jimmy had a clearer idea of the significance of the message. *Charlie Hall was plainly code for Terminal C at Logan, right?*

D-hour was 0800, and a couple of right fucking nutters had just tried to blow up the freakin' airport. Holy shit!

That apartment on Commonwealth Avenue plainly held the key to this latest terrorist assault on an American city. At least it used to. But despite the presence of a dozen forensic guys combing through the place for clues, it was now just another dead end. Ramon Salman had vanished and taken his secrets with him. Maybe the police would pick him up somewhere. Maybe not. America's a very big place in which to get lost, and the Arab had probably taken off around 0300, six hours before the airport closures. J. Ramshawe knew *the murderous little bastard could be anywhere.*

He also knew that even the massive resources of Crypto City, the insiders' name for the National Security Agency, would not be effective against a foe who had disappeared off the charts. So far as Jimmy could tell, the only chance was to get after the wounded Reza Aghani and persuade him to talk.

Meanwhile, so far as Jimmy was concerned, the rest of the message was nothing short of a *bloody PITA*—that's Australian for pain-in-the-ass. And Jimmy, born in the USA of Aussie parents, retained at all times the rich Aussie accent and the quaint, colorful inflections of the outback west of Sydney, where his family traced their roots. His office was where Clancy of the Overflow met James Bond. *G'day, Admiral—no worries.*

Meanwhile, the second part of the transmission to Syria was giving him a whole stack of worries. Reza was accounted for, and Ari was dead. But the "headquarters in Houston" was a complete blank, and that was where Reza was supposedly headed. The Texas police were concentrating a search for Ramon Salman in the Houston area, but there was no Flight 62 on any airline going anywhere near the southern Texas area.

The number 62 of course could have meant anything, and the codebreakers in Crypto City had come up with over seven thousand computerized possibilities, which included just about every takeoff in North America that week, including the Space Shuttle.

The wording did suggest that Flight 62 was the one the terrorists were supposed to be on, and that probably had meant their leaving the country ASAP. And yet, in Jimmy's mind, he saw that last short sentence, *Flight 62 affirmative,* as something separate. Like a possible second hit.

He had been ruminating for a half hour on this and had twice tried to speak to his mentor, the Big Man, Admiral Morgan himself. But Mrs. Morgan thought Arnold was in Norfolk with Jimmy's boss, Admiral Morris, on board a carrier, but he would be at the White House later for lunch with the president if Jimmy's business was vital.

"Might not be vital now at 11:30," he said as he put down the telephone. "But it sure as hell might be at lunchtime."

Meanwhile, back in the Oval Office, President Bedford had just been briefed that Reza Aghani was conscious, the bullet had been removed from his arm, and he was drinking tea, resolutely refusing to utter one word to any of the six police officers currently guarding his room both inside and out.

"How long before they charge him?" asked the president.

"Maybe twenty-four hours," replied Alan Brett. "But the CIA thinks this cat is a really dangerous little character, almost certainly an Iranian Shi'ite, based in either Gaza or Syria, probably Hamas. They're scared some civilian court will free him and he'll hit back at us somehow."

"Can we make a case that he's military?"

"Well, he was carrying a bomb with him."

"Can that make him military?"

"I'll ask the Pentagon."

"Okay, Alan. I'll see you after lunch. I'm expecting Arnold Morgan in the next few minutes. He'll probably want Aghani shot at dawn, no questions asked."

The professor chuckled. "Not a bad plan, that," he said archly, as he let himself out.

Two minutes later, the president's clock ticked over to noon and the door opened. The president did not look up, because he found the scenario more amusing that way.

"Eight bells, sir," rasped a familiar voice. "Permission to come aboard?"

President Bedford looked up, smiling, face-to-face once more with the immaculately dressed Admiral Morgan, clean-shaven, dark gray suit, white shirt, Annapolis tie, black shoes polished to a degree appropriate to a Tiffany display case.

"Goddamned towelheads hit us again," Morgan growled. "How does it look?"

"Lousy," replied Paul Bedford, who was long accustomed to the admiral's propensity to dispense entirely with formalities like "Good morning," or "Great to see you," or "How you been?," or "How's Maggie?"

This applied particularly when there were matters on the desk that involved even the slightest problem of a Middle Eastern nature.

Straight to the gun deck was Admiral Morgan's policy, and the president gave it total respect. "I guess the only good part, Arnie, is we have one of the two terrorists under arrest, in Mass General Hospital."

"Is he under civilian or military guard?" The admiral's tone was sharp.

"Civilian right now—six Boston cops."

"Better change that immediately."

"Huh?"

"Get those civilians outta there right now. Call in a Navy guard and move the little sonofabitch to the Navy Hospital in Bethesda. Let's get some control right here."

"But he might not be well enough to travel."

"He's well enough," replied Arnold Morgan. "And anyway, who gives a rat's ass? He just tried to blow up a thousand people, didn't he? The hell with him. Let's get him under military arrest."

"I'm not absolutely clear why that's so important at this time, Arnie. The guy's plainly not going anywhere."

"You want me to tell you why?"

"Of course."

"Because sometime in the next twenty-four hours, a couple of highly paid lawyers are going to show up, probably paid for by bin Laden's Saudi relatives, and announce that this poor little guy made the mistake of getting into the wrong limousine, found himself in the middle of a gunfight, got shot, burned, and shockingly ill-treated, and not only *must* be released, but also is entitled to massive compensation from the trigger-happy Boston Police Department."

The president was thoughtful. But then he said, "Arnie, I am advised that there were two highly respectable Boston businessmen who will swear on oath that this was the man who abandoned the briefcase bomb, in the line in Terminal C."

"And within a very few hours there'll be about fifteen Arabs ready to swear to Allah that this Reza Aghani has never even owned a briefcase, never had one single conviction in his entire life, has no connection whatsoever with any terrorist organization, is a practicing Roman Catholic, and the Boston businessmen must surely be mistaken.

"And how could it possibly be Reza's fault if some crazed Boston cop took it upon himself to blow up the parking garage at Logan, while his buddy gunned down a passing limousine driver?"

"Arnie, in front of a jury, no one could possibly get away with that. . . ."

"O.J. did."

Paul Bedford was silent for a moment. "What do you want me to do, Arnie?"

"Have the Pentagon announce that this atrocity was the work of some Arab outfit that constantly refers to the Islamic *Jihad.* That's holy war, and since war traditionally gets fought by armies, we have deemed that this man is an illegal combatant, arrested by an eyewitness. He has thus been taken into military custody, and will face military interrogation and military incarceration until the matter is resolved."

"Okay. I'll get it done."

"And remember, Paul, if anything else happens, our only lifeline to serious information is this little prick in Mass General. Let's get him under real tight arrest. And the media the hell out of the goddamned way. We just don't want a whole lot of bullshit being written about people being held without trial, or even charged."

"Guess we ought never to forget, Arnie," said the president, "the media wants only a story. They do not think the national interest has anything to do with them."

"Just so we never forget, right here in this sacred office, the *only* thing that matters is the national interest and our ability to protect our people. Nothing else."

"Sometimes, Admiral, you can be quite surprisingly philosophical."

"Bullshit, Mr. President," replied Arnold, briskly. "Just don't want to take our eye off the ball, right?"

"Nossir, Admiral. Just hold everything for a minute while I brief Alan Brett to put our new operation in place. Then we'll find some lunch."

The commander in chief picked up the telephone and outlined his current view about Reza Aghani—"Just have the Navy take over, Alan, and get him into Bethesda, under heavy guard—and tell State, willya?"

He replaced the telephone and said, "Okay, old buddy, where do you want to eat? Right here, or in the private dining room?"

"This is not a private-dining-room day, Paul. I got a gut feeling we better stay right here on the bridge."

"Good call. I'll send for the butler."

Three minutes later, the White House butler came in and mentioned two or three dishes he was already preparing for visitors.

Arnold said, "Before I answer, can I just check if Maggie is now in residence?" He referred to the svelte and beautiful Virginian horsewoman, Maggie Lomax, who had married her childhood sweetheart, Paul Bedford, just as soon as he resigned from the Navy for a political career.

"Hell, no, she's out somewhere in Middleburg with her mother," replied the president.

"Okay, Henry, I'll have a roast beef sandwich on rye, mustard and mayonnaise. And coffee, black with buckshot." The butler smiled. He'd known the admiral for many years.

"Same," said the president. "Hold the buckshot."

The president, having declined the little sweetener tablets the admiral used instead of sugar, watched the butler leave and then inquired, "Can you tell me why my wife's presence affected what you ordered for lunch?"

"Sure, she's going out with Kathy tomorrow. Some ladies' fashion show, and I didn't want to risk being seen eating anything except grass, dandelions, and cottage cheese, the way I'm supposed to."

President Bedford chuckled. "You don't think I'd be eating roast beef and mayonnaise if Maggie was anywhere near, do you?"

1206 Same Day
National Air Traffic Control Center
Herndon, Virginia

With eight major international airports closed down for both takeoffs and landings, this had been an extremely hectic morning. Aircraft were being diverted inland, or to smaller airfields in central Florida or the Carolinas. Large nonstop passenger jets moving north were being diverted out to the west. Herndon could put up with almost anything except congestion over the East Coast airlanes, where a national emergency red alert was currently operative at all altitudes.

Reports, which on a normal day were critical, today faded into background cackle . . . *We got a medium system out to the southwest, not too big, moving westward . . . nothing on the president's schedule . . . Andrews quiet . . . American 142, make a 32-degree left turn, divert to Pittsburgh . . . good morning, United 96 . . . sorry about this . . . make a 40-degree left for Cincinnati . . . right now JFK's closed.*

Even the significant news that a United States Navy carrier was conducting a series of air-combat exercises eighty miles off the Norfolk approaches scarcely raised a ripple in the control room, save to make damn sure that nothing strayed into the path of an F-16 fighter-bomber screaming at eight hundred knots through cloudy skies.

Everyone was at full stretch, scanning the screens, checking out flight after flight, diverting, canceling, refusing permission either to land or leave. Their overriding task was to clear the decks as the airports evacuated the passengers, just in case al Qaeda was going to Plan B.

And right now, there were only two identified men who could help. One was Reza Aghani, still lying in Mass General with a sore arm and a firmly closed mouth. The other, Ramon Salman, had vanished not only from Commonwealth Avenue, but also off the face of the known world.

"*SUPERVISOR! RIGHT HERE!*" There was a sudden and unmistakable note of pure urgency in the voice of Operator Steve Farrell, a heavily overweight 25-year-old with a deceptively quick brain that might one day carry him straight into the director's chair.

"*I got a bolter,*" he snapped.

"You got a what?"

"A bolter. Pilot's ignored orders from the tower and pressed right along."

"Where is he?"

"Right here, sir, 'bout three hundred miles south of us, heading north. He just crossed the Cape Fear River in North Carolina."

"You got his last instructions?"

"Right here, sir. Ten minutes ago I sent him clear orders to make a thirty-degree course alteration to his left and to take a swing left around Cincinnati, leaving Northern Kentucky International to his starboard side."

"Where's he bound?"

"Montreal, sir."

"Start point?"

"Trinidad, sir. Refueled Palm Beach, Florida."

"Aircraft?"

"Boeing 737, sir."

"Is she squawking?"

"Nossir."

"You tried High Frequency?"

"Yessir. I went to SELCAL [selective calling] seven minutes ago. And I tried the private voice channel. I just hit the two cabin warning lights, let 'em know we're trying. Nothing."

"You sure she's still flying?"

"No doubt, sir. She's headed straight over the southern part of the state of North Carolina, slightly right of the city of Raleigh."

"Airline?"

"Thunder Bay Airways, sir. Canadian. She has no scheduled stops in North America. Her fuel stop was not on her flight plan, according to the Miami Tower."

"They probably ran out in Barbados."

"Guess so. But what do we do?"

"Well, right now she's flying over some lonely country. But I want you to alert the agencies. CIA, National Security, then White House Security . . . that'll do it. They'll take it from there."

"What do I tell 'em, sir?"

"Tell 'em we got a fucking bolter! What else? And keep trying the cockpit, Steve. You never know. Could be an electrical problem."

1213 Same Day
National Security Agency
Fort Meade, Maryland

Today Lt. Commander Ramshawe was hot on the trail of anything to do with aircraft. The short, low-key signal on his screen was informing him that some nuthouse Canadian pilot was ignoring warnings from the control tower and appeared to be heading for the North Carolina swamps. This hit him like "Houston, we have a problem" had hit the NASA ops room on April 13, 1970.

Jimmy Ramshawe grabbed the phone, direct line to his assistant. "Get me Herndon on the line right now," he snapped.

"National Air Traffic Control Center, Operator Simpson speaking."

"Operator, this is Lt. Commander Jimmy Ramshawe at the National Security Agency, Fort Meade. Please have the operator dealing with the

Thunder Bay Airlines off-course Boeing 737 call me back right away. Military Intelligence Division."

As always, the words *National Security Agency* worked their magic. Inside seven seconds, Steve Farrell had dropped his donut, mid-bite, and hit the phone.

"This is Steve Farrell, sir. You wanted me."

"G'day, Steve," said Jimmy. "This Thunder Bay flight. Where is it right now?"

"Sir, I'm showing it just southeast of the city of Raleigh, making around 380 knots through 35,000 feet. They've ignored my orders to swing left, refused to answer my signals, and stopped squawking. Just silence, sir. Like they'd gone off the charts."

"You're certain they haven't."

"Dead certain, sir. We got a radar paint on relay. They're up there, sir. And right now they're flying where they ain't supposed to be."

"They stuck to their original course all the way?"

"Nossir. After the Palm Beach refuel, they were directed out over the water and were scheduled to stay off the East Coast until they made landfall over Connecticut, and then proceed on up to Montreal. But we got a Navy Exercise in operation off Norfolk, so we redirected 'em west, back over land."

"And they heard that okay?"

"Yessir. And obeyed it."

"So they didn't ignore the towers until they were diverted from their northerly course off the Carolinas?"

"Nossir. That's when they went quiet. Soon as I told them to head for Cincinnati, Ohio."

"Is the aircraft full?"

"Nossir. It's not logged as heavy. But we don't have a passenger count."

"Who owns Thunder Bay Airways?"

"No idea, sir. They usually fly out of Downsview Airport, Toronto."

"Where's their home base?"

"No idea, sir. We don't see them that often. Tell you the truth, I think this might have been a private charter."

"Got a flight number?"

"Funny you should ask, sir. I've been checking. But I've had two different answers, 446 and 5544, almost like they filed two different flights."

"Steve, you sound like a very smart guy. I'll find out who owns the airline; you nail down their flight number. And keep tracking that bastard, will you? Call me in five with the flight number and gimme a projected route, okay?"

"You got it, sir. Be right back."

Lt. Commander Ramshawe hit the line to Military Intelligence Research and instructed them to run Thunder Bay Airways to ground and find out how many were on board their flight from Barbados to Montreal this morning. "And get the name of the pilot while you're at it."

Then he hit his own desktop computer, which took all of two minutes to inform him that Thunder Bay was situated way up in northern Ontario, on the northwest shore of Lake Superior. The city was very small, mostly a ski resort, but it most certainly did have an airport.

Three more minutes went by, and the phone rang again: Steve Farrell, to give the pilot's name, Captain Mark Fustok, plus the Boeing's current projected route.

"If she doesn't deviate," said Steve, "this bearing will take her four miles to the right of Raleigh, North Carolina, then straight over the middle of the city of Richmond, Virginia, across the Potomac, up the eastern shore, and on over the very center of Washington, D.C. There was still no accurate flight number."

"Gimme her last known," snapped Jimmy.

"She's just crossing the Virginia border," replied Steve, "close to a little place called Greensville. Still making 380 knots, still at 35, still defying every fucking thing she's been told to do."

Ramshawe liked that. Farrell was an earthy character, feet on the ground, hard to fool, no bullshit, moving fast, right next to a half-eaten donut.

"Stay with it, kid," he said.

At that moment, his screen lit up the way it did when there was incoming data from Military Intelligence Research. He swiveled around and watched the signal, which informed him that Thunder Bay Airways was about two years old, registered in Canada, excellent safety record, with servicing facilities at the local airfield. It ran regular flights to the Caribbean throughout the winter, with specialized vacation programs available throughout the year to a series of luxury hotels, all of them in the Middle East, Dubai, Saudi Arabia, Qatar, Egypt, Tunisia, and Morocco.

There were no American-based directors, and only two Canadians. Ninety percent of the shares were held by an overseas trust based in the

Bahamas. There was an office on the airfield at Thunder Bay, dealing mostly with their flights from Toronto and Montreal, transporting skiers. The president was listed as Mr. Ismael Akhbar, an Iranian-born naturalized Canadian, who held a master's in engineering from McGill University.

Jimmy glanced at the phone number and called the office in Thunder Bay. He explained to the girl that he was trying to trace a passenger on the flight but could not locate a flight number.

"Well, that's because we have no scheduled stops in the USA—it's not necessary to file flight details if you're going straight over. We never stop in the USA. Sir, what was the name of your passenger?"

Jimmy trotted out the name of his maiden aunt Sheila, who was currently located on a sheep station 746 miles southwest of the Great Dividing Range in New South Wales, Australia. He added that he was real anxious to make contact.

"I'm sorry, sir," replied the girl from Thunder Bay. "I can confirm that Miss Sheila Wilson was not on that flight from Barbados. There are only twenty-seven passengers aboard, and she is not among them."

"Okay, Miss," said Jimmy. "By the way, what was that flight number?"

"Our nonstop Barbados–Montreal is under charter today. It's TBA flight number 62," she replied.

Jimmy Ramshawe's heart stopped dead. When it restarted, he murmured, "Say again."

"TBA 62, sir. Will that be all?"

"Just say hello to Aunt Sheila if you see her."

He slammed down the phone and yelled into the intercom, *"Get me the White House!"*

It took three minutes to open his line to the Oval Office, and he told the president's secretary that he needed to speak to Admiral Morgan urgently.

Ten seconds later, he heard the familiar growl: "Morgan. Speak."

"It's Jimmy here, sir. Have you yet read that intercept message from Boston to Syria?"

"Of course I have. What's up?"

"Arnie, I've just found Flight 62—the one they mentioned affirmative. It's what air traffic control calls a bolter—it's refusing to obey orders from the tower, and right now it's headed for the city of Richmond, Virginia. Its present route will take it straight over the center of Washington."

"You in touch with the operator supposed to control it?"

"Yessir."

"Is he worried? Doesn't think it's just a mistake or anything?"

"Hell, no. He thinks this flight is very deliberately ignoring all instructions and flying straight down the course it wants to take."

"Where is it right now?"

"Making 380 knots at 35,000 feet. It's 1225 now. She's covering a little over six miles a minute, which would put Flight 62 around thirty-six miles north of the Virginia border, over Dinwiddie County, maybe fifteen miles south-sou'west of Richmond. . . ."

"What's Richmond from Washington, Jimmy? About a hundred miles?"

"Correct. Maybe thirty minutes from now if she slows down some, losing height."

"*Slows down!* You think she's planning a second hit?"

"Arnie, there's no doubt in my mind. There's only twenty-seven people on board. This is an Arab airliner, and it's plainly intent on hitting the city. I'm assuming that, sir. And I'm staying right on it, trying to get a visual. Sir, please tell the president to scramble the fighters; we're gonna have to shoot this fucker down."

For the first time in his life, Jimmy Ramshawe hung up on the admiral, who was thus left holding the president's silent phone inside the Oval Office, right in front of the boss.

"Sir," said Arnie, "National Security believes there's a rogue Boeing 737 heading for Washington, D.C., with a view to crashing into a major population center. Generally speaking, they believe it's the same gang that just had a shot at blowing up Logan this morning."

"What do we do?"

"What d'ya mean, 'we'? You, Mr. President, scramble Langley and Andrews—*battle stations, fighter jets RIGHT NOW!*"

"Are you telling me to order the United States armed forces to shoot down a passenger jetliner in cold blood?"

"I'm telling you to give them permission to fire at will. That way, the military has a free hand to do as they think fit."

"But, Arnie, what about civilian loss of life?"

"Guess that was worrying everyone on 9/11. And that's why close to three thousand people died in the World Trade Center. If our Air Force pilots had dropped the fuckers straight into the Hudson River with a couple of Sidewinders, it would not have happened."

"I know, I know. They didn't get 'em into the air quick enough, right?"

"Not quick enough to nail American Flight 11, or even United 93. Military commanders were not informed of that hijack until four minutes after it crashed in Shanksville, Pennsylvania. Basically, everyone was scared shitless of shooting down unarmed passenger jets."

"I am too."

"Don't be, Paul. Get the fighters in the air, and tell them to open fire on sight. The passengers die anyway. But don't, for the sake of all that's holy, let that fucking plane ram the Capitol or the White House. That would be absurd, given how much we already know."

"I guess," said the president slowly. "There's no getting away from one simple truth: on 9/11, the only one of the four hijacked aircraft that did not reach and hit its target was the one in the field at Shanksville."

"Spoken like a naval officer, Paul. And there's no escaping the fact that on 9/11 the fighters were not ordered into the air in time. They were still on the ground when the Towers were hit, still on the ground when the last terrorist flight hit the field in Pennsylvania. Don't let that happen again."

1231 Same Day
Command Center, Northeast Air Defense
Rome, New York

Colonel Rick Morry came out of his desk chair like a Saturn rocket. His computer screen was showing a possible hijack or terrorist takeover of a Boeing 737 passenger jet in the area of Richmond, Virginia, heading north toward the nation's capital. More importantly, President Bedford had already given clearance for the military to locate, engage, and if necessary shoot it down.

And these orders came straight from the Oval Office, with all commands, as usual, directed through Northeast Air Defense control, way out there in upstate New York, west of Syracuse, about forty-five miles from the freezing shores of Lake Ontario.

"*MAJOR FREEMAN!*" snapped Colonel Morry. "Right here we got a real-world possible hijack or takeover of a passenger jet over Virginia headed direct to Washington, D.C. We have permission to shoot it down direct from the commander in chief. *LET'S GO!*"

Scott Freeman picked up his phone and called out: *"LANGLEY AND ANDREWS—GO TO BATTLE STATIONS RIGHT NOW—WE GOT A NO-SHIT SITUATION—BATTLE STATIONS RIGHT NOW."*

The control room at Northeast Air Defense went stone silent. Every eye in the room was on Major Scott Freeman. Two minutes went by, and then he spoke.

"Four F-16s Langley. Andrews scrambled. Copy that. In the air eight minutes. Copy that. Takeoff 1241. Will advise precise location of Boeing 737. No other passenger jets in the area, flights grounded since Logan incident 0800. Rome control over and out."

Colonel Morry walked over to the command console on Major Freeman's desk and informed him that the civilian flight controller monitoring the Boeing was Steve Farrell at Herndon Flight Control.

"Langley naval fighters 160 miles to ops area south of Washington 14 minutes. Steve, give me an approximate on Flight 62 at 1255?"

"She's already losing height and speed, sir. She's projected over Woodbridge, Virginia, fifteen miles south of the city at that time—that's 38.38 North, 77.16 West. Right now she's making 260 knots through 28,000 feet. We have her over King William County right now, approx twelve miles north of Richmond."

"Thank you, Herndon. Copy that."

Colonel Morry: *"Rick, we got three F-16s in the air at Langley 1239—headed 335, speed 685—projected ops area 1249."*

"Roger that."

"Herndon to ADCC Rome—we have a Navy aircraft returning Norfolk moving southeast across Virginia—just picked up a real weird transmission . . . foreign voice background only passenger jet—something about executing will of Allah—on you I depend. There's a lot of screaming in the background. No visual. Suspect traveling north."

"Copy National Security Agency. Langley Birds moving in."

"This is Herndon—this is Herndon. All tracking techs on full alert—we got Flight 62 on scope—no course change on primary target—but he's descending rapidly—right now 21,000 feet still descending. Not responding."

"Langley Birds closing. Andrews fighters in the air headed directly for the city."

"This is Herndon—emergency, emergency—Flight 62 is descending rapidly below 15,000 feet—no clearance—repeat no clearance—descending all on its own."

"Langley—Langley to Northeast Command: leading F-16 pilots have Flight 62 on visual now heading north across Charles County, Maryland."

"Herndon to Northeast Command: *we just got another report from that Naval aircraft—picking up sounds of screams and panic on board Flight 62—someone shouted something about the will of Allah.*"

"Copy that, Herndon. Ordering F-16s to close one mile astern Flight 62— port and starboard wing. F-16s reporting 11,000 feet—confirm, please."

1250 Same Day
The White House

The president replaced the receiver. "Arnie," he said, "we got a couple of F-16s right on 'em heading north up Charles County. . . ."

"Both armed?"

"Yup. Air-to-air missiles. That was Langley, I guess checking once and for all that I wanted the aircraft obliterated. . . ."

"Before it obliterates the government of the United States, right?"

"You really think it will?"

"Either that, or it'll take a swerve at the White House, and I gotta say that doesn't have much appeal. At least, not right now."

"Arnie, I followed your advice. Almost three thousand people died on 9/11 because of indecisiveness. That's not going to happen again. You heard me just say *affirmative*?"

"I did."

"That was in answer to the question, *Do we have your absolute permission to shoot down Flight 62, if it refuses to obey commands from the tower?*"

"That's a good decision, Paul. You may get some flak about being a little hasty. But nothing like the flak you'll get if that sonofabitch drives straight through those ten-ton bronze doors to the Capitol and blows up the largest legislative chamber in the world."

President Bedford shook his head half in bewilderment, half in disbelief.

"C'mon, Paul," said Admiral Morgan. "Our first president, General Washington, laid the foundation stone for the Capitol over two hundred years ago. It's your privilege to be the president who saved it."

Northeast Air Defense
Command Center

"Northeast Air Defense Rome to Air Force North: Combat Command, Florida, we're tracking Flight 62 right now—two F-16s out of Langley, one mile astern and closing, positioned port and starboard. Permission requested for pilots to open fire at will?"

"Air Force North Combat Command, Florida, copy that, permission granted."

National Air Traffic Control
Herndon, Virginia

"Flight 62 reduces speed to 220 knots, altitude 8,000 feet, still descending, approaching Chicamuxen Creek, appears to be following Potomac River. She's not squawking, repeat not squawking, ignores all communications from U.S. Air Traffic Control."

"Northeast Air Defense to Herndon: did Flight 62 just make a slight course adjustment?"

"Affirmative, Northeast: Flight 62 came three degrees left toward Woodbridge. Speed remains 220 knots, still descending rapidly, we're projecting 5,000 feet over city of Woodbridge—that's 38.38 North, 77.16 West."

"Herndon, is she still out over the river?"

"Yessir. Right over the widest part where the stream splits into the wide estuary heading northeast up Occoquan Bay. Right here we got width seven miles."

"Northeast Air Defense, we're gonna take her out right now. Over and out."

Same Day
Over the Potomac River
Cockpit, U.S. Navy F-16 Fighter-Bomber

"Green Leader roger that, Langley. Weapons armed, firing both missiles starboard engine Boeing 737."

"OKAY, CHUCK—CLEARANCE RECEIVED—HIT THE PORTSIDE ENGINE RIGHT NOW!"

The four Sidewinder missiles dropped from the wings of the two pursuing U.S. Navy aircraft. All four ignited, accelerating forward. They flashed into their heat-seeking mode, leaving fiery trails as they cleaved through the clear skies, straight toward the massive engines of the 737.

All four hit, blasting the engines to smithereens, blowing apart the wings of the big passenger jet, which lurched forward for perhaps four hundred yards and then turned turtle and plummeted out of the sky. Thunder Bay Airlines Flight 62 twisted and turned in a ball of fire until it plunged, with a thunderous crash, into the Potomac River less than a mile below.

"Target destroyed. Repeat, destroyed. Birds climbing to ten, course one-six-zero. Returning Langley, returning Langley."

National Air Traffic Control
Herndon, Virginia

"Herndon to Northeast Air Defense—1257—Flight 62 disappeared from all screens. Last known fifteen miles south of Washington, D.C., making course north 4,000 above the Potomac River."

"Roger that, Herndon. Over and out."

1305
The White House

"Jesus Christ, Arnie, they splashed it!"

"Mr. President, like we say back home in Texas, sometimes a man's gotta do what a man's gotta do."

"Well, I agree that that's a phrase heard more often in the Wild West than in Virginia, but, hell, this is going to raise all kinds of havoc in the media."

Admiral Morgan looked quizzical. Then he said, "You mean there's some kind of imperative, weighing down upon us, to make this all public? So far as I know, some charter flight company from north of the border misjudged his instructions from the tower to head inland, and crashed his ole Boeing 737 straight into the goddamned ocean. Lightly loaded, thank God. None of 'em Americans."

"You mean we make some kind of a false announcement to the press?"

"Certainly not. We make a very sinister announcement about the Boston bomb. Then we allow the flight-control guys to issue a press release revealing that an overseas flight apparently ditched into the Atlantic several hours later. Bit of a coincidence really. Same day and everything. But the United States government will be making no statement until more facts are known.

"The air traffic department of Public Affairs should mention that there may have been a hydraulic problem in the 737, and the pilot was flying in a prohibited area off the coast of North Carolina, east of the Outer Banks, less than fifty miles from a U.S. Navy exercise.

"He ignored all our advice and then disappeared from all screens. No wreckage has yet been located. The military will of course say nothing, know nothing, and suggest nothing."

"How about people who may have seen the missiles hit the aircraft over the Potomac?"

"Unlikely, Paul. The plane came down in one of the widest parts of the river, almost seven miles across. And it was certainly on fire on impact. There may be a very few claims to have seen something, but in the end it'll be like a sighting of a UFO: interesting, but unproven."

"Kinda like that TWA flight that went down off Long Island twenty years ago—there were a few reports that something hit it, but nothing ever was accepted as a fact."

"You got it, Paul. And before Henry comes back, we have to do a few things—first, get the military and flight control on the same page. Then someone's got to brief the CIA. We can leave that to the National Security Agency. Meanwhile, have Alan Brett call the Defense Department and get the Navy moving on lifting that wreck out of the river. Top secret, obviously. Last, make sure the damned towelhead has been moved out of Mass General and into Bethesda."

At which point, Henry the butler reappeared with two king-sized roast beef sandwiches, a few potato chips, and a large bottle of fizzy water. "Just the way you like 'em, Admiral," he said, addressing his remark firmly away from the president, as if conscious of the terrible sin he had most certainly committed in the eyes of the absent First Lady. At least he would have, had she been present.

The two men divided the spoils, the president pouring the springwater into two crystal glasses. They each took a luxurious bite from what Kathy Morgan described as the billion-calorie-an-inch sandwiches.

"Jesus, these are great," said the president. Arnold Morgan, chewing dreamily, had a look of such supreme happiness on his face that a reply was strictly redundant.

Henry brought them coffee ten minutes later and clicked the sweeteners into Arnold's cup from the little blue tube.

"Thanks, Henry," said the admiral as the butler made his exit. Then Arnold turned to the president and inquired, "What time do you plan to address the nation? In time for the evening news?"

"Me?" replied Paul Bedford. "You think I have to make a formal speech?"

"Absolutely," said Arnold. "Reveal that this nation has been attacked yet again by the rabid fundamentalists of Islam and that only the prompt and courageous action of the two Boston policemen prevented a massive loss of life inside the terminal at Logan. Tell them we have the main perpetrator captive and that a huge inquiry is under way. There will in due course be substantial U.S. retaliation."

"And what do I say when some journalist wants to know if there is any connection between the airport bomb and the mysterious crash of the 737 into the ocean?"

"You say very simply, sir, the aircraft that went down was a lightly loaded, foreign, civilian Boeing 737 which had been overflying U.S. territory and U.S. waters. Neither the White House nor the Pentagon has been briefed about the precise circumstances of its disappearance. If and when the security agencies become involved, the media will be kept informed."

"You think they'll buy that?"

"Mr. President, Marlin Fitzwater, Reagan's man, used to describe the White House press corps as 'the lions.' He reckoned they needed feeding late every afternoon. That bomb story and the attendant terrorist implications will be like throwing those lions fifty of these roast beef sandwiches apiece. They won't be hungry. Just keep telling them we will seek revenge. They'll love that."

CHAPTER 2

Even the phone had an irritated ring to it when the Big Man called. Lt. Commander Ramshawe picked it up, and the rasping tones of Admiral Morgan snapped down the line. "JIMMY! Just give me one straight, no-bullshit assessment of our actions this morning."

"Sorry, sir. What's that you need?"

"I want to know your degree of certainty on the correctness of our actions."

"One hundred percent."

"REASON?"

"Sir, the CIA picked up a one-way transmission to Damascus that started off by correctly revealing the bomb at Logan International, time and place, plus operatives. Secondly, it confirmed that some kind of terror operation was happening with a Flight 62.

"Next thing we know, some fucking nutcase is driving a bloody great Boeing passenger jet straight at the city of Washington, D.C. Diving low, directly at the buildings, in defiance of our air traffic orders. What was its flight number? Sixty-two. As forecast. That's game, set, and match, old mate. Game, set, and match."

"Thank you, Jimmy," replied the admiral. "Just wanted to hear the reason again. I must be getting old."

"Not you, Arnie . . ." replied the lieutenant commander. But he was too late. The admiral had already rung off and was staring into the log fire in his study at the big house in Chevy Chase. He was staring at the flames, and thinking of the bomb, and the Boeing, and the endless evil these Middle Eastern fanatics were capable of visiting upon the United States of America.

"Fucking towelheads," he grunted. "But today belonged to us. We blew out their kamikaze airliner, and we screwed up their airport plan, captured the lead man. And the quicker we get him into Guantánamo Bay, the better I'm going to like it."

1700 Same Day
Mass General Hospital
Boston

The Sikorsky Sea King, a Navy search-and-rescue helicopter from New London, Connecticut, came clattering north up the Charles River. It came in a hundred feet above the Longfellow Bridge, banked right over the impressive edifice of Mass General, and landed with polished dexterity on the great hospital's sixteenth-floor rooftop helipad, atop the Ellison Building.

Commander John Fallon stared out at the assembled crowd that awaited him—six orderlies, six Boston cops, one white-coated doctor, two nurses, and three very obvious CIA men, big tough characters dressed in dark overcoats, narrow-brimmed hats, and thick scarves.

They all surrounded one medical gurney upon which was a tightly strapped hospital patient, lashed to the safety rails with the kind of wide security belts normally associated with the criminally insane, psychopaths like Hannibal Lecter. King Kong would have been hard-pressed to break free.

"Who the hell's that, the guy on the gurney?" Commander Fallon asked his loadmaster.

"Search me, just so long as he doesn't get loose with us."

"No chance of that," replied Fallon. "Those three CIA guys over there are coming with us."

The loadmaster opened the door and jumped down onto the roof. The gurney was wheeled over, and the stretcher that rested between the rails was lifted up by the orderlies and the patient carried into the helicopter.

The CIA agents climbed in, the doors were slammed tight, seatbelts buckled, and the Sea King lifted off from the roof. Not a word was spoken, especially by the patient, who had, incidentally, remained totally mute since five minutes past eight that morning, since Pete and Danny had hauled him out of the burning limo.

The helicopter immediately turned southwest, but within minutes came thirty-five degrees left, banking around onto a more southerly course, heading straight for the clear skies above the icy waters of Narragansett Bay and Rhode Island Sound.

The CIA guys sat stone-faced next to the patient as the Navy pilot and his navigator headed out to sea, clattering down the East Coast, exchanging friendly information with the control tower at Groton while they crossed the submarine roads off Block Island.

Commander Fallon again swung the Sea King south, heading out into the Atlantic, leaving Montauk Point on the eastern tip of Long Island to starboard, and staying out to sea all the way down the long New Jersey coastline.

The Sea King made its westerly turn as it reached the wide waters of Delaware Bay and flew swiftly over the eastern shore, making a beeline for Annapolis and then the northern suburbs of Washington, D.C. It flew low directly toward Bethesda, Maryland, and circled the extensive grounds of the National Naval Medical Center.

Commander Fallon could see that the wide concrete helipad below was surrounded by the type of guard strength you might expect for the arrival of a stricken U.S. president, for this place would be his first stop. Indeed, the body of the slain John F. Kennedy had been brought here immediately after Air Force One returned from Dallas.

The great tower of the hospital was Fallon's landmark, as it had been to generations of Navy pilots ever since its completion a little more than a year after President Roosevelt had laid its cornerstone on Armistice Day, November 11, 1941.

Commander Fallon made his approach into the midst of Navy staff vehicles and police cruisers. He had no idea of the identity of his wounded passenger, but he understood one thing: someone believed this guy was of serious importance. If he'd recognized the big black Humvee parked in a strictly no-go area right at the hospital entrance, he'd have understood better just how important.

Admiral Arnold Morgan was already in residence, sipping black coffee in the private office of the hospital commander, Rear Admiral Adam Roberts. Also in attendance were Lt. Commander Jimmy Ramshawe and Professor Alan Brett. That was the measure of importance concerning Mr. Reza Aghani, currently under arrest, shot, burned, strapped down, and interrogated after a busy morning at Logan.

Aghani entered the hospital on the double, six orderlies running the wheeled gurney through the automatic doors. They were surrounded by three Secret Service agents from the White House, four armed Navy guards, four Washington cops, two nurses, and two doctors.

Once inside, they headed directly toward the section reserved for the President of the United States: five darkened rooms, quivering with ultra-sensitive pressure plates on the floor all along the approach. At the entrance to the suite stood two White House agents, direct from the Secret Service Command Post immediately below the Oval Office. They alone knew the numbers that would open the industrial-strength cipher locks which guarded the gateway to the presidential quarters.

And here, in this rarefied interrogation center, as designated by Paul Bedford and Arnold Morgan this very morning, the first-ever non-president of the USA would become a resident. Only briefly. But nonetheless a resident. Mind you, if President Bedford as much as complained of a head cold, Reza Aghani would have been outta there in about one minute, dispatched immediately to some kind of basement lockup. Right now, however, he was in the relative comfort, but high security, of the Presidential Rooms.

As Arnold Morgan had stated earlier today, "I can put up with damn near anything except someone silences this guy with a bullet or a bomb. He's all we got, and this is a day which someone planned to be another 9/11."

The orderlies placed Aghani in a bedroom normally reserved for Secret Service agents who might be guarding a sick president. Two armed Navy guards were posted in the room, with two more outside. The terrorist's first visitor was Admiral Morgan himself, who was immediately followed by Lt. Commander Ramshawe. Instantly, Aghani closed his eyes and sank back into the pillow, as if aware that no one had yet told him this was going to be unpleasant.

"Reza Aghani," said the admiral, "you are being detained by the United States government as an illegal combatant, more specifically for heading up a terrorist team that tried to blow up a passenger terminal in Logan International Airport. You of course were transporting the bomb.

"You are no longer in the custody of civilians. You are under tight arrest by the United States military. And we have fewer restrictions. The good news for you is that we *may* stop short of beheading you.

"However, you should not rule out other methods of persuasion. I will be back here twenty-four hours from now, and if you have not told us truthfully what we want to know, I will have you immediately transferred to a military prison and interrogation center. And there you will be subject to more stringent questioning and may be executed."

Admiral Morgan did not wait for a reply. Nor even to check whether the man understood what had been said. The admiral merely turned sharply on his heel and jerked his head at Jimmy Ramshawe, signaling that he too should depart.

Once outside the room, Admiral Morgan headed immediately to the exquisitely furnished presidential drawing room, slung his overcoat over the back of an eighteenth-century Chippendale chair, and sat down, somewhat luxuriously, in a softly upholstered dark green chaise longue probably worth a hundred thousand dollars.

The cost of refurbishing this room had been some kind of White House joke, ever since thieves had somehow gained entry and stolen around $600,000 worth of antiques, Sheraton furniture, crystal chandeliers, paintings, and god knows what else. It had happened on the watch of Jimmy Carter, the no-frills, no-alcohol, cost-cutting president, and, understandably, it embarrassed the hell out of him.

It did not, however, embarrass the hell out of Admiral Morgan, who slipped into the high life as if to the manor born. "Coffee, James," he commanded. "And see if they can rustle up a few cookies, while we attempt to frighten the truth out of that goddamned little fuckhead with his eyes closed next door."

"Right away, sir," snapped Jimmy, adopting the subservient tone of a lieutenant commander to an admiral. "Be right back."

Jimmy left. The admiral mused. A log fire crackled in the grate. Absently, he reached for the television remote and flicked on Fox News. The entire channel was devoted to the events at Logan that morning, the reporters complaining of a news blackout but revealing that the president would address the nation at 7 P.M.

In the principal part of the newscast, no mention was made of the downed airliner currently resting on the bed of the Potomac estuary. At least not until a small segment on the rest of the day's news was *précised* by the female anchor. It was based on a short press release issued by the National Air Traffic Control Center, Herndon. This had stated merely that an unknown, lightly loaded Canadian-based Boeing 737, carrying no U.S. citizens, had vanished from their screens, somewhere out over the Atlantic off the Virginia coast.

Admiral Morgan, who had written the release himself and had the president's press office transmit it to Herndon, was somewhat smugly pleased. As he had intended, there was no suggestion of what fate had befallen it, no accurate location.

The spectacular-looking young redhead who delivered the broadcast may not have been employed by the television station solely for her vast experience of journalism and international events. But she was very beautiful and confirmed that no details had yet been released.

She then interviewed, on a link, a member of the International Air Transport Association and wondered what the mood was like in their office with a large passenger jet missing. "Is there a sense of failure?" she suggested.

The exec from IATA blinked and said, "I'm sorry. Would you rephrase that?"

"No, well, I mean, it's kind of your responsibility, right?" she added. "I guess you guys somehow let us down?"

"Ma'am, we do not actually fly the aircraft."

"No. But they're your pilot members, right?"

"Fuck me," said Arnold and hit the OFF button, astounded as ever by the blissful manner in which modern "journalists" are prepared to get something completely wrong, broadcast it to millions, and not appear to care one way or another.

Jimmy returned, followed by a waiter with cookies and coffee. The waiter poured from a priceless-looking engraved Georgian silver coffeepot, which had presumably been standard issue during the elegant age of the Georgian peanut farmer.

"You know, Arnie, I've been thinking," said Jimmy. "This really would have been another 9/11, and that means there must be a very active al Qaeda cell working right here on the East Coast. Because 9/11 was not just one jet aircraft, and they did not intend just one hit on one target: there were four attacks aimed at four different targets, all on one day."

"And I guess that's got you thinking there could be another this evening?"

"Darned right it has," replied Jimmy. "Do you think they could break that little sonofabitch next door in the next hour?"

"Probably not, kid. Our best chance might be in Houston, if they can locate the missing Ramon Salman. But even that's a long shot."

At that moment the door opened and the tall, angular figure of the president's national security adviser, Alan Brett, came into the room. "You ready for the CIA guys, Arnie? I have them outside right now."

"Gimme five, would you?" replied the admiral. "Have a cup of coffee and tell me your views. We haven't had much time for a chat."

"Tell you the truth," replied the professor, "I'm real nervous they might try to hit us again. This guy next door is an obvious hard man, not scared of us, accustomed to being put under pressure, and full of hatred and defiance. You can tell a lot about a character who simply does not react."

"He's pretty small to be an obvious hard man," muttered Jimmy Ramshawe in his deep Australian drawl. "Doesn't look to me like he could hold down a baby kangaroo."

"Guess you could say the same about the diminutive Julius Caesar," replied Alan Brett with a grin. "And *he* managed to conquer most of the known world."

"Well, this bastard had a serious shot at conquering the Boston airport," interjected Arnold Morgan. "And he must be interrogated as if he's some kind of a monster."

"I think the CIA guys know that," said Alan Brett. "How long have they got?"

"I'm going to tell the president to ship this guy out directly to Guantánamo Bay at noon tomorrow," said Arnold.

"Then the interrogators right here have around eighteen hours."

"No more than that," said the admiral. "But they really should operate as if they've got about two hours. Any news on the 737?"

"Just before I left, the president was talking to the CNO. Sounded like the Navy was about to take over the salvage and investigation."

"And Houston? No sign of Ramon Salman?"

"Not a thing."

"Okay, Alan. I don't need to brief the CIA guys. Just tell 'em to get going."

2030 Same Day
The White House

"Nice speech, Paul," said Admiral Morgan. "Let's keep the focus on the heroism of the Boston cops, because that'll shut the media up for a few days—keep 'em prancing around trying to speak to their goddamned relatives and schoolmasters, while we quietly turn the screws on the terrorists."

"You mean 'terrorist,' old buddy. Right now we've only got one."

Arnold Morgan surveyed the interior of the Oval Office and then muttered, "With all the great resources of the American empire at our disposal, we *have* to be able to find the missing Ramon Salman, and that's what I'm counting on."

The president nodded and then added, "By the way, Arnie, you probably could get a job as a press officer if you really tried. You sure as hell threw 'em off the scent of the missing airliner."

"I was actually thinking of taking out an ad," replied the admiral. "Lies, evasions, subterfuge a specialty. Expert at vanishing tricks. Morgan the Magician."

Paul Bedford chuckled. Then he looked up, much more seriously. "Will anyone ever find that aircraft and discover what really happened?"

"Not if I have anything to do with it."

0200 Saturday 15 January
United States Naval Station
Norfolk, Virginia

The night was clear, freezing but cloudless, over the world's largest naval station. A hard frost was already forming all along the 8,000-acre waterfront sprawl, home to the breathtaking oceanic muscle of the United States.

Lights gleamed from the massive nuclear-powered aircraft carriers berthed along the piers, the USS *John C. Stennis, George Washington,* and

Theodore Roosevelt. All of them glowered in the bright moonlight, great bruising veterans of the world's most troubled regions, frontline keepers of the honor of the United States of America.

There was hardly a sound in the vast naval complex, which in its way is just about landlocked, save for the narrow throughway out of the Hampton Roads, past Old Point Comfort and Fort Monroe to port and Fort Wool to starboard. But tonight the thin freezing air magnified the sounds. The very occasional helicopter landing echoed on the night air; mobilized guard patrols drove slowly to and from the long, frosty jetties. Footsteps sometimes accompanied the watch changes. But none of the forty warships in residence was moving.

At 0200, the incoming tide was rising all the way down the long "inland" coastline, which joins the naval station to the shipyard thirteen miles to the south. And out to the northeast, beyond the protective land, lies Chesapeake Bay, its waters ebbing and flowing with the tides of the Atlantic Ocean.

But the tide rises silently along the Navy piers, and the sudden throb of four powerful Caterpillar diesels driving a 4,200-hp ship north in the dark caught the attention of anyone who happened to be out in this cold night, either on deck or onshore.

There's a bush telegraph in Norfolk, and most people knew when any warship was scheduled to clear the station in the small hours and make an exit to the open ocean. But right now, no one had the slightest idea what kind of vessel was steaming straight up the exit channel. Equally, no one much cared. It was just a bit unexpected, even though she was showing all the correct navigation lights and had plainly come up from the repair berths down in the shipyard.

The reason for her late, or early, departure was mainly due to an intense evening of painting that had eliminated every marking that showed this was a Navy vessel.

But now she was "clean," the 2,880-ton *Safeguard*-class salvage ship USS *Grabber*, fully disguised as a civilian, smelling of fresh paint, and moving as fast as her engines would allow. That was twelve knots, and she was being closely followed in line astern by a couple of flatbed Navy barges, self-propelled and in a similar state of newly painted self-denial.

There was no insignia, and in the dawn there would be no Navy pennants flying. This had become, in a few hours, just a tiny fleet from a private salvage company, heading through the night, toward the hottest political hot potato in the entire country; orders of the commander in chief, acting personally on the advice of the Big Man, Admiral Morgan.

On board the lead ship was an extremely unusual cast. There was the normal team on the bridge: helmsman, navigator, watchkeepers, and in this case bosun. But they were all under the command of Bob Wallace, a newly promoted commander, ex-submariner, qualified Navy diver, who'd never been on a salvage ship in his life.

There were also sixteen more divers waiting below, led by Chief Petty Officer Mark Coulson, a U.S. Navy SEAL who had been flown to the Norfolk Shipyard from the SEAL base at Virginia Beach just before midnight. He brought with him an LPO, Ray Flamini, mini-submarine driver, SEAL underwater specialist. There was also a special team of Navy salvagemen and crane operators, men who would handle expertly the steel cables attached to the two big rigs, positioned fore and aft, each capable of a 65-ton dead lift.

Most of them were sleeping now, and would do so throughout the fourteen-hour, 160-mile run out into the Chesapeake and then onward up the dark and silent Potomac River toward Washington, D.C. There would not be much sleep after that. This was an urgent mission, and it needed to be accomplished fast and secretly. No mistakes.

Slowly they chugged across the west-facing naval station, coming eighteen degrees to starboard as they approached the gateway to Chesapeake Bay. The stark outline of Fort Monroe was dark in the moonlight to port as they began their left turn northward. The water was rougher here, and there was a slap-and-swish to the freighter's bow wave as she cut through the incoming tide.

The big heavy barges directly astern rose up laboriously before wallowing back into the troughs as their helmsmen swung the wheels left, expertly allowing these cumbersome floating freight platforms to find their shallow lines.

Grabber led them out to the north-running channel, and within two hours they had crossed the bay and run past Cape Charles on Virginia's eastern shore. A little over four hours later, they crossed the unseen frontier where all north-going ships steam into the waters of the state of Maryland. Eight bells chimed on the salvage ship's bridge, signaling the start of the forenoon watch: 0800 on this bright midwinter morning. But the sun was still low off her starboard quarter as they swung forty-five degrees left, up through the wide tidal waters of the Potomac estuary.

Point Lookout was silhouetted clear in the morning light, lancing out from the long Maryland peninsula like a black snake on a silver carpet. The estuary was calmer here, and all along the portside of the three ships, the long, shallow, bay-strewn shore of Virginia stretched to the north, for forty miles, up toward the big S-bend where the river narrows and in places becomes deeper.

This is a mighty waterway. From its icy, gushing source way up in the Allegheny Mountains beyond the Shenandoah Valley, the Potomac runs 160 miles along the South Fork alone before reaching Harper's Ferry and turning east toward Washington, on its final 160-mile journey to the sea.

Grabber and her consorts still had a hundred miles to run in broad daylight, and all along the route she kept strict radio silence. Occasionally they passed a freighter running south but made no signal of greeting, friendship, or recognition. The watch changed at noon. Lunch was served to all personnel on board the salvage ship, but the men on the barges settled for beef sandwiches and chocolate with mugs of hot coffee.

The afternoon wore on, and a deep chill set in long before the sun began to set. By 1500, they had cut their speed to eight knots and the navigator was studying the GPS intently, calling out the numbers. As they passed Quantico, Commander Bob Wallace made contact with the United States Marine Corps airbase at Turner Field.

They came slowly past Chicamuxen Creek on the starboard side and, almost drifting now, came alongside the low-lying peninsula of the Navy's surface warfare center at Stump Neck. Right here, Commander Wallace ordered a course change, and USS *Grabber* came thirty-eight degrees left into the middle of the stream, onto a 360-degree bearing, due north.

Sonars active.

The navigation officer was calling the GPS numbers now, and he did so for three more miles. It was almost dark now, and in the failing light, with the sun disappearing behind the long, low shoreline of Charles County, Commander Wallace called for the helmsman to hold course, but for engines to reverse, and for the barges to do the same. The firm voice of the navigator could plainly be heard:

Thirty-eight spot thirty-eight north, seventy-seven spot zero-two west.

"Thank you, Tommy," said Commander Wallace quietly. "All stop. Drop anchors fore and aft. Diving Team One prepare to go. Check marker buoys, load sea anchors, and lower the Zodiacs away. Ops area teams prepare to leave."

Grabber was suddenly a fast-moving U.S. Navy warship. There was no enemy, of course, in the middle of the Potomac a few miles south of Washington, D.C. But there had been, and right now it was hard to tell the difference between battle stations and peacetime action stations. No one was standing still. Or sleeping. Or sipping coffee.

The shouts and commands of the petty officers, chiefs, and lieutenants crackled in the gloom of the early evening. Lines were made fast, anchor chains howled, heavy metal hit the riverbed sixty feet below, underwater lights were tested, scubas checked, ropes, lines, and marker buoys prepared. Away to starboard, four miles through the fast-encroaching darkness, the powerful night scopes of the watchmen at the U.S. Navy surface warfare center peered out from Indian Head. Tonight and until this mission was completed, they were watchdogs.

Two patrol craft, engines running, were moored on the jetty. The slightest suggestion of an intruder would have them racing at flank speed for the *Grabber,* armed to the gunwales. That small ops area in the middle of the Potomac River was no place to be. Not tonight.

Commander Wallace and his men were acting under orders direct from the Pentagon. And right now their mission was one-dimensional. Everything else was Phase Two. Before dawn, they must locate, and mark with floating buoys, the shattered wreckage of TBA 62.

They had the last known GPS numbers the airliner had shown on the screen before everything went fizzy. However, those numbers may have been her final position when the missiles hit, or they may have been her final position when the 737 hit the water.

The operators at Herndon were of the opinion the air control radars would have continued "painting" her until she plunged beneath the surface. The missiles were known to have severed her engines and blown off the wings, but the general opinion was that the fuselage had stayed intact until the moment of impact with the Potomac.

Thus, Commander Wallace had positioned his little flotilla exactly at Flight 62's last known position. In his opinion, that wreck would be dead beneath the ships. If the divers failed to find anything, it meant the blasted aircraft had vanished from the screens maybe twenty seconds before she hit the water. Twenty seconds at 220 mph is equal to two thousand yards.

Essentially, *Grabber* was positioned at the near end of Flight 62's range of descent. If the divers found nothing, the fuselage of the aircraft was lying on the riverbed up to two thousand yards closer to the city. Commander Wallace believed, from all his reports, that the fuselage had been in one piece when it hit the water, and the numbers 38.38N 77.02W signified the precise position of impact on the water, not the position 1,500 feet above the water where the missiles struck home.

The commander left the bridge and walked down to the lower deck, where SEAL Chief Coulson and LPO Flamini were preparing to go over the side. Seamen were making last-second checks on all the equipment. For the initial search, two more Navy divers were going with the SEALs.

The lights from the patrolling Zodiacs cast a brightness upon the water, but the depths looked black, and Commander Wallace wore a look of admiration as the four black-suited figures rolled backward, down into the water, kicking hard into the depths, their flashlights casting strong beams out in front of them.

The dive control operators began communications almost immediately as the SEAL leaders, using their regular attack boards, kicked along the bottom, the GPS figures stark before them, keeping them straight, warning them when they strayed too far from the direct line of flight of the Canadian bolter.

Twenty minutes went by. Then five more. And the SEAL leader had specified that since this work was likely to go on more or less indefinitely, it should be conducted in thirty-minute takes. Four more Navy divers were preparing to go overboard when one of the controllers called, "*Sir, they got something.*"

Every eye swiveled around toward the men with the headpieces, standing on the deck talking to the men below the surface.

Chief Coulson's saying there's something there, maybe a hundred yards off our bow.

Another three minutes passed, close to the limit of the SEALs' time underwater. And then the controller called again. . . .

He's telling us to watch for the buoy, coming directly up from the smashed window of the cockpit.

The big light on the roof of the bridge suddenly blazed into life, ripping a beam through the dark and onto the surface of the river. Seconds passed, but they seemed like minutes. Then a scarlet Navy marker buoy bounced out of the water and settled.

Two minutes later, Chief Coulson surfaced next to the *Grabber*'s portside hull and called up, "We got her, sir. Those numbers were right on the money. Haven't found the wings yet, and the fuselage is split almost in half. If we lift her, she'll break. But if the cranes get two cables on her, she'll come up one section at a time."

"Will she take one around the tailplane and one through the cabin?" asked the commander.

"Not a chance," said Chief Coulson, hauling himself up the ladder. "Tailplane broke off on impact. I never even saw it."

"Can we get cables underneath the main fuselage?"

"I don't think so, sir. She hit the riverbed pretty good and then skidded some. I'd say she's embedded maybe three feet."

"What's the bottom like?"

"Kinda high-class mud. Doesn't look dirty, more like silt, light-colored, and more holding than plain sand."

Commander Wallace held out his hand and gave the chief a pull over the gunwale. "Great job, Mark. What next?"

"Get the diving engineers down there right away. Let's get some decisions made. But one thing's definite: she'll come to the surface. No doubt in my mind."

"How about the bodies?"

"Didn't see too many of them, sir. I took a quick look, and everyone was still strapped in."

"Do we move them now, or bring 'em up with the wreckage?"

"I'd bring the whole lot up together. Mostly because it'll be a darn sight easier to get 'em in body bags up here than it will underwater."

"Okay. Now you go and get some food and hot coffee. We'll talk again in an hour . . . and Mark, thanks a million."

Five hours later, the decisions were made jointly by the engineers, the SEALs, and the commanding officer. It was plainly too difficult to get cables right under the fuselage of Flight 62—at least, it was without very sophisticated equipment, the kind of hydraulic air pumping used for dock piles, driving out the seabed and hammering them in through soft disturbed sand. But that's conducted from the surface. And it's a whole lot more difficult to transfer this technology to operate sixty feet below the waterline. And a lot too slow.

Far better to thrust the lifting cables straight through the cabin, heave her out of the silt, and haul her in. As Chief Coulson had observed, the hull of the aircraft was split. She'd break as soon as the cranes moved her, and she'd come up cleanly in two parts. Meanwhile, a separate team of divers would begin the search for the tailplane and whatever fragments of the obliterated wings were still recognizable.

The Big Man had apparently stressed that no part of that aircraft must be left on the riverbed, since he didn't want some smart-ass television monkeys groping around down there and coming up with *Mystery Air Crash Baffles Government.*

There was not, of course, an imminent danger of that, since the only information available about TBA Flight 62 was she had disappeared fifty miles offshore, out over the Atlantic Ocean, east of North Carolina, 180 miles away.

It was almost midnight now, and the temperature had plummeted to twenty-one degrees Fahrenheit. An icy wind whipped across the surface of the water, and there was no moon. Commander Wallace decided to have the cables attached to the hull of the airliner through the night, but not to attempt to lift the wreckage aboard the barges until after dark the following day.

It was slow going working underwater, and the engineers estimated it would take up to ten hours to fix cables to both ends of the fuselage. Meanwhile, the Navy divers would work in shifts through the night, using underwater metal detectors, trying to locate the smaller sections of wreckage that had broken off during the downing of Flight 62. Especially hardware from the engines.

To the northern end of the ops area, a four-foot-high floating notice board, anchored to the bottom, read: PROHIBITED AREA—U.S. NAVY EXER-CISE IN PROGRESS. *STAY RIGHT OF THE BUOYS.*

To the south, an identical sign ordered northbound shipping also to keep right of the area. A line of flashing buoys now provided guidance, forcing any vessel to give the *Grabber* an extremely wide berth. The proximity of the Navy's Surface Warfare Center on nearby Indian Head fortuitously gave the operation complete credence.

This was plainly a legitimate naval operation. It was very public; at least it was to passing captains and seamen. It most certainly did not give the appearance of a clandestine mission, designed to carry out one of the biggest, most diabolically deceptive tasks ever undertaken by the United States military.

In peacetime it was almost unprecedented. Politicians were shy of indulging in such adventures because most people still did not recognize the War on Terror as a true war. Still, it had taken the Flat Earth Society more than a century to disband.

Right now, it was hell on earth out on the freezing decks of the *Grabber,* colder than it was sixty feet below on the riverbed. The blue-twisted steel cables had to be hooked onto the lifting cranes and then lowered away over the side, down to the divers, who were anxiously awaiting the engineers' clearance to begin running them through the cabin. Everything was heavy, everything was freezing. Commander Wallace changed shifts all the time, allowing no one to work out there for longer than one hour at a stretch.

By the time dawn broke over the Potomac, there were eight scarlet marker buoys in place, bobbing brightly on the surface, identifying accurately the positions of various hunks of wreckage. The SEAL leading petty officer, Ray Flamini, had personally found the tailplane, lying forlornly on its side half-buried, snapped off on impact, around a hundred yards short of the main hull, directly under *Grabber*'s bow.

And all through the morning, the underwater men worked at securing the cables, in order to avoid breakage and facilitate a neat, clean lift from the riverbed. In the opinion of Chief Coulson, the critical moment would come when the aft section of the fuselage was lifted and, hopefully, snapped off from the for'ard part.

If the metallic outer skin did not break, they would probably have to blow it apart with explosive, and that was never easy underwater. It was easily achievable but inclined to make one hell of a mess. However, *Grabber*'s cranes would not lift the whole fuselage, and time was not on their side.

By 1530, they were ready for the lift. But there was traffic on the river, and Commander Wallace was not about to begin lifting what he called "darned great hunks of civilian jetliner" out of the river, in broad daylight, in full view of anyone who might be looking.

Their journey from the shipyard had been conducted in the utmost secrecy, with nothing to announce they were Navy ships. And once on station, even with periodic visits from the patrol vessels out of Indian Head, they appeared just like a regular Navy exercise from the Surface Warfare Center. Strictly routine.

Every twenty minutes, two divers returned to the riverbed to check that all was well, and the rest of the salvage crew just hung around, glad to be warm, hoping to hell the fuselage of Flight 62 would not fall off the goddamned crane or some other unforeseen bullshit.

Winter darkness descended over the river before 1700. The flashing lights of the buoys went active; the big deck lights, fore and aft, illuminated the lifting tackle. Chief Coulson and LPO Flamini were over the side in company with six other divers, tending the huge cables. Signals were given, the controllers snapped out commands, and at 1724 *Grabber*'s foredeck crane began to lift.

Swimming slowly through the water, thirty yards off the starboard beam of the aircraft wreckage, Chief Coulson watched the cable take the strain. Slowly the rear section lifted out of the silt, dragging with it the still-attached front section.

For a split second, the chief thought the whole fuselage was going up together. But then there was a crunching thud, like a *POP!* played in slow motion. And the for'ard cabin vibrated, then snapped off, dropping back into its hole and sending a massive cloud of silt and sand billowing into the calm water. It would take two hours to clear. But, fortunately, the second set of cables was already attached.

Chief Coulson moved slowly upward, through the water, with the smashed hull in front of him. He could see a barge being moved into position for the crane to deposit its load onto the deck. By the time the chief had surfaced and once more climbed aboard *Grabber,* the aircraft hull was on board, with a team of twenty seamen swarming all over it, covering the huge cargo with tarpaulin and lashing it down in preparation for the journey back to Norfolk.

During the next three hours, many of the other remnants were brought up and loaded, until all the pieces of Flight 62, save for the tailplane and the front section of the cabin, were on board and covered. At 2300, the barge pulled out between the buoys and turned south for Norfolk.

To both port and starboard were escort patrol boats from Indian Head. Leading the way was a Navy frigate, which had materialized from nowhere. Just like the Big Man had specified. No chances. Take no chances whatsoever. The Navy escorts would stay close to the barge for the first hundred miles until dawn, and would then peel away, permitting the big unmarked vessel to continue her journey alone in broad daylight. The barge, however, with her highly classified load, would never be out of sight of the escorts.

On board *Grabber,* the teams took a break for an hour; shortly after midnight, the divers returned to the riverbed and hooked up the cables on the final, smaller section of the main fuselage, the part that contained the cockpit and first-class kitchen.

Having already been hauled off the bottom, this time it came away easily, moved slowly up through the water, and swung onto the second barge. The tailplane was easiest of all, comparatively light and manageable. The crane lowered it onto the stern part of the deck, and immediately the engineers set about cutting off the jutting, perpendicular part. They used oxyacetylene cutters and sledgehammers. The exercise took almost an hour. Finally the second barge was ready, its load covered, unobtrusive.

In company with *Grabber,* it turned south, back along the Potomac. Every last piece of the aircraft, every piece that could be located, had been gathered up and brought to the surface. No one would ever know her fate. A subsequent search, out in the deep Atlantic, of course, yielded nothing. Flight 62 was officially deemed "lost over the ocean, no trace, no evidence."

Her passengers and crew would never be found. Only the barest details of their existence were discovered when the Navy searched the bodies before placing them in coffins. Passports yielded names, but the fire on board in the moments before the crash had incinerated all paperwork in the forward section before the waters of the Potomac extinguished it. Only fifteen coffins were required. No one else was left; the swift-running tidal waters through the aircraft had carried the ashes away.

They had not, however, carried away the big metal boxes in the hold which contained a quarter of a ton of TNT, hidden under papers and books. The explosive was wired but not activated. Detonation devices were identifiable in the forward section where the fire had obviously been most ferocious.

The Navy investigators came to the conclusion that the Sidewinders had hit with such sudden and devastating force that the terrorists on board were taken entirely by surprise. And all of them were in the forward section. There had been no time to arm their somewhat crude bomb to explode on impact.

Had they done so, however, and managed to hit the Capitol as planned, that much high explosive coming in from the southwest would have blown the Capitol building straight into the Reflecting Pool, and with it all the hundreds of government workers who served there. In his tenure as President of the United States, this was most certainly Paul Bedford's finest hour. And no one would ever know. Well, not many people.

All fifteen of the recovered bodies carried Canadian passports. None of them had Middle Eastern names, and all of them were from either Montreal or Toronto. It was plain that the terrorists had effectively been cremated during Flight 62's long, burning fall from five thousand feet. They left no trace behind.

Inquiries made at Palm Beach airport yielded little. Yes, the 737 had requested a refueling stop, and yes, permission had been granted. Further inquiries in Barbados revealed that no, the airport had not run out of fuel, and Flight 62 had taken delivery of all the jet fuel it required.

This particular piece of information caused Lt. Commander Jimmy Ramshawe almost to have a seizure. And his thoughts were clear:

This means there's some kind of terrorist agent operating right there in Palm Beach airport. They did not have to stop there; they chose to. And if they don't discover that the explosive was loaded right there in Palm Beach, I'm a fucking wallaby . . . GET ME ADMIRAL MORGAN RIGHT NOW.

1630 Tuesday 18 January
15,000 Feet above West Virginia

Meanwhile, there was the somewhat vexing problem of getting rid of the fifteen Canadian bodies. Thus it was that a three-engined Sikorsky Super Stallion helicopter was making its way across the Allegheny Mountains on a 700-mile journey to the enormous military base of Fort Campbell, which lies fifty miles northwest of Nashville, right on the Tennessee-Kentucky border.

They were flying through the last of the light, even at this height. In place of the standard cargo of fifty combat Marines, the Super Stallion now carried fifteen coffins.

In a remote corner of the military base, down to the southwest, near the banks of the wide Cumberland River, there was a small graveyard, unused for decades. Tonight it would be used for a mass burial, the grave would be unmarked, and the huge mechanical diggers, already waiting, would accomplish their task very quickly.

The country around the little graveyard was soft, picturesque, and wooded. It was a fitting place, perhaps, for those who had died violently, unknowing victims of Muslim terror, and silent guardians of a very deadly secret.

The big Navy helo would be refueled and back in Norfolk before midnight. Less than a dozen people would ever know the purpose of its mission.

Lt. Commander Ramshawe raised a very loud alarm. His call to Admiral Morgan took mere moments, and the sudden realization that Palm Beach International Airport housed a treacherous jihadist who had assisted in a plot to kill hundreds of Americans caused an electronic vibration of anxiety to shudder through CIA headquarters in Langley, Virginia. As an operation, the CIA prided itself on staying at least two steps in front of the National Security Agency at Fort Meade, and several more in front of the FBI and all of its branches.

Ramshawe's call caught them on the hop. An unnamed terrorist working in a U.S. airport represented a five-alarmer, and there were a thousand questions to answer. These included: Precisely who gave Flight 62 permission to land? Were the security operators informed? Who designated the stand she should occupy during refueling? Was there an opportunity for five metal trunks to be loaded into her hold? Was anyone paying attention?

The answers to the latter questions were most disturbing. Yes, there had been an opportunity for those trunks to be loaded on board. No, no one was paying the slightest attention to this Canadian 737 that apparently wanted extra fuel. No problem.

Florida's state police, keen to assist in any way, joined forces with the CIA and the local branch of the FBI, and they swooped down upon that airport like a 21st-century Gestapo. They confiscated miles of closed-circuit television film, and one by one they interviewed employees.

In the end, it transpired that the five metal trunks with the illicit cargo had been wheeled into the near-empty baggage room at 0300 on the morning of Friday, January 14.

Around 0930, they had been quietly attached to a line of baggage trucks being towed out to an aircraft. However, a new baggage tractor then came out into the area and unhooked the last cart from the main line of six being loaded onto a United Airlines passenger jet. No one took the slightest notice.

But right now there was a quarter-ton of TNT being towed around the loading area of Palm Beach International Airport, by an employee, wearing the right uniform, on a properly qualified vehicle. Again, no one noticed. Why should they have noticed?

At 0945, Flight 62 from Barbados came in to land and was directed to a stand in the refueling area. She took on board her jet fuel, and, while she was doing so, one single employee brought out a luggage cart on which were five identical boxes. The pilot ordered his engineer to unlock the door to the hold, and the boxes were loaded. Everything looked absolutely normal. And no one batted an eyelash. The al Qaeda hitmen were in business. Before Flight 62 took off again at 1040, she had been converted into a massive flying bomb, and she was headed directly to Washington, D.C.

The question for the CIA to answer was, plainly, who was the mysterious truck driver who delivered the explosive to the aircraft? The answer was not long in coming.

The man had avoided the CCTV cameras, but everyone knew who he was. A youngish guy, aged around thirty-four, named Mo Dixon. He was in bed in his apartment when the CIA men burst in at four o'clock in the morning in West Palm Beach. The place was clean, but that was not Mo as in Maurice; it was Mo as in Mohammed. The police found two passports, one of them Syrian. One American. Both of them featuring Mo, unsmiling, innocent-looking.

Under questioning, he revealed he had worked at the Syrian embassy in Caracas, Venezuela. Then he'd conned his way into the USA on a false passport back in the year 2001. He'd had a variety of jobs, with long periods of doing nothing. Well, nothing useful to the USA. Mohammed Rahman was a Syrian agent with close ties to the Middle Eastern terror organization Hamas.

In the opinion of Lt. Commander Ramshawe, he must be subjected to the most rigorous military questioning—mostly to see if he could be connected to the missing Saudi, Ramon Salman. Admiral Morgan arranged for the obvious illegal combatant, Mohammed Rahman, to be transported forthwith to Guantánamo Bay.

The New York City Police Department is mildly jumpy about two main subjects, drugs and street crime, mostly because the first infuriates the government and the second infuriates the mayor. But there is one subject, above all others, which makes them *really* nervous. That's terrorism. That infuriates everybody.

And all through the city, there were small mom-and-pop stores that had literally had the "frighteners" put upon them by New York's finest. Mostly they sold electronics, batteries, timing devices, plugs, wires, lightbulbs, and electrical fittings. But some sell industrial fertilizer, various chemicals, small electric motors. The kind of stuff that might be needed by someone planning to blow something up.

The New York Police Department stayed in touch with these store-owners on a regular and consistent basis. They asked very little, except to be informed of any suspicious-looking characters who might be purchasing any commodity that could possibly be used in the construction of a bomb.

At 9 P.M. the previous evening, Mr. Sam Goldblum of downtown West Broadway had called his two pals at the precinct and informed them he was preparing a timing device for a couple of guys who stated they were fitting a homemade alarm system into their warehouse in the Bowery.

Sam did not believe them. He had family in Tel Aviv, and in his opinion his two customers were either Palestinian or Iranian. Either way, he did not trust them one inch, and suggested that Officers Mike Carman and Joe Pallizi might like to pay him a visit in the morning and take a look at the device Sam was building for them.

Mike and Joe turned up at 9:30 sharp. The electronic timer was being attached behind a small clock face, geared to go active any time in a

24-hour cycle. The two cops were not world-class experts on live detonation gear, but they disliked what they saw, and they decided to wait it out until noon and then apprehend the two suspects and find out what the hell was going on.

They took up their positions on Prince Street, south of Washington Square, just east of West Broadway, and watched. At 11:02 A.M., two young men hurried across the street and entered the shop. Officer Carman's cell phone bleeped.

Mike—they're here.

Got 'em, Sam. Thanks a lot.

Ten minutes later, the two men emerged from the shop, both of them wearing black sneakers, heavy jackets, and scarves. One of them carried a large white plastic bag marked *Goldblum Electrics.* Sam was right. Both of them were distinctly Middle Eastern in appearance.

The two cops broke cover and walked quickly toward the two men, coming from behind. Mike Carman overtook them and motioned for them to stop. Joe Pallizi, standing right behind them, drew his service revolver and ordered them against the wall. Mike grabbed the package and demanded to be shown what it contained.

"It's just a burglar alarm, man," said one of them.

"Then I guess you won't mind us coming home with you, to check out what kind of device it is and where it's going?"

This was not greeted with absolute joy by either man, and one of them attempted to run for it. Mike grabbed him by the neck and Joe snapped the bracelets on the other man. They were marched at gunpoint to the home address printed on a New York driver's license found in the pocket of the man who had tried to escape.

The result was an outstanding arrest and a spectacular discovery of a bomb-making factory just around the corner, in a fourth-floor apartment. It contained bags of chemicals, enough bundles of dynamite to knock down the George Washington Bridge, a large sealed container of white powder that would later be identified as anthrax, and enough electrical wires and batteries to light up Yankee Stadium.

The two cops made their report instantly by telephone, and before they even left the premises, before even the forensic guys were in, the main security agencies had been informed of the police coup.

Jimmy Ramshawe, firing questions at the precinct chief in downtown Manhattan, demanded, on behalf of the National Security Agency, to know the address of the premises where the arrest was happening.

"Wait a minute, sir . . . okay, right away . . . it's 75 West Houston, corner of Broadway."

"*Mother of God,*" breathed Jimmy. "Don't let any of them leave. No one leaves. Everyone stays right in that apartment. Don't let anyone make a phone call, 'cept for your own guys, right? Just wait."

"You got it, sir."

One hour and ten minutes later, the Boston terrorist mastermind, Ramon Salman, formerly of Commonwealth Avenue, walked into the al Qaeda headquarters, straight through the door of Apartment 4D, 75 West Houston, New York. Mike Carman and Joe Pallizi, who had bound and gagged their original captives, instantly grabbed the startled Ramon in a headlock and an armlock, and he offered no resistance.

Twenty-four hours later, Salman was with his highly lethal buddies, Reza Aghani and Mohammed the baggage man, in Guantánamo Bay, Cuba, special courtesy of Arnold Morgan and the President of the United States.

Lt. Commander Ramshawe slightly sheepishly informed the CIA that the intense police search for Salman, currently in progress in Houston, Texas, could now be called off.

"That bloody Ramon," he muttered, as he rang off. "That's one cunning little Arabian bastard, and no error."

Almost fifteen hundred miles to the south, lost in the gigantic sprawl of the oldest overseas base ever occupied by U.S. forces, Salman, Aghani, and Mohammed Rahman faced up to the rigors of military interrogation in the chilling regime of Guantánamo Bay.

Here on the 45-square-mile compound there are still close to ten thousand U.S. troops, training and working, right on the southeastern edge of Cuba, on the only U.S. base in the world located on Communist soil.

No interrogation center in the free world has a more feared reputation. Outside of the more barbaric nations, no interrogation center has ever been more successful at prying information out of known terrorist hard men, at mentally breaking down illegal combatants, at making them reveal to the U.S. military precisely what their cutthroat brothers-in-arms are planning.

Almost all the West's major hits against terrorist organizations come as the result of "information received." Guantánamo Bay, and its interrogation teams, are entitled to a massive share of the credit for that. They are not, of course, ever going to get it, since, in their trade, credit is an almost unheard-of commodity.

Those teams confer in secret, they work in secret, they turn the screws in secret, they make their demands on prisoners in secret, and they report in secret. Over the years, thousands of lives have been saved, hundreds of plots have been exposed, thanks to the skill and determination of America's unseen maestros in the cages of Guantánamo Bay.

The Cuban government has for years loathed and detested the American presence down there in the remote razor-wired compound which lies nearly five hundred miles from Havana, Cuba's capital city up on the northwestern shore. But America came by this territory thanks to a treaty signed by Cuba's first president, Tomas Estrada Palma, in 1903.

To this day there are God knows how many clauses, steel-rimmed, protecting America's rights—"complete jurisdiction and control," "perpetual sovereignty over Guantánamo Bay," "lease termination requiring the consent of both governments."

Fidel Castro once made a determined attempt to break the lease by citing the 1969 Vienna Convention. And by asserting that any agreement between the U.S. and Cuba had been dependent upon the threat or use of force by the Americans.

But Uncle Sam banged an iron fist on the table and told Comrade Fidel he was talking nonsense, and reminded him he had accepted a substantial lease payment from them at the outset of his rule, thus ratifying the lease agreement. The Americans were not going anywhere.

Unsurprisingly, diplomatic relations could not exist between the two countries, and cooperation was zero. But the great sheltered Bay of Guantánamo is essentially a U.S. naval base, and is easily supplied from the American mainland.

Independent, a law unto itself, secretive, and highly successful, this hot, dusty, subtropical detention center can more or less do what it likes. Hated and feared by the jihadists of the Middle East, Guantánamo has been home to operatives from Hamas, Hezbollah, and just about every Muslim terror group including al Qaeda and the Taliban.

The dread of every terrorist commander in Iraq, Iran, Afghanistan, or Pakistan is that one of their senior men will end up in the Cuba facility and spill the beans, as many of them have. The seizure and subsequent transportation of Ramon Salman, Reza Aghani, and Mohammed Rahman sent a shiver of dread through clandestine enclaves in Damascus, Gaza, Tehran, Kabul, and the high caves in the Hindu Kush.

Could these three important al Qaeda men withstand the mental onslaught of U.S. interrogation—a process which would not only be relentless, but also conducted in secret? All of the Middle East terror organizations had access to lawyers, and they frequently succeeded in presenting them at civilian proceedings in the U.S., and, more especially, in England. Also they had a thousand hotlines to the Arab television network, al Jazeera, which often cited examples of brutality, bullying, and torture by the West. But none of this applied to Guantánamo.

The procedures there were strictly on American terms, just the way Admiral Arnold Morgan liked it. And this was about as bad as it gets, if you had just attempted to blow up a U.S. airport, or, worse yet, the Capitol building in Washington, D.C.

It was not much comfort that things might have been a lot worse. Back in the early days of al Qaeda and Taliban interrogation, in 2002, temporary holding facilities for three hundred detainees were built at Guantánamo Bay right out in the open.

This was the feared Camp X-ray, where satellites occasionally photographed prisoners kneeling, shackled, or squatting under a burning hot sun with no overhead cover, in the presence of armed guards. Many prisoners were also seen to be wearing earmuffs, face masks, and covered goggles.

The more modern Camp Delta was quickly constructed for two thousand detainees, but Middle Eastern propaganda television stations still refer to Camp X-ray, because of its association with harsh treatment for its inmates. Human rights groups have called such measures "sensory deprivation," citing such levels of restraint as unnecessary and inhumane.

Never mind that most of them had been caught trying to kill, maim, or murder U.S. servicemen or civilians and were meeting a far less onerous fate than prisoners of the jihadists so often do. It might have been tough or even humiliating, but no one had their head cut off. Or worse.

Within a couple of years, there were six separate detention camps at Guantánamo (named 1, 2, 3, 4, Echo, and Iguana), three of them maximum security, capable of holding eight hundred prisoners between them, all living in solitary confinement.

Inside these camps, there were numerous detention blocks, each holding twenty-four units. These oppressive cells are eight feet long by six feet eight inches wide, and eight feet high, constructed of metallic wire mesh on a solid steel frame. A couple of hundred prisoners were released to other governments in 2005, but over five hundred were left.

Ramon Salman landed in Guantánamo after a direct flight from the U.S. Naval Air Station at Boca Chica, near Key West, fifty miles off Florida's south coast. He was immediately manacled and walked to a reception area, where he was issued the usual prisoner's gear: two orange boiler-suits, a foam sleeping mat, one blanket, two buckets, a pair of flip-flops, washcloth, soap, shampoo, and a copy of the Koran, in case he thought Allah might have abandoned him.

Salman was then walked slowly to a detention block, a separate one from either of his two cohorts, neither of whom did he realize was in captivity less than two hundred yards from where he stood.

And from there he was, for a while, left to his own thoughts. And these were private. Salman had not uttered one word since the New York cops had grabbed him in the Houston Street apartment the previous day. He must clearly have been stunned by the experience, seeing his two colleagues bound and gagged in the presence of Officers Carman and Pallizi.

But he had offered nothing, refused to give even his name, and was identified one hour later only by the police photographs which had been taken outside his apartment on Commonwealth Avenue. Since his arrest: nothing. Not a word on the military aircraft. Not a word to anyone since the flight. His entry card to Guantánamo read simply:

Ramon Salman, last known permanent address 2, Commonwealth Avenue, Boston, Massachusetts. Arrested in known terrorist HQ at 75 West Houston Street, New York City, on suspicion of terrorism against the United States. Believed involved in Logan airport bombing, 01/15/12, and other plots to murder and maim involving aircraft. This prisoner is designated ILLEGAL COMBATANT. NON-COOPERATIVE. Possibly Syrian. No passport located.

At 1900, they brought him an evening meal with the rest of the prisoners. It consisted of white rice, red beans, a banana, bread, and a bottle of water. The guards stared at him for a while, noting his unshaven, dark, swarthy Middle Eastern appearance, the pure hatred in his eyes, and the defiant curl to his upper lip.

This was the man, they knew, who had made the phone call from his apartment to Syria, the call that had betrayed so much. This was a critical figure in the al Qaeda system. He was, as yet, undetected as a disciple of bin Laden, and nothing was known about him. But he had been coldly planning to blow apart hundreds of innocent American citizens in the airport. But for the sharpness of the Boston financier Donald Martin in spotting the briefcase, he would have succeeded.

Salman's current plight may have incensed, or at least drawn sympathy from, the human rights groups. But it did not impress the U.S. guards, one of whom muttered, as they walked away, "For two bits, I'd kick the little fucker's nuts into his lungs."

Happily for Salman, there would be the kind of legal restraint common in the United States military, but there would be little mercy when the interrogation began at 0100. Still, they probably would not behead him.

The lights in his holding pen went out at 2100. It would be a long time before he was allowed out of the darkness, since the principal objective of interrogation, in its initial stages, is total disorientation, the prisoner not knowing whether it's day or night.

They came for him on time at 0100, and immediately placed a hood over his head. He was then manacled, placed in a chair, and the senior interrogator said quietly, "Okay, Ramon. We know you speak English, and we also have in custody your colleagues, Reza Aghani and the Palm Beach baggage man Mohammed Rahman.

"They have both been sensible and told us everything we need to know, including details of your own part in the attempted atrocities against the United States on January 15. However, I would like to clarify your personal details. I believe you are Syrian, like Mohammed?"

That last remark was a wild swing in the dark, based upon Mohammed's admitted job in the Syrian embassy in Caracas and the almost certain destination of that phone call from Commonwealth Avenue.

Salman made no reply. Was he related to Osama bin Laden, whose Saudi-based cousin still owned the Boston apartment? Nothing. Had he worked for Osama? Nothing. Was he an active jihadist? And, if not, why had he delivered the critical phone message back to Syria? Zero. No response. No reply to anything.

They kept it up for four hours, never threatening. Just probing. Then they took him back to his holding cell, still manacled, still hooded, still in the dark. Every half hour, someone came in and shook him awake. He ate his meals in the dark, he drank his water in the dark. Four times a day, and every night, he was questioned. Ramon Salman was never allowed to sleep.

At midnight on Friday, January 21, they turned on the pressure. Salman was by now completely disoriented. He did not know whether it was night or day. He did not know what day of the week it was; he had lost count of the number of days he had been in captivity.

He had not spoken, but he was clearly becoming distressed and was beginning to hallucinate, mumbling incoherently, the guards assumed in Arabic. As Friday turned into Saturday, they suddenly piped deafening music into his cell, cheap rock 'n' roll, blasting in the confined space. He was not manacled at the time, and the guards watched him clamp his hands over his ears.

At which point, they walked in and grabbed him, replacing the manacles and the handcuffs and the hood, and then left him for one hour with the music still blaring. When they returned, the tone was very different. "SALMAN! GET UP! SIDDOWN! And listen carefully, because our patience just ran out, and if we don't get some answers we're going to beat the living shit out of you."

Right then they pulled off his hood, and Salman's eyes, accustomed only to the dark, almost exploded as they were hit by viciously bright interrogation lights, aimed right at him.

Simultaneously, from out in the corridor came penetrating screams of pure terror, the sounds of hell, the unmistakable sounds of the torture chamber. There were sounds of men being beaten, of slashing whips, cries and whimpers of appallingly injured people. As fake tapes go, this one often did the trick down there in Guantánamo. The wretched Salman gritted his teeth, clenched his fists, and said nothing.

"SALMAN!" roared the interrogator. "Right here I'm holding a U.S. Army officer's baton, and two minutes from now I'm going to smash it right across your mouth. You got just one way out. Answer this question: are you Hamas, Hezbollah, Taliban, or al Qaeda?"

Ramon Salman spoke not one word. He just sat there, hunched up, listening to the screams echoing in the corridor. He was shivering now, but something seemed to tell him the Americans were not going to smash his face. Everyone knew the West was soft.

He kept up this defiance for one hour. And the guards began to think he never would give in. They were wrong. The following night, Salman cracked.

1930 Sunday 23 January
Guantánamo Bay

Reza Aghani had been kept outside under the hot Caribbean sun all day. He'd been kept in one highly uncomfortable position for more than ten hours. They gave him food and water, but he was not allowed to move, and there he had remained, isolated, disoriented, hallucinating, probably wishing to hell he had never asked Elliott Gardner to look after that briefcase in Logan's Terminal C.

They took him back to his cell and fed him his evening meal at 1900, just bread, beans, rice, and an apple. Then they turned up the music, and left him under rock 'n' roll assault for an hour. When the guards returned, they turned off the music, manacled and handcuffed him, and asked him the questions he had refused to answer maybe a hundred times.

Who is your immediate superior? Who gives your orders? What is his name?

Aghani had had enough. The wound in his upper arm, where he had been shot by Officer Pete Mackay, was throbbing. His resistance had ebbed away. There was nothing he would not do to end this interrogation. And he was very afraid the Americans might just kill him, and no one, including his wife and family in Tehran, would ever know what had become of him.

His hallucinations were very bad now, and he swayed through some kind of a no-man's-land, not comprehending the difference between reality and fantasy. He looked at the guard who asked the question. And he thought it was his father. The room kept dissolving into a café he frequented on the Vali-ye Asr. He could not even remember the question he had been asked ten seconds ago.

The American officer asked it again, and, as he did so, Aghani caved in. "Salman," he said. "Ramon Salman. He's my senior commander." With his last ounce of defiance, he blurted out, "But you'll never find him—he's gone home."

That's Hamas, right? asked the interrogating officer, taking yet another wild stab in the dark, but acting on certain knowledge that the new links between al Qaeda and the Iranian/Palestinian terror group were growing stronger with each passing year.

The title al Qaeda had become almost generic, and it had ceased to mean anything, certainly not sufficient to pinpoint a terrorist operation. Al Qaeda was operational all around Baghdad and Basra in Iraq, in Iran, in both the south and northeast of Afghanistan, and in the mountains of Pakistan. It meant nothing to an intelligence agency, whereas Hamas very definitely did. It meant Tehran, or Damascus, the Syrian capital, which Salman had called on his cell phone from Boston the night of January 14. And that mattered.

Reza Aghani elected to answer. He seemed only semiconscious, and he had been deprived of sleep for a long time. He just sighed, and then mumbled, "Yes. Hamas." Then he slumped forward, and the interrogator shouted for a stretcher to cart the unconscious Iranian terrorist to Guantánamo's small, twenty-bed hospital.

The seventeen words Reza Aghani had uttered, under stress, bore all the signs of a man who had given up. The interrogators assessed he had been telling the truth. And they returned with new vigor to the cell occupied by Ramon Salman.

They shook him awake and turned up the music, slammed the door, and left him. When they returned an hour later, he was rocking backward and forward, in the manner of the insane, and not in time to the fifth-rate rock 'n' roll. They ripped off his hood and turned on the arc lights, almost blinding him.

Right now, Ramon Salman did not know if he was in heaven or hell, though he suspected the latter. He could not work out whether he was in a dream or in reality. Like Aghani, he was hallucinating beyond reason, murmuring in Arabic, trying to work out why his children were in the room, why he kept drifting in and out of his favorite underground teahouse in Damascus, the one in Al-Bakry Street, near his home in the Old City.

SALMAN! YOU KNOW WHAT WE WANT. AND YOU'ALL GONNA TELL US RIGHT NOW. The words bore the drawn-out inflection of the Carolinas, and they were being yelled by a former graduate of The Citadel military academy.

GIMME THE NAME OF YOUR HAMAS COMMANDER IN CHIEF!!

Ramon Salman's head lolled back, and his eyes rolled. He seemed to slide into sleep, and now he was still, his eyes unseeing, facing up to the ceiling.

The southern infantry colonel's voice was softer now. And he spoke, quietly: "Come on, Ramon. You haven't got one thing to gain by keeping quiet. Come on, tell me your commander's name. Was it the Englishman, the SAS major who joined Hamas? Come on, boy, let's end this shit right now. Just tell me the truth. Who is he? And where does he live?"

Ramon Salman looked up and said softly, "Damascus. He lives in Damascus. Sharia Bab Touma."

"HE'S RAVI RASHOOD, RIGHT?" The voice from South Carolina was harsher now. *"FORMERLY KNOWN AS MAJOR RAY KERMAN OF THE BRITISH SAS.* That's who you work for, *RIGHT?"*

The yelled final word almost made the Syrian leap out of his skin. He began to tremble as if terrified that one more word would seal his death warrant.

"ANSWER ME, YOU LITTLE BASTARD!!" The American voice was now full of venom, edged with menace, as he went in for the kill.

"WAS THAT WHO YOU CALLED FROM COMMONWEALTH AVENUE LAST WEEK?"

Salman could stand no more. And he closed his eyes against the pitiless glare of the hot arc lights. "Yes, sir," he murmured in a barely audible whisper. "My commander in chief is General Ravi Rashood."

CHAPTER 3

The communiqué from Guantánamo Bay came ripping through cyberspace at 2100 and landed simultaneously on the screen of Lt. Commander Jimmy Ramshawe and that of his boss, the director of the National Security Agency, Rear Admiral George R. Morris.

Within moments, it was linked to the CIA's Middle East desk in Langley, and to the Surveillance Division in Washington, D.C. All the intelligence agencies were alerted. Ramon Salman had spilled the beans. The attempted atrocities on January 15 were a Hamas plot, masterminded by General Rashood, whose address they now had.

The information confirmed what U.S. intelligence chiefs had long suspected: Al Qaeda had dissipated into a kind of rabble, no longer coordinated without the cash and discipline of their erstwhile leader Osama bin Laden. The real, burgeoning power of the jihadist movement was held by the ruthless military council of Hamas and their ruthless military C-in-C, General Ravi Rashood.

The duty officer working the first night watch on the second floor of the Ops-2B building saw his own screen flashing the letters *GBI*. That meant Guantánamo Bay Intelligence coming through. He knew the drill and hit the direct lines to both Admiral Morris and Lt. Commander Ramshawe.

The admiral was 170 miles away in the Norfolk yards, and Ramshawe's home telephone was patched through to the Australian embassy. Behind those great wrought-iron gates on Massachusetts Avenue, the young Aussie assistant to the director was having dinner with his fiancée, Jane Peacock, daughter of the ambassador.

Jane handed him the phone, heard him snap *I'll be there,* and groaned. Jimmy kissed her and said, "I'm sorry, really sorry. But this is important."

"It always is," she replied. "See you tomorrow?"

"No worries," he called, as he headed for the stairway. "We're going out. Pick you up at 1900."

"When the hell's that?" she muttered. "Nineteen hundred! Jesus, what does he think I am, a midshipman?"

On his way around the Beltway, heading east toward the Parkway, Jimmy called the Big Man and told him to stand by for a call in thirty minutes on a more secure phone from his office. When he arrived, he was immediately informed that Admiral Morris was on his way in by helicopter from Norfolk. The breakthrough in Guantánamo Bay was the last piece in a long-running jigsaw puzzle.

All of the Western world's intelligence agencies knew of the astonishing defection of SAS Major Ray Kerman during a pitched battle in the Israeli city of Hebron in the summer of 2004. They knew he had found some reason to kill two of his colleagues, and then had vanished.

Over the next five or six years, there were a number of daredevil attacks by the warriors of Hamas, involving highly trained troops and even submarines. The West suspected there was only one man capable of leading such sophisticated adventures, and it plainly had to be the work of Major Kerman, who was, even by SAS standards, a brilliant operator.

However, no one ever knew for sure. The name General Rashood surfaced every now and then, and informers referred to him by name, but no one ever found out who Rashood was, or anything about his background.

Admiral Morgan and Jimmy Ramshawe were darned sure he was Major Kerman, and a couple of times the U.S. military came within an ace of catching him. But he always got away, and still no one was ever certain of his true identity.

They were now. The transcript of the interrogation in Guantánamo made it quite clear that the question had been put to the terrorist Salman in an unambiguous way. Major Kerman and General Rashood were one and the same. Better yet, there was now an address, Bab Touma Street in

Damascus, a street that ends at the Bab Touma Gate, the eastern approach into the city through the ancient Roman wall.

The last line of the communiqué from Guantánamo stated that in answer to the question *What number Bab Touma?* Salman had replied, *within a hundred meters of the Gate.* And that was enough. That was actually plenty. The CIA would take it from there. The important thing was that General Rashood was right now living the last few weeks of his life. There would be no mistakes. The reign of the world's most lethal terrorist was drawing to a close.

Jimmy Ramshawe called Admiral Morgan on an encrypted line. He told him Admiral Morris was on his way. Arnold did not hesitate. "I'll be right over," he said. "Gimme forty-five."

"No speeding, for Christ's sake. I don't want to send someone to get you out of the slammer."

"On this little mission, young Jimmy, anyone stops my car, the whole goddamned police department will be looking for new jobs tomorrow morning."

The likelihood of any Washington cop pulling over the admiral's White House limousine *(for life)* driven by a White House driver *(until he was late)* was remote. In all the many years Arnold Morgan had served his nation, only one cruiser had ever dared to take such an action.

The popular story goes that the driver, overtaken by Admiral Morgan's car, which was making about 105 mph around the Beltway, switched on his lights and siren and came screaming up behind him, muttering, "I don't care who's in that car, I'm pulling the crazy sonofabitch over and he's going to pay the *biggest* fine. I might even have him jailed for three months."

When the two cars came to a halt, the policeman took one look at the figure glowering in the back, and the blood drained from his face. He just said swiftly but sheepishly, "Oh . . . er . . . good afternoon, sir . . . I just wondered if you needed an escort."

The admiral just growled, "Sure, if you can keep up . . . *NOW HIT IT, CHARLIE!*" And the big limo hurled gravel as it squealed off the hard shoulder, leaving the cop in a cloud of dust, cursing his bad luck.

Forty-four minutes after Jimmy's phone call, Admiral Morgan, who had once been the director of the NSA, came thundering into the Ops-2B

Building, under escort by two young guards who were both on the verge of nervous breakdowns, so urgent did the Big Man's mission appear to be.

Which office, sir?

"The goddamned director's office, of course. Where d'you think I want to go, the mail room?"

One of the guards went white. The other tried to turn away, but he caught the sly wink the admiral gave him. At the hallowed door of the director of the National Security Agency, one of them stepped forward to tap on the door. But the admiral just grabbed the handle and opened it, strode across the room, and sat down hard in the director's big executive chair, which had once been his.

He always sat there when he visited Admiral Morris. It seemed, in its way, correct for the most respected man who had ever worked in U.S. military intelligence to be sitting right there. Admiral Morris considered it an honor. In lighter moments, even the President of the United States often asked Admiral Morgan if it would be okay for him to sit behind his desk in the Oval Office. It had been a standing joke between them ever since Arnold Morgan had swept him to power two years previously.

The door opened again, and this time Lt. Commander Ramshawe came through. "Admiral Morris has landed, sir," he said. "He'll be here in five."

"Does he know I'm here?"

"Arnie, there are twenty-eight thousand people currently employed at this agency. Every last one of 'em knows you're here."

"Would that include the guys who bring the coffee?"

"Yessir, it's on its way, nuclear hot with buckshot the way you like it."

"Outstanding," replied the admiral. "Now tell me about the little Arab who caved in under interrogation."

"Well, it seems the Guantánamo guys got their lead from Reza Aghani, the one who got shot at Logan and went to Bethesda. He knew only a little, and took his orders from Ramon Salman, the Commonwealth Avenue guy who we picked up in New York. That confirmed Hamas.

"And then they went right to work on Salman, broke him down without laying a finger on him, and he confessed he worked for our old friend General Rashood, aka Major Ray Kerman. Once he'd gone that far, he apparently told the guys the precise whereabouts of the general, some side street in Damascus, and I guess that's what we're here to discuss."

"Was that who he called in Damascus, the night before the Logan bomb?"

"Damn right it was. And he admitted it."

The door opened again, and Admiral Morris walked in followed by the waiter. Admiral Morgan stood up and clasped his hand. "Good to see you, George," he said, and for a few fleeting moments the ex–nuclear submarine commander from Chevy Chase stood and smiled at the former carrier battle group commander. They were two old warriors, friends for thirty years, patriots, and both still capable of cold fury at any threat to the United States.

"Arnie," said Admiral Morris, "am I right in thinking we've got this Rashood character cornered in Damascus?"

"Well, not quite. But at least we know where he lives, which is a darned sight more than we have ever known before."

"We don't want him alive, do we?"

"Hell, no. This is one murdering sonofabitch. He's blown up power stations, refineries, volcanoes, and god knows how many people. He's smart, trained, and damned dangerous. Rashood is one of those people you kill, no questions asked. Nothing announced. Nothing admitted. Just get it done."

"As I recall, Arnie, you're kind of good at that sort of stuff."

"Guess you could say I've had my moments. But not for a couple of weeks." For the second time in a half hour, Admiral Morgan offered a conspiratorial wink, this time at Jimmy Ramshawe, who grinned and shook his head.

It was almost midnight now. Admiral Morris poured the coffee, firing a couple of buckshot sweeteners into his old friend's cup. Jimmy delivered it to the big desk, and Arnold Morgan said crisply, "Okay, boys, whaddya think, do we shoot him, poison him, blow him up, or bomb the whole street?"

"Why not the whole city?" said Admiral Morris benignly. "Might as well start World War III while we're at it."

Arnold Morgan chuckled. "George, I'm more or less serious. It will probably not be that long before the Hamas leaders discover that someone has spilled the beans. Maybe a matter of three or four weeks. At which point, they're going to move their General Rashood to a very different, much safer place. Maybe even to a different country, but certainly to a different city. Then we've lost him again. So we better get moving if we want to take him out."

"I presume you rule out a full-frontal assault?"

"Christ, yes. We can't do that, not with the new Middle East peace talks coming up."

"Then you're thinking straightforward assassin? CIA or even special forces?"

"Quite honestly, George, I'm not mad about either. First, we don't really know how much protection Rashood has, how many bodyguards or even military security. And second, it'll take us a while to find out. And even if we could get a team in place, or even a single sniper, we have no guarantee our man could get away; and if he were caught, there'd be hell to pay."

"How about a bomb?" said Jimmy.

"Well, that's a possibility. But we got so much trouble in the Middle East, it would probably turn out to be a bigger risk than the president would be prepared to take. Can you imagine the uproar if we either got caught, or somehow got the blame?"

"I could imagine it very easily," interjected George Morris. "The liberal press would crucify us, behaving like gangsters, bullies, murderers, and Christ knows what else—reverting to the standards of our enemies and all that."

"Don't remind me, George," replied Admiral Morgan. "But these things have to be considered. And in the end, we might have to get someone else to do it for us."

"What? Go in and assassinate General Rashood? And then be prepared to take the rap for it if necessary?"

"There's only one group who would fill those boots," said Jimmy. "And that's the Mossad."

"My own thoughts precisely," said Arnold Morgan. "Remember, Israel wants General Rashood dead worse than we do."

"Remind me?" said Admiral Morris.

"Well, for a start, in the original battle in Hebron, he turned traitor against the Israeli forces, which counts as high treason and is punishable by execution. Then he masterminded those two huge bank robberies in

Jerusalem and Tel Aviv, Christmas 'bout eight years ago . . . what was it? A hundred million minimum?

"Four months later, he led an assault force on the Nimrod Jail and released just about every one of Israel's major political prisoners, killing almost the entire prison staff while he was at it. A couple of years ago, the Mossad thought they had him trapped in some restaurant in France. But Rashood turned the tables on the Mossad hitmen and killed them both. And the Israelis, as we know, never forgive."

"Are they still looking for him?" asked George Morris.

"They never forgive, or give up," replied Admiral Morgan. "Guess that's why they're still breathing as a nation. They're still looking for him, all right, but no one ever told me they came even close to finding him. Rashood's probably the most dangerous and clever opponent the West has had since bin Laden retired."

"I don't think we'd even need to ask the Mossad to help us," said Jimmy. "Just tell 'em where he is. Assure them of the validity of our sources, and they'll be grateful. We can probably leave the rest to them."

"They might not acknowledge we're asking for a favor," said Arnold. "But they'll sure as hell know why we're telling them."

"Do we need to involve the government and the president and everyone else?" asked Admiral Morris.

"Hell, no," said Arnold. "This will be just a friendly chat between intelligence agencies. My view is the less said, the better. Until one day we get a call from an informer letting us know the archterrorist General Rashood has been killed by a bomb in Damascus."

"How do you know it'll be a bomb?"

"It just happens to be the Mossad's preferred method of operating. Less risk of missing the target, and the ability to be far away when the timing device explodes."

"How do we start?" asked Admiral Morris.

"That part's easy," replied Arnold. At which point he picked up the telephone on the big desk and said sharply, "Get me the Israeli embassy, would you . . . right away."

Moments later the call went through, and Admiral Morgan ordered whoever was at the other end, "Put me through to the ambassador, would you?"

Sir, I would need to know the nature of your call before I am permitted to do that.

"I'm not at all used to explaining things," replied Arnold, curtly. "Just tell Ambassador Gavron to return my call immediately. That's Admiral Arnold Morgan. I'm in the director's office at the National Security Agency, Fort Meade. And tell him to look sharp about it."

Crash. Down phone. The young Israeli girl on the line at the embassy instantly realized that in her experience no one had ever passed on a message like that to Ambassador Gavron, and she knew the name Arnold Morgan. Precisely twenty-three seconds later, the phone rang in George Morris's office.

And the other two heard Arnold say cheerfully, "Hello, David. Yes, I appreciate you tried to look sharp about it!" And they watched the great man chuckle at the minor explosion he had put under the switchboard at the Israeli embassy. At least, it was minor compared to the one he was planning for Bab Touma Street, Damascus.

"Urgent? Hell, no. I just decided it was too long since I'd seen you, and I'd made a highly classified decision to buy you dinner—tomorrow night?

". . . What d'you mean, only if Kathy comes? I know she's better-looking than I am . . . of course we're going somewhere halfway decent. I'll get a table at Matisse. And, no. That does not mean I must have an ulterior motive. Seven-thirty. See you then."

Admiral Morgan had just reentered, in his customary rambunctious manner, the life of one of the Mossad's most revered former commanders. Which, happily, always amused the life out of the battle-scarred Israeli general.

David Gavron was a true sabra, an Israeli of the blood, and a patriot from his bootstraps to the jagged scar that was slashed like forked lightning across the left side of his face. He was six feet tall, lean, upright, very obviously ex-military, with a fair, freckled complexion, deeply tanned, with piercing blue eyes.

His sandy-colored hair, receding, still seemed bleached from the Sinai Desert, where, thirty-nine years ago, as a young tank commander, he had fought a desperate battle for his own life and for that of his country.

The bitterness of the Yom Kippur War remained for years in the hearts of the Israeli army commanders; but, for some, there burned a flame of pure fire that would never die. David Gavron was one of those.

On that most terrible day, October 8, 1973, Captain Gavron was twenty-six. And he was caught up in the frenzied rush to join General

Abraham "Bren" Adan's tank division. He was alongside the general as they charged out into the desert to face the massed ranks of Egypt's well-prepared troops sweeping across the canal.

The Egyptians had slammed into the Israeli defenses while the entire nation was at prayer. When the two armies finally came face-to-face in the Sinai, General Adan was still unprepared. He was stunned by the suddenness of the attack, and every advantage was with the invaders. The Egyptian troops, backed up by literally hundreds of tanks, dug in, calmly, to await the hopelessly outnumbered Israelis.

General Adan and his men attacked with stupendous courage, and for a half hour it looked as if the Egyptians might lose their nerve and retreat. But in the end, their superior numbers held sway, and after four hours the bloodstained, battered Israeli armored division was forced back.

Hundreds had died. David Gavron was wounded, shot as he tried to drag an injured man from his burning tank. Then he was blown twenty feet forward by an exploding shell that seared the entire left side of his face. At that point, Israel's fate hung in the balance. They were temporarily saved only by the gallantry of their teenage infantrymen, who fought and died by the hundreds trying to hold the Egyptians back until reinforcements arrived.

For a while, the Sinai was the Somme with sun and sand. But finally, assisted by Captain Gavron, General Adan re-formed his front line and once more they rolled forward into the teeth of the Egyptian attack.

David Gavron, his arm bandaged, his face burned, fought only thirty yards from "Bren" Adan. To this day he is still haunted by the memory of that moment when "Bren" raised his right fist and bellowed the motto of his embattled army—*Follow me!* It was, he says, the sheer nobility of the man.

No one who was there would ever forget that roar of anger and leadership, as the guns of the Israeli tanks once more opened fire. No one heard it louder than David Gavron, as his tank rumbled forward, and there, to his starboard side, was General "Bren," right fist still clenched, at the head of his battered division, pounding toward the heart of Egypt's Second Army.

The Israelis opened fire. They threw everything they had at the Egyptians, whose commanders finally lost their nerve completely and gave in. Nine days later, General Adan, with the always-faithful Captain Gavron, drove on and crossed the Suez Canal, and proceeded to smash the hell out of Egypt's Third Army, before leaving it isolated in the desert.

Decorated for gallantry beyond the call of duty, David Gavron was promoted to become one of the youngest colonels ever to serve in the Israeli Army. He was groomed for many years to take up his position as head of the Mossad.

For all of their lives, the legendary General Adan and the subsequent prime minister, General Arik Sharon, would regard David Gavron as perhaps their most trusted friend.

Arnold Morgan knew every line of the above. He did not expect the ambassador to regard Ravi Rashood as anything less than a reptile that must be beheaded at any cost. David regarded any enemy of Israel in that light, as indeed Admiral Morgan did enemies of the United States. They were two military leaders who, through no fault of their own, considered their nation's problems to be theirs to rectify. They were born that way.

The plush Matisse restaurant tonight would not be an ideal place for any terrorist to look for mercy. Especially if he happened to be General Ravi Rashood. Admiral Morgan anticipated having the upper hand, since he alone could tell the Israeli ambassador the whereabouts of the Hamas military leader.

Geographically, the restaurant was perfectly positioned, just about midway between the Morgans' home at the edge of Chevy Chase Village, and the Israeli embassy, which was situated three miles north of downtown D.C. off Connecticut Avenue. The other attraction of Matisse was that it was generally regarded as among the top five restaurants in the Washington area, a favorite haunt of presidents and senators.

With its superb design inspired by Henri Matisse's work, its gleaming white tablecloths, and French Mediterranean cooking, the restaurant felt no obligation even to put prices on its menu. The introduction of crude commercial considerations would doubtless have caused the head chef to have a nervous breakdown.

Arnold Morgan lived only a mile away, and he was a regular. For this night, he chose a corner banquette in the cozy back dining room, with its cheerful limestone fireplace. It was automatically assumed that a member of the proprietor's family, the lovely young Deanna, would serve the table personally.

Admiral Morgan arrived first with his wife, Kathy. His driver, Charlie, dropped them right outside the door on Wisconsin Avenue, and they stepped out into a biting January wind gusting out of the northwest. As soon as they were seated, the admiral ordered a bottle of supreme white burgundy, his favorite Meursault, Premier Crus Perrières 2004, made by the maestro Jean-Marc Roulot at his small domaine off the main road through to Puligny.

He was certain this would please General Gavron, who, despite hardly touching alcohol while he was involved in the Mossad, these days had mellowed and hugely enjoyed a glass of what Arnold described as *snorto-de-luxe.*

This was plainly a phrase more befitting the torpedo room of a nuclear submarine than the fabled small chateaux of the Côte d'Or in central France. But it did not disguise the admiral's knowledge and enjoyment of great French wine, and tonight was an occasion to be savored.

If it were successful, the admiral's selections ought to be paid for by a nationwide donation drive of pure gratitude by the American people.

In the absence of that, Arnold would probably toss the check at the Oval Office for a refund. As for charging one dollar for his time and skill, the admiral would have had the same stunned reaction as the Matisse head chef if anyone happened to mention money.

At 7:42 P.M., Ambassador Gavron's driver dropped him off outside the door. He arrived at the admiral's table dressed in a dark blue lightweight suit, with a white shirt and a blue silk Israeli Navy tie. He leaned over to kiss Kathy's hand and then shook the hand of Arnold Morgan.

Just then the chilled Meursault arrived, and the waiter poured three glasses. David Gavron raised his and said quietly, "To the United States of America."

"Thank you, David," replied the admiral, who usually presumed he *was* the United States of America, particularly in the event of trouble.

"Before we begin, let me have them prepare a bottle of Bordeaux for our main course," said Arnold.

"No argument from me," chuckled the Israeli, flashing his wide smile, which Kathy, along with several other beautiful women, some of them divorced, considered so engaging. It made him one of the most attractive men in Washington. Especially if anyone knew his background: decorated warrior, the Mossad's James Bond, and latterly a high-ranking diplomat on the world stage.

Arnold studied the wine list, which he normally referred to as the race card, and chose a third-growth bottle from Margaux, the 1996 Château Palmer, which sits on the left bank of the Gironde, just west of the junction with the mighty Dordogne River.

"I think we'll be okay with that," he said. "Sixteen years old from the slopes near the village of Margaux, where they once grew the favorite wine of Thomas Jefferson . . . and you know something? People still say that after a really hot summer, those wines still surpass all others grown in the High Médoc."

"Arnie, how the hell do you know all this stuff?"

"David, you may, during the course of this evening, become astounded at some of the things I know."

"Not for the first time, old friend," said the ambassador. "And, I hope, not for the last, given your predilection to share the *snorto-de-luxe* . . . by the way, this white burgundy is probably the best I've ever had."

"They keep a darned good cellar here," replied Arnold. "Shall we just sit quietly and have a drink, or do you want to have a look at the menu?"

Kathy spoke first. "Let's just have a drink," she said. "Unless David's in a rush."

"Not me, my dear," he said courteously. "I'm happy to sit here with my two favorite people and sip the finest wine on earth until midnight if necessary."

"That's good," said Arnold, sipping luxuriously. "Because there's a character who looms from our past who's just become highly topical."

"There is? And who might that be?" asked the ambassador.

"Do you remember General Ravi Rashood?"

"Remember him! Jesus Christ, I still wake up in the night thinking about him. What's he done now?"

"Well, nothing we actually know about. But we have some interesting new information about him."

"And I bet I know where you got it."

"I bet you don't."

"Okay, how about Guantánamo Bay, where you're grilling the Boston airport bombers?"

"Now, how the hell do you know that?" asked the admiral, plainly incredulous.

"During the course of this evening," said the Israeli, deadpan, "you may become astounded at some of the things I know."

Both men laughed. But Arnold Morgan looked serious when he said, "No one knows who we have and who we don't have in Guantánamo. Except, apparently, the Mossad."

"We don't know much," said Gavron. "We just heard from one of our lawyers that both the wounded man who had the bomb, and the big cheese you picked up in New York, have been removed from the U.S. civilian justice system. We actually guessed the rest. Guessed, specifically, that you would want both terrorists out of the way, under military security, where you could interrogate them in peace and hopefully get some answers."

"And that brought you to Guantánamo?"

"Absolutely. But I'm not going to ask you to confirm that. Because it's none of our business. But I'll say one thing: we would be inordinately grateful if you could help us to nail that terrible bastard Rashood . . . sorry, Kathy."

"David, you forget, I live in the ops room of a nuclear submarine. Even our clocks chime the bells of the watch—I haven't known the correct time for years, and I'm really used to sailor's language."

David Gavron smiled. "Of course," he said. "Anyway, back to that terrible bastard Rashood . . . we'd do anything to find him. But he's always escaped us, in Israel, in Syria, in France, once even in London. He always seems to be one jump ahead."

"So you'll be pleased to know I may have a permanent address for him?" interjected the admiral.

"Pleased? My entire country would be thrilled. He's done us a huge amount of damage, and he's still out there. Somewhere."

Arnold Morgan, sensing an advantage, decided to keep his guest on the hook for a while. "Okay, let's have a look at the menus, shall we? David, I don't want you to get overexcited on an empty stomach."

They read through the short list, three appetizers, four entrees. "All fresh, nothing frozen, and no bullshit," said Arnold, glancing up at the newly arrived Deanna and saying, "Crab cakes, and then rack of lamb, please. . . . Kathy?"

"Sea scallops and grilled rockfish, please."

David Gavron went for gravlax and then breast of duck with risotto, spinach, and port sauce. All three of them were accustomed to making swift, firm decisions.

"Arnie, do you really have an address for Rashood?"

"Of course I do, and since you plainly know our source, you'll understand we have assessed it as highly reliable."

"Will you tell me?"

"Got a pen?"

David Gavron produced a slim gold ballpoint and a wafer-thin leather notepad, and looked up expectantly.

"He's in Syria," said Arnold. "Damascus, Old City, right inside the Roman wall near the eastern gate. Bab Touma Street. Less than a hundred yards from the Bab Touma Gate itself, left-hand side of the street coming in from the Barada River bridge.

"Sorry we don't have a street number, our informant did not know, and if he had known he'd have told us. He said it's a big eighteenth-century house right around the corner from the Elissar restaurant."

"That's fantastic, Arnie. Does he live there with his wife?"

"What wife?"

"Oh, a Palestinian girl he met right after he defected from the Israeli army. I heard they were married almost immediately. She's supposed to be very beautiful. And she's also very dangerous—apparently gunned down two French secret servicemen a couple of years back, in Beirut."

"She had a good tutor," said Admiral Morgan.

"None better," said David Gavron. "Ex-SAS major, wasn't he? His background's still a mystery, and the Brits won't tell even us who he really is."

"Nor us," said the Admiral. "I think the guy embarrassed the hell out of 'em. Ramshawe says he's from a rich family, Iranians living in London. He went to Harrow School and then the Royal Military Academy at Sandhurst, ended up commanding their top special forces, and then jumped ship and joined the goddamned Palestinians."

"Harrow's one of their top private schools, right?" asked Kathy.

"Sure is. Churchill went there. Guess they taught him about patriotism."

"Probably taught the former Major Kerman too," said David. "But he couldn't sort out who he was, not until he ended up back in the desert.

Funny, isn't it? Turning his back on everything like that, becoming an enemy of everything he'd ever known."

"Sure as hell is," responded the admiral. "Can't hardly imagine waking up one morning as a decorated, serving British Army officer, and suddenly deciding to be a goddamned Arab terrorist! Jesus Christ. Must have been some turning point."

"Arnie, are you planning to get after him?" asked the ambassador.

"Not right now. Not with the Middle East peace talks coming up. We couldn't afford to get caught, or even suspected."

"Happily, my former organization suffers from no such constraints. You may leave it to us."

"I had hoped so, David."

"Yes, I guessed as much. There is, after all, no such thing as a free dinner. Especially one as good as this."

1645 Monday 6 February 2012
Mossad Headquarters
King Saul Boulevard
Tel Aviv

Inside the briefing room, the atmosphere was subdued. The Israeli general, a man in his sixties, standing in front of the big computer screen on the wall, spoke quietly and firmly, pointing with his baton at the illuminated map of Bab Touma Street, Damascus.

"Right here," he said, "we have rented an apartment on the third floor. It's pretty basic, but it has a bathroom, cold water only, and electricity. Our field agents have moved in a couple of mattresses and some blankets. But you're going to be uncomfortable. There's no workable kitchen and nothing to cook on. We have installed an electric kettle and a coffeepot. There's not much else."

Before him, sitting at the conference table, were four ex-military secret service officers. All of them, for the moment, wore olive-green uniforms and had duffel bags slung on the floor next to them, alongside their M-16 machine guns. Two of these men wore the coveted wings signifying membership in Israel's elite parachute division. They both wore officers' bars on their shoulders. All four of them had the distinguishing three small Hebrew letters stitched in yellow above the breast pocket.

"You will see from the map, gentlemen, that this apartment has a commanding view of the big house directly opposite, and we were damn lucky to get it. An old Arab man used to live there, and we paid him generously to get out. While you are in residence, you will ignore his mail, answer the door to no one, and use cell phones only under the most dire circumstances.

"You will eat a proper meal only once a day, and that will be after dark. For that you will leave by the back door, and never, under any circumstances, use the same restaurant twice. Fortunately, Damascus stays open very late."

One of the paratroopers asked about the getaway, and the general answered sharply. "Right here," he said, pointing with his baton, "one street back, is a locked garage, right before house number 46. You will of course recce this, and inside that garage you will find a very old, battered-looking wreck of an automobile, plainly on its last legs.

"However, it has been expertly converted, four new tires, new transmission, brand-new Mercedes engine, everything directly out of the showroom. When you leave, you will be in Arab dress and you will make your escape in the old car, which will run like a Ferrari and attract the attention of no one. There will be two heavy machine guns in the back in the event of an emergency.

"You will drive out of the east gate and turn hard right down to the circle, and then it's marked, straight down the highway to the airport that lies to the southwest of the city.

"Two of our field agents will meet you. One will get rid of the car; the other will escort you to a private Learjet, and you will take off immediately for Israel. The agent already has your passports. You will not need them for entry into Syria. There will be no record that you were ever in the country."

The general, whose name was never mentioned, stood before them in full uniform, his steel-gray hair cropped tight, his posture still rigidly upright. His face was a picture of military sternness as he outlined the operation designed to execute Ravi and Shakira Rashood, the sworn and proven enemies of Israel.

There have always been officers in the Israeli Army whose determination borders on fanaticism. They are men who will stop at nothing to keep their nation safe, and this particular general was most certainly one of them.

As a twenty-year-old infantry lieutenant, he had fought shoulder to shoulder against the invading Egyptians with General Avraham Yoffe, when they smashed their way through the Mitla Pass in the Sinai during the Six-Day War in 1967. They were six bloodstained days of pure heroism by the Israelis. In less than a week, they destroyed four armies and 370 fighter-bombers belonging to four attacking nations.

The general had not been brought up to drop his guard against enemies of the state.

And here in the plain white-walled briefing room, in the heart of Israel's Institute for Intelligence and Special Operations, he was once more planning a deadly strike against a couple of Palestinian terrorists who had posed more trouble for his nation than the Egyptian Second Army had done thirty-nine years previously.

It was a typical Mossad briefing. Two guards on the door, no cell phones permitted. The four men who were going in tonight had made their wills and had their last contacts with home. They would not carry any written notes with them when finally they were released, and they would leave from the rooftop, by helicopter, to the Israeli Army's Northern Command HQ base for a short stopover. The sixty-mile onward flight to Damascus would take them over the Golan Heights, along the north-running 1974 Ceasefire Line, and then east over the desert into the southern area of the city.

The leader, sitting pensively, listening to the general, was Colonel Ben Joel, fortyish combat veteran, unshaven, former Special Forces, who had been involved in the revenge attack on Yasser Arafat's house in Gaza. Ben was an infantryman, a ground-to-air communications officer, and an explosives expert, more accustomed to fighting with a club and tear gas against rioting crowds of Arab youths.

His number two was Major Itzaak Sherman, son of a true Israeli patriot, the legendary, highly decorated Sergeant Mo Sherman, who had gone into Entebbe Airport alongside Jonathan Netanyahu to rescue the hostages in 1976. Sergeant Sherman was a choral conductor in Tel Aviv, and no one in the aircraft ever forgot him, standing up as the commandos screamed in from the east, low over the pitch-black northern waters of Lake Victoria. Sergeant Sherman conducted these armed daredevils as they sang at the top of their lungs that most haunting patriotic song of Israel, "Onward—we must keep going onward!"—shutting out the fear of the great unknown that faced them when they landed.

As they dropped below a hundred feet, howling toward the runway, Mo Sherman hooked up the sound system to the bittersweet anthem written by Paul Ben-Haim and each man grappled with his onrushing task to the glorious strains of "Fanfare to Israel."

Those who were there swear to God that that music made them all feel fifteen feet tall, revved them up for the murderous firefight to come in the airport, the fight in which Yanni Netanyahu was mortally wounded. Mo Sherman, brokenhearted, helped carry the young leader's body into the aircraft for the homeward journey.

And here was Mo's son, Major Itzaak, preparing to go into another hostile foreign country and carry out his unquestioning duty on behalf of his government. His father's last words to him were simple: "Go bravely, son, and make sure you do not let anyone down."

The third man was another ex-member of the Israeli Special Forces, a newly promoted Mossad agent, Lt. Colonel John Rabin, aged forty-one. His own father had died in the Sinai on the opening morning of the Yom Kippur War, along with hundreds of young soldiers facing the Egyptian tanks. John never knew him, but followed in his footsteps as a career combat soldier. Like Ben Joel, he was an explosives expert, but a specialist, said to be the best in the Israeli Defense Force.

The fourth member of the team was one of those Mossad hard men whose background was not publicized. He was a five-foot, ten-inch iron man from a small town south of Hebron. He was massively strong, skilled in close combat, and a maestro with a knife, a man who'd kill you as soon as look at you. His name was Abraham, and he was on the team as a personal bodyguard to the other three.

His wide smile and cheerful manner did not provide any clue to his true disposition. But the others liked him immensely and were delighted, to a man, that Abraham would be with them.

Midnight, 6 February
Northern Command HQ, Galilee

The wide single rotor flailed the cold night air as the Texas-built Sea Panther lifted slowly off the runway. It rose vertically for fifty feet, then tilted north toward the Sea of Galilee and rocketed away into the night, climbing to five thousand feet. When it reached the Ceasefire Line, it would drop down drastically, in order to come in under any Syrian radar that might be active. Unlikely, but remotely possible.

To the rear of the pilot sat the four Mossad special operators: Colonel Ben Joel, Major Itzaak Sherman, Colonel John Rabin, and Abraham the bodyguard. All of them were in Arab dress for the insert. And each one of them carried his personal light machine gun, strapped beneath his white robe.

They carried only food and water in their traveling bags, and no identity. All of their operational equipment was already installed in the apartment on Bab Touma—the high explosive, the detonators, the timing devices, the electronic wiring, the tool bag, a laptop computer, a long-lens camera, the binoculars, two cell phones, the front and back door keys, four mugs, one spoon, a bag of Turkish coffee, and a bag of sugar, plus two thousand Syrian *lira*.

They flew at almost two hundred miles an hour, in silence, for a half hour before the pilot called back, *"We've cleared the Heights and we're descending to around fifty feet . . . get ready . . . ten minutes."*

The Sea Panther came clattering over the cold, silent desert at the farthest possible point from Syrian military radar. None of the operators detected them; no one had the slightest idea they were there. The pilot used night goggles to spot the road running up from the south, and then called:

"This is it, guys, we're landing."

The army helicopter touched down just before 0100. The loadmaster jumped out and held open the door, with his other arm pointing toward the road. All four of the Mossad hitmen followed him out and, without a word, walked away from the aircraft, which was up and flying home thirty-six seconds after it had landed.

After a hundred yards, they reached the long straight road that led to Damascus, and they stood on its edge in the dark. In the distance they could see headlights coming toward them, very fast. When the vehicle reached them, it skidded to a halt. It was a big old clapped-out American Ford, its side door dented, one window cracked, in desperate need of paint, or even a clean. On the plus side, it was right on time.

Abraham automatically climbed into the passenger seat; the other three piled into the back. The driver, an Israeli field officer known to Ben Joel, just said, "Hi, Ben. Everyone aboard? Okay, let's go."

They were around thirty miles shy of the city, and the car was as quiet and fast as a brand-new Mercedes Benz. According to the driver, they had taken a new Mercedes, stripped off the body, and somehow fitted an aged, rusting thirty-year-old substitute over the chassis.

It now looked as if it belonged in an Arab side street, which was, after all, where it was now headed, and where it would spend the rest of its life, a totally forgettable, undercover adjunct to the most dangerous secret service on earth.

"Did the pilot contact you, Jerry?" asked Ben Joel.

"No need. I had your ETA and GPS numbers. I just waited a mile up the road until I heard the helo. Then I hit the gas pedal and here you all are."

"Pretty neat," said Colonel Joel. "Are we likely to be stopped or checked at the edge of the city?"

"Hell, no. This isn't Baghdad. And even if the police were on the lookout for someone, they'd never check this thing. We look like a group of local Bedouin bringing vegetables to the market. No problem."

The car sped on, straight up Route 5, over the railroad and down the freeway into the city. They hardly saw another car until they reached the streetlights of Damascus. Jerry took a swing to the western side and came in along Kalid Ibn al-Walid Avenue. They swung right just before the Hejaz Railroad Station and skirted around the north side of the Old City wall.

They drove through the Bab Touma Gate and headed down the street of the same name. Jerry took the second right, drove for fifty yards, and parked in the dark, right next to a grim-looking back door to somewhere. He ordered them all out, produced a key, and opened it.

"There's no light in here," he whispered. "Follow me up to the third floor." And in single file they crept up the narrow staircase. Finally, on a narrow top-floor landing, he groped for another door, opened it with a key, and switched on a light.

"There's one other apartment on this level," he said. "We had to buy the fucker, make sure no one was in residence." Abraham and Itzaak both laughed.

Jerry waited around for less than five minutes, just pointing out the bathroom and the coffeepot, before he showed them the view. And now he turned out the light and walked to the window. "That's your target right there," he said, pointing directly across Bab Touma Street. "That big place with the steps up to the front door. There's two guards right inside it. Be careful at all times."

And with that, Jerry was gone, leaving Ben Joel and his men staring out at the two-hundred-year-old townhouse across the street, where Ravi and Shakira Rashood, protected by at least two armed guards and probably more, were doubtless sleeping the untroubled sleep of the innocent.

Colonel Joel called his team to order. "It's almost 0220. We'll have something to eat, get some coffee, and begin the operation at 0300," he said. "Four-hour shifts. Abraham, Itzaak, you crash out on those two mattresses in the bedroom. John and I will open the surveillance chart, and maybe Abe will fire that computer up while I get the range on these binoculars.

"We'll watch the house in twenty-minute takes, and John can start preparing the weapon. We have no schedule for H-hour—that's H for Hit. It's entirely up to us. We just need to call home base when we're going in.

"Problems?"

The other three shook their heads. And Colonel Joel put out the light, while he drew back the thick black curtain that covered the window. He raised the binoculars and focused on the house across the street.

"Okay," he murmured, "there are curtains on the windows in the upper floors, but none on the street level. The main reception room is situated to the left of the front door looking in. There's a glass-patterned window above the front door. I can see the light from the passage spilling in. I guess the guards are stationed right there where it's light."

Roger that, sir. Abraham was instantly on the case, typing out every word uttered by his team leader.

Ben Joel drew the curtains over the window. And turned on the light. He reached for his sandwiches and chocolate and said quietly, "Since we are under orders to make the hit in the hours of darkness, it's going to be in that front room left of the door. It's the only one we can see into after dark. That's if we use a controlled explosion. Otherwise we'll have to knock down the entire house, and that would cause havoc."

"Whatever it takes," said Itzaak. "The mission is to kill Rashood, and we've got enough high explosive in here to knock down the Wailing Wall. We'll just do what we must."

"Correct," said Colonel Joel. "Let me have some of that coffee, will you?"

"Looks like we'll have to get rid of the guards," observed Abraham.

"No way we'll get in there without," replied Ben. "Unless there's some time in the day when the house is left unprotected."

"Can't imagine that," said John Rabin.

At 0300, they started work. Colonel Rabin was locked in the tiny kitchen with his explosive and detonators. Ben Joel stood in the dark with his glasses trained on the house across the street. Three times every hour, they changed places, while Ben entered the surveillance chart on the computer, mostly reporting no movement.

A little after 0600, there was a change. The front door of the Rashood residence opened and two youngish men dressed in jeans and loose white shirts emerged into the dawn. Colonel Joel grabbed the camera and fired off six pictures of them.

They turned left out of the house and walked together down Bab Touma toward the Via Recta. Ben looked carefully for the arrival of two more guards, but none showed up. But then he saw movement in the main downstairs room of the house: two other men, both carrying machine guns, were standing there staring out of the window. The powerful Mossad binoculars picked them up starkly. Neither one of them was Ravi Rashood.

When the watch changed and Colonel Rabin emerged from the kitchen to take over at the window, Ben Joel told him, "The guard duty changed at 0600. Two of them left, but the other two, who took over, did not come in through the front door. That means they were already in there. It's a big house. There may be a guard room where they can sleep."

"Unless there's a back door they use?"

"We'll recce that today, and maybe watch that door for a few hours—check when it's used."

"Okay. Do we need more help? Two watches will stretch us a bit."

Colonel Joel was pensive. "Quicker we get this done, the quicker we can get the hell out. Let's just go for it—I'll get around the back end of the house this morning around 1100. Is the weapon ready?"

"Affirmative. I need about thirty minutes to check the timer. Any time after that, the bomb can be put in place."

"Size?"

"I've made it in two halves. If we just want to blow that front room to eternity, we use just one. If we don't mind knocking the fucking house down, we use the lot."

Ben Joel chuckled. "Okay, John. It's getting light; stay back behind that curtain. I've cut two holes in it for the binos. Don't take your eyes off that place even for twenty seconds. I'll get us some coffee."

The watch changed at 0700. Abraham and Itzaak came on duty. Abraham left immediately to check out the garage where the getaway car was hidden. Then he skulked around the side streets and finally walked slowly into the street right behind Ravi Rashood's house, adopting the gait of an old man.

There was a small backyard to the property, and that yard was surrounded by a twelve-foot-high wall. A hefty wooden gate, painted green, was shut tight, and it was secured by a chain and a large padlock.

"Jesus," breathed Abraham. "You want to get in there, you'd have to blow that gate down with dynamite."

Right now the street was absolutely deserted. And Abraham took a risk. He walked along the wall and stopped at the gate, pretending to take a rest. But he had a good look at the padlock, and found what he was searching for, rust. And there it was, right there on that thick, curved steel bar. No one had opened that door for a very long time. Abraham kept going, slowly, his white robe billowing in the light February breeze. The street was still deserted.

He walked past the back of the next house and saw a white truck parked against the high wall. For a split second he debated climbing onto its roof and taking a look into the backyard, but he dismissed that as too risky.

He continued for another hundred yards, and to his mild surprise saw a builder's ladder lying on the ground, alongside a house on the left-hand side of the street. There was also a group of paint cans and a small cement mixer. This was work in progress.

Abraham considered borrowing the ladder and using that to take a good look into the Hamas colonel's backyard, but thought better of it. *I could give it a go after dark,* he decided. *Wouldn't take more than five minutes.*

Once more he took a devious route, checked out local cafés and a couple of restaurants, and then made his way back to the rear door of the apartment building, used a key to let himself in, and climbed the stairs.

Ben Joel, still unshaven and still awake, was talking to Itzaak at the window. Abraham told him the car was in place, keys under the front seat, and that the back entrance to Mr. and Mrs. Rashood's home was bolted and barred, unused, and obviously secured.

He also explained he had not looked over the wall, but had found a way to do so, by borrowing a ladder and maybe using it after dark.

"I'm not too certain about that," said the colonel. "What if you got caught?"

"Then I suppose I'd have to kill someone," said Abraham, shrugging his shoulders.

"I don't think so," said Ben. "The last thing we need is a murder hunt conducted by the police in a back street behind Rashood's house."

"Hadn't thought about that," replied the Mossad hitman, gloomily. But then he brightened and said, "Ben, that back gate is never used. I know that. Right here we got a one-door house."

"That's what I'm working on. Thanks, Abe. The next hour should tell us something."

And at that precise moment the front door of the big house on Bab Touma opened, and into the now-bright morning light stepped General Ravi Rashood, followed by his wife, Shakira, and a bodyguard holding an AK-47 Kalashnikov. Ben Joel stared at their photographic evidence, which was very little: two quite good pictures shot by the Americans of Ravi on a high cliff in the Canary Islands, and a better-quality print of Major Ray Kerman, supplied, reluctantly, by Great Britain's SAS.

The images matched, no doubt. The man leaving the house on Bab Touma was General Ravi Rashood, commander in chief of Hamas. The woman accompanying him was plainly his wife, and the field agent's description of her was accurate. She was indeed tall, dark-haired, and spectacularly beautiful.

It was 0900 and a cool fifty-eight degrees. The general was dressed in Western style, light blue jeans, a white shirt, and a brown suede jacket. Shakira also wore light blue jeans with high black boots, a blue shirt, and a leather jacket. Ben Joel grabbed the camera, pressed the long-range button, and snapped four close-ups of the Hamas terrorist and his wife.

The men from the Mossad watched as the guard stepped back and took up his position on a white bench set against the wall on the right-hand side of the front door. General Rashood and his wife walked down the steps alone and turned left toward Via Recta. They were in fact making their way over toward the Madhat Pasha Souq and a little restaurant where they often had breakfast.

Ben Joel did not care one way or another where they were going. He cared only what time they left, what time they returned, and the movement of the guards at the big house. With Ravi and Shakira still within sight, there was another change. A second guard came outside and sat on the opposite side of the door. Ben photographed both men, talking and smoking, their Kalashnikovs resting against the wall.

These were the 0600 men, who had begun their watch in that front room, moved out into the inside passage, and then taken up position outside at 0900. At noon, Ravi and his wife returned, walking slowly, reading newspapers.

They reentered the house, and almost immediately there was a guard change. Two young men arrived from the north end of the street. The men on the door handed over their AKs and left. The new arrivals sat outside. By Ben Joel's calculations, there were no other guards inside the house.

Aside from several occasions when the guards went inside, always one at a time, the situation remained unchanged until 1800. At this time, four new guards came along the street together, the other two left, and the night watch took up position.

Colonel Ben Joel spent the afternoon sleeping, but now he had it clear in his mind. The four new arrivals guarded the house through the night, taking it in turns to eat and sleep. The photographs on the computer matched. The two men he had seen leave at 0600 that morning were the same two who now slipped inside the front door. The others stayed outside in the last of the light and the warmish air.

Much depended on General Rashood's plan for the evening. If he went out for dinner, the two guards must be removed quietly before he returned, killed and hidden. The bomb must then be planted in that front room. If Ravi did not go out, they would have, somehow, to remove the guards, and then, in the immortal words of Colonel John Rabin, knock down the fucking house. No survivors.

As it happened, General Rashood dined out every evening, either alone with Shakira, or with friends.

At 1945, a taxi pulled up outside the house. There were no guards at the door, but almost instantly one of them came out and ran down the steps to speak to the driver. Five minutes later, Ravi and Shakira walked outside and climbed into the cab.

Colonel Joel, Colonel Rabin, and Abraham watched it pull away.

"John, any reason why we should not go in tonight?" asked Ben.

"Not at all. The weapon is absolutely ready. You just need to decide whether we design it to obliterate that one room, or demolish the building."

"Okay. Let's say we expect the general to return around 2300, or even later. According to our estimations, there will be a guard change at midnight. But we cannot wait until then. We need to take out and remove these two Hamas thugs guarding the door around 2230, and hope to Christ no one disturbs us."

"And if anyone does?"

"Eliminate."

"Guns?"

"Knives."

"Messy?"

"But quiet. And that's better."

"That way, we're counting on the general arriving back between 2300 and midnight?"

"Not necessarily."

"But what if the second shift of night guards turns up and their colleagues are not there, deserted, gone missing?"

"What can they do but remain on station, wait for the boss, and then tell him two men have vanished? We don't care. The bomb will be in place."

"Okay, what if the general then decides to search through the house, and then goes straight to bed?—and with a wife like that, who could blame him?"

Colonel Joel laughed, knowingly. "I was coming to that," he said. "We take out the two guards at 2230, as planned, insert the big bomb. And blow the bastard up as soon as Ravi enters the house and shuts the door. That way we don't care which room he is in."

"No, I guess not. But it does mean we won't have much use for the timing device."

"Not at all, John. We wait for that door to close behind the general. We set the timer for ten minutes. And then we leave. We just bolt down the stairs, straight to the garage, and we're gone, out of here. We'll be about four miles away when the blast occurs. All we need to know is that Ravi's in there."

"Can't fault that, boss," said Colonel Rabin agreeably. "Shall we go out for an hour?"

"Good idea. We haven't eaten all day. Tell Abe and Itzaak we'll be gone for a while and we'll bring food back."

Two hours later, the Mossad's hit team was in order. Everything was packed away in a couple of big mail bags, which Jerry would pick up later that night. At 2225, Itzaak and Abraham, still in Arab dress, went downstairs and walked the short distance into Bab Touma Street, which was very quiet, though not entirely deserted.

They crossed the street and walked up the steps to the front door of the Rashood stronghold. Major Itzaak Sherman rapped sharply on the door, which was instantly opened, and the Israeli found himself looking at the barrel of an AK-47.

The guard spoke in Arabic—*What do you want?*

Itzaak just said, "Please, sir, I need to speak to General Rashood." The guard hesitated and stepped forward, saying, "I thought there were two of you—" But he was too late. Abraham swooped out of the shadow and rammed his combat knife straight into the man's heart. It was a deadly blow, viciously hard and accurate. The guard gasped, tried to yell, but he was dead before he hit the floor.

From inside, there was a call of "Rami, who is it?" And the second guard stepped out onto the front porch and met with an identical fate when Abraham, using a second knife, plunged it into the man's heart.

By this time, Colonel Ben Joel had crossed the street, carrying the bomb in a leather duffel bag. He raced up the stairs and into the room on the left. Right behind him came John Rabin. They both hit the floor and began to screw the device to the underside of the big heavy table in the center of the room.

Meanwhile, the other two were dragging the two bodies down the steps and into a small open front yard, below the main street window. This area was unkempt and overgrown, and it had a gateway but no gate. The walls around it were two feet high. It took exactly one minute for Abraham and Itzaak to dump the dead men into the far corner of the tiny yard, where they would never be discovered until it was light, and maybe not even then.

At this point, Major Rabin was working alone on the electronics of the bomb, with Abraham standing guard on the door, in case either of the sleeping second-shift guards heard something and came to investigate. But the house was deathly quiet.

Colonel Joel hurried back across the road and opened up a connection from his cell phone to that of Colonel Rabin, who was still under the table in Ravi's house. They spoke briefly, for no more than eight seconds, and then John Rabin screwed in the last wire, set the detonation mechanism to coincide with the electronic box up in the apartment, and left.

Carefully, he made certain that the front door did not lock automatically, since they did not want Ravi and Shakira to be locked out. They just hoped the couple would return before the midnight watch change.

Meanwhile, they regrouped in their observation post and watched. The small black box that would activate the bomb was resting innocently on the window ledge.

It was 2315 now, and there was no sign of the general. But Abraham saw it first, the lights of a taxi coming around the corner from Al-Bakry Street, swinging right into Bab Touma. It pulled up directly in front of the house they watched.

"Here we go, boys," breathed Abraham, who was apparently unaffected by the double murder he had committed less than an hour previously. "They're back."

And all four men saw the lovely Shakira emerge from the back left-hand passenger seat of the cab. From the other side, there emerged her escort, who took her arm and walked up the steps.

They reached the front door and knocked, but the door opened even at Shakira's light touch. She was doubtless mystified by the absence of the two guards, but she entered the house, followed by the man, presumably Ravi, who was somewhat lost in the shadows. But at least neither of them had noticed the two hidden bodies.

Colonel Joel saw the light flood into the front room. Toward the rear he could see a male figure. Shakira was nowhere to be seen.

"That's it, John," snapped Ben. "That'll do for us. Set the timer for ten minutes and let's go."

John Rabin turned the dial, pressed the activate button. The residents of the house on Bab Touma were on borrowed time. The four Mossad men stampeded down the stairs and out into the dark. They ran through the back street behind the apartment and reached the garage. The key fitted easily, and they pushed the door open.

And there, inside, was the converted Mercedes Benz. Colonel Joel jumped in the front passenger seat. Abraham rummaged for the key and started the motor. Major Sherman jumped in the backseat, and John Rabin waited outside to shut and lock the garage door.

The car moved forward. The last member of the team climbed into the rear seat, and Ben Joel hit the button to inform the field agent Jerry that they were on their way. Abraham drove swiftly to the Bab Touma Gate and swung right onto the road that would take them down to the airport perimeter road.

But before they reached that crossroad, John Rabin's bomb went off with a crash that ripped into the night sky. It was so powerful that it blew the roof thirty feet into the air. The entire building went up with a stupendous blast, exploding the ancient cement and brickwork into the street, outward and upward. Flames leapt into the air. Rubble, glass, and stonework rained down from the sky. The world's oldest continuously occupied city shuddered on its sandy foundations.

"Holy shit!" yelled Abraham. "We just did it. Tel Aviv, here we come."

Ten minutes later, as Abraham gunned his supercharged wreck down the airport highway, Ravi Rashood arrived back from dinner with the wife of his close friend Abdul Khan, one of Shakira's half-brothers.

The scene of pure devastation was beyond belief. The entire street was blocked with rubble. Two police cars were already there; a fire engine was trying to get in from the wrong end of the street. Sirens were blaring, blue lights flashing, women screaming.

Ravi raced to what was left of the front of his house. But that was simply pointless. There *was* no front to his house. Rudy Khan was hysterical, but Ravi had no thought for anyone except Shakira, and he ran with a helpless desperation around to the back of his former home.

He reached the padlocked green gate, and, from behind it, he could hear a woman screaming, incoherently, plaintively. He spotted the white truck, and with one bound was on the hood, and then the roof, staring down into his own backyard. He could see that the inside door to the yard was open, and there, crouched on the ground, was Shakira, terrified, covered in blood, but alive.

Abdul, who had brought her home to make coffee, was not with her. Instinctively, Ravi knew he was dead. He also knew if he jumped over the wall, he and his injured wife would both be trapped. There was no way out through the collapsed house.

He jumped down to the street, and ran back around to the front of the house and yelled for help. The police and the ambulance crew were only too glad at least to save someone's life. Six of them arrived at the gate and the cops blew the lock away with a submachine gun, taking care not to allow bullets to penetrate the green gate.

Twenty minutes later, Shakira and Ravi were on their way to the President Hassad General Hospital, where fifteen stitches were required to repair a cut on her head, sustained in the basement-level kitchen when a part of the ceiling had caved in.

She was also in severe shock, and the surgeon decided she should stay overnight. Ravi remained with her, and most people in the drama were happy. The Hamas terrorists were merely thankful that Shakira lived.

And the Mossad men boarding the Learjet were in self-congratulatory mood. Mission accomplished. Nearly.

CHAPTER 4

The shuddering blast which knocked down the entire northeastern end of Bab Touma Street caused newspaper editors and television stations to work most of the night. Reporters swarmed around the site of the bombing and quickly realized that many neighboring houses and apartments were either crumbling or dangerously shaken on their foundations.

Miraculously, while there were several people injured in adjoining houses from falling debris and collapsed floors, there were no deaths, except for Abdul Khan, who was known to have been in the house where the bomb went off, but whose body had not yet been recovered.

Ironically, the bodies of the two murdered guards were currently buried under the rubble that had cascaded into the street when the blast detonated outward from the house.

The front-page headline in the English-language *Syria Times* read:

MIDNIGHT BOMB BLAST ROCKS OLD CITY STREET
Homes destroyed. One dead.
Many injured. Police mystified.

Beneath this was a photo taken at the scene, in the dark, showing the lights of the police cars and ambulances illuminating the pile of rubble. The caption read: CHAOS ON BAB TOUMA AS OFFICIALS SEARCH FOR BODIES.

On the eight o'clock morning news broadcast, on Syria 2, the reporter stated, *"Among those saved and admitted to hospital was Mrs. Shakira Rashood, who was believed to have been in the house where the blast went off. She survived mostly because she was in her kitchen, downstairs on the basement level, and that lower floor had held up while the rest of the house was blown sky-high.*

"Mrs. Rashood's half-brother, Mr. Abdul Khan, was also in the house and police say there is no possibility he could have survived. Early this morning, she was too upset to make a statement, but is expected to leave hospital with her husband, Mr. Ravi Rashood, sometime this morning."

Jerry, the Mossad field agent, watching the broadcast at his home in the Saahat ash-Shuhada area (Martyr's Square), was astounded. His apartment was in the far end of the Old City from Bab Touma, but he had heard the blast. When he moved in to clear out the hit team's apartment, he had stayed west of the devastated area, keeping to the dark side streets.

He could not believe that proven special operators like Ben Joel and John Rabin could possibly have made such a mistake. The entire plan, he knew, had been to wait and watch for the Rashoods' return.

He accepted that Shakira was alive. The journalists must have picked up her name from the hospital register. But General Ravi? How could that possibly have happened? The guys must have seen him enter the building. Otherwise they would not have detonated the bomb.

Jerry was mystified, like the police. But he walked out into the square and called the office in the Hada Dafna Building on King Saul Boulevard, reporting what the Damascus news services were saying. The Mossad chiefs had not yet seen the Syrian newspaper, nor had they heard the broadcast, but they knew Ben Joel and the team were safely home and had reported in during the small hours, *mission accomplished.*

As screw-ups go, considered Jerry, *this one was well on its way.*

At 11 o'clock that Wednesday morning, February 8, Ravi and Shakira walked out of the hospital toward a waiting taxi. They were greeted by a scrum of reporters and photographers, yelling questions . . . *how did you escape? . . . do you have any idea who could have done this? . . . Shakira! Shakira! . . . this way. Mr. Rashood! Did you save your wife's life?*

This was a terrorist commander's nightmare. Personal publicity, photographs, questions. But he faced the media with equanimity. "Yes, I am the husband of Shakira Rashood . . . no, we did not leave the restaurant to-gether . . . my wife came home with her stepbrother to prepare coffee and pastries . . . twenty minutes later I followed with Abdul's wife, Rudy. Yes, of course, both women are extremely upset."

In answer to the question *Mr. Rashood, do you think someone was try-ing to kill you?* he replied, "I doubt it. This was either a complete accident, or a badly mistaken identity."

For several hours, this innocuous statement held good. Ravi and Shakira moved, temporarily, into the Barada Hotel, on Said al-Jabri Avenue. But as the afternoon wore on, the police were wrestling with one problem: *this was one hell of a bomb—who the hell detonated it, and why?*

It was plainly not some Molotov cocktail put together by a disparate group of jihadists. This was a major, professional weapon, assembled by an expert, and somehow smuggled into that house on Bab Touma and detonated within minutes of Shakira and Abdul's return.

This was no accident. This was a plan, which may have gone wrong, but was nevertheless a premeditated action. There was not the slightest sign that it was a suicide bomb. In the opinion of the Damascus Police Department, this bomb had been detonated by a remote-control device and it was meant to kill Mr. Rashood, and perhaps his wife. The trouble was, no one knew who the devil Mr. Rashood was.

And while the Syrian police pondered the mystery, the Hamas War Council moved with lightning speed. They sent a car and two jihadist war-riors into Damascus from an outpost they maintained in the southern border city of Der'a and scooped up General Ravi and his wife with mili-tary efficiency.

They headed back south and crossed the border into Jordan, providing for their esteemed guests passports upon which the ink was barely dry. They kept going south for another fifty miles until they reached the capi-tal city, Amman, where the Rashoods checked into the Rhum Continental Hotel as Mr. and Mrs. Anwar Mehadi, in accordance with their passports. The men from Hamas had, in fact, moved so fast that Mr. and Mrs. Ra-shood had vanished from the face of the earth.

Which left the Syrian police, and the media, in something of a quandary. Senior law-enforcement officials understood perfectly well that the bomb had been executed with great precision. They also believed someone wanted to kill, at least, Ravi Rashood very badly.

But like the journalists, they had no idea who he was and why he might have such determined, maybe fanatical, enemies. He had, apparently, lived in Damascus for a few years now, and there had never been one hint of trouble before.

By 1900 something had, however, become clear. The police not only had no idea who he was, they also had no idea *where* he was. They posted men at the airport and at the train station and the bus station. They checked out the Barada Hotel, but he had very obviously left.

As for the Mossad, they were following events blow by blow through the guile of Jerry, who, not wanting to call attention to himself, could do no more than follow events through the television and radio news and the afternoon newspapers.

Thus the Mossad, in the split second of the midnight blast, had lost all of their advantages. So far as they were concerned, General Rashood was as elusive as ever. They no longer had an address for him, they no longer knew even the country he was in, and they no longer knew under what name he was traveling.

BOMB SURVIVOR AND HUSBAND VANISH, confirmed the *Syria Times.* "Jesus Christ," said Jerry.

It took another twenty-four hours before journalists cottoned on to the fact that this Ravi Rashood and his wife might well have had sinister connections. The principal clue came when the bodies of the two guards were found. They did not have the AKs with them, since Abraham had "confiscated" those. But they both had spare ammunition clips, and neighbors stated there had often been armed guards in front of the house. On Thursday evening, the police confirmed that both men had been knifed through the heart, which suggested that the bombers had first unloaded the sentries.

Whichever way anyone looked at it, this was a military-style hit, one that had only narrowly missed succeeding. And there were two outstanding questions that badly needed answering—who was Ravi Rashood, and who wanted him dead?

The trouble in Damascus was that anyone who actually knew who he was, most definitely was not divulging anything. And the only other person in the city who knew the identity of the assassins was Jerry.

Which left the media to speculate, blindly. Was it a gangland killing concerned with drugs? Was Rashood a terrorist the West wanted removed? Had he been attacked by Muslim extremists for whatever reason? Or was this just a local dispute between families or acquaintances?

The latter might have been the favorite explanation but for the enormous size of the bomb. And since no one had any real information, the story quickly died the death. By the weekend, nobody gave it much thought, except for those whose houses had been wrecked.

In Washington the story was barely covered. The agencies picked it up from the *Syria Times* and transmitted a short item headlined BOMB BLAST IN DAMASCUS. It read:

Damascus. Tuesday. A bomb that detonated in the Old City at around midnight killed at least one man and injured several more. Many houses in ancient Bab Touma Street were damaged, and one was destroyed. The police refused to confirm that it was the work of a jihadist group. But they stressed that it was a very large explosive device, much bigger than those usually associated with suicide bombers.

The *New York Times* used it at the low end of one of the Middle East pages. The *Washington Post* used it way inside on an international page. And the *Boston Globe* omitted it altogether.

Lt. Commander Jimmy Ramshawe caught it in the *Post,* and instantly thought that was the end of General Ravi Rashood, since Bab Touma Street was the name stated by the imprisoned Ramon Salman.

He called Admiral Morgan, who had already spotted the news item, and had a call in to David Gavron at the Israeli embassy. When the ambassador called back, however, Admiral Morgan detected an air of uncertainty in his responses that was highly atypical of the Israeli general.

Arnold Morgan smelled a rat. And one hour after Jimmy Ramshawe, David Gavron called back and said, "Strictly between ourselves, old friend, there's been a bit of a foul-up."

He recounted in some detail how the plan had misfired, and explained that no one really held the Mossad team to blame. "It was a hundred-to-one chance they would return home at different times, with different people," said the ambassador. "I'd say anyone would have made the same mistake."

"Yeah. I agree," replied Arnold Morgan. "And I guess we've now lost him. I'll have the guys in Guantánamo check whether Salman can give us that cell phone number he called in Syria, but I expect he'll say he can't remember it. Even if we persuade him differently, you can bet it will have changed after an attempt like that one on Ravi's life."

Meanwhile, Ravi and Shakira, now wearing Arab dress, were given exquisitely forged documents and the passports that identified them as Mr. and Mrs. Mehadi, who were supposedly Jordanian travel authors, working on a new publication highlighting the historic wine-growing districts of Egypt, Israel, and other Middle Eastern vineyards. Shakira carried a long-lens camera for authenticity.

Any journey into Israel is fraught not with peril, but with eccentricity. It's only twenty miles from Amman to the King Hussein Bridge, which straddles the Jordan River north of the Dead Sea. But the Jordanians insist that you are not leaving Jordan at all, even though they declared, in 1988, that they no longer had any ties with the West Bank.

On crossing the bridge to leave the country, they do not actually give you an official stamp, but instead give you a permit stating that you are not going any farther than the West Bank. No one admits they are going into Israel; but halfway across, as travelers enter the Holy Land, the span over the river is suddenly named the Allenby Bridge.

The Israelis immediately stamp you into their country, just as soon as you set foot on the West Bank. But they do it on a separate sheet, since everyone knows passports with an Israeli stamp are bad news when traveling in Arab countries. So right there, standing on the West Bank, you are in two countries at once, never having officially left Jordan.

This was all slightly nerve-racking for the world's most wanted terrorists; but, coming out of Jordan, the King Hussein Bridge is the only way over the river. There is also only one way to make it over the bridge. You take one of the JETT minibuses, which are the only vehicles permitted to make the crossing. You can't walk. You can't drive, you can't cycle. And you sure as hell can't hitchhike.

Ravi and Shakira came by taxi to the foreigners' terminal and proceeded to the minibus. They crossed the Jordan and went into the Israeli terminal, avoiding as much as possible the closed-circuit surveillance cameras. Both were in heavy disguise, Ravi with a full beard, Shakira wearing spectacles and walking like an elderly woman in black robes.

They were each issued a government-stamped document that welcomed them officially into Israel. The problem for their pursuers was the documents did not reveal they were Mr. and Mrs. Ravi Rashood. And they did not look anything like Mr. and Mrs. Ravi Rashood.

They walked for about a mile, carrying only one small leather bag, and then paused as a black sedan, bearing the blue license plate of "The Territories," pulled up beside them. A chauffeur signaled them to climb aboard and immediately drove west. In the plush backseat, Ravi and Shakira removed their disguises and sank back gratefully, traveling once more in the style of a commander in chief and his greatly revered wife.

And traveling, moreover, in a car that would not attract a throng of stone-throwing youths once they reached their destination. That only happens to cars bearing the yellow Israeli license plate.

They covered the thirty-eight miles to Jerusalem in a half hour, moving swiftly along the highway. From the Holy City, it was a two-hour run to the Gaza Strip on the Mediterranean coast. They went through the Israeli military checkpoint with barely a word, thanks, no doubt, to the blue license plates. From there into the town of Gaza was a matter of minutes, and in mild traffic they proceeded to the long Omar el-Mokhtar Street, which runs out of the main Shajaria Square all the way to the seafront.

Gaza has been destroyed by war more than any other town in the world, occupied in its long history by Crusaders, Turks, Muslims, the British, and even by Napoleon's troops.

As befits an endless battle zone, Gaza is a coastal eyesore, a squalid place of ruined buildings and constant running fights, Arab against Israeli, Palestinian gangs against the IDF, the haves against the have-nots, right against wrong, neither side prepared to give an inch, which is, of course, the trademark of all wars.

Ravi and Shakira drove through the sandy streets, past people who had somehow lost everything and whose presence now renders Gaza the "Soweto of Israel." Arab women, clad in black robes, balancing baskets on their heads, walked through the streets, heading mostly for one of the eight refugee camps, lending a biblical mood to a vicious, thoroughly modern conflict. These are the displaced Palestinians, thousands of them refugees, blaming the West, blaming especially America and Great Britain, blaming the Israelis. None of it without reason.

Yet this was the spiritual home of Ravi Rashood, the Iranian-born, Harrow-educated British Army officer, who had answered the mystical call of the desert, and its people, after rescuing a Palestinian girl, whom he later married.

For here, in the 3,500-year-old city, lay the roots of his new calling, the foundations of the terrifying fundamentalist organization, Hamas. It all began right here in Gaza, in 1987, when this often-savage branch of the Islamic Resistance Movement was born, created by the fanatical Sheik Ahmed Yassin.

The word *Hamas* means enthusiasm and exaltation of the Prophet Mohammed, whose grandfather Hamesh is entombed somewhere here in the city. The organization has always claimed much more modern roots, however, with connections to the fabled Muslim Brothers formed in Egypt in 1929.

It is best known for sensational acts of violence, bombs, shooting, and general mayhem against Israel. Hated by the rest of the country, Hamas operated for years in some kind of chaotic murder rampage. It was not until the former SAS major Ray Kerman appeared, first as an experienced officer and then as their fully fledged C-in-C, that Hamas truly did replace the Palestine Liberation Organization as the undisputed front-line muscle of the movement.

In a sense, as they drove through the dusty streets of Gaza, Ravi and Shakira were both coming home. They had spent little time here since Major Kerman first fled the authorities with his young bride-to-be. But now they both sensed a warm welcome awaited them behind these rubble-strewn living areas.

And as they drove on toward the relatively less damaged area of Omar el-Mokhtar Street, they found themselves in a kind of suburb, with white-walled courtyards, palm trees, and green shrubs.

Shakira, who had been born here in the city, just smiled and said, "I always liked it here, Ravi. I think we'll be very happy." Ravi, ever the pragmatist, still shaken by the mini–atom bomb which had nearly sent him over the bridge into the arms of Allah, looked nothing like so sure, and not even remotely cheerful.

The car turned into a side street, and then into a labyrinth of small apartment blocks. At the end of the second street, they pulled alongside a high wall, this one red brick rather than whitewashed cement. In the center, it contained a glossy black-painted wooden gate with a six-inch-square door placed in the center around head height.

The chauffeur climbed out and tapped on the big gate. The smaller door opened inward and a voice spoke in Arabic.

"Please, sir, madam, you come now," said the chauffeur, and they both stepped out of the vehicle into the bright sunlight. The big gate opened and a sentry, holding an AK-47, saluted as Ravi and Shakira walked through into a shaded stone courtyard with a large fountain splashing in the center.

"Perhaps you would like some water," said the sentry. "Please wait, sir, while I fetch the colonel."

Ravi filled two small stoneware cups from the fountain, handed one to his wife, and glugged the other one himself. Almost immediately, the door to the house, which was situated at the north end of the courtyard, opened and Colonel Hassad Abdullah emerged, an old comrade of Ravi's from the attack on the Nimrod Jail.

The two men stared at each other in the unmistakable way of the Bedouin, and then they clasped hands and hugged with the reserved joy of fighting men who somehow had lived to tell the tale.

"General Rashood!" exclaimed the colonel. "I cannot tell you how pleased I am you came today. We will dine together tonight. But then I must go. I think you understand that our High Command is very concerned about the bomb that almost killed you. Well, they've appointed me to investigate. I leave for Damascus early tomorrow."

"Now, that is very sad," replied Ravi. "I was hoping we might have a few days together. Talk over the past, and, of course, the future."

"Alas, we have only this evening," replied the colonel. "That bomb in Bab Touma has sent shockwaves through our entire community."

"I suppose they still have no idea who was responsible?" asked Ravi.

"No one's told me. But I have been posted immediately to Damascus."

"Who does that leave in this house?"

"Just the servants, and two guards at all times. Only you and Shakira."

"You think it's safe here?"

"Oh, most definitely. Particularly since no one has even the slightest clue who you are."

0900 Sunday 12 February
Bab Touma Street, Damascus

Colonel Hassad Abdullah had been patrolling the street since first light, trying to ascertain where the men who had tried to blow up General Rashood had been stationed. The police report, stressing that the bomb had gone off within minutes of the arrival home of Shakira and Abdul, made it absolutely certain in the minds of the Hamas High Command that someone had been watching.

Only by discovering from where they had watched could the Hamas colonel work out who might have done it. There must be clues. There were always clues. The issue was, where to find them.

Right now he had narrowed it down. The forensic investigators had ascertained that Abdul had been in that front room when he died. So had the bomb. The shards of a big table were so small that it had definitely been right in the upward path of the explosion.

Therefore, whoever had watched had had their eyes on that room. That meant the opposite side of the street, which narrowed down the options. There were only about three places where a would-be assassin could observe the Rashood residence. And only one of them was empty.

Colonel Abdullah had been met with total noncooperation from the real estate agent, and that heightened his suspicions. Which was why he and a young Hamas freedom fighter were about to break into the back entrance of the apartment block lately vacated by the Mossad hit team. In fact, the younger warrior had just wrenched the back door lock open, and was now beckoning the colonel to join him in the building.

Five minutes later, they were both outside the top-floor apartment. The building was quiet, and the colonel himself, using a small crowbar, ripped open the lock to the sound of splintering wood, and they were in.

Silently they moved through the deserted rooms. All empty. Too empty. Someone had wiped out everything. At first sight, there was not a trace that anyone had ever been there, and Colonel Abdullah stood gazing out of the window, muttering to himself, "These were real professionals."

For in his honed, alert, and instinctive terrorist soul, he sensed he was in the right place, enjoying a perfect view of the gaping hole where once there had been a house, right across Bab Touma Street.

Quietly, he drew back the curtains. Very slightly. They were made of brand-new material, too good for an old slum of a place like this. And then he peeped through the space between them, thinking to himself how little he would have liked that, even if the room was dark. Anyone looking out of the old Rashood residence could have seen the telltale gap. And perhaps wondered who was up there, spying. Especially if they were trained security guards.

And then Colonel Hassad Abdullah spotted a flaw in the obviously new curtain material. Not so much a flaw, actually: a hole, very deliberately cut. And not just one hole. Two of them, about four inches apart.

He poked his fingers through, and tried to look through, out across the street. But the holes were too wide apart. *Hmmm,* he thought, *perhaps just right for binoculars.*

They searched for another half hour, but Jerry had been thorough. There was indeed nothing to discover. This had been a ruthlessly planned, most daring and savage attack on the commander in chief. Hamas, in their bloodthirsty and vengeful creed, were vowed and determined to catch, and execute, whoever had been responsible.

But all Colonel Hassad Abdullah had to show for his investigation were two small holes in the curtains. And in his opinion, that was quite sufficient.

Because that apartment had confirmed a great deal. First of all, the place had been rented for only one month. Second, the other apartment on the top floor had been purchased by the same people, and was now for sale. The real estate agent had provided at least that.

Third, it was the perfect observation post. Those three facts alone suggested that the attempt on General Rashood's life had been conducted by a professional organization, almost certainly state-sponsored. The newly cut curtains, the sheer size of the explosion, the perfection of the cleanup. It was all carried out with absolute professionalism.

This was no murder attempt by a bunch of hoodlums. This was military. And that really narrowed it all down. Because in all the world, General Rashood had only two copper-bottomed, grudge-bearing, rich, relentless enemies—the United States of America, and Israel's Mossad. No one else could possibly hate like them.

In the city of Gaza where the High Command of Hamas was ensconced, the first minister, Commodore Tariq Fahd, was already following the case along those lines. And he had a set of circumstances that were leading him ever onward.

He called a meeting at the secret underground situation room in the house where Ravi and Shakira lived. Colonel Abdullah was back from Damascus; his second in command, Major Faisal Sabah, was in the city; and two other senior Hamas councillors, Ahmed Alaam and Ali al-Fayed, were also summoned.

They gathered together at 10 A.M. on Wednesday, February 15, six jihadist warriors, plus Shakira, who would, if required, kill her Western opponents without mercy.

There were no chairs in the room, just a table. They sat beneath plain whitewashed walls on big colored cushions set upon the sandy floor. There was no window in the room, but there was a stone air vent which led outside into the garden. Lengths of four-inch-thick wood had been carved into elaborate double doors, beyond which were four armed guards.

Commodore Tariq Fahd greeted everyone, and the house servants came in with pots of Turkish coffee, served in plain glasses set into silver holders. They also brought two trays of the sugared, almond-flavored pastries that are so favored in that part of the world.

"It is, of course, obvious now, certainly to all of us, that someone has tried, very determinedly, to execute our commander in chief. Thankfully, we are all able to welcome him and Shakira here today, and to swear, by the blood of the Prophet, vengeance upon these enemies."

He hesitated for a moment and sipped his coffee. "I should like, if I may, to outline the sequence of events that I believe will lead us to an inevitable conclusion. I should add that I am using only known facts rather than any form of supposition.

"Therefore, I will begin in the small hours of January 15, when we know beyond any doubt that our brother Ramon Salman made a call of confirmation to our command headquarters on Sharia Bab Touma. General Rashood himself took the call and was informed the attack on the Boston airport was a go." General Rashood nodded in agreement.

"A few hours later," continued Commodore Fahd, "that attack was foiled, principally because our senior operations man somehow allowed the briefcase carrying the explosive to fall into the hands of a policeman.

"We were then delivered two terrible blows. Our second field operator was shot dead by the Boston police, and the injured Reza Aghani was taken into police custody. We know he went into Massachusetts General Hospital, but from there we are ill-informed.

"Our lawyers say Aghani was almost immediately removed from the United States judicial system. Which most certainly means he was transferred to a military interrogation center. In the opinion of our lawyers, that most certainly means Guantánamo Bay, given the enormity of his potential crime.

"For the purpose of this meeting, we will assume he reached Cuba by January 18. And then, in a very bizarre twist of fate, the New York police picked up Ramon Salman in the Houston Street apartment within a day of that happening. He too was removed from the U.S. justice system, and that much is definite. We have no proof he was also transported to Guantánamo Bay, but our American lawyers say he almost certainly was.

"So we may assume that by January 23, after three days of torture and brutal U.S. interrogation, Ramon Salman may have told them what they wanted to know."

Commodore Tariq Fahd paused theatrically, and then said, "Four days later, installed in the house directly opposite General Rashood's residence on Bab Touma, there is a hit team which makes a thoroughly professional attempt on his life, murdering his guards first, in the classic manner of trained Special Forces."

Colonel Abdullah turned to Ravi and said, "How good were your guards? Are you surprised they were dispensed with so efficiently?"

The terrorist C-in-C looked pensive. Shakira stood up and walked to a table and poured more coffee for her husband. "On reflection, Colonel," he said, "I am extremely surprised. One of those two guards had fought with me at the Nimrod Jail, and you may remember him yourself. He was the one in the hood, the one who hit the gatehouse, blew away the guards, and smashed the communications system. He was top-class."

"Of course," said the commodore, "it's always easier to succeed when you have the element of surprise on your side. At the jail, the man in the hood had every advantage. Not so on Sharia Bab Touma, hah?"

"Correct," replied Ravi. "Nonetheless, it remains difficult to imagine how my highly trained bodyguards could have succumbed so quickly to an outside attack."

"The men who killed the guards were either Israeli or American," said the commodore. "Of that we can be certain. I do not think the Americans would have moved Special Forces into Damascus so quickly. But I accept they might have."

General Rashood added, "Whoever it was had all the skills of U.S. Navy SEALs. It was either them or the Mossad. No one else."

"How about Great Britain's SAS Regiment, which did so much for the Israelis?" asked Colonel Abdullah, smiling. "Could they have done it? I am sure the general here will attest to their efficiency."

"I think they could most certainly have done it. But that last Labour government in Westminster did so much damage to the armed forces, I don't think they've ever recovered. Or ever will. No, the Brits could no longer move that fast. Only the Israelis or the Americans."

"And which one would you favor?" asked the commodore.

"I'd say it was a combination," said Ravi. "The Americans have the peace talks coming up in a few weeks. The last thing they need is to get caught blowing up hunks of historic old Damascus."

"Well, if I had to guess," said Tariq Fahd, "I'd say the hideous Americans tortured our people, wrung the information out of them, and then tipped off the Israelis to come in and nail the Hamas C-in-C, the man Ramon Salman telephoned the night before the Logan airport bomb."

"I'd go with that," said Ravi. "And I should remind all of you, the Mossad always favors the bomb against the bullet. And I doubt they have ever forgiven me for the death of their senior operatives in the restaurant in Marseilles."

"Not to mention wiping out the entire jail staff at Nimrod, and, in one hit, liberating every last one of the most sworn enemies of Israel." Tariq Fahd looked wistful.

"Do any of you think we should seek revenge, on behalf of Allah and the Prophet?"

"Always," said General Rashood. "We should never accept a strike against us on this scale without an immediate response. The problem is, the Mossad probably considers its operation in Bab Touma to have been the most terrible failure. And anyway, you all understand how difficult it is to mount an attack on the Israelis. They're liable to come back and flatten this entire city. If they suspect Hamas."

"They won't just suspect Hamas," said the commodore. "If anything happens to them, they'll *know* it was us, before the dust clears."

"Nonetheless, I think we should most certainly devote some time toward planning a major strike against either the Mossad or the USA," said Ravi. "Something devastating, something that will surely grab the headlines. Make 'em sit up and listen to us, as they have never really done since 9/11. Never done since our beloved Osama bowed out."

"Could we blow up their entire headquarters on King Saul Boulevard?"

"Only if we did not mind losing possibly twenty of the highest-qualified personnel we have," replied General Rashood. "Because that's what it would take, and that's what would happen. We'd never get out alive."

"And that would be an awful waste," replied the commodore. "By the sword of the Prophet, that would be the most awful waste. But Allah will guide us."

"Allah is great," intoned Ravi. And he was joined in that Muslim exaltation by everyone in the room. And in the silence that followed, they repeated the following lines from the Koran, the prayer of the jihadist:

> . . . *from thee alone do we ask help.*
> *Guide us on the straight path,*
> *The path of those upon whom is thy favor,*
> *. . . Light upon light,*
> *God guides whom He will, to his Light . . .*

Washington, D.C.

Not every member of President Bedford's White House staff was absolutely thrilled about the continued presence of Admiral Arnold Morgan at the elbow of the chief executive.

And in particular, there was a small cabal of the president's speechwriters who considered the admiral a gross intrusion upon their ambitions. These were youngish men, three of them, highly educated, who believed to the depths of their egotistical souls that they alone knew what the president should be saying.

The problem with such people is they also believe they know what he should be *doing*. Not all the time. But enough of the time to make certain senior staffers extremely wary of them.

The business of writing speeches for the boss has, over the years, developed into the function of a committee. First draft, rewrite, alterations, new thought, new draft . . . *Christ, he better not say that . . . why not? He is the president, right? Yes, but the media will go for him . . . they'll go for him no matter what . . . yes, but . . . yes, but . . . yes, but . . . yaddah, yaddah, yaddah.*

This crowd, bursting with self-importance, would rewrite Shakespeare—*To be or not to be* (delete the last "to be," superfluous), *That is the question* (delete "question" and substitute "problem," it's more positive, less indecisive).

Writers and editors, the endless war . . . *I don't think you should say this, or indeed that.*

Yeah, but where were you, asshole, when the paper was blank?

After a couple of years of this internal strife, these literary staffers quite often lose track of the fact that what a president says has nothing whatsoever to do with what he does.

They begin to believe that their thoughts and words represent actual policy. And when a tyrant like Admiral Morgan comes rampaging in, not giving a damn, one way or another, who says what, only about what the president does—well, that causes inevitable friction among the scribes.

They are also apt to rear up a bit when he writes something down, tells someone to type it out and then release it immediately, on behalf of the president—*and someone tell those assholes who work here not to touch one single word of it, if they want to stay employed.*

Staff relations were never a strong point with Admiral Morgan—though, when he commanded a U.S. Navy nuclear submarine, the crew, to a man, believed him to be some kind of a god.

When he headed up the National Security Agency at Fort Meade, he conducted some kind of a reign of terror, growling from the center of a vast spider's web, striking fear into the hearts of agents, field officers, military commanders, and foreign heads of state.

When the previous president brought him into the White House as his national security adviser, he caused havoc among senior members of the staff, bypassing some people completely, speaking only to the president. He treated the chain of command as if it were not there, riding roughshod over anyone who intervened.

That first president, the one who recruited the admiral, trusted him totally. As did the present incumbent of the Oval Office . . . *If that's Arnie's opinion, that's the way we go.*

The president who served between these two was virtually frog-marched out of the Oval Office by the United States Marines. Directly into resignation, because he thought he could ignore the advice of the old Lion of the West Wing, the man every serving chief in the armed forces revered above all others.

Arnold Morgan was the Top People's Man. Only the truly brilliant truly liked him. The rest regarded him with the suspicion that lurks only in less able minds. And this was a quality that had no place in an assessment of Admiral Morgan. He was selfless, demanded no financial reward, and had no personal ambitions.

He had sufficient patriotism to last ten lifetimes. And when he walked through the corridors of the White House, he still nodded sharply to the portrait of the former Supreme Allied Commander, President Dwight D. Eisenhower.

On the wall of his study at home was a portrait of General Douglas MacArthur. Any time Arnold sat alone wrestling with some awkward problem, he invariably ended by muttering, *That's the way the United States of America should go. Maybe not Great Britain, or any of those lightweight foreigners over there. But that's the way for the U.S. of A.*

And then he would look up at the general's portrait and snap, *"Right, sir?"* As if expecting a confirming, "Affirmative, Admiral," from the stern face that gazed out from the east wall of the study in toney Chevy Chase.

How could such a man possibly be understood by youngish graduates consumed by their own ambitions? How could a man who had commanded his mighty nuclear boat in the freezing depths of the North Atlantic ever expect to be comprehended by the president's speechwriters?

The truth was, the old Cold Warrior, with his innate mistrust of Russia and dislike of China and the "Towelheads," expected nothing from those he brushed aside in Washington. Except for loyalty to the country, support for the military at all times, and unquestioning obedience.

The speechwriters did not like him, this immaculately dressed bull of a man who held no torch for anyone and whose only concern was for the good of the USA.

The speechwriters were held, literally, at arm's length by the president throughout the entire day of the Logan bomb. He and Admiral Morgan were closeted in the Oval Office for hours. The admiral drafted the president's speech; the admiral made the decisions on who was going into military custody and who was not.

As for that missing Flight 62, the one that apparently crashed into the Atlantic off Norfolk. There was rumor all over the White House, but no facts, because the president discussed the issue with no one except for the admiral. Only the serving national security adviser, Professor Alan Brett, was confided in by Paul Bedford.

And anyway, so far as the speechwriters were concerned, Professor Brett, West Point lecturer, Army Commander, and all that, was too much like Admiral Morgan to be trusted.

Neither the president nor Admiral Morgan was a political animal. Neither of them had antennae for personal danger, plotting, and scheming. In a Medieval royal court, the pair of them would have lost their heads in the first ten minutes. They simply did not do intrigue.

And intrigue was brewing in Paul Bedford's White House. Hints were being dropped to the media . . . *the president did not see a reason to brief on that . . . the president decides such things entirely on his own, consulting only Admiral Arnold Morgan . . . there is less cabinet government in today's White House than at any time in the last forty years.*

It was only a remote drip. The press did not pick up the undercurrent of unrest among staffers, and no one thought anyone was briefing seriously against the president and his hard-man buddy. And they were wrong.

The speechwriters had limitless access to the news media, and columnists, and broadcasters. It was just a matter of time before one of them decided to help some writer construct a major feature article about the overpowering presence of Admiral Morgan in the Oval Office. And they could start with one question, of "national importance"—*what the hell went on with Flight 62?*

The White House staffer who ultimately did the deed was Anthony Hyman, a 31-year-old English graduate with a master's from Yale and a postgraduate doctorate in political science from Balliol College, Oxford.

Anthony had strict personal goals. He expected to become the president's chief speechwriter within eighteen months. He expected to have a position with a senior senator, hopefully from his home state of Connecticut, within five years, and to run for office as a congressman well before his fortieth birthday.

He was a tubby person, inclined to sarcasm and impatient with those of less obvious qualities than his own. He blinked at the world through thick lenses set into gold wire spectacles, and he possessed an ego approximately the size of the Smithsonian.

Anthony Hyman's personal confidence was little short of atomic. He walked on the balls of his feet with a quick, short, bouncy stride and the manner of a busy debt collector. His hair was longish and curly, and his suits usually needed pressing.

He was quick-witted, and no one was in any doubt he was the best writer in the building. A lot of people did not like him. But these were few compared with the long list of people Anthony himself disliked. This included almost everyone, for a vast variety of reasons. But the one at the very top was Admiral Arnold Morgan.

There had, apparently, been an occasion when Anthony had drafted a press release specifically to mollify the liberal branch of the media. It was not altogether necessary, and since the matter was military, the president checked it out with Admiral Morgan, who immediately ripped it up and threw it in the wastebasket.

A few months later, on the day of the Logan bomb, the admiral himself wrote out the main points for Paul Bedford's forthcoming evening speech. And three people heard him growl, "Better get this polished up, but don't for Christ's sake give it to that fat fucker who hasn't got the brains he was born with."

Anthony Hyman had just enough enemies for that little episode to be relayed onto the White House grapevine, and in the end, of course, someone made certain he heard about it personally.

The tubby speechwriter seethed. And he planned to strike back, using his particular buddy in the media, the *Washington Post* political columnist, Henry Brady. And on a chill February evening in a small, unobtrusive bar in Alexandria, Virginia, Anthony Hyman spilled the beans on Arnold and the president. Much like Ramon Salman had done with Ravi Rashood.

They ordered a couple of beers, and the White House man began by explaining the close personal relationship between the two men, how their wives were friends, how Arnold never even knocked when he called at the Oval Office, a habit which had annoyed a succession of secretaries and aides.

He described how President Bedford never even sought another opinion when Admiral Morgan had made a decision. He described how the president took his cue on the phrasing of awkward matters, how he never even consulted his speechwriters when Admiral Morgan issued him with a first draft.

"I'm telling you, Henry," he said. "This president's got a lot of brainpower in his writing pool, and a lot of talented advice surrounding him, but there are times when he uses none of it. And it's usually when that boorish old bastard from another age comes calling."

"I hear what you're saying, Anthony," said the newspaperman. "But Admiral Morgan commands huge respect in the international intelligence community, and he has cracked some big issues on behalf of the United States, more than most people will ever know. And what you're telling me is certainly excellent background material, but it's not what you might call hot. . . . "

"I'm coming to that—I'm coming to that," said Anthony. "Be patient. We're not in a hurry, are we?"

"No, Anthony, of course not, but no one's very interested in running a big anti–Arnold Morgan story without some heavyweight information. He's one powerful dude. And he hates the media, anyway."

"Okay, okay, keep listening, okay? Now let's take the Boston airport bombing. I'm here to tell you, the admiral was in the Oval Office, right there with the president, through the whole day. And there were a lot of decisions made that day, especially about the captured terrorist, and how and where he would be interrogated.

"I know he refused to speak to anyone, and I also know it was Arnold Morgan who had him removed to the Naval Hospital in Bethesda—first step in getting him under strict military control, right?"

Henry Brady's interest visibly heightened. "Well, I admit I did not know that."

"Neither do you know where that terrorist is right now?"

"We assume still under guard in Bethesda."

"Wrong, Henry. He's in Guantánamo Bay, has been for nearly two weeks."

"Seriously? Hell, that's news."

"And I'll tell you something else. The New York cops picked up some other terrorist plot two days after Logan, and they arrested the mastermind behind the airport bomb. Right there in the city."

"Yeah?"

"And you know what? Admiral Morgan had him removed instantly to Guantánamo Bay, alongside the other guy."

"How do you know?"

"Because I talk to all the other people who should have had a part in that, and none of them did. The whole thing was Morgan and the president acting alone. They never even took the requisite legal advice."

"You mean the whole fucking place is being run like some kind of military *junta*?" replied Henry, who was ever keen to speak strictly in newspaper headlines.

"Precisely," smiled Anthony, amused at the phrase. "And since then, the president has spoken to the nation twice, and on neither occasion did he even consult with his team of writers.

"And now, Henry, I want to get to the really interesting bit. You may not remember, but on that very same day, there was a civilian air crash, out in the Atlantic, fifty miles or so off Norfolk. Naturally, some of you guys asked formally if there was some kind of connection with the bomb. And you were told a categorical 'no' by the White House press office.

"In his speech, the president glossed over the coincidence, and muttered about having no information about the flight or the airline that owned it. Air Traffic Control confirmed that it was a Boeing 737 and it went down in deep water. And that was supposed to be the end of it."

"Okay?"

"Well, Henry, as you know, the White House is a village, nothing more, nothing less. Gossip gets around real fast. And an awful lot of people who should know better think there was a lot more to it than that.

"What's more, they think Admiral Morgan was in it, up to his elbows."

"Jesus."

"Henry, I've spoken to people who think January 15 was targeted to be another 9/11; that al Qaeda intended to blow up the busiest passenger terminal in the Boston airport, to commemorate American Airlines Flight 11 and United 175. The aircraft that hit the North and South Towers. Both of 'em, as I'm sure you remember, took off from Boston.

"On January 15, three or four hours after the disaster in Terminal C, those al Qaeda guys intended to slam another airliner into the Capitol building in Washington. That was Flight TBA 62, which mysteriously vanished into the Atlantic before it got there."

"But no one knows why?" said Henry.

"No one has the slightest idea why. And no one's gonna tell you anything. But I have spoken to a very senior man right here in Washington. And he thinks Admiral Arnold Morgan told the President of the United States to order U.S. fighters to battle stations, and to shoot the fucker down, laden with civilians."

Henry Brady's jaw dropped about three inches.

"And my source told me, Henry, the president went right ahead and did just that."

"As secrets go, that one's pretty good, eh?" The newspaperman took a long draft of his beer. "You could work on that for years, Anthony, and never get a hint of the truth," he said. "Like you said, we don't even know where it went down."

"I accept that," said Anthony Hyman. "But you could begin by finding out all about Thunder Bay Airways. They owned the aircraft, they know who was on board, and they might even know where it is. They just might have received a final destination from the pilot. But I'll tell you one more thing. Thunder Bay Airways is Arab-owned."

Thus it was, on Thursday morning, February 23, the *Washington Post* carried a two-page feature on Admiral Morgan, cross-referenced on the front page. It was the biggest feature story Henry Brady had ever written.

The headline read:

THE RETURN OF THE OLD LION OF THE WEST WING
Is Arnold Morgan actually running the country?
Is the president now isolated with the fire-eating admiral?

The story ran and ran. It detailed the principal events in Admiral Morgan's career, listed his triumphs, found no disasters, and talked openly of how Paul Bedford had been swept to power when the previous president had refused to tackle a flagrantly vicious terrorist attack on the USA.

It pointed out how reliant so many people had been on the admiral's support, how the military counted on him to raise hell if their warnings were not heeded.

But it also pointed out how easily he could put people's noses right out of joint. How he gathered devotees and enemies in equal numbers, how he did not give a damn what anyone thought, just so long as it was right for the USA.

The story stated that President Bedford refused to make big international decisions without him. And that he was ignoring the advice of once-trusted colleagues. Mostly the sentences of Henry Brady started with *Insiders say,* or *Sources close to the president believe,* or *Staffers fear.* Never a name.

Nonetheless, the message was clear. Admiral Arnold Morgan had a great deal to say about the actions of the United States on the international stage, and whereas some people thought "Thank God for that," there were others. Others who thought this was all very unhealthy, a swerve in the wrong direction, too much power vested in two men, with too little consultation.

Essentially, this very large spread of newspaper type was divided into two sections. The second one occupied a massive "box," on the right, over three columns, running down most of the page. There was a full-length picture of the admiral, in uniform. In the background was a sinister-looking *Los Angeles*–class nuclear submarine moored on the jetty. The headline here was:

DID THE ADMIRAL TAKE OVER ON JANUARY 15?
And what really happened to the missing Arab 737?

The drift of the story was that the public had never been informed of the true scale of the terrorist plot. They had not even been told that it was, without question, the work of either al Qaeda or an associate organization with close links to Hamas, the Palestinian group.

Henry Brady revealed, flatly, that the man who was shot and then taken, in police custody, to Mass General was now in Guantánamo Bay.

A series of judicious inquiries in New York then led Henry to discover that there had been three arrests at an apartment on Houston Street on January 18, and that one of the men had been flown immediately to Guantánamo Bay. In Henry's opinion, the other two were on their way, and all of this was on the specific orders of Admiral Morgan.

"No civilian," wrote Henry, "no retired officer, unelected, unappointed, in the entire history of the United States has ever wielded such formidable power in the Oval Office. Except for Admiral Morgan these past several years."

He then moved more pointedly to the precise events that took place on January 15. This part of the story was pieced together after a series of interviews with the press office at the Air Traffic Control Center in Herndon, Virginia. Henry had conducted these in person, driven out there and informed the receptionist he was Henry Brady of the *Washington Post,* and he wished to talk to someone in a senior position, orders of the editor.

The editor of course was in no position to order anyone to do anything at Herndon, but it startled the receptionist and Henry was given access to a couple of public affairs officers.

He made the most of what he was given. Which, in fairness, was not much. Yes, the ATC operators had locked on to Flight 62, which had maintained course, despite being instructed to make a change and swing left inland. It had continued north out over the ocean.

"Why was the course change ordered?"

"I'm sorry, sir. That is classified information."

"Military?"

"I'm sorry, sir, I cannot answer that."

"Is it classified?"

"Yes, sir."

"For how much longer, after the 737 ceased to obey orders from Herndon, did you track it?"

"Sir, I did not say it ceased to obey orders. I said it continued on its northerly course."

"In flagrant defiance of the ATC instructions, right?" Henry was trying to close in.

"Not necessarily, sir. There may have been an electronic foul-up. Flight 62 may not have been receiving us. We were not in communication. And that would make it an accident, sir. Not defiance."

Henry persisted. "Okay, let me rephrase. For how long were you able to track the aircraft after you first noticed it was not obeying instructions?"

"I would say less than an hour, sir. We had it on radar, fifty miles off-shore, east of Norfolk, Virginia."

"And then it vanished?"

"Yes, sir."

"Do you have a record of the height the aircraft was flying when it disappeared?"

"I am certain we do."

"Could I see that record?"

"I am sorry, but everything's gone to the government department that investigates such matters."

"Would anyone remember whether Flight 62 was at thirty thousand feet or two thousand feet when it vanished?"

"Possibly, but that information would be classified right now until the documents are released by the government and a satisfactory explanation has been found."

"Okay, I'm just trying to establish whether that aircraft, packed with civilian passengers, who are now dead, disappeared from your screens way up there in the stratosphere, either because of a bomb or some other explosion. Or perhaps it just suffered what you guys call catastrophic mechanical failure and plunged into the ocean?"

"I'm sure one day, sir, this will all come to light. But right now that is not possible."

Henry Brady tried to pull rank. "I represent the most powerful political newspaper in the United States," he said. "And in my opinion, the citizens of this country have a right to know what happened if Americans died in any kind of disaster."

"Sir, there were no Americans on board. The aircraft was Canadian-based, Canadian-owned. It was not scheduled to stop in the USA."

"How do you know this, if you were not in communication?"

"Sir, every flight has a number which betrays its origins. This was TBA 62. We have of course been in contact with its parent corporation."

"That's Thunder Bay Airways, right?"

"Correct. And they may be able to help you more than we can."

That last sentence had Henry on the line in double-quick time to the little airline on the freezing north shore of Lake Superior. And there he discovered the aircraft was very lightly loaded, it had made a fuel stop in Palm Beach, unscheduled, and there were no Americans on board.

The chief executive confirmed the flight had been lost, out in the Atlantic, according to the Americans. So far as the airline was concerned, no one had any idea where the wreckage was, not within an area of 2,500 square miles. So far as they were concerned, no further search-and-rescue operations were being conducted.

Yes, they could confirm that the senior directors of the airline were of Arabian descent, and yes, the majority shareholders were extremely wealthy Saudis. That was public record.

Henry at that stage had a smattering of facts. And a very big mystery. So far as he was concerned, that was perfect. So long as he could ascertain that Admiral Morgan was right in the middle of it.

And that would take several leaps of faith, all of them slightly shaky. But Henry was a newspaperman, and his business was not to establish the pure unbridled truth. He worked for a commercial corporation. His business was to sell newspapers, to write a slightly sneering, cynical story against the government, not to establish unbridled truth. Henry was quite prepared to take those leaps of faith.

And he was prepared to take a really big one on the subject of TBA's Flight 62.

This is what he wrote: "*So what was the true fate of that innocent passenger jet, flying through peaceful American skies, lawfully taking its people home? Was it really subject to 'catastrophic mechanical failure'? Or did something more darkly sinister befall it?*

"*As a reporter of more than 20 years' standing, I am acutely aware of evasiveness; I am tuned to understand when people do not want to answer my perfectly reasonable questions, on behalf of my readers.*

"*And in this case they most certainly were reluctant to tell me anything, save for the obvious, that the aircraft disappeared off the screens. We do not know why, and since its communications with the tower were down, we do not know precisely where, although it was out over the deep Atlantic.*"

Henry could really go no further. But this feature story was designed to be about Admiral Morgan, and Henry was obliged to end it with a bit of a flourish. This he managed to do:

"*Perhaps, then, I should offer this: Could the aircraft have been subject to a planted bomb? Or was it in any way possible that this Arab-owned Boeing 737 was somehow connected to the gang that tried to bomb Logan International?*

"*And might it have been cold-bloodedly shot down by American military fighters, on the specific orders of the President of the United States, on the advice of his permanent right-hand man, Admiral Arnold Morgan? There are those close to the president who believe this is the real truth."*

Henry Brady realized this ending was based on the flimsiest of suppositions, but he remembered Anthony Hyman's words, that this suspicion had been raised by a very senior man in the White House.

Like many another journalist, Henry had decided to take his chances. If there was a stern White House denial, so what? It all added to the controversy. If nothing was said, then that made his conclusions look even better.

What Henry did not know was that his story about Admiral Arnold Morgan would have massive ramifications. And that they would begin in an underground room at the back end of Gaza City, six thousand miles away.

General Ravi Rashood was devoted to newspapers. When he and Shakira had lived in Damascus, they had bought a selection of foreign newspapers from the most famous bookshop in the city, the Librairie Avicenne, three times a week. He rarely missed purchasing irregularly available copies of the *New York Times, Wall Street Journal, Washington Post,* and London *Daily Telegraph.*

Here in Gaza it was more difficult. Foreign papers arrived only sporadically, and often the Hamas field agents were slow to grasp important items. However, no one missed Henry Brady's story in the *Washington Post,* and three copies of it arrived from different sources, in the mail, at the house off Omar el-Mukhtar Street on Monday morning, March 5.

Ravi sat outside in the courtyard, sipping coffee and contemplating the significance of the strange and powerful man who sat effortlessly at the right hand of the President of the United States.

He knew precisely who the admiral was, and had indeed given serious thought to assassinating him in London six years previously. But it had proved impossible. The admiral's security staff, when traveling, rivaled that of the president himself.

At least it did when he was on official business, as Ravi had assumed he had been, that summer in London.

Shakira brought him some more coffee and asked him what he was reading. "Oh, nothing much," replied her husband. "Just some newspaper articles about an American admiral."

"Well, if it's not important, why do you have three copies of it?"

"How do you know I have three copies of it?"

"Mostly because I am able to count," said Shakira sassily. "One in your hand, one sticking out of this envelope, and one on the floor."

"I don't think that makes them important," said Ravi.

"Someone did," she said. "Three people did. Otherwise why did they send them to you?"

"They actually sent them to Colonel Abdullah, who used to live here."

"Well, if they are not important, why did they send them to him?" A part of Shakira's charm was her determination to go on asking the same question, over and over, until she received the answer she thought she deserved.

Ravi thought she should have trained as a trial lawyer, rather than a terrorist, but nonetheless declined to mention this to her while she was pouring the coffee.

And it did not escape her attention that throughout the entire morning, the general was very much within himself, thinking, reading and rereading the newspaper cutting, which displayed for all to see the man who was the real nemesis to one of the biggest terrorist operations in the Middle East.

Shakira left him for an hour but returned to find him still staring at one of his three newspaper cuttings. She picked up one of the others and said, "So who is this man here, the one you spend all day looking at? What's his name, Admiral Morgan? I've heard that name."

"In our business, everyone's heard that name. That man is the biggest reason in the world why the Great Satan believes that America still has the right to dominate the Middle East, to buy and sell our oil, arm the Israelites with the most terrible weapons against us, and station their armies upon our lands whether we like it or whether we don't."

"Why is he such a nuisance?"

"He's worse than a nuisance, my darling. He's an ogre, nothing less."

"What's an ogre?"

"A giant, with a club, which he uses to smash people from poor nations, to beat them because they cannot defend themselves against the military strength of the USA."

"Well, we have whacked the USA a few times, hah?"

"Yes, but never as hard as we wish. And it seems to me that every time we can get a plan together, for a major strike against them, this guy ruins it."

"What does he ruin?"

"Everything. He lost us two nuclear submarines. And he got his hands on our operatives in Boston and they all ended up in Guantánamo Bay. One of them obviously was forced to tell them where we live. That's why someone tried to kill us both."

"How do you know it was Admiral Morgan?" said Shakira, who privately thought the admiral, from his picture, was a handsome and rather cheerful-looking older man. Not at all like an ogre.

"So how do you know?"

"I'm reading this story about him. It seems even the Americans are worried he has too much power. Some Americans, anyway."

"Perhaps we should offer him a job?" said Shakira, laughing. "Then he can get back at the Americans who don't like him. He sounds to me like he'd make a good terrorist."

They both laughed. But suddenly Mrs. Rashood had a flash of memory, and she said to her husband, "You remember when we went to Paris a few years back, and you went to London for a few days for an assassination. Was that anything to do with Admiral Morgan?"

Ravi stared admiringly at his beautiful wife. "You remember?" he said. "All that time ago."

"That was the only time I ever heard you wanting to take the life of one specific person. And I remember you mentioned an admiral."

"And this is the very same man, and the very same problem, his hatred of us and his determination to crush us."

"Then you must be very careful," she replied. "Because I know it did not work out last time. This is obviously a very clever and dangerous person."

"The last time, when I watched him in London, I was only mildly interested. I was just testing the waters."

"Will you try again now because of the attempt to kill us in Damascus?"

"Yes, little Shakira. I must. I feel differently now, ever since I saw you in our backyard, trapped, crying and covered in blood. I thought you might die. And that would have broken my heart.

"And this newspaper has given me all the information I need. I will assassinate Admiral Morgan. And this time, I will not fail."

CHAPTER 5

Four Months Later
Wednesday 20 June

British Airways' morning flight from London was right on time at Logan, and the line for the "U.S. Citizens Only" windows was a lot shorter than the one for visitors and legal aliens.

Window three, sir, straight along to the left . . . this way, please . . . window 10 . . . stand right behind the red line. The bewildered-looking foreigners moved slowly along, moving up to the glass booths, being fingerprinted, checked, by steely-eyed immigration agents.

This was the last line of defense at the American borders. This was where illegal entrants were questioned, then grilled, then sent right back where they came from if all was not in order—passports, entry forms, visas.

At the right end of the line, where American citizens go through, things were a little more relaxed. The words "Welcome home, sir" were used often. And the agents occasionally wanted to know where a traveler had been abroad. But all U.S. passports were nonetheless scanned and checked. No fingerprints.

Correctly dressed businessmen and -women seemed always to get through quickest. America runs on business. These people always receive respect. And the very smart young woman in her late twenties, dark suit with a skirt, white blouse, computer, and briefcase, stepped confidently into the booth and handed over her passport.

She actually thought her heart might stop as the agent opened it and stared at the first page. Martin, Carla, birth date 27 May 1982, birthplace Baltimore, Maryland. The two long lines of numbers at the bottom. The picture of her, staring out.

The agent flipped to the back page and scanned the barcode through his machine. He glanced at the screen and stared at Carla's very striking face, which looked Spanish, could have been South American. Then he stamped her officially into the USA, smiled, and said, "Welcome home, ma'am."

Thus Carla Martin slipped into the United States of America on an exquisitely forged passport, a sensational copy of a passport belonging to another person. Only the picture showed a slight variance, but Carla's hair was swept up in the precise manner of the original owner, and in the photograph she wore the same necklace, a pendant with a red garnet stone set into a silver loop.

When she retrieved her luggage downstairs, just one suitcase, there would be another passport tucked away inside, with only three changes: birth date, birthplace, and name. This one would be in the name of Maureen Carson, born in Michigan, a year younger. This one would be used only to exit the country. The Americans, like all other nations, are disinterested in who's leaving. Only in who's trying to break in.

Carla walked down the steps and waited for her suitcase. Officials with dogs were working around the baggage conveyor. When she grabbed her suitcase and lifted it onto her cart, no one took any notice. She walked to the exit door, where the customs official took her form and nodded briskly.

Outside the terminal, she waited for a few moments on the sidewalk, and then a jet-black Buick pulled up alongside her. The driver stepped out and opened the rear door before loading her luggage into the trunk.

When he was back behind the wheel, Carla said quietly, "Thank you, Fausi. Am I ever glad to see you!"

"Was it nerve-racking?"

"Very. I was terrified he'd notice the variations in the picture. She looks a bit like me, but not that much."

Fausi, a dark, swarthy intelligence officer at the Jordanian embassy in Washington, chuckled. "I knew you'd hold your nerve. And everything was on your side. All the numbers, codes, and details in that passport were absolutely correct and legal."

"I know. But the photograph was my weak point. What if he'd noticed, accused me of being a different person? Arrested me? Traveling on a false passport."

"He'd have refused you entry," replied Fausi. "And they would have put you on the next plane back to London. It's not a hanging offense. And you're not a known criminal. It would just have been a plan that went wrong. Inconvenient, but not life-threatening.

"Besides, you carried with you a Carla Martin Social Security number, three Carla Martin credit cards, and a Carla Martin Maryland driver's license. Everything was in your favor, photograph or no photograph. It was a slight risk, and you took it very well."

"Thank you, Fausi. I'll leave the rest of the journey to you."

The Jordanian agent gunned the car out of Boston, straight down to the Massachusetts Turnpike and southwest to Hartford, Connecticut, and New York. Four hours later, they hit traffic coming to the Triboro Bridge, and it was almost 7:30 in the evening when Fausi pulled up outside the Pierre Hotel.

His passenger left him there, and, as the doorman took her suitcase, she called out, "Early start tomorrow."

Fausi answered as he drove off down Fifth Avenue. "No problem, Shakira, right here, nine o'clock."

One hour later, the beautiful Shakira Rashood walked elegantly into the Pierre Hotel's dining room and joined a smoothly dressed Arab sitting at a corner table, nursing a glass of chilled white wine.

He stood up as she approached, smiled, and said, "So you are the legendary Shakira. I was told you were very beautiful, but the description did not do you justice."

"Thank you, Ahmed," she said. "I have heard many good things about you too."

"I hope from your husband. He is a great hero, both to me and many other devout Muslims."

"Yes," she replied. "And he is very impressed with your work here on our behalf."

"And now you must remember," he said, "as we all do in the USA, to take extra care at all times. The Americans are a friendly, trusting people, but if the authorities here get a smell that something is wrong, they are absolutely ruthless in hunting down their enemy."

"And that would be us, correct?"

"That would most certainly be us."

The waiter poured Shakira a glass of the wine and took their order, grilled sole for both of them. She listened while Ahmed explained how his duties in the Jordanian embassy as a cultural attaché allowed him access to many American institutions.

His embassy, situated just along the road from the Israelis on International Avenue in Washington, was mostly trusted, although not by the CIA. And definitely not by Admiral Morgan. But, broadly, Ahmed was allowed access to any cultural affairs in the nation's capital and in New York. It had been his job to set up Shakira in the correct place to carry out her mission.

And he had achieved that, more or less accidentally, by attending a recent cocktail party for a cancer charity at the John F. Kennedy Center for the Performing Arts, right on the Georgetown Canal behind the Watergate complex.

To his utter delight, he realized Admiral Morgan and his wife were in attendance, and he was swift to move into prime position for an introduction to Mrs. Morgan, who served on the committee. The Jordanians were often extremely generous in their support of these Washington charities.

It was obvious, in the first few moments, that the admiral was bored sideways by the small talk, and he swiftly left to speak to an official from the State Department.

It was a moment that effectively chopped several months off the preparation time General Rashood had allocated for the hit against Morgan. Because Arnold's departure had left Ahmed sipping champagne (cheap, New York State, horrified Arnold) with Kathy Morgan.

"And were you originally from this part of the world?" he asked her.

"Well, a long time ago," she smiled. "I was married before, and we lived for several years in Europe, but then I came home."

"To Washington?"

"Well, to Virginia. My mother still lives there. Little country town called Brockhurst, way down near the Rappahannock River. It's very pretty."

"So you have a nice drive down to see her when the big city gets too much?"

"You're right," said Kathy. "I do like going down there. That's where I was born, but there aren't many people I still know. Mom's on her own now, and she gets a bit lonely sometimes. And you?"

"Oh, I am from a place called Petra in the south of Jordan. My parents have a small hotel there."

"Petra," said Kathy. "I know about Petra. That's where they discovered the lost city carved into the rock. Burial grounds, palaces, temples, and God knows what. Pre-Roman."

"Well, that's very impressive, Mrs. Morgan," said Ahmed. "And you are right. There are still very important excavations taking place down there."

"I'm afraid there's nothing that dramatic happening in Brockhurst when I go home," said Kathy, laughing. "Just Emily working in her garden."

"Emily?"

"Yes, that's my mom. I always called her Emily. She's Emily Gallagher."

"Then you are of Irish descent," replied Ahmed, with the skilled dexterity of an international diplomat. "Like my own mother."

"Well, yes, I am—I was Kathy Gallagher. All four of my grandparents were immigrants from Kerry in southern Ireland. But your mother sounds really interesting."

"Her family came from County Cork, but she met and married my father when he was a Jordanian diplomat in Dublin. He hated the weather, so they returned to Petra and bought a hotel."

At this point, Kathy excused herself to assist the chairman with her gratitude speech, and she moved away unaware that she had been speaking to one of the most sinister, dangerous undercover terrorists in the entire United States.

Ahmed hated the West, and everything it stood for. He was a rabid extremist for Islam, though not in the front line of strikes against the Great Satan. He operated behind the scenes, and was probably Hezbollah's most valuable intelligence gatherer. He also helped Hamas whenever he could. Ahmed was permitted to take no risks.

And now, sitting quietly in New York's Pierre Hotel with Shakira Rashood, he would put his knowledge to work. "Take notes, but destroy them before you get on station," he ordered. "Your mission is to befriend a Mrs. Emily Gallagher. She lives in a small town called Brockhurst, down where the Rappahannock River runs out into Chesapeake Bay."

"Have you been there?"

"Yes. I drove down. It's about 120 miles from Washington. But it's a good road, Interstate 95 until you hit Route 17, then straight down the right bank of the river."

"Did you see Mrs. Gallagher's house?"

"I did. That part was easy. It's a white stone colonial building on the edge of the town. I think she might be rather a grand lady. So please be extra careful. Those kinds of people are usually a lot cleverer than we may sometimes think."

Shakira wrote carefully in a small leather-bound notebook. "Did you see her?" she asked.

"No. But I saw the house."

"And the hotel you mentioned?"

"That's in the center of town. Quite an old building, with a bar and a restaurant. And quite busy."

"And I am either to stay there or work there?"

"Correct. But much better to work there if you can. I have an apartment for you about twenty miles north of Brockhurst in a new complex. It's the penthouse on the twenty-first floor, and I have right here the lease agreement, which you must sign and present to the management when you get there."

Ahmed reached into his pocket and produced the document, with a banker's draft made out to Chesapeake Properties for $9,000, the amount of four months' rent.

"That's a lot of money," said Shakira.

"It's a very nice place," replied Ahmed. "Private. Penthouse, balcony, two bedrooms, nicely furnished. Big living room, kitchen, two bathrooms, and a small utility room. The building has a doorman 24/7."

"I probably won't want to leave," smiled Shakira.

"You probably will *have* to leave," said Ahmed. "As we all do. In the end."

They concluded their dinner with a cup of coffee at around 10:30. "I must go," Ahmed said as he stood up from the table. "I have to get back."

"To Washington?"

"Yes, I have a driver outside. We'll make it in four hours. Remember, I'm supposed to be at the Whitney Museum for a reception this evening. I'll be expected at my desk on time in the morning."

Shakira thanked him for everything, but before he left, Ahmed placed on the table a long, thin cardboard box. "This is for you," he said. "I hope you never need it, at least not during your stay in the USA." And with that, he hurried toward the Fifth Avenue entrance and was gone.

Shakira picked up the box and made her way up to her seventh-floor room. Once inside, she opened it and stared at a long, slender Middle Eastern dagger, its blade very slightly curved, its handle set with red, green, and blue stones. There was also a brief note, written in Arabic. Shakira translated automatically—*Do not under any circumstances leave your home without this. Strict orders from General Rashood. Ahmed.*

Shakira smiled. *I'll keep it inside a wide belt, in the small of my back, like Ravi.* And then, thankfully, she went to bed, exhausted by the tension experienced by all subversives at the start of a clandestine operation.

Almost all transatlantic passengers from Europe wake up at some ungodly hour on their first morning in the United States, mainly because at five o'clock in the morning on the East Coast, it's 10 A.M. in London, and the body clock has not yet adjusted.

Shakira was awake at 5:30 and spent the next couple of hours watching television, trash on three channels, which she loved. By eight o'clock, she was having a light breakfast of orange juice, fruit, and coffee. By 9 A.M., she was outside waiting for Fausi, who was right on time.

They headed down Fifth Avenue, slowly in the morning traffic, and crawled their way west toward 10th Avenue and the Lincoln Tunnel. The traffic pouring through into the city from New Jersey was extremely heavy, but not too bad outward-bound.

The line for the tunnel was slow; but once inside, everything sped up. Fausi accelerated into New Jersey, collected his toll ticket, and headed fast down the turnpike. They were past Philadelphia in ninety minutes, past Baltimore in three hours, and around Washington heading south in four.

Just after 1 P.M., they stopped for gas and coffee; then, with a little over a hundred miles in front of them, they set off for Brockhurst, arriving there after a drive on a narrow, winding road in hot, clear weather at 4:35.

Fausi parked the car on a deserted street six hundred yards from the Estuary Hotel, and Shakira, who was dressed in light blue jeans, an inexpensive white shirt, and flat shoes, walked the short distance.

The front door of the Estuary led into a wide, rather dark interior hall, carpeted in dark red. There was a long wooden reception area, behind which was a middle-aged man, fiftyish. To the left was an obvious bar, with the same carpet, soft lighting, and bar stools. It was completely deserted. To the right was the dining room/restaurant, with a desk at its entrance. Unoccupied.

Shakira looked doubtful. No customers. They wouldn't need any staff. Nonetheless, she walked hesitantly to the front desk and said, politely, "Good afternoon."

The man looked up, smiled, and asked, "And what can I do for you?"

"Well," said Shakira, "I am looking for a job, here in Brockhurst, and I wondered if you had a vacancy. I can do almost anything—maid, waitress, receptionist."

The man nodded and stood up. He offered his hand and said, "Jim . . . Jim Caborn. I'm the manager here. And you?"

"I'm Carla Martin. It's nice to meet you." Shakira had been well versed in American niceties.

"Well, Carla," said the manager, "I'm afraid I don't have anything right at the moment. However, I do have a barman leaving in a week. Can you do that kind of thing?"

"Oh, yes. I worked in a bar in London for three months. Does this place get busy?"

"All the time," replied Jim. "From about 5:30 in the evening onward. And especially on weekends in the summer." He stared at her very beautiful face and swept-back raven hair, and wondered about her background; he asked, "Do you have an American passport?"

"Oh, yes. I'm American. I've just been away for a few months."

"And what brings you here to Brockhurst?"

"I'm visiting an aunt near here in a little place called Bowler's Wharf, and I think this is the nicest and biggest town."

"Honey, it's not Washington, trust me."

Shakira smiled. "Well, I like it. And I'm fed up with big cities."

"Listen, Carla, running a bar in a busy place like this is not easy. You understand how quick and accurate you have to be, and how you must understand the drinks, and the cocktails, and be able to make Irish coffees and all that."

"Jim, I worked in a really busy bar in Covent Garden—that's downtown London. But if you will employ me, I'd be happy to put in a week, at my own expense, working with the man who's leaving. That way I'd be organized for when I was on my own."

The offer of free help almost tipped the balance with this hotel manager. But not quite. He had one more question. "Do you need to live in the hotel?" he asked.

"Oh, no. I'll go back to my aunt's house. I have a small car."

"Okay," said Jim, who was surprised she had not mentioned money. "I'll pay you four hundred bucks a week. I have to deduct taxes off the top, but you keep whatever tips you get. When do you want to start?"

"How about tomorrow?" she said.

"That'll be fine. I'll need your Social Security, a look at your passport, and references if you have any. If you don't, give me a couple of numbers I can call."

Shakira told him that was not a problem, and returned to the car for the documents. Fausi was asleep, as well he might have been after the long drive from New York. She retrieved the passport and SS card and reached into her bag for the correct references, all of which had been beautifully forged by the same man who did her passport in the depths of the Syrian embassy in London's Belgrave Square.

She selected two that pertained to her skills behind a bar. She had others for her work as a housekeeper in a country hotel; others for her efforts as a maid; a couple for her prowess as a waitress; and three more for secretarial jobs, not one of which she had ever held.

The two she chose for Jim Caborn were from the Mighty Quinn Bar in London's Neal Street, Covent Garden. It was written on letterhead and assured the reader that Miss Martin was truthful, honest, hardworking, and always punctual. The other was from the Hotel Rembrandt, in Buckingham Gate, where Miss Martin had managed the downstairs bar, and again it testified to her reliability.

It was all plenty good enough for Jim, who made careful notes on a blue file index card and gave everything back to Shakira. "See you tomorrow," he said. "You can work the 4 P.M. 'til eleven o'clock shift. That's when you'll learn the most."

Shakira thanked him. They shook hands. And Jim watched her admiringly as she walked out. He was pleased with his new recruit, and was blissfully unaware that he had just hired the most dangerous woman in the United States.

Outside, she paused to assess her surroundings. The Estuary Hotel had stone white walls with mock Tudor beams, and it stood on a corner of the main street, which ran down to an area on the banks of the Rappahan-nock and then swerved around to the right.

Shakira guessed that from the top floor of the hotel there would be a view right across the wide river, as indeed there was from the parking lot of the supermarket that was situated on the opposite side of the main street.

Brockhurst had been here for a long time, and developers had taken care to protect its original character. There were many newish buildings, deliberately constructed to reflect the early twentieth century. There was the usual number of real estate agents and boutique gift shops. This little town attracted visitors all through the warm months. And the only place in town to stay was the Estuary, which had twelve rooms with baths in the main building and an outside annex with a dozen more.

Shakira walked around to the back of the hotel. There was a parking area in the rear, big enough for a large delivery truck to unload supplies. The street that ran along the side of the hotel was narrow and lonely. There were two small stores, one selling hardware, the other children's clothes.

More certain of her bearings now, she walked back to the car and woke Fausi, who was asleep again. She climbed into the backseat. "Get moving," she said. "I've just been hired, but I'm not living here. I start tomorrow afternoon."

"Beautiful," replied Fausi. "Now I'll take you to your new home." He turned the car north, and they drove back up Route 17 for a couple of exits and then swung down a tree-lined road to a new apartment block, cleverly set back into surrounding woodland.

The sign at the entrance said CHESAPEAKE HEIGHTS, which was interesting since the land in this part of the Virginia peninsula, which lies between the Rappahannock and York rivers, was almost geometrically flat.

It was 6:30 now, and the light was just beginning to fade. Shakira signed her lease, paid the money, and moved into the top-floor apartment. Fausi went off to buy her some groceries, just regular stuff: bread, milk, butter, preserves, cold cuts, eggs, fruit juice, rice, a few spices, cheese, Danish pastries, apples, grapes, peaches, and coffee. He delivered them in a couple of big boxes, one at a time.

"Will you need me tonight?" he asked, conscious of his 24-hour duties as Shakira's driver, bodyguard, and personal assistant.

"No," she replied. "But I'd like to make a tour of the area tomorrow morning. How about 10:30?"

"No problem," he said. "I'd better get moving."

Fausi was staying in a small hotel twelve miles away. His own anonymity was as important as hers. Nothing should connect them. Nothing should suggest that he was some kind of a boyfriend, or even a colleague. Nothing that would ever give any law enforcement officials the slightest clue as to the identity, or whereabouts, of either of them. Even the license plate on Fausi's car was false.

In the ensuing weeks, he planned never to come to the main entrance of the apartment block, never even speak to the doorman, never enter the Estuary Hotel, or even park within its precincts. Fausi was a ghost, just as much as Carla Martin was.

Shakira utilized the first three days of her trial run behind the bar to familiarize herself with the locals. She quickly located the home of Mrs. Emily Gallagher, and once, parked along the street in Fausi's car, she caught a good look at the lady as she tended her roses along the post-and-rail fence of her front yard.

She also watched when Mrs. Gallagher took her dog for a walk. He was a big, rather fluffy golden retriever and usually looked as if he were taking *her* for a walk, rather than the other way around.

On her fourth night in the bar, a fairly quiet Monday, the regular barman took off early, and Shakira, wearing her name tag with CARLA inscribed on it, had her first real break: Mrs. Gallagher came into the hotel with a friend and entered the dining room. At 10 P.M., she and the friend walked across the hall to the bar, where Mrs. Gallagher ordered two Irish coffees, which Shakira made.

At 10:20, the friend left, and Mrs. Gallagher stayed to order one more regular coffee. There were only two other people still in the bar, and Shakira ventured to ask the elderly lady whether she had enjoyed her dinner.

"Oh, yes," she replied. "I always have a grilled piece of sea bass here on Mondays. They get a fish delivery here, my dear, at noon, straight from the wharf down at Gloucester Point. It's always delicious."

"They didn't offer me any," said Shakira, laughing.

"Oh, I'm not surprised," said Mrs. Gallagher. "Between you and me, that Caborn character is frightfully mean-spirited. He probably said you could have a cheeseburger."

"Meatloaf," said Shakira. And they both laughed.

"You're new here, aren't you?" said Mrs. Gallagher.

"Yes. I just started on Friday."

"Well, I hope you stay for a while. Most of them don't, you know. That's the trouble with the young. Very restless, don't you think? No time to enjoy anything."

Shakira moved to her right at this point, to serve a final drink to the remaining two customers, residents of the hotel, and then returned to Mrs. Gallagher, who was preparing to leave.

Before she went, she said to Shakira, "My name, by the way, is Emily Gallagher. I usually come in on Thursdays as well, so I expect I'll see you again. Good night, my dear."

"Good night, Mrs. Gallagher."

"Oh please, Carla, call me Emily. Otherwise you'll make me feel ancient."

There seemed to be no question of anyone paying a bill, so Shakira just ignored it, and assumed, correctly, the check would be added to some kind of monthly account.

And with a friendly little wave, Emily Gallagher left her longtime local hostelry for the short 200-yard walk, straight up the well-lit main street, to her home.

Shakira smiled a smile of pure contentment.

The following morning, Fausi dropped her off in the main part of the town. She shopped in the supermarket, placed her packages in the car, and asked Fausi to meet her at one o'clock. She walked toward Mrs. Gallagher's house, and at 11 A.M., right on time, she watched the old lady come out of the house with her dog on his leash.

Timing her walk perfectly, she arrived at the front gate twenty yards behind, and noticed how difficult it was for Emily to control the bounding big retriever. Catching up quickly, she said, "Good morning, Emily. Would you like me to help you with this ridiculous person? What's his name?"

Emily Gallagher turned around, and laughed when she saw who it was. "Oh, it's you, Carla. You're right. He is ridiculous, and his name's Charlie."

"He's very good-looking," said Shakira, "and handsome people get away with a lot."

Charlie, sensing, as dogs do, that he was in the presence of another friend, turned to Shakira and planted his front paws on her belt, his tongue lolling out, his tail wagging fiercely.

She reached for the leash and said, "Let me take him. I'll walk with you for a while."

Emily looked relieved. "He is a terrible handful," she said. "But I've had him for seven years now, and I would miss him terribly. He is a good companion for me, now that I'm alone. I usually take him about a mile down here, to the bend in the river.

"Last week, he got loose and jumped into the river. I thought he'd end up in Chesapeake Bay. But he just swam back to the shore and soaked me, shaking water everywhere."

Shakira shook her head. "He's almost too big for you," she said, firmly pulling Charlie into line.

"I know he is," replied Emily. "And, you know, if I ever miss a day taking him for a walk, he gets so boisterous, rushing around the house, knocking things over."

Carla smiled and said, "Well, I love dogs, and I love walking. Would you like me to take him out sometimes?"

"Oh, my dear, that would be such a huge help. But would you mind? I hate to be a nuisance."

"No, I should like it very much. I don't have many friends around here yet. And he is the most gorgeous dog."

Thus Carla Martin and Emily Gallagher became firm friends. Carla walked Charlie, three or four times a week, sometimes with Emily and sometimes not. Sometimes she had a cup of tea with the old lady before starting her shift at the Estuary, and occasionally they had lunch together.

Meanwhile, at the hotel she had become extremely popular, particularly with a youngish crowd who were in the hotel bar three or four times a week, always on Thursdays and Fridays, sometimes on Saturdays, and always on Sunday nights.

Despite all her efforts to play down her obvious charms with loose sweaters, wide skirts, flat shoes, no makeup, and her hair tied back in a plain ponytail, Shakira could not avoid attracting the attention of young men.

Among the group she saw most was Rick, the local computer engineer; Bill, whose father owned the supermarket; Eric, who had inherited one of the local building firms; Herb, who ran a photographic business; and Matt Barker, who had built and owned the local garage and Toyota dealership. Matt was older, maybe thirty-four.

The best-looking was Eric, twenty-four, divorced and the local golf club champion. Rick was the most studious and well-informed; Bill was the richest; Herb was showy and overconfident, with not much money but a lot of ambition to work in New York in fashion; and by far the most consistent in his admiration for Shakira was Matt Barker, who drove a Porsche and asked her to have dinner with him every time he saw her.

Shakira used all of her guile to remain remote from them. She hinted at a serious boyfriend in London; she always closed the bar by 11:30 and left by the back door, running swiftly across the parking lot and around the corner into a dark street, where Fausi awaited her, engine running.

She never said she was leaving, and her routine was not varied. She always pulled on a pair of short leather driving gloves, which she knew suggested she had her own car, and in turn that would discourage anyone from asking if they could drive her home. And once the gloves were on, she just slipped away, leaving the security to the night porter who supervised the last nonresidents, seeing them out, and then locking up.

After a couple of weeks, she became a woman of mystery. The guys used to ask each other, "When did she go? Which way did she go? She never even said good night."

And she never would. Shakira had no intention of being alone outside the hotel with this high-spirited but well-mannered group of young bucks, the well-heeled middle-range stratum of Brockhurst society.

On busy nights, there were often girls from the town in the bar, but they tended to be those whose education or background had not taken them to a good university and on to Washington or New York. And Matt Barker and his guys had no serious interest in dating also-rans.

They had no idea who Shakira was (*she thanked God*), but they definitely knew she was not an also-ran. There was a poise about her, an aloof quality, like someone with more important things on her mind. And boy, did she have important things on her mind.

And every time the group came in, one of them, sooner or later, asked her out. With Bill and Eric it was slightly frivolous; Rick and Herb seemed earnest and genuinely were looking for more permanent girlfriends. Matt Barker, however, from across the bar, was falling in love.

Shakira determinedly kept him at arm's length, spending less time chatting to him than she did with the others, but sensing him watching her, admiring her, wanting to talk to her.

He was a big man, always well dressed, clean-shaven, with longish blond hair. At first sight, he could easily have been mistaken for a city lawyer or financier, except for his big hands, which were slightly rough from years of grappling with car engines, brakes, and chassis.

"Hi, Miss Carla," he would say when he walked in. "Have you changed your mind about me yet?"

Shakira did not wish to offend him, and she tried to be evasive . . . *oh, you know I can't, Matt . . . I'm very involved with someone . . . I might even be married before the end of the year.*

Matt did not buy it. He sensed she was alone, and at times, late at night after a few beers, he found her the most sexually alluring woman he had ever seen. He would stand looking at her back, watching the firm tilt of her hips as she hurried about her duties. Matt actually dreamed about her, dreamed she was naked in his arms, imagined the feel of her, longed for the moment when she agreed to go out with him, as he believed she would. One day.

But night after night, she always slipped away, vanishing into the dark, leaving Matt bereft of the only woman he believed he could ever love. The trouble was, Matt believed Carla Martin was simply playing hard to get, and that she too lay in bed at night thinking of him in a similar light. Which was about eight hundred light-years from the truth.

It was a Monday morning when Shakira finally hit pay dirt. She called at Mrs. Gallagher's house to collect Charlie and went in for a cup of coffee. She sensed that Emily was about to ask her for a favor, and her instincts did not let her down.

"Carla, my dear," she said, "I have been so terribly worried. My daughter has asked me to look after her dog for a month, and very foolishly I said yes. But I just don't think I can cope, not by myself."

"Name and make?" asked Shakira.

"I'm sorry. I didn't quite catch that."

"Name and make?" repeated Shakira, laughing. "Of the dog, I mean."

"Oh, how foolish of me," chuckled Emily. "He's called Kipper. A King Charles spaniel. My son-in-law says he's as silly as a sheep."

"Has he been here before?"

"Oh, yes. Lots of times. He's really quite charming, nothing like so boisterous as Charlie, nor so greedy. Of course, he's considerably smaller."

"Emily, I don't think you should be let loose on the public road with two dogs in hand. Especially since one of them's Charlie."

"Well, I'm sure that's true. And I was almost afraid to ask you, but do you think you could help? I'd pay you to do this."

"Of course I will. When do we expect Kipper to make his appearance?"

"Four weeks from today. That would be Monday, July 30, the day Kathy and her husband are leaving. She's delivering Kipper, then taking the evening flight to London."

"So you enter this two-dog frenzy the next day?" Shakira had learned everything she knew about humor from Ravi, and he learned it at Harrow. For an Arab, she really could be quite droll.

"Well, yes," said Emily. "By that Tuesday morning, I will probably be at my wits' end. Could you possibly be here early that morning? Just to help me get them under control."

"Of course," replied Shakira. "I usually come at eleven. While you have both dogs, I'll be here at ten, starting July 31." She produced her little leather-bound notebook and wrote in the dates. On the previous page were the words: *TARGET EMILY GALLAGHER. Brockhurst, Virginia.*

Shakira sat back and sipped her coffee, glancing up just once at a framed photograph she had seen before. "Is that your daughter there, in the photograph?" she asked.

Mrs. Gallagher picked up the picture and smiled. "Yes, that's Kathy," she said.

"Gosh, she's pretty," said Shakira, looking at the wedding-day picture, which showed Arnold and Kathy standing outside the offices of the justice of the peace who had married them in Washington.

"When was this?"

"Oh, just five years ago," said Emily.

"Then it must have been a second marriage," smiled Shakira. "No girl can be that pretty and remain single for that long."

"You're correct. Kathy was married before. He was rich but a frightful, selfish man. I'm just so glad she's found real happiness now. Her husband is not everyone's type, but he makes her happy. And I like him very much."

"Are they going somewhere wonderful after Kipper gets dropped off?" said Shakira.

"Well, I never really know where they are," replied Emily. "He's some kind of very high-powered diplomat. All Kathy said was they were flying to London, staying at the Ritz Hotel for a few days, and then going to Scotland."

"Doesn't sound too bad," said Shakira.

"Indeed it doesn't. The Ritz! It always reminds me of that English wartime song 'A Nightingale Sang in Berkeley Square'—that line, *There were angels dining at the Ritz.*"

Shakira looked thoughtful. Mrs. Gallagher really was the most charming lady, kind, generous, and so proper. For a split second, she wondered how she could possibly be sitting here in this lovely house, subversively planning to have Emily's son-in-law murdered.

But again she forced herself back to The Cause, to remember the terrible plight of the Palestinians. The poverty, the suffering, the lack of medical supplies, the cruel arrogance of the Israelis, and above all the hatred, the hatred of the Great Satan, and her husband's unflinching view that the West must be driven out of the Middle East forever and that Israel must be destroyed.

Of course, Mrs. Gallagher had nothing to do with any of this. But she was part of America, that monstrous nation that had somehow crushed her own and now stood smiling with its great white teeth, basking in its inestimable wealth, sucking the underground wealth of the Arab nations dry, while her own people lived and died on the precipice of destitution.

Ravi had been definite. America must be attacked, because they will take notice of nothing else. Americans react badly to loss of life, and they really hate loss of assets and loss of money. They are not true warriors, though they have highly efficient armed services and a truly devastating arsenal of high-tech weaponry.

But they will be brought down: perhaps not defeated, but forced to retreat behind their own borders, leaving the Muslims to create a new empire stretching from the Horn of Africa to the Atlantic. That remained Ravi's dream and the dream of the ayatollahs, and the imams, and all the holy men.

That is the will of Allah, and that is the stated opinion throughout the Koran . . . *Death to the infidel.* And right here she, Shakira, was, sitting with one of them, the matriarch of the family of the man most feared by the Middle East's jihadists—Admiral Arnold Morgan.

Yes, she would carry out her mission. She would inform Ravi of precisely where he could locate the admiral. And although she would not wish personal harm to Emily Gallagher, neither would she forget her purpose in this life. Which was to carry out the will of Allah . . . *Allah is great.*

She glanced at her watch. It was time for prayers. *Which way was Mecca? To the east, out across the river.* And Shakira turned toward the window, feeling, unaccountably, the deep comradeship and belief of the Muslim world holding her within its cocoon. Allah, she knew, would forgive her for failing to pray this morning, sitting here with this infidel, so long as she was carrying out His work.

"A penny for your thoughts, Carla," said Emily. "What about some more coffee, and one of these cookies?"

"Oh, gosh, thank you," she replied. "I think I was daydreaming. This is such a comfortable house."

No sooner had the word "cookie" been uttered than Charlie came thundering toward them from four rooms away.

Shakira took charge. She stood up and said, "CHARLIE. SIT DOWN." Charlie sat. "I give you one little piece, if you behave." Charlie wagged his tail in anticipation. "But if you jump on me, or your mistress, and spill coffee, you're not getting anything."

Charlie, who plainly understood English, looked inordinately sad, cocking his head to one side in that timeless stricken pose of the retriever, which suggested that he had been given nothing to eat for at least a year. Shakira's heart melted. And she gave him a cookie. Charlie crunched it instantly, swallowed the lot, and readopted the stricken pose.

"I'd better take you out," said Carla, who then turned to Emily and said, "It looks a little like rain. Why don't you stay here, and I'll just take him to the river? Back in forty-five minutes."

As she gathered up the dog leash and clipped it on, Mrs. Gallagher looked at her quizzically. She had noticed, as educated people often will, one tiny slip in Carla's diction; the mistake of a foreign person. She had said, "I give you one little piece, if you behave." Not, correctly, "I *will* give you one little piece." Future conditional.

It was not much, but Mrs. Gallagher could not help wondering if Carla had perhaps had one foreign parent, or had been brought up somewhere else with English as her second language. One thing she did know, however, was that *"I give you one little piece"* was not the diction of a proper American national.

It was, of course, in the great scheme of things, completely irrelevant. Shakira Rashood had already accomplished her mission on behalf of the fanatical warriors of Hamas. And she had completed it right here in Brockhurst, courtesy of Emily Gallagher.

The Ritz Hotel, check-in Tuesday morning July 31, until Thursday morning August 2. Admiral and Mrs. Arnold Morgan. No problem.

Outside on the street, Shakira walked briskly, all the way along to the bend in the river, where she entered the little park that Charlie loved and stared across to the far bank, easterly.

The park was deserted, and she began to whisper—

Allahu akbar . . .

Ash hadu an la ilaha Allah . . .

Ash hadu an-an Muhammadar rasulul-lah . . .

La ilaha ill Allah . . .

No one could hear. Except for Charlie. And even he did not understand that.

It was, of course, the 1,400-year-old prayer of devotion from the Koran: *God is most great.*

I bear witness there is none worthy of worship but God. I bear witness that Mohammed is the Prophet of God.

There is no Deity but God.

She unclipped Charlie and stood for a few moments. Then she quoted, quietly in English, direct from the Koran, the words of Allah as stated by the Prophet: *Remember me. I shall remember you! Thank me. Do not be ungrateful to me. You who believe, seek help through patience and prayer.*

At this point, Charlie charged straight into the Rappahannock, and Shakira ran to the bank, shouting at him in words that may not have been entirely understood by the Prophet. But they were understood by Charlie, who charged back out again, shook himself, absurdly, all over Shakira's jeans, and then went back into the river again.

Finally he came out, shook himself again, and allowed himself to be clipped back onto the leash and walked home. He was, however, such a wreck with river water and mud that Shakira took him to the garden hose, washed him, and left him outside to dry.

Emily came out and said, "I suppose he ran into the river again, Carla. I'm so sorry to put you to all this trouble. Are you staying for lunch?"

The familiarity between them was now complete. And Shakira felt almost sad that soon she would leave and never again see this calm, pretty

American house. And she found herself wondering if she and Ravi would be happy here together. But that was impossible, and Carla politely declined lunch and said she would see Emily in the evening at the hotel.

Somewhat wistfully, she walked back to the center of town, where Fausi had the car waiting, to drive her to a lonely spot down on the estuary of the river, where she could make contact on her cell phone with the High Command of Hamas.

She had already chosen the place. A near-deserted beach down near Grey's Point, ten miles south of Brockhurst. The land was flat. The road was hardly used, and indeed petered out into a sandy track as it neared the water. She would stand right there and make the satellite call on one of the most expensive phones of its type in the world, with the American T-Mobile service. No mistakes for the 21st-century terrorist.

Fausi dropped her off at the point where the beach road dissolved into sand. Shakira walked for a couple of hundred yards down to the water, then began punching in the numbers for the house where Hamas kept a 24-hour communications center, and where she hoped Ravi would be, to know she was safe.

The house was situated south of Tel Aviv because the Gaza phone system was so unreliable. Israel itself has always been rather shaky at telecommunications, but it was a whole lot better than Gaza.

Shakira dialed the country code—011-972—then three for the area south of Tel Aviv, then the secret number. There was no reply until an answering machine clicked in. Shakira spoke in her well-practiced operative's voice, much the same as Ramon Salman had done from Boston to Syria almost six months before: *Virginia calling—the Ritz Hotel, London, Tuesday, January 31, to Thursday, February 2.* Not another word. No clues, no indications, nothing to reveal Shakira's personal plans, nothing to identify the target. Plus the usual Hamas code for months—six forward—thus July becomes January, and August turns into February.

If there had been a wiretap on the Hamas phone south of Tel Aviv, that message would have revealed only inaccurate information. But there was no tap. And that message almost caused the roof to fall in, so incendiary were its ramifications.

Because General Rashood would now have to enter England, which was almost catastrophically difficult. Air travel was out of the question.

Ravi was one of the most wanted men on earth. If he presented any passport, forged or genuine, at Heathrow's immigration desk, the computer would probably explode.

A clandestine landing by sea was no less hazardous. The new antidrug culture had put the entire British Coast Guard on red alert. There were Royal Navy ships patrolling the English Channel like bloodhounds. Every radar dish, civilian or military, was sweeping the coastline for intrusive small aircraft.

There was only one way in, only one that carried an acceptable risk, and that meant Ravi had to move very fast. As it happened, he was in the house when Shakira called, and he wished fervently that he could speak to her. But he knew better, and he tried to shut her from his mind as he prepared for the immediate conference of the Hamas High Command and the two visiting senior members of Hezbollah. It was 9:30 in the evening.

Shakira arrived back at Chesapeake Heights at around 2 P.M. Fausi dropped her off and drove away. She greeted the doorman and made her way to her top-floor apartment. The day was hot but cloudy, with a slight but increasing breeze that might easily turn into a thunderstorm.

She made herself a sandwich of roast beef and goat's cheese and houmus on the bread. It gave it an offbeat Middle Eastern flavor, and it made her homesick, and she wondered if she and Ravi would ever make it home together.

But most of all, she wondered where he was and what his plans were. She had, she knew, fulfilled the relatively easy part of the Hamas scheme. All she wanted was to be with him again, and to help him in his mission and protect him if she could.

She took a chair out onto her wide penthouse balcony and sat reflectively, staring out over the wide green treetops toward the river. She knew so little of this evil country. All she knew was the great highway that had brought her from Boston to Brockhurst, to this peaceful place with its wide river and warm climate.

She had met with only friendliness here. The cheerful officer in the Boston immigration booth, who had welcomed her home; the big doorman at the Pierre who had carried her bag; Freddy, the nice, helpful doorman downstairs here; agreeable, trusting Jim Caborn, her boss; and her new best friend, Emily.

So far as she could tell, America was very short of archvillains, the kind her husband always railed about. But she had never really been anywhere until she met Ravi, and he had taught her almost everything she knew.

She supposed he must be right about America. But she had not seen anything yet, firsthand, to suggest a terrible land populated by ogres like Admiral Morgan. No, she had definitely not seen any of those.

She ate her lunch thoughtfully, and drank some fruit juice. And she wondered how and when she should extricate herself from here before going to meet Ravi. She most certainly would not tell Emily she was going, which would leave the old lady in a bit of a spot when Kipper arrived. Not, however, in so bad a spot as the one in which Kipper's master, Admiral Morgan, might shortly find himself.

Shakira would have liked to say a proper good-bye to Emily and perhaps make plans to stay in contact. But that could never happen. The truth was, if she just vanished, it would take maybe a day, or even two, before anyone even realized she had gone. If she announced her departure, a lot of people would know she was leaving before she even started. No, the only way was to vanish, and she had to organize that.

Her cell phone rang, and she rushed back into the apartment to retrieve it from her handbag and answer it. There could be only one person in all the world calling that number, but she knew he would not be there personally.

She pressed the receiving button and heard a voice recording. It intoned only a dozen words: *Dublin. Ireland. The Great Mosque in Clonskeagh. 1700. July 16 to 18.* The line went dead.

And Shakira clicked off the phone. The message had, she knew, been overheard by no one. And it meant she must be in Dublin by the evening of July 15. That was a week from Sunday. She must be on her way, on a flight from the USA by Friday night, July 13, at the latest.

She plugged her computer into the Internet connection and decided the best flights were Aer Lingus. She was flying first-class, and her very expensive ticket could be switched to another airline, from British Airways, which did not fly direct to Dublin.

She returned to the balcony with a new glass of fruit juice. And she sat there for a half hour, reading one of the celebrity magazines she so loved and wondering if Emily and Charlie would ever think of her.

In her mind, there were two people, two Mrs. Rashoods: the Shakira who tried to be polite and helpful, the one Emily had grown fond of; and then there was the other Shakira, the assassin's ruthless assistant. She did not like to think of herself as one and the same.

Midnight Same Day (Monday 2 July)
Gaza City

General Rashood was invited to chair this meeting as the most senior member of the Hamas military. Once more, they were seated on cushions in the whitewashed situation room in the basement of the walled house off Omar el-Mokhtar Street.

He opened the discussion by pointing out that in the short time that had passed since he had first seen the *Washington Post* story on Admiral Morgan, there had been a serious uproar in the liberal media back in the USA. People were beginning to ask important questions about the presence of Arnold at the right hand of the president.

They had trotted out all the predictable platitudes: *Just who does this admiral think he is? Why does a modern USA require this aged Cold Warrior? Is Arnold Morgan leading us back to gunboat diplomacy? Just how dangerous is this ex–nuclear submarine commander? President Bedford must explain to the American people . . . If Arnold Morgan wants this much influence, he should run for office.*

The television networks seized upon the theme. Political "forums" were established specially to wreck the admiral's reputation. And very quickly, the Arab al Jazeera television station leaped onto the bandwagon with such "documentaries" as *The Terrorist-Buster in the White House*— an in-depth look at President Bedford's Hard Man.

General Rashood was as utterly disinterested in this outpouring of indignation in the USA as Admiral Morgan was himself, regarding all media journalists as a bunch of know-nothing, half-educated, hysterical charlatans. Or worse.

What concerned the general was the intelligence between the lines: that Admiral Morgan had indeed been the principal force that sent three of the top Hamas field officers to Guantánamo Bay, probably for the rest of their lives. That there was a definite chance that the suicide Boeing 737,

Flight TBA 62, going for the Capitol building, had been shot down by the U.S. military on specific orders from Admiral Morgan.

In General Rashood's opinion, the jihadists were fighting a war against one man, and losing it. Time and again. Militarily, there was only one option. And he would carry out that option himself. They now had a time, a place, and the target. All that remained was to enter England in a thoroughly clandestine way.

Colonel Hassad Abdullah interrupted to report that the Iranian Navy had one of their Russian-built *Kilo*-class diesel-electric submarines in the Mediterranean, patrolling somewhere off Lebanon. It had been refueled at the north end of the Suez Canal, and its task was, essentially, to stand by to help the holy warriors of Hezbollah should they require it. The Iranians, however, would be only too delighted to help General Rashood on his mission.

This was the best possible news, because without that submarine, it would be nearly impossible to land General Rashood in the operations area. Even now, time was extremely tight. Southern Ireland was the obvious landfall for anywhere in Great Britain, although the distance was somewhat daunting. From Lebanon, it was approximately 3,900 miles by sea, straight through the Med to the Strait of Gibraltar, a distance of 2,500 miles, then 1,400 more north across the Bay of Biscay to the open Atlantic and on to the coast of County Cork.

The 3,000-ton Kilo could probably make twelve knots all the way. But she would have to run at periscope depth, snorkeling throughout the journey, to keep her massive batteries charged. That would be noisy, but unavoidable, because the diesel generators, running hard, needed air.

Her greatest strength, her stealth, would thus be compromised. Because, running deep and slow, she was a deadly quiet underwater combatant, totally silent under five knots. Undetectable, with a 3,650-horsepower electronic running capacity on a brilliantly engineered single shaft. But for this mission, speed was the deciding factor, the intention being to land Ravi somewhere on the south coast of the Irish republic on the weekend of Saturday, July 14.

From there he must make his way to Dublin, and then to England, on one of the busy ferry routes, arriving at one of the less stringently patrolled terminals. But first there was a question of arming him.

And even at the ferry ports, there was no possibility that Hamas would take the risk of sending someone through with a sniper rifle. That was the way to a British prison and certain exposure. If they caught him, the Brits would probably hang Ravi for high treason against the state. He had, after all, shot two SAS men in cold blood. His own people. In a sense.

No, he must collect his weapon in England. Collect it, use it. And somehow leave without it. There was no other course of action open to him. The details would be handed over to the Syrian embassy in London, and perhaps the rifle could be handmade in time for Ravi's arrival.

Time, once more, would probably be pressing. So the rifle would need to be constructed in London, since there would be so little time for the ace terrorist to be running around all over England to collect and test it. The arrival of Admiral and Mrs. Morgan was cast in stone. The early morning of Tuesday, July 31. The Ritz Hotel, on Piccadilly.

And such a destination, busy, public, and always secure, would undoubtedly require a great deal of time for reconnaissance. Which, as every military man knows, is always precious and sometimes priceless. It is time seldom wasted.

The Hamas general would need to be on station, in London, by July 20. Only with that timetable could he possibly have the sniper's rifle perfectly primed, his hiding place perfectly sited, his escape route from central London perfectly organized, and his rendezvous with the submarine timed to perfection.

The general would need a car and money, lots of it, since he might have to rent, or even buy, a space somewhere along the north side of the wide thoroughfare of Piccadilly, opposite the great hotel. Real estate in that area was scarce and astronomically priced. The Syrian embassy would be called upon to assist in this commercial end of the plot.

All this was for the elimination of one man. And there were three oil-rich Middle Eastern states involved in the planning and financing: Jordan, Syria, and Iran. But the power behind the decision was Ravi Rashood, the world-class, SAS-trained sniper-marksman, the Islamic terrorist mastermind, who would trust no one else to carry it out.

The general's overall reasoning was simple: "Every operation we undertake against the USA will stand a 100 percent better chance of success if

Admiral Arnold Morgan is in his grave. And that is where I intend to put him."

1900 Monday 2 July
The Estuary Hotel

Shakira was busy for a Monday night. The local group—Herb, Bill, Rick, and Matt Barker—were into their second beers, and there were several residents who had stopped for a drink before going into the dining room. The restaurant was filling up, the kitchen was busy, and tonight's special, sea bass, was awaiting Emily Gallagher and her friend, for whom the same table was always reserved.

The two ladies arrived at 7:15 and made their usual stop at Shakira's bar for a glass of white wine. At the time, Matt Barker was proposing that Shakira meet him as soon as she finished and he would take her to a beautiful spot on the water for a nightcap. The Porsche was outside.

As ever, Shakira was making her excuses to the doe-eyed Matt and was inordinately grateful for the arrival of Emily, who was watching her with an amused smile. Shakira broke away from Matt and moved quickly to pour the wine for Mrs. Gallagher, who said quietly, "I sense that young garage man is making a slight nuisance of himself?"

"Oh, he's all right," she replied. "But he does seem to have a crush on me."

"It's his age, my dear," whispered Emily. "He's too old to be some kind of a lovesick teenager, and too young to be a suave, wealthy, middle-aged Lothario. The trouble is, to people like us, he'll always be a garage mechanic. Not good enough for you, Carla. Stay well clear."

Emily offered a conspiratorial smile and retreated into the crowd. A few minutes later, Shakira saw her cross the hall into the restaurant, and thought enviously about that freshly caught baked sea bass. She had been offered only a cheeseburger for her own dinner.

But she could never, of course, betray to Jim Caborn the irritating fact that, to her, money was absolutely no problem whatsoever. She could have bought the fishing trawler, if she'd felt like it. On a mission such as hers, finance was not a consideration, not for the most wealthy of the jihadists.

Matt Barker once more stepped up to the plate. "Carla," he said, "I really want to take you out tonight. We know each other well enough by now. And anyway, I have a little gift for you."

"Matt," she replied, "that is very sweet of you, and I appreciate it. But I have tried to tell you, I am engaged. There is no way I can go out with you. It wouldn't be fair to Ray." She spoke the name without thinking, almost without realizing; it had been her husband's name in another life.

And anyway it did not make a shred of difference to the way Matt felt about her or his overwhelming desire for her. But he tried to hide it, shrugged, and said, "Well, okay. I just wanted you to know how much I respect you, and how much it would mean to me, if you would ever go out with me."

"Not in this life, I'm afraid," she said jauntily. "You need to find an unattached girl. Not someone who is planning to marry someone else."

Matt, stung by the double-edged poison of rejection and envy, ordered another beer.

The evening wore on, and although Matt Barker and his friends were drinking only some kind of light beer, they were, all of them, showing signs of becoming increasingly drunk.

At ten o'clock, Emily and her friend returned to the bar for Irish coffee. They sat at the counter while Shakira made it, and stayed on their bar stools to drink it. Matt, noticing Shakira's obvious fondness for the old lady, called loudly for the Irish coffees to go on his tab.

Mrs. Gallagher was far too wise to argue with a rowdy group of men who'd been drinking the entire evening, and she nodded a polite sign of thank-you to the garage owner, and then hissed to Shakira, "Don't you dare put it on his tab."

Slightly to her surprise, Matt Barker drained his beer, paid his check, and was the first to go. "Early start tomorrow," he said. "Washington. Again. Still, the new Porsche knocks it off pretty sharply."

By 10:45, there were just a few residents left. Matt's crowd had gone, and so had Emily and her friend. Shakira was tired, and she asked the night security man to take over for the last few minutes.

Then she slipped through to the small room behind the bar, put on her short jacket and her driving gloves, and headed for the back door. She ran down the steps and across to the dark side of the parking lot, and there, waiting in the shadows, was Matt Barker.

"Oh, hi, Carla," he said, stepping toward her. "I told you I had a little present for you, and I'm here to give it to you." And with that, he lunged for her wrists, drawing her toward him and then ramming her against the wall.

She could feel his hot, beery breath as his right hand reached down and pulled her skirt up around her waist. He pressed against her, clamping his huge hand over her mouth. She could feel him ripping down the zipper of his pants, and suddenly thrusting his hard cock right between her legs, forcing her to sit astride him, protected only by the thin silk of her panties.

"Let's see whether little Ray can do this to you," he grunted, tearing her shirt, groping for her breasts. "Come on, Carla, you've been waiting for this. And you know it."

She leaned back almost submissively as he tried to force her underwear aside. In his eagerness, he did not notice her right hand slipping surreptitiously behind her back, toward the thin, jeweled dagger she carried, holstered in her wide leather belt—the present from Ahmed.

Matt now cast care to the winds and used both hands to tear down her panties, and, as he did so, Shakira Rashood, aka Carla Martin, shoved the lethal dagger directly between his ribs, all the way to the hilt, cleaving his heart almost in two. It instantly went into spasm and then stopped. Ravi had shown her how to achieve that.

Then she let go and twisted away, watching Matt Barker slide slowly, face forward, down the wall. He was dead before he reached the ground. Carla rearranged her underwear and skirt, refastened the only three buttons she had left on her blouse, leaned back, and delivered an almighty kick to Matt's twisted face. "You stupid little bastard," she breathed.

And with that, she turned onto the side street behind the Estuary Hotel, leaving the corpse, with the dagger still protruding, lying on its side on the edge of the parking lot. There was blood on the ground now, seeping slowly out into the night.

But there was none on Shakira, who had been well taught that there is almost no risk of a killer being bloodstained if the weapon is left in the body. Knives and daggers betray people, when they are pulled—messily—out. Because they bear DNA samples, not to mention fingerprints. Shakira's dagger would betray nothing, thanks to her driving gloves.

Those had been Ravi's idea. "You are armed at all times," he had told her. "So you must always wear your gloves when you are alone at night. That way, you can eliminate your enemy and leave behind no clues."

The unlit side street was deserted, and Shakira walked swiftly without breaking into a run. When she swerved onto a piece of waste ground, she could see the Buick, engine running.

Fausi looked up at her and sensed in the dark that she was slightly disheveled. He jumped out and opened the door for her.

"What happened?" he asked.

"Oh, nothing much," she replied.

"Someone attacked you?"

"Afraid so. One of those local guys tried to rape me in the parking lot."

"So I'm guessing he's dead?"

"Correct," said Shakira. "He was too big for me to fight, so I had no choice. Now let's get out of here—for good."

CHAPTER 6

Fausi turned the Buick north. He drove fast out of Brockhurst to Route 17. It was a hot, cloudy night, very dark, and very light traffic. The Buick clocked 80 mph all the way, since Shakira believed a speeding ticket was a lot better than becoming a suspect in a brutal murder.

When they reached Chesapeake Heights, she got out, on the road, and walked to the front entrance, a distance of 150 yards. She moved fast, straight past Fred, the doorman, to avoid his observing her slightly hectic appearance, and immediately took the elevator to her apartment.

Once inside, she grabbed her suitcase and placed it on the bed, wide open. In a blur of activity she hurled her clothes, shoes, possessions, laundry, and toiletries inside. She changed her shirt, forced the suitcase shut, and put on a denim jacket.

She checked every cupboard, checked under the bed, checked the kitchen and the bathroom. Throughout her stay, she had been careful to accumulate nothing. She stripped the bed of sheets and pillowcases, gathered up two damp towels, scooped up a couple of dish towels, and raced for the incinerator hatch, down which residents could get rid of any rubbish they no longer required. She dumped anything that might bear DNA samples straight down the chute. Shakira would leave her apartment carrying only what she had brought with her.

She took her cell phone onto the balcony and dialed the numbers for

152

the house in Gaza. No reply. She had not expected one. She just left the briefest of messages: *Evacuating immediately. Cell phone active.*

Then she dialed a local number, let it ring twice, and pressed the cut-off button. Downstairs, Fausi pulled into the drive, his headlights off. He parked in the shadows, rendering the car almost invisible.

Then he walked around the side of the building, selected an expensive Lincoln Continental, picked up a stone from the rock garden, and hurled it through the windshield.

The alarm system went off like a klaxon, echoing through the deserted parking lot. Fausi raced back to his own car and swept up to the front of the building. He charged through the door, still in his chauffeur's uniform, and yelled through to the little anteroom where Fred was watching television.

"Excuse me, sir, I think I just saw two guys break into one of the residents' cars. I heard a crash and then they ran right past me. I didn't realize anything was wrong until I heard the alarm go off."

Fred, a heavyset former Green Beret, came out of his chair like a bullet. This would not look good for him, a professional security officer. "Thanks, pal," he called, as he raced across the foyer. "I'm right on it."

The big doorman rushed outside, following the sound of the blaring car alarm. And as he did so, the elevator door slid open. Fausi beckoned Shakira to come out, and she edged her way through the foyer, turning deliberately away from the door and covering her face with a copy of *American Vogue.* She walked slowly, in a stooped fashion, like an old woman.

Outside, Fausi grabbed her suitcase, and the two of them slipped swiftly through the shadows to the Buick, which was running quietly. Fausi shoved the suitcase onto the passenger seat and climbed in behind the wheel, while Shakira prostrated herself on the backseat.

The black car, displaying no lights, sped off down the drive, swung right toward Route 17, and moments later was hurtling up the highway. No one at Chesapeake Heights, especially the night doorman, knew that Carla Martin was no longer a resident.

It was almost midnight now. Back in Brockhurst, Emily Gallagher was sound asleep, content in the knowledge that Carla would take care of Charlie in the morning. Jim Caborn was upstairs watching television, feeling self-congratulatory at the competence of his latest bar manager. And the undiscovered body of Matt Barker seeped blood, silently, in the shadows of the hotel parking lot.

By 1 A.M., Fausi had reached the junction with Interstate 95, the endless highway that runs north-south down the entire length of the eastern seaboard of the United States.

Once more they turned north, and Fausi asked, "Okay, where's it to be, Shakira? Washington Dulles, Philly, or New York?"

"Boston," she replied.

"Wow!" said Fausi. "That'll take us another eight hours. That's a long way. I guess you mean nonstop?"

"I most certainly do," she replied. "And I am sure you understand, Fausi, that right now this car is my best friend in all the world. Every mile we travel is one more away from Brockhurst. Every mile means I am just a little more remote."

"When do you think they're going to find that body?" he asked.

"Probably early in the morning. When one of the hotel residents drives out that way. I suppose around eight o'clock. I'm hoping they'll think it's a local murder and concentrate their search for the killer in the Brockhurst area."

"You want to go straight to Logan?"

"Oh, I think so. Then I'll get the first flight to Europe I can." Not even Fausi was permitted to know her destination. And he knew it. Never even asked. He just said, "I'm going to miss you, Shakira. It's been tense, but enjoyable."

Shakira had never heard those two adjectives used together, and, as a student of language, she found herself laughing. "Very nicely stated, Fausi," she said. "I think you are better at speaking English than I am. Which is important, because I am really good."

"Thank you, Mrs. Rashood," he replied. "I'll accept the compliment."

It was forty miles more from the I-95 junction up to Washington, which they made by 1:45 A.M. They avoided the city, because 95 swings sharply right on the southern outskirts of Alexandria and sweeps across the Potomac on the Woodrow Wilson Memorial Bridge, straight into the state of Maryland.

From there it makes a huge easterly sweep, combining with the Beltway, right around the outside of the nation's capital for about twenty miles, running directly past Andrews Air Force Base, and then, in Fausi's case ironically, veering resolutely off-course, diametrically away from the National Security Agency at Fort Meade.

The Buick angled back to its northeasterly route at around 2:30 A.M. and headed for Baltimore. They were past that city by 3:15 and heading on up to the Philadelphia area. Shortly before first light, they crossed the Delaware River at Trenton and made the New Jersey Turnpike, toward New York and the long wooded highways of New England.

They stopped for gas and coffee somewhere north of New Brunswick, and kept going to the George Washington Bridge. Traffic was beginning to build even at 5:30 in the morning, but it was still flowing fast, and Fausi crossed the Hudson at high speed, gunned the Buick along the north end of Manhattan, and then straight up the New England Thruway.

Three and a half hours later, they were approaching Logan airport, and they pulled into the international building, Terminal E, at 9:15 A.M. Their parting was achieved in under five seconds; they shook hands, and Shakira grabbed a nearby baggage cart and walked into the terminal.

At precisely this time, seven states away in Virginia, the pace was less frenetic. Matt Barker's body was discovered in the parking lot, not by a departing resident but by a member of Jim Caborn's cleaning staff who always entered the hotel that way, and who almost tripped over the body.

She stood there in the parking lot and started screaming at the top of her lungs. It was never made clear whether this was because Matt's cock was still sticking ramrod-straight out of his trousers, or because the hilt of the jeweled dagger did suggest he had been murdered. At any rate, Mrs. Price did some world-class screaming.

Jim Caborn, who was in his office, heard the commotion and came running outside, thinking someone was being murdered. Close. But the deed had taken place many, many hours before. Jim reached in his pocket for his cell phone and dialed 911.

Within ten minutes, the local police chief, in company with two officers, a detective, and the pathologist, arrived at the parking lot. An ambulance came five minutes later. The body was photographed and briefly examined by the pathologist, who took the temperature and pronounced that Matt Barker had died around midnight or before.

The detective in charge of the investigation considered that there would be no point in casting a police cordon around the town. If the killer had left, it was too late. If he was still in the area, he would almost certainly remain in place. There was no harm in having the body removed to the nearest mortuary, since it was obviously not a perfect advertisement for Jim Caborn's Estuary Hotel.

"Thanks, Joe," said Jim, as the ambulance pulled away. "Now come in for some coffee, and I'll arrange for you to speak to everyone you want."

All three of the principal men in this sudden, unexpected small-town saga on the banks of the Rappahannock had known each other since childhood. Detective Joe Segel had been at school with Matt Barker. Jim Caborn had played football with Joe at Virginia Tech in Blacksburg, out in the foothills of the Appalachian Mountains in the western part of the state. This was a very local murder.

Inside the hotel, Jim made a list of everyone he thought might be able to throw some light on the final hours of Matt Barker, which had plainly been spent in the Estuary Hotel bar with his buddies. Top of Jim's list was Carla Martin, who often talked with the big garage owner. He also gave Detective Segel the full names of Herb, Rick, and Bill, who were presumably the last people to see Matt alive.

"What time does Miss Martin show up?" asked Detective Segel.

"Five o'clock sharp," said Jim. "And she's never late."

"I'll be here," he replied.

0930 Tuesday
Logan International Airport, Boston

Shakira made a split-second decision not to use her Carla Martin passport to exit the USA. Instead, she went to the one copied from that owned by Michigan-born Maureen Carson, thirty. She walked to the Aer Lingus ticketing desk and asked if she could travel first-class to Dublin on the airline's new morning flight, leaving at 10:30 A.M., arriving Dublin at 2240 with a stop at Shannon.

"Yes, I have seats available on that. May I see your passport?"

Shakira handed it over, and the Aer Lingus girl gave it a cursory look, checked the photograph of Maureen against the dark-haired lady who stood in front of her, smiled, and said, "How do you wish to pay?"

"American Express," she replied, knowing the card had been issued to an attaché in the Jordanian embassy in Neuilly-Seine, Paris, and that she, Shakira, was a secondary signature on the card and in possession of the PIN.

She punched it into the machine, for a ruinous amount of money, more than six thousand dollars. "Is there anything else we can do for you?" asked the girl.

"I wonder if you could book me a room in the Shelbourne Hotel in Dublin, and tell them I'll be arriving quite late?"

"Will you require them to meet you off the flight?"

"No. I'll take a cab," said Shakira, ever alert for the necessity of anonymity whenever possible.

She picked up her bag and walked to the first-class desk. One hour later, Shakira took off for southern Ireland. The Aer Lingus Airbus was climbing steeply out over Boston Harbor just as, six hundred miles to the south, Detective Segel was preparing to return to the police station.

By any standards, the Estuary Killer had well and truly flown the coop.

1430 Same Day
Brockhurst Police Station

Detective Joe Segel had little to go on. Someone in the hour before midnight had plunged a dagger into Matt Barker's heart, and, according to the doctor, killed him instantly.

The police search of his body had revealed a wad of twenty-dollar bills, adding up to over $300. His credit card wallet was intact, no one had taken his cell phone, and there was no sign of a fight save for a nasty bruise on the left-hand side of his face, which could have happened when he slid, face forward, down the wall.

And yet . . . someone had wanted to kill Matt Barker very badly. Detective Segel spoke to his close friends, particularly those who had been in the bar with him the previous evening. None of them had the slightest idea what could possibly have happened to him. They were obviously all extremely upset. Herb and Rick were both in tears at the death of their lifelong friend.

Which, essentially, left the Virginia detective holding the dagger. He sat in his office, wearing white linen gloves and handling it carefully. There was no maker's mark on it, which was unsurprising since it did look as if it had been manufactured somewhere in the Middle East.

And those jewels in the handle—Jesus! If they were real, the darned thing was worth a fortune. And yet it had been abandoned, jutting out of Matt Barker's body, in the manner of a true professional, someone who knew the blood would not flow immediately if the weapon was left jammed in the wound.

This was someone who knew how to make an escape unscathed by the detritus of the crime. The forensic boys had already made a thorough search, and the dagger bore not one trace of a fingerprint.

In the next twenty minutes, he expected to see the local jeweler, who would tell him, one way or another, whether or not the murder weapon was worth several thousand dollars. As a matter of fact, it wasn't. The jeweler turned up right on time and told Joe Segel the stones were just colored glass set into brass. Pretty, but worth no more than $50.

The biggest concern for Detective Segel was Matt Barker's cock. What the hell was that doing, sticking out into the morning light? There's only one reason for that—sexual passion. And whoever Matt had intended to stick that cock into had obviously had second thoughts. Male or female? Friend or stranger? Who had taken such an elementary dislike to Matt Barker that, instead of fucking him, they had stabbed him to death?

It beat the hell out of Joe Segel. But one thought was uppermost in his mind. The killer could not possibly have been a girl. At least, no ordinary girl. That death blow to Matt Barker's ribs had been delivered with terrific strength, an upward thrust into precisely the correct place to inflict death.

Hell, thought Joe Segel, *was old Matt some kind of a faggot? All these years, and no one's ever known that. No one I ever met. I'll be real interested to hear the opinions of Miss Carla Martin when she turns up for work.* According to Jim Caborn, that would be another hour.

Joe was sitting in the front hall of the hotel as the old grandfather clock struck five times. He waited patiently for five more minutes. Then ten. Then he stood up and walked to the desk and said, "Jim, old buddy, you said she was never late."

"Joe, old buddy," replied the manager, "she never was. Not 'til today."

"I'm gonna sit here for another twenty minutes," said the detective. "Then I have to go find her. This Carla may have been the last person not only to talk to him, but also to see him.

"His three guys all thought he spoke to her, then drank his beer and left. Said something about going to Washington early in the morning. That was around 10:30. And before eleven o'clock, Miss Martin had packed up and left the hotel. Out the back door, directly into the parking lot where Matt's body was found."

"Is she a suspect?" asked Jim.

"She sure as hell is. But right now I personally don't think she did it. And if she'd turned up for work on time, she wouldn't be. Get me her phone number and address, will you?"

Jim Caborn flipped through his card index file where he kept details and locations for all of his staff. But he was basically wasting his time. Shakira had long ago removed her card, which bore her passport number, Social Security number, reference details, and the name of her "aunt's" village, Bowler's Wharf. She had replaced it with a simplified one, which listed only her address—the Estuary Hotel, Brockhurst.

Jim Caborn could not believe his eyes. He turned to Joe Segel and said, "I just cannot understand this."

"Understand what?"

"I filled out a detailed card with a lot of stuff about Miss Martin, including her Social and passport numbers. I even wrote down the names, addresses, and phone numbers on her reference letters. I made a note of her aunt's name in Bowler's Wharf where she lived."

"Did you get her car registration?"

"She never told me."

"Did you ask?"

"Twice. And both times she said she'd get it and fill the card out for me. I assumed she'd done it."

Joe Segel's hackles were up and bristling. "I'm not being critical, Jim. Believe me. But I want to get this very clear. This girl gets a job here when?"

"Couple of weeks ago."

"Okay, and you're sure you filled out that card?"

"'Course I'm sure. I've done it for everyone who's ever worked here. Both her references were from London, England."

"Okay. So here we have Little Miss Nobody. She destroys all her records, right here in this hotel. She writes out an address for your file, where she does not live. Someone gets murdered, an obvious sex crime, and Little Miss Nobody vanishes off the face of the earth.

"How old was she?"

"Now that I can recall. She was thirty. I remember looking at her birth date on her passport. It was May 1982. You know how I remember?"

"Lay it on me."

"I graduated from college that month. . . . But wait a minute, Joe . . . wait a minute. She said she was living with this aunt in Bowler's Wharf. I think she said her name was Leno. Jean Leno. I remember. It reminded me of the *Tonight Show*."

"Jim, let me tell you something. This lady went to a whole hell of a lot of trouble to brush away her footprints. Five dollars gets you a hundred if we find a Jean Leno in Bowler's Wharf."

"That's a bet I'm not taking. Not now."

"Was this Carla good-looking?"

"She never made much effort, but anyone would consider her really beautiful. Dark-skinned, black hair, slim with amazingly long legs. A lot of the guys could hardly take their eyes off her."

"How about Matt?"

"Especially Matt."

Detective Segel looked up. "Did she go out with him?"

"I don't think so. I heard a couple of the guys joshing him a few days ago. You know, saying it was sad, a man of his stature getting blown off by the barmaid. So I guess she refused to go out with him."

"Look, Jim, I've known Matt for years," said Joe. "So have you. But I've learned you never really know everything about a person. You don't think Matt attacked her, do you? Or tried to? And Miss Martin stabbed him to fend him off."

"Matt!" The hotel manager was incredulous. "Hell, no. There wasn't a shred of malice in him. He was a big soft puppy."

"It might seem that way," said Joe. "But he didn't get that Porsche by being a big soft puppy."

"He probably hadn't paid for it," chuckled Jim Caborn.

"Yes, he had."

"How do you know?"

"We checked. This morning."

"So where does that leave us?"

"It leaves us with one very large missing piece. Because everything any detective could want to find out about Matt Barker is right there on the table. We know his friends, his acquaintances, his customers, his relatives. I doubt there's a suspect among them. They all live right around here."

"And Carla's the missing piece?"

"She sure as hell is. And what, Jim Caborn, was said by the greatest detective who ever lived?"

"You got me."

"When you have eliminated the impossible, only the truth remains. Sherlock Holmes."

"So what happens now? A nationwide manhunt for my barmaid?"

"I wouldn't go that far. But we sure as hell need to find her. And I've got a real strong feeling the lady ain't coming to work."

2225 (local) Tuesday
Shannon, Southern Ireland

The Aer Lingus Airbus had completed its short stopover in the sprawling international airport of Shannon, which was for many years the first transatlantic refueling stop for every passenger aircraft incoming to Europe from the United States and Canada.

Even today it's a favorite departure point for thousands of Americans wishing to visit Ireland's great southwestern beauty spots—the Ring of Kerry, the Lakes of Killarney, and the coastline of West Cork. Which is why Aer Lingus flights from the United States stop there every day on the way to Dublin. And why an exhausted Shakira Rashood was sitting by the starboard-side window, almost alone, in first class, as the half-empty aircraft taxied to the end of the dark Shannon runway.

She glanced at her watch, which was still on American time, five hours back. "Twenty-five minutes late for work," she murmured. "I wonder if they've missed me yet."

The wind was gusting out of the southwest tonight, directly off the Atlantic, and they took off in that direction. The lightly loaded Airbus climbed steeply away from the airport peninsula at the head of the Shannon estuary and swung hard right over Ireland's greatest river.

It was just a short twenty-minute flight to Dublin, straight across the lonely heart of the Emerald Isle. They would scarcely fly over any towns. After crossing Lough Derg, their route would take them only above an endless dark green patchwork of fields.

Shakira was awakened after perhaps ten minutes of sleep, when the captain told the passengers he was beginning the descent into Dublin airport. Eight minutes later, they were on the ground. And Shakira's nerves began to tighten.

As a first-class passenger, she was among the first to disembark from the aircraft, and she walked briskly to the passport control booth. There were only two officers on duty, and both of them gave the impression they could think of better things to do at this late hour on a Tuesday evening.

She handed over her perfectly forged copy of Maureen Carson's passport. The officer opened it and put a large green port-of-entry stamp on one of the pages. He looked at her, smiled broadly, and said, "Welcome to Ireland. Have a nice stay here." Shakira wondered whether he said that to everyone, and decided, on reflection, he probably did. As usual, she tried not to think of these people as part of the Great Satan.

The baggage area was quiet, and she walked through the green nothing-to-declare area, which was totally deserted. She did think this was strange, not being attuned, as yet, to that crystal-clear Irish logic, which reasoned: *Now, what would be the point of putting a customs team in there when no one has anything to declare?*

Shakira climbed into a taxi and asked the driver to take her to the Shelbourne Hotel. However, when they arrived in St. Stephen's Green half an hour later, she realized she had no Irish currency. No euros. "Oh, I'm sorry," she said. "Please wait. I expect the hotel will change me some American dollars."

"Ah, Jesus," he said, "don't be worrying yourself. I'll take 'em—it's twenty-eight euros. The dollar's about one and a half. Say forty-two bucks."

Shakira gave him a $50 bill and said, "Keep the change, and thank you."

"Ah, you're a Christian," he replied in the Irish idiom, grinning broadly, delighted with his tip, and certainly not realizing how utterly wrong was his statement.

The doorman took her bag, and she checked in. The Shelbourne is an innately Irish hotel, its bars the favorite watering holes for generations of Dublin's scholars, poets, and businessmen, from Brendan Behan on down. They mostly don't have any nonsense with passports, especially for their American clients.

And they never even asked for Shakira's. "Just a quick swipe of your American Express card, and it's fine," said the desk clerk. "Niall, over there, will take your bag up, room 250, enjoy your stay. Anything you need, just pick up the phone."

No, it couldn't be possible. These cheerful, welcoming people could not be part of the Great Satan's world domination. She would forbid Ravi and his men to make any kind of attack on any Irishmen, anywhere.

She unpacked some of her suitcase and hung a few things up. Then she took a long, luxurious bath in deep fragrant water and climbed gratefully into bed. Shakira had had little sleep, indeed she had not even been in a bed since eight o'clock on Monday morning. And now it was midnight Tuesday.

She relaxed on her pillow, worked out that it was 7 P.M. in Brockhurst, Virginia. *They've probably missed me by now,* she thought. *But I still doubt they'll connect me with the death of Matt Barker.*

Like the cab driver's, that was another truly astounding misjudgment.

1900 Same Day
Bowler's Wharf, Virginia

Four state police cruisers were parked on the main street of the little village on the banks of the Rappahannock. House by house, the troopers banged on doors, asked if there was a Mrs. Jean Leno in residence, asking if anyone knew of a Jean Leno in residence, finally asking if anyone had ever even heard of a Jean Leno in all of their lives.

The answer was negative, to all three questions. Jim Caborn's shrewd decision not to risk his five dollars betting with Joe Segel was looking better by the minute. The troopers' secondary question was whether a very beautiful woman, in her late twenties, name of Carla Martin, had been living in the village for the past couple of weeks, going to work in a small car in the late afternoon.

That last one elicited a veritable salvo of completely blank stares. No Jean. No Carla. No luck. The young lady had flown the coop. Detective Segel had a photo-artist identity kit prepared by two police artists, who were guided by Jim Caborn and one of Matt Barker's buddies. And, in truth, they came up with a pretty fair likeness of Shakira Rashood.

Segel ordered hundreds of "wanted" posters to be distributed all over the area. *Hell, someone must have seen her. No one can just disappear off the face of the earth. And what I really need to know is where did she live. She must have lived somewhere. And somewhere close. And someone must have seen her.*

At 7:30 P.M., he held a press conference at the Brockhurst Police Department, having tempted the broadcasters and journalists by announcing that the police were treating the death of a local man, Mr. Matt Barker, as murder.

This is not absolutely unusual when a body is found with a dagger jutting out of its chest. But the word "murder" has a shock-value ring to it, particularly when the media does not even realize there has been a death, never mind a homicide.

Detective Segel had deliberately withheld the announcement all through the day, since he did not want small afternoon newspapers running away with the story. He wanted blanket coverage, big dailies, network newscasts, wall-to-wall radio bulletins. Lights, cameras, music. Detective Segel wanted The Big Show. Because he believed that was the way to nail Miss Carla Martin. He believed someone would come forward with information about the vanishing Estuary Killer.

His judgment in the first part was excellent. The idea of a middle-class, well-to-do, Porsche-driving proprietor of a garage being stabbed to death in the parking lot of the local hotel was very appealing to those who essentially make a lavish living out of other people's misfortunes.

And journalists drew a careful bead on the tiny township of Brockhurst. The first to arrive were the camera crews and presenters from the big 24-hour news networks, CNN and Fox. Both of them have running news programs, all day and night; and a story like this, a classic whodunnit, would keep them topical for at least two days, maybe four.

Reporters from the three main Washington newspapers, the *Post,* the *Star,* and the *Journal,* came down in a shared helicopter. CBS thought it worthwhile to send a full camera crew down, plus presenters, in a truck the size of the Pentagon.

NBC thought it was a good story, but was happy to rely on stringers and a local camera crew. ABC sent no one, but E-mailed a local reporter and told him to keep them posted. The newspapers from Richmond and

Norfolk, both situated around fifty miles from Brockhurst, sent in reporters and photographers.

And there were about a dozen representatives from local weeklies based around the Rappahannock River and Chesapeake Bay area. And the same number of radio reporters, five of them local and five down from Washington. It was, without doubt, the biggest assembly of media personnel ever seen in Brockhurst. The whole town was talking about it, and, within a couple of hours, the name Matt Barker would be heard more often than that of the President of the United States. There's one thing about meeting a violent death. It really gets your name out there.

Detective Joe Segel started the proceedings by announcing the fact that Mr. Matthew Barker, a well-known member of the local community for many years, had been found dead outside the Estuary Hotel this morning. He was thirty-four. A jeweled dagger was protruding from his chest. It had been driven into his heart, right up to the hilt, and death had occurred at around midnight.

He added that no one had been arrested, but that a friend of Mr. Barker's, the barmaid at the Estuary Hotel, Miss Carla Martin, was almost certainly the last person to see him alive, and had mysteriously vanished.

There was available to the media an excellent identity-kit picture, a very close likeness of Carla, which reporters could pick up from the table at the back of the room. Before taking any questions, Detective Joe Segel said, "We are extremely interested in speaking to this lady, because we believe she may be able to assist us with our inquiries."

Does this mean we got a murder hunt right here?

"Well, not precisely, because we really do not have any evidence whatsoever against Miss Carla Martin. But she was most certainly the last person seen speaking to him before he left the bar. And she may have seen him again in the parking lot of the hotel when she left. Mr. Barker's body was found at the street end of the parking lot."

How long after he left did Carla exit the bar?

"We believe twenty minutes maximum."

Was she in love with him? You know, were they going out together?

"So far the answer to that is a very definite *no*. According to his close friends, Mr. Barker had asked her out, but she always refused."

Where did Carla live? In the hotel?

"Good question. She did not live in the hotel, and it appears that she removed her identity card from the manager's file. We thus have absolutely no idea where she lived. But it must have been quite near. She came to work every day, right?"

When did she quit her job?

"She never did. She just failed to show up today. She was due to start at 5 P.M. What is it now? Eight o'clock? And she's never been late before. Don't hold your breath."

Pretty suspicious, right?

"Pretty suspicious," agreed Joe Segel. "But that does not mean she murdered him."

A lot of people wouldn't agree with that. This is a murder hunt, sir. You must know that.

"No, it's not. She may have just fled because of something she saw out there in the parking lot and did not wish to get involved, for whatever reason. And even if she did kill him, it may have been self-defense. We don't know that he didn't attack her. He was a big man, and his fly was undone."

Jesus Christ, Joe. You mean the whole world could see his pecker?

"Well, only the members of the world who happened to be walking past the western end of the Estuary Hotel parking lot, right after first light today."

You think he had tried to sexually assault Carla?

"Well, I wouldn't rule it out. But this entire case rests on us finding Carla Martin. And I want you to help us get that done."

A few members of the press corps nodded their assent and asked for more details about Matt Barker's home and relatives. A couple of them wanted to know a lot more about the sex side of the case. And Joe told them he would be happy to see members of the media privately in his office any time during the next hour.

He knew the value of the publicity the case would receive from this. And he knew the value of that kind of exposure. Not Matt's kind. And he was not about to discuss the Barker Pecker again, not in front of a mixed audience.

As it happened, there were enough journalists asking questions to keep Detective Segel busy for another hour and a half, at which point he called an end to the evening's proceedings. He turned out his office light, locked the door, and walked briskly up the road to the Estuary Hotel for a night-cap, as he often did.

But when he opened the front door, the journalists were packed in there, most of them staying, all of them trying to obtain interviews from locals, as they prepared to hit the world with:

VIRGINIA TOWN IN SHOCK AT COLD-BLOODED MURDER
State Police Launch Dragnet in Hunt for Mystery Woman

Detective Joe Segel retreated toward home. He had answered quite enough questions for one day. And with a major media outburst scheduled in the next few hours, he needed to be up early.

Nonetheless, Joe walked rather disconsolately home, knowing he would be greeted by an equally disconsolate wife, Joanne, who would tell him she could hardly remember what he looked like, the way she always did when he was involved in a major case.

Joe, who was forty-six, had married late in life, and Joanne, who was much younger, in her late twenties, was already showing signs of exasperation as the wife of a police officer. She had given up preparing a late dinner long ago.

And there would be questions about this Mystery Woman, he knew that. Which was why he had stopped off for a drink at the Estuary. To get away from it all, just for an hour. To tell the truth, Joe was pretty fed up with the Mystery Woman himself. Where the hell was she? Still, he had a good chance of some answers tomorrow.

At the time, the Mystery Woman was dead to the world, sound asleep in a luxury room, four thousand miles away, in Dublin's Shelbourne Hotel. She was beyond the dragnet, perhaps beyond the law, exactly the way she had planned it. The Virginia police did not even know her name.

The late-night news bulletins on American television were full of it. The story had "more legs" than anyone realized, especially the bit about the Barker Pecker. By 10:30 P.M. on the East Coast, Detective Joe Segel's name was a household word, more or less.

The Fox Channel led with it. The newscaster, filmed standing outside the Estuary Hotel, announced: "This was the sex attack that went violently wrong. Right here in this rather sleepy little town, way down on the Rappahannock River, a highly regarded local businessman was found dead this morning with a jeweled dagger jutting from his chest.

"He was in a state of disarray, and police believe, judging by his condition, he had been involved in some kind of sexual assault on another person.

"He was found in the parking lot of the Estuary Hotel in the town of Brockhurst, Virginia, and police say he was killed around midnight. Right now there is only one suspect, the beautiful barmaid from the hotel, Carla Martin.

"The dead man, Mr. Matt Barker, owner of a local garage, had been drinking there during the evening, and was believed to have asked Miss Martin out, but she refused. The two left the bar twenty minutes apart, and Miss Martin, say police, has vanished, leaving a perfectly ordinary little American country town in a state of shock."

At this point, the newscast switched to interviews, showing footage of the detective in charge of the crime, Joe Segel, stressing the importance of finding Miss Martin, who, he said, had taken a great deal of trouble in covering her tracks.

Then they went to one of Matt Barker's friends, Herb the photographer, who was unable to shed one scrap of light on the reason for Matt's death, or indeed the whereabouts of Carla.

The next lady had been saved by the news producers for the big payoff line. Mrs. Price, the hotel cleaning lady who had first discovered the body, said, "Well, it gave me a very nasty shock, I can tell you. Matt Barker lying there with that big thing sticking out of him."

Mrs. Price, I assume you mean the dagger?

"Nossir. I do not mean the dagger."

Cut to studio. Smiling anchors, serious man, dazzling blonde. Really great television. Half the country was rolling about laughing. That's what it's all about, right? Leave 'em laughing. Even in the middle of a murder hunt.

The morning newspapers tackled the Brockhurst killing boldly. The *Washington Post* made it the second lead on the front page under the headline:

MURDER MYSTERY STUNS VIRGINIA TOWN
Police Seek Vanished Barmaid.

Other publications were more lurid. One of the tabloids came up with:

SEX-CRAZED GARAGE MAN MURDERED BY BARMAID

Another went with:

SEX BRAWL IN HOTEL PARKING LOT ENDS IN DEATH

So far as Joe Segel was concerned, the only thing that mattered was that they all carried the identity picture of Carla Martin. And they all stressed the importance of locating the Mystery Woman. Joe hoped that by lunchtime they would have some serious leads. This was the kind of high-profile local murder that could not be allowed to go unsolved.

It was Wednesday, July 4, a national holiday, but murder hunts do not stop for those. Joe had set up a reception desk with three operators drafted in from another town to take the calls. And there were calls, dozens of them. But they were geographically hopeless. Joe had drawn a large circle on his wall map of the area, a sixty-mile diameter, with the town in the middle. That's thirty miles in any direction.

Almost all the calls named or identified suspects outside the murder zone, places too distant for Carla to have made it to work every day. She had stated to Jim Caborn that she wanted to live in or near Brockhurst. And in Joe Segel's opinion, that absolutely ruled out anyone more than thirty miles away.

There were leads that needed to be followed, but Joe's policeman's instincts, honed by a lifetime in the force, were telling him they were not yet on the right track. At least they were telling him that until the phone rang for him personally, and Mrs. Emily Gallagher informed him that she would very much like to see him at her house, something concerning Matt Barker's murder.

Mrs. Gallagher was a lady who commanded enormous respect in the area, with which she had a lifelong family association. There were also those who knew her daughter was married to one of the most important men in America. Joe Segel was rather proud she had called him, and he asked one of his team to drive him immediately to her house and wait.

When he arrived, Mrs. Gallagher had recovered her decorum, having almost been pulled into the Rappahannock by Charlie an hour before. She had made some coffee, and now she was ready to talk to Joe about the pretty dark-haired girl who had suddenly vanished from her life, as thoroughly as she had from Joe's.

The detective listened wide-eyed to Mrs. Gallagher, who swiftly established that she knew more about Carla Martin than anyone else he had spoken to. Admiral Morgan's mother-in-law recalled a conversation in which Carla had mentioned her "apartment," and once her "doorman."

She also had a fleeting suspicion that Carla either may have been foreign or had lived abroad for a long time. She had never forgotten that sentence *"I give you one little piece, if you behave."* Future conditional. The mistake of a foreigner. Joe Segel really liked that.

Emily also recalled once asking what Carla had been doing on such a fine day, and she had mentioned that she just sat on her balcony and read some magazines. *Apartment, doorman, balcony.* Vital observations, not because they led to anything specific, but because they ruled out so much.

But the key point Mrs. Gallagher raised was the conversation she had in the hotel, possibly an hour before the killing. "That Matt Barker was harassing Carla," she said. "I saw him, and I heard him. I told her to be careful, he was entirely the wrong type of person for her to go out with."

"Careful, Emily," said Joe. "He was successful, well-liked. And he did drive a Porsche."

"He also had some very rough edges, entirely inappropriate for my friend Carla," she replied. "I just hope this is all sorted out soon. And that she can come back to help me with Charlie and Kipper."

"Who's Kipper?" asked Joe.

"Oh, he's my daughter's spaniel. She and Arnold are going to Europe for three weeks, and I'm in charge of the dog."

Joe smiled. He really liked Mrs. Gallagher, and he asked her once more, "You really have no idea where she lived?"

"Absolutely none. But it could not have been very far away. She was always on time, and I presumed she left her car in the parking lot at the hotel. But I never saw it. Not here. She always walked."

So far as Joe was concerned, the mystery, if anything, deepened. And Mrs. Gallagher should have been a detective. He was grateful to her, and interested in how genuinely surprised she was that Carla had left without a word.

Noon, Wednesday 4 July
National Security Agency
Fort Meade, Maryland

Lt. Commander Jimmy Ramshawe was on duty. His boss, the director, Admiral George Morris, had been away since the previous weekend, visiting his son in New York. He would not be back until tomorrow morning.

This left Jimmy at the helm. The agency had many more senior officials in residence, commanders, captains, admirals, colonels, and brigadier generals. But Ramshawe had the ear of the mighty, and everyone knew it. He punched far above his weight in his job as assistant to Admiral Morris, thanks in no small way to his known friendship with the Great One, Admiral Arnold Morgan.

Everyone kept Jimmy posted, willingly and without rancor. Admiral Morris trusted him implicitly. If you wanted to get something urgent done, in any department, have a chat with young Jimmy. Everyone knew that rule. Indeed, most everyone believed that one day Admiral—or at least Captain—Ramshawe would occupy the Big Chair. Admiral Morgan said his protégé was the most natural-born intelligence officer he had ever met.

The downside, of course, for one so respected, was you had to work on national holidays. Jimmy's fiancée, Jane Peacock, the Aussie ambassador's daughter, was particularly peeved because she had wanted to dazzle the local populace of Chesapeake Beach on her surfboard, Bondi beach goddess that she was. But Jimmy swore to God he'd be at her house for dinner by 7:30 P.M.

Meantime, he had spent the morning catching up on the foreign papers. He never got to the local ones until quite late, and even then concentrated principally on overseas news.

However, the Estuary Killer was crowding in on him, since it was mentioned on all the front pages and he had heard mention of it on television news. He picked up the *Washington Post* and could scarcely miss the second lead, accompanied as it was by a large photo-artist identity of Carla Martin and a photograph of Matt Barker.

"Hello," he muttered to himself. "Here's the bloke who died with his pecker out." He recalled the cleaning lady mentioning that it was jutting out there, large as life.

But it was not the pecker that arrested Jimmy's attention. It was the dagger, which he thought sounded extremely old-fashioned. *You just don't hear it much, that's all. You hear about knife crime, and stabbings, but you don't hear about daggers. Except in* Macbeth, *or* Julius Caesar—*"Is this a pecker I see before me?"*

Jimmy chuckled, floored by his own amazing humor. But he was taken by the jeweled dagger, taken by its off-key presence and by its suggestion of the Middle East, like something out of *Arabian Nights* or the Crusades. *I don't care what anyone says,* he mused. *There's no daggers in 21st-century Virginia. Guns, yes. Knives, yes. Maybe even bombs. But no daggers. And that's final.*

Jimmy read on. And then he stopped dead. *Brockhurst, now where the hell's that? And where have I heard the name before? It's too familiar. Someone has mentioned that town before.*

He poured himself a cup of hot coffee and tried to concentrate. Then he went to his computer database, hit search mode, and punched in *Brockhurst*. Nothing. He'd never filed anything that included that name before. He called Jane, and she could not even remember hearing the name.

"See you later," he said. "Call me if you remember anything."

"Don't be late," she replied, archly.

He summoned up a big computerized wall map and searched for Brockhurst. Found it in the middle of nowhere, and confessed himself more baffled than he was before. *Jesus, that place is in the bloody outback,* he confirmed to no one in particular. *I just can't remember where or why I ever heard that name before. But I did.*

He glanced through the paper to check whether anything truly diabolical had happened, and was glad to see nothing had. Iraq was quiet, Afghanistan was quiet, and Iran for once was behaving itself. The right-wing French president was threatening to quit the European Union, and the Brits were running out of North Sea oil, probably going broke with their massive welfare programs and no resources.

Then he had a brainwave. He called Jane and checked whether they had the embassy to themselves tonight, and, if they had, would she object to asking Arnold and Kathy to join them for dinner?

"Well, Mum and Dad are going out, and we do have the staff on duty. I don't really have a problem with inviting them. Do you want me to call Kathy?"

"They probably can't come," said Jimmy. "But we've been to at least three really expensive restaurants with them lately, and it would be a good chance to repay something. You know Arnold always pays."

"Okay. I'll call. Will he be all right with Aussie wine?"

"I doubt it. He'll call it grape juice. If they're on, call me and I'll try to do something."

Brockhurst. The word was revolving around in Jimmy's mind. He sat quietly and racked his brains. And suddenly, thinking of Arnold's predictable reaction to Australian Shiraz, it hit him.

"It's Kathy's mum! I got it. That's where she lives. I've seen a photograph of her house there. A picture of Kathy with two dogs, a big golden retriever and Kipper. That's where Kathy goes when she visits."

Jim was proud of that. He rewarded himself with a fresh cup of coffee and sat for a few moments pondering the world. He picked up the *Post* and read the story in more detail. Beyond the Pecker, as it were.

And he read with immense awareness of the hunt for the missing barmaid. Dark, beautiful, may have been the victim of a sex attack, covered her tracks and vanished. No other suspects.

He read some other newspapers. He read all the accounts and assessed the many facts that were spread out before him. And as the afternoon wore on, he came up with one question, as he so often did when trying to solve something: *what was this Middle East weapon doing rammed into someone's body, two hundred yards from Kathy's mum's house?*

Did he like it? Absolutely not. And he cast his mind back to that big story in the *Post*, three or four months ago, the one that had painted Admiral Morgan as the archenemy of all Middle Eastern terrorist groups.

Here we have a new situation, he pondered. *From right out of the wide blue yonder, we have the first murder in a hundred years in the town of Brockhurst, Virginia, international crossroads to nowhere. The crime was committed with an obvious Middle East weapon, a jewel-encrusted dagger, which, from the photos, looks like it belonged to Abdul the Turk or someone.*

But it bloody didn't, did it? It belonged to someone in Brockhurst, visiting or resident. Now what the hell's a resident of a nice Virginia community doing with something like that? And then stabbing a bloke to death right down the road from the mother-in-law of the jihadists' number one enemy. Don't understand it. But I don't like it.

Jane called back. "Arnold and Kathy can't come. They're going to the Bedfords."

"Well, at least we tried."

"And we might have to try harder," added Jane. "They're going on vacation in three weeks for most of August. Kipper's going to Virginia."

"Okay, see you later," said Jimmy.

Right now, it seemed to him, the local police detective was certain that this Mystery Woman had probably committed the crime, stabbed this Barker character for whatever reason. And Jimmy was inclined to go along with that, because people do not make really elaborate plans to remain anonymous, cover up every one of their tracks, and then leave the area. *Not without they were bloody well up to something.*

For Jimmy, that Middle Eastern dagger was critical. Because it had "jihadist" written all over it. He sipped his coffee and frowned. And he decided, then and there, that he would take a drive down to Brockhurst early tomorrow morning, try to get his facts in a row. Right now he would call Arnold, set out his suspicions, and then ask if it would be okay for him and Jane to visit Kathy's mum while they were in the area.

He would mention to the admiral what a coincidence it was that they were headed down to the Brockhurst area on an entirely separate matter. But he understood with unerring certainty that there was about as much chance of Arnold believing that coincidence as there was of Copernicus joining the Flat Earth Society.

He picked up the phone and dialed the admiral's number. Arnold answered in person and immediately said how sorry he was they could not join Jimmy and Jane at the embassy. But then he paused, as if sensing that Jimmy was all business tonight.

"What's on your mind, kid?" he asked, flatly.

"Well, it's about that murder down in Brockhurst," he began—

"Guy with the pecker and the dagger?" interrupted Arnold.

"That's him," said Jimmy, aware that the admiral's voice betrayed impatience with a very large capital "I." "And don't you think it's kind of strange that some Arab murderer, a professional by the look of it, should be plying his trade a half mile from Kathy's mum's house?"

"Two things, Jimmy. One, the newspapers think the murderer was probably a girl. Two, the fact that the dagger was made in the Middle East does not mean it was being wielded by an Arab. Could have been used by a fucking Eskimo, for chrissakes. Ramshawe, you're getting paranoid."

"It's my job to be paranoid."

"Jimmy, right now there's no connection whatsoever between this barmaid and the murder, except they left the hotel within twenty minutes of each other. But let's say she did kill him, by accident if you like; then, so what? She didn't kill Kathy's mom, did she? She didn't go to live in Brockhurst for that, did she?"

"Then why did she go to live in Brockhurst?"

"Christ knows, old buddy. It's all a bit far-fetched for me. Coincidences. Disjointed, unconnected facts."

"Anyway, Arnie, the real purpose of my call was to ask you if it would be okay for Jane and me to visit Mrs. Gallagher while we're in the area tomorrow."

"'Course it would be fine. But what the hell are you two doing in the area?"

"Oh, Jane's got some kind of art project down on the estuary, you know, teaming up with a few other students in the wetlands."

"Yeah, right," said Arnold, and hung up the phone.

Jimmy chuckled. "Cunning old bastard," he muttered to himself. "But he's being a bit bloody hasty on this one. I'm not done with it yet. Not by a good long way."

Jimmy's evening at the Australian embassy passed with its customary luxury, the white-jacketed butler serving dinner to Jane and her fiancé as if Jimmy were the ambassador himself. The following morning they set off at 8 A.M., down Interstate 95 to Fredericksburg, and then to Route 17, which followed the Rappahannock River all the way to its estuary and the little town of Brockhurst.

Jimmy and Jane parked his Jaguar behind the Estuary Hotel, not twenty-five yards from where someone had rammed an Arabian dagger into the heart of Matt Barker. Jimmy walked to the end of the parking lot. There was an obvious bloodstain on the wall and on the concrete surface of the area. They walked in through the rear door of the hotel and inquired if they were too late for breakfast. The manager smiled and said, "Go through to the dining room and we'll fix you up."

It was almost 11 A.M. when Jimmy ordered eggs, bacon, sausage, and toast. Jane settled for cereal, yogurt, and fresh fruit salad. They were sitting in companionable silence when Jimmy stood up and walked through to the hotel foyer and spoke to the manager.

"Sir, are you Mr. Jim Caborn?"

"That's me."

Jimmy offered his hand and said quietly, "I'm Lt. Commander Ramshawe, National Security Agency. Could you find time to join me in the dining room? There's a couple of things I'd like to discuss."

The hotel manager looked suitably impressed at the mention of America's most secret intelligence agency. "Why, certainly, Commander. I'll be right in." Jimmy returned to Jane, and Caborn came in and pulled up a chair and sat with them. He was a naturally friendly man, and he poured himself a cup of coffee.

"I'll get some fresh if we need it," he said, and offered his own right hand to Jane Peacock with the practiced aplomb of all hotel managers. "Glad to meet you, ma'am," he said.

She shook his hand and replied, in the unmistakable style of a true Australian, "G'day, Jim. Nice little place you've got here."

The hotel manager grinned and said: "Now what would a high-ranking young officer from the National Security Agency be doing down here—as if I didn't know. It's Carla, isn't it?"

"Of course it is," replied Jimmy. "And I want you to answer my questions with great care." He reached into his pocket and pulled out his identification pass, which allowed him to enter, every day and any night, the innermost sanctum of the front line of America's military security.

Jim Caborn gave it a cursory glance and handed it back. "I don't need to see that," he said. "If the hotel business teaches you one thing, it's to spot genuine. I knew you were on the level, first time I saw you."

"Did you feel that way about Carla Martin?" asked the commander.

"Well, she had an American passport and all the right references. But there was something about her—she was kind of a mystery. I never felt I knew one thing about her background."

"Did you ever think she might be foreign?"

"Not consciously. But now you mention it, she did sometimes say things kind of strangely. You know, like a French person—fluent in English, but sometimes saying things not quite the way we would."

Jimmy nodded. "I guess you never knew where she lived?"

"No. I never did. No one did. Still don't."

"Do you think she murdered Matt Barker?"

"Jesus, I've always found that darned near impossible to grasp. She was a very nice girl, educated, polite, and very efficient. But I guess you have to consider, she covered her tracks and vanished the night of the murder. Never been seen since."

"You have no documents or records of her?"

"Hell, no. Either she or someone else cleaned out her file. We have absolutely nothing to show that she ever existed."

"Very professional," murmured Jimmy.

The manager looked at him quizzically. "Professional?" he said. "I'd say more like cunning."

"We're in different trades, mate," replied Ramshawe.

They finished their coffee, paid the bill, and said their good-byes; but as Jimmy and Jane walked across the parking lot, she turned and said, "Jesus, Jim, there were a whole lot more questions I could have asked him."

"I'm not trying to solve this murder," he replied. "I'm trying to identify Miss Carla Martin, nothing else. I don't give a flying fuck about Matt Barker or his death."

"Well, where are we going now?"

"We're going to the police station, mostly because I want to have a look at that dagger."

They'd driven past Detective Segel's office on the way to the hotel, and now they strolled through the warm summer morning, leaving the car parked behind the hotel.

Both of them wore light blue jeans and loafers. Jane had on a crisp white shirt, and Jimmy a dark blue short-sleeved polo shirt. His shock of floppy dark hair, which so irritated the crewcut Admiral Morris, blew in the light wind. As did Jane's spectacular blonde mane, bleached all through her teenage years by the hot sun that warmed Sydney's Bondi Beach. They were, by any standard, a striking couple.

When they reached the police station, Jane said she'd rather wander down to the wide river, and Jimmy walked alone to the duty officer's desk. He asked to see Detective Joe Segel, whose name he had read in the newspaper as the man leading the murder inquiry.

His NSA identification dispensed with any waiting. Within one minute, Lieutenant Commander Ramshawe was shown into the office of Brockhurst's top investigator. They exchanged greetings, but Jimmy was aware of the natural reserve all local law officers display in the presence of officials from the FBI, the CIA, or, even more sinister, the National Security Agency.

Detective Segel smiled. "And to what do we owe this great honor?" he asked.

"Oh, nothing much," said Jimmy, cheerfully. "I was just trying to get a handle on this vanished Carla Martin. Tell the truth, we think she might be foreign, and we'd very much like to know precisely what she was up to, working here in this small Virginia town."

"But what caused you to care so much, you drove personally all the way down here? Your card says you're the assistant to the director."

"Two things, Joe," replied Jimmy, slipping easily into the naturally casual way of the Aussie. "One, Miss Martin apparently took a great amount of trouble removing every trace of identification at the hotel. I'm assuming the murder of Matt Barker was a sudden and bloody inconvenient occurrence, and merely hastened her departure. Like no one thinks she came down here just to murder Matt.

"Two, that dagger was Middle Eastern in origin, and America's most important terrorist hunter, Admiral Arnold Morgan, just happens to have a mother-in-law who lives right here in this town. I guess a few hundred yards from where Carla Martin worked so anonymously. We don't like the coincidence."

"Stated like that, I'm not sure I do either," replied Detective Segel. "I do, of course, know Emily Gallagher. And I have, of course, had a chat with her about Carla Martin. I've spoken to most people in the area, especially those who frequent the Estuary Hotel. But I'll admit that it had not occurred to me that Mrs. Gallagher was the prime reason for Carla's presence right here in Brockhurst."

"Different mindset, old mate," said Jimmy. "You're trying to solve a murder. I'm looking at the possibility of a future attempt on the admiral's life. Although I've kept that one to myself. And I sure as hell haven't told the admiral!"

Detective Segel laughed. "Good idea," he said. "Might make him nervous."

"Not him," said Jimmy. "He'd just laugh and say he wasn't sufficiently important for that. But even he'd know that was pure bullshit."

Detective Segel frowned. "You mean Carla Martin was here as a kind of jihadist outrider, trying to find out the future movements of Admiral Morgan and his wife?"

"I think she might have been. But first, could you and I have a look at the murder weapon?"

"It's right here . . . let me give you a pair of rubber gloves to handle it with. The forensic guys might want to look at it again."

Jimmy pulled on the gloves and removed the dagger from the plastic evidence bag. He pulled a small folding printmaker's glass from his pocket, and he stared hard at the area where the blade joined the handle. And there he saw what he had come for. A small mark, perhaps a hieroglyphic, possibly Arabic writing, no more than a half inch long. It began with a shape like a small letter "a" with two dots above and below, then two curves like a "j" and then a "9," finally a "w."

Jimmy pulled a small white card from his pocket. It contained an alphabetical list of fourteen Middle Eastern countries, from Bahrain through Egypt, Iran, Iraq, and Jordan to Yemen. Next to the name of each country was the Arab translation. The markings on the dagger fitted precisely the country listed eleventh from the top, Syria.

"Well, Joe," said the commander, "at least we know where the murder weapon was made."

"Does that help?"

"Not much. But it might. Especially if your Carla Martin made her way here from Damascus and tucked this little devil right here in her suitcase."

"You think she might have?"

"If she did, I'm rapidly losing interest."

"How come?"

"Joe, at the National Security Agency, we only look for very big fish. If this barmaid took a chance and stuffed that dagger into her luggage, running the risk of a U.S. airport security man finding it . . . well, that would not be the action of a professional. A true terrorist agent would never do that, because for them, discovery is unthinkable. If you find her, which I doubt, make sure you find out where she got that dagger."

Detective Segel nodded thoughtfully. "If indeed it was hers," he said. "You are not interested in the murder, are you?" he said.

"No, I just want to know who Carla Martin really is, where she came from, and what her purpose was here in Brockhurst."

"A pretty tall order, right? Where's your next stop? Mrs. Gallagher?"

"Correct," said Jimmy. "We're friends of the family, and I do not believe the sole reason for Carla coming here was to murder this somewhat insignificant garage owner. And I don't need to tell you how important it is for you to keep us informed, the moment you find her."

"If we find her."

Jimmy stood up and handed the Brockhurst detective a card with his name and phone numbers written on it. "Any time of the day or night, Joe. This could be a whole lot more important than you think it is."

"Give my regards to Mrs. Gallagher."

The two men shook hands and Jimmy walked out into the sunlight, where Jane was peering through the window of the local sports shop. Three minutes later, they were approaching the front gate of Mrs. Gallagher's house, where the golden retriever Charlie was prostrate on the front stoop of the tall white colonial.

The front door opened, and Emily Gallagher stepped outside and welcomed them warmly, telling them Kathy had called and that she was delighted they had come to see her. Without further ceremony, she asked them to come inside for some iced tea and for a conversation about the missing Carla Martin, which she was certain they had hoped for.

Jimmy and Jane sat through the preliminaries—the possibility that Carla might be foreign, her politeness, her reliability, and the utter unsuitability, as an escort, of the late Matt Barker. Finally, on his second glass of iced tea, Jimmy ventured to ask whether Emily had told Carla when Arnold and Kathy were leaving for vacation.

"Well, I suppose I must have," replied Mrs. Gallagher. "I had to tell her when the two dogs needed walking, and I am sure I mentioned the precise day when Kipper was due to arrive. That's about three weeks from now."

"Mrs. Gallagher, did you tell her where Arnold and Kathy were going?"

"Not very accurately, because I don't really know myself. But I think I told her Kathy was coming here first, and then driving back to Washington, for the evening flight to London with Arnold."

"You didn't mention the airline, did you?"

"Certainly not. I don't know it. But I did suggest that Carla might like to come over around noon, to have lunch with Kathy and myself and acquaint herself with Kipper, who is very slightly crazier than Charlie."

"Did you give her any further details of their stay in London?" asked Jimmy.

"I'm sure not."

"Do you know *where* they're staying?"

"I expect the Ritz in Piccadilly," she replied. "Arnold always stays there; says he likes the tea they serve in the Palm Court."

"Did you mention that to Carla . . . ?"

"You know, I think I must have. I seem to remember her saying something about cucumber-and-marmite sandwiches, her favorite, that she and an English army officer she once knew always went there for tea, as a special treat."

"Jesus Christ!" said Jimmy.

"I'm sorry?" replied Arnold's mother-in-law.

"Oh, nothing, Mrs. Gallagher. I was just remembering I stayed there once myself, with my dad. I was only about fourteen years old, but I remember those sandwiches."

Emily laughed and wished she could have been more helpful. Her parting words to Jimmy and Jane were "Quite frankly, I hope Carla turns up. She was such a very nice girl. And so good with Charlie."

CHAPTER 7

Lieutenant Commander Jimmy Ramshawe gunned his beloved Jaguar north up Route 17 without uttering one word for twenty minutes. Jane Peacock would have mentioned his uncharacteristic silence, except she was asleep in the passenger seat. Finally, as they ran through the flatlands of Essex County, three things happened. Jane awakened. Jimmy spoke, or rather cursed. And a Virginia state trooper pulled him over for speeding.

When he produced his driver's license, he also handed over his National Security Agency identification. The officer looked at both.

"You going straight through to Fort Meade, sir?"

"Right now I'm headed for the Australian embassy."

The policeman nodded, handed back the documents. "Trouble?"

"Big."

"Okay, sir. You need an escort?"

"I guess not. I'll keep it down on the highway."

"I'll track you up to Fredericksburg. No problem, and, hey, thanks for what you do for our country."

The state trooper, who was in his late twenties, offered his hand and confided, "I tried out for the Navy SEALs a few years back, down at Virginia Beach. Too tough for me. But I still appreciate what all you guys do. . . . So long, Commander."

Jimmy pulled back onto the road and accelerated once more toward Washington. The police cruiser sped along fifty yards in the rear, its blue lights no longer flashing.

Jane shook her head. "It's a bloody miracle what those three little words mean in this country," she said. "National Security Agency. It really matters, doesn't it? Sometimes I forget how much."

Her fiancé was pensive. After a few seconds, he said, quietly, "Speaking of miracles, I'll tell you about another one. . . ."

"You will?"

"Yeah. Because that's what it will be, if that Brockhurst detective ever finds Carla Martin—you know what? He's never going to find Carla Martin."

"How do you know? Half the country's looking out for her."

"Half the country's whistling Dixie. Because Carla Martin no longer exists. She died with Matt Barker."

"Died!"

"Figuratively, I mean. Carla Martin was a professional agent, almost certainly operating on behalf of an Islamic terrorist group. She came here to Brockhurst to set up a field office, with the express purpose of finding out when Arnold and Kathy were leaving the country."

"Well, where is she now?"

"Dunno, babe. But if I had to guess, I'd say Syria."

"What do you mean, Syria? How could she get there?"

"No trouble. Air France to Paris, from either Washington or New York. Then on to Damascus. Same airline."

"And how, Great Oracle, do you alone come to be in possession of these facts? You alone, out of the entire country?"

Jimmy took his right hand off the wheel and tapped the side of his nose with his forefinger. "Mostly because I alone do not give a rat's ass about the murder. I'm looking for something else, and I just found it."

"I don't know why you have to be so dismissive about the life of Matt Barker."

"Because he was just a big stupid accident who blundered into the path of a major Islamic terrorist operation. Of course she killed him, but it's about as important as having a cup of coffee. And I'm the only person right now who is aware of that."

"Well, the media don't seem to agree with you. They are possessed by this murder."

"If his bloody pecker hadn't been sticking out, none of 'em would have given a damn. It just gave a salacious flavor to a routine country killing. And that'll do it every time. They wouldn't recognize the real truth behind the story if it bit 'em right in the ass."

Jane chuckled. "Christ, Arnold Morgan has had an effect on you," she said.

"I take that as a compliment," he replied. "But just ask yourself. This murder has all the hallmarks of an international terrorist operation. And how many times has any newspaper, radio, or television outfit mentioned that obvious truth? I'll tell you. None. And how often have they mentioned Matt Barker's pecker? About eight zillion times."

Again Jane laughed. "I guess his brains ended up *in* his pecker," she said. "A darned expensive move—cost him his life."

"Right. And a very dangerous one for Carla. Just a bit of bad luck. This randy bastard from the garage waits outside the hotel and tries to give her the Big What-Ho. Attacked her in some kind of sexual frenzy. For Carla, there was no alternative but to kill him. Quickly. And efficiently, like all special operators.

"And that meant she had to get the hell out. And now she's gone, probably abroad, certainly under a different passport. She'll never be found."

"How do you know that?"

"For a start, no one knows her name, no one has the remotest idea what country she's in, and she left, apparently, no trace. No one even knows where she lived."

"Okay. But the truth may come out in the next few days."

"I wouldn't put your life savings on it. Miss Carla was a complete professional. Assume, just for a moment, I'm on the right track, and then look at what she did. Her objective is to find out from Kathy's mum when Arnold is going on vacation.

"She enters the country almost certainly on an American passport, otherwise the forgery would have been picked up at the immigration desks at the airport. She makes her way to Mrs. Gallagher's little town and immediately gets a job at the local hotel. She befriends no one, except for one person—Mrs. Gallagher, surprise surprise.

"No one ever sees her arrive at the hotel, and no one ever sees her leave at night. No one has ever seen her car, not even Mrs. Gallagher. You know why?"

"No, 'course I don't."

"Because she never had a car."

"So how did she get to work and home at night?"

"She had a chauffeur, who dropped her off at different places close to the hotel, quiet streets only. And at night he waited for her at an agreed place. She just slipped across the parking lot and ran to where her car was waiting. Until the night when Matt Barker decided to ambush her."

"Was the chauffeur her boyfriend?"

"Christ, no. More likely a fellow member of Hezbollah or Hamas, or maybe even from a Middle East embassy. Someone right here in the USA gave her that dagger to protect herself if necessary. She'd never have tried to bring it through airport security herself."

"Well, it all sounds plausible, and I do remember that hotel manager saying she must have removed her documents from the file. And she plainly gave a false address, that Bowling Wharf or whatever it was."

"Listen, Jane. Sooner or later, someone's going to report a missing tenant in an apartment block. Remember Emily's words, apartment, doorman, balcony. And the police are going to trace Carla Martin's passport, and it will be a dead end, and no one will ever have heard of her.

"And we'll still be the only people who care about her real purpose. Because Emily told Carla all about the admiral's trip to London, his hotel, date and time of departure from Washington. And someone is going to be waiting for him. And that someone is going to try to kill him. Arnold's life is in the gravest possible danger."

"Is anyone going to believe all this?"

"I doubt it. Certainly not Arnold."

"So what are you going to do?"

"I'd like to stop him from going. Which will be a lot like trying to stop a freight train with your bare hands."

1000 Friday 6 July
Police Station, Brockhurst

Detective Joe Segel had more "information" on his plate than he knew what to do with. There had, so far, been more than sixty-five "sightings"—people who claimed to have seen a youngish lady fitting Carla's description driving toward Brockhurst during daylight hours.

The vehicle identifications were more diverse than the geographic locations, ranging from small compact automobiles to huge SUVs. A few callers claimed to know where she lived, and Joe Segel had been moving police cruisers all over the area to check out the possibility of "apartment, doorman, balcony," as reliably mentioned by Emily Gallagher.

Three had emerged as possibilities, but police checks had revealed no one answering Carla's description in residence, no one having gone missing, and no female who was out after 10:30 P.M. on Monday night. All three of these expensive apartment blocks employed assiduous doormen who logged in every resident on a computer, every night. None of the buildings was named Chesapeake Heights.

Joe considered all of that added up to a huge disappointment. But the biggest stone wall he ran into was the identification of Carla Martin. Computerized records revealed only three white females of that name born in the USA in May 1982. Joe Segel trusted Jim Caborn on that one.

Further checks revealed that two of them had never applied for passports. The other Carla Martin had been born on May 27, 1982, in Baltimore, Maryland. She was unmarried and now lived in Phoenix, Arizona, where she worked at a high school, teaching physical education. There were approximately 278 students, about 19 teachers, and 67 parents perfectly willing to swear that Miss Martin had been running three soccer games last Monday until seven o'clock in the evening, nine o'clock in Brockhurst. No, she did not have a part-time job moonlighting in a hotel bar 2,350 miles away in Virginia.

The local Phoenix police did interview Miss Martin, but only halfheartedly, since she was plainly innocent of any crime. They thus failed to discover that her first cousin on her mother's side, Kathy Streeter, was married to Mr. Dori Hussein, a cultural attaché at the Jordanian embassy, in northwest Washington, D.C.

Like his colleague, Ahmed, Mr. Hussein was a field officer for Hezbollah. And a good one. Documents were his specialty, having graduated from the Rhode Island School of Design.

Well, how the hell did the Brockhurst Carla get ahold of the Phoenix Carla's passport? That was essentially what Joe Segel wanted to know. Although he realized it was a blind alley, because the passport Carla showed to Jim Caborn was blatantly a forgery, and could have been scanned and copied in a dozen different ways. The forgers might even, in a blind coincidence, have invented all the names, dates, and places.

And had Carla used it to enter the United States, IF she was foreign? *Who the hell knew?* And anyway, that was none of Joe's business. All he wanted to know, for chrissakes, was who had killed Matt Barker. And the only certainty with which the day had presented him was that a lady who taught sports at an Arizona high school was not guilty.

A blanket check of all ports of entry on the East Coast of the United States had revealed nothing. There was no record of any Carla Martin. And the fact that Joe Segel did not even have a proper name for his prime suspect was really bothering him.

But at ten minutes before noon on that Friday morning, he got one. Fred Mitchell, the ex–Green Beret who manned the door by night at Chesapeake Heights, called in to reveal that he almost certainly knew the barmaid the police were seeking. Better yet, he knew her address and apartment. "Sir," said Fred, "she lived right here in this building, and I'm afraid she might be dead."

Detective Segel rounded up two officers, boarded a police cruiser, switched on the warning lights and siren, and sped out to Chesapeake Heights. And there Fred informed them that one of the tenants looked exactly like the photo-kit versions he had seen in the local newspaper last night and on a television news program. What was more, she worked nights, usually arrived home around 11:30 P.M. Yes, all apartments above the tenth floor had balconies. There was an especially large one on the penthouse floor where the lady lived.

"However, sir," said Fred, "she wasn't no Carla Martin. Nossir. Her name was Jane Camaro. She had been in residence for only a couple of weeks. On a four-month rental lease she had paid for in advance. Cash, the evening she arrived."

Detective Segel nodded, unsurprised by any of this. "And why do you think she is dead?" he asked.

"Sir, we had a little trouble last Monday night. Coupla hoods broke into one of the tenants' cars, brand-new Lincoln out back. It happened just after Jane arrived back, like I said, around 11:30 P.M., maybe a little after that.

"Anyway, I saw her come in, and then I had to go and check out the break-in. I came back in, maybe five minutes later, contacted the tenant whose car windshield had been smashed, and told him to call the police. Then I logged Miss Jane in on the computer, and no one's seen her since. Brad—he's the daytime doorman—has not logged her out since then, and I have certainly not logged her in."

"Can we go take a look at her apartment?"

"Sure we can. I got keys to all the apartments here. But I sure ain't looking forward to this. Nossir."

"You think she's died?"

"Well, I don't know what else to think. No one can get in or out of this building without one of the doormen seeing 'em go."

"How about she has a boyfriend in this building and moved in with him for a few days?" offered Joe Segel. "Just gone AWOL. That's absent without leave."

Fred grinned. "I know all about that, sir. I did fifteen years in the Green Berets. I wouldn't say there was any chance of that, sir. Right here, we got mostly married couples."

"Well, if we don't find her, my men will have to interview the residents."

"I understand, sir," said Fred, as the elevator came to a halt on the twenty-first floor. The four men turned to the left and walked along the corridor, led by the doorman. At the second door, Fred inserted his key and pushed open the door, tentatively. Inside, there was nothing much to see. The apartment had been abandoned in a major hurry.

In the bedroom, the wardrobe and drawers were still wide open and there was nothing left, not even bed linens. The bathroom yielded not so much as a spare toothbrush. The kitchen was bereft, the refrigerator empty, nothing whatsoever in the cupboards. There was one clean plate, one knife, one fork, one glass, two coffee mugs. All in the dishwasher, all thoroughly cleansed in scalding-hot water. There was not one single trace of either Jane Camaro or Carla Martin.

There was not much else to do except to leave. And Fred was relieved that Jane Camaro was not dead. "Wouldn't look good on the résumé, right?"

But on the way down in the elevator, Detective Segel asked him one specific question: "How do you know that no one left the building while you were away from the desk, for maybe ten minutes?"

Fred beamed. "We got closed-circuit television right here, sir. One small camera right above the door, another at the far end of the foyer. When you gentlemen have left, I rewind the film, right there at the desk, and check out if anyone entered or left. The film displays the correct time."

"How about someone you cannot identify?" asked Joe Segel.

"Nothing's perfect, and that's a flaw. But I sure as hell could identify Miss Jane Camaro. That was one great-looking chick."

"Did you check the film after the break-in, you know, maybe catch a glimpse of her leaving?"

"No, I didn't bother. I was only out at the side of the building for three or four minutes, and I'd have known if anyone came in or left. Head-lights, car engines, and all."

"How long would it take to run the film back right now so we could take a look?"

"Maybe coupla hours. There's a lot of film in that system."

"Okay. Perhaps you'd do it when you got some time and let me know?"

"No problem, sir."

"Did Jane have a car?"

"Well, she never filled out the vehicle identification form for a reserved space in the parking lot. But she must have had a car. Ain't no other way to get out here in the country. I guess she must have forgot."

"Is the management strict about these procedures?"

"Hell, no. This parking lot's half empty most of the time. Ain't some-thing we take very seriously. But since you mention it, I never saw her be-hind the wheel of a vehicle. But that don't mean she didn't have one."

Joe thanked Fred for his help and said they'd be in touch, with regard to police interviews with the residents. When he arrived back at the precinct, he picked up the telephone and dialed the personal number of Lieutenant Commander Jimmy Ramshawe at Fort Meade.

1530 Same Day
National Security Agency

The call from Detective Segel, in Jimmy's mind, caused more questions than answers. How long after "Jane" came home did the break-in occur in the parking lot? Who told Fred it had happened? Precisely what was on that film during the few minutes Fred was out? And what the hell was someone doing smashing the windshield of the Lincoln? No one breaks into a car like that, especially one with an alarm system.

In fact, these days, very few people break into cars at all because the systems are so good. Whoever broke into that Lincoln certainly did not want to steal it and then drive around with no windshield. And through the windshield was no way to get inside the car.

No, pondered Jimmy, *that made no sense, unless it was pure vandalism. And who the hell would want to do something that stupid, knowing they might get caught when the alarm went off?*

There's only one person who logically might have broken that windshield, and that was someone who wanted Fred away from his station for a few minutes. Time either to get into, or get away from, Chesapeake Heights.

He picked up the phone and called Fred, who jumped right to attention at the contact from a Navy lieutenant commander at the National Security Agency. He promised to call back in two hours with some answers. And, when they arrived, every one of those answers was precisely what Jimmy guessed they would be.

The break-in occurred eighteen minutes after Jane Camaro returned home. Fred did not hear the alarm because he was watching television. He was alerted by a chauffeur who rushed in through the front door and said he saw a couple of hoodlums running away from a big Lincoln automobile with a smashed windshield and an alarm blaring.

Fred saw the chauffeur fleetingly, and identified him as a guy who could have been Italian or Puerto Rican. And yes, he had studied a rerun of the film and identified a figure leaving the building who could have been Jane. But she had turned away from the camera as she walked through the foyer, covering her face with a magazine. It may not have been Jane, because she was walking kind of funny. But it could have been. Anyway, she was carrying a medium-sized suitcase.

Carla Martin, you are one very professional lady. Jimmy Ramshawe's admiration was sincere.

Right now, he had about three hundred coincidences. And in Jimmy's mind, they added up to one large warning light. Someone was most certainly determined to eliminate Admiral Morgan. But he doubted Arnold would believe him.

He was right about that too. "I guess it's possible," the great man grunted. "But I'm not running my life around the antics of some goddamned barmaid. I got a lot of security, and it'll be as good in London as it is here. Jesus Christ, Jimmy, leave it alone. Why don't you check out that Iranian submarine at the eastern end of the Med? I see it's only about two hundred miles from a U.S. carrier. That's too close. Call me."

The phone went down with a crash. Arnold, of course, never said good-bye to anyone. Not even the president. Jimmy usually chuckled at this gruff eccentricity. But he found nothing amusing today. Absolutely nothing.

0400 Saturday 7 July
In the Mediterranean Sea

The Russian-built Type 877 *Kilo*-class submarine, owned by the Iranian Navy, slid through clear ocean waters five hundred miles south of Italy's Gulf of Taranto. Her captain was Mohammed Abad, who had twelve offi-cers, fifty-three crew, and one guest under his command. The guest, Gen-eral Ravi Rashood, C-in-C Hamas, had come aboard off the coast of Lebanon, delivered by a Syrian Army helicopter.

These were strange seas for the Iranians, who normally patrolled only the Gulf and the Arabian Sea. But this particular submarine had just emerged from refit conducted in her birthplace, the Admiralty Yards in St. Petersburg, on the shores of the Baltic. It had been commissioned back in November 1996, and it had not been necessary to return to Russia since then. The engineers at Iran's submarine base, Chah Bahar on the north-west shores of the Gulf of Oman, had been more than competent.

However, Hull Number 901 had experienced some major mechanical difficulties eighteen months previously and had missed an Indian Naval Review. With her propulsion system on the blink, the Kilo had been towed behind a Russian frigate all the way back to the Baltic. Now, re-stored to pristine fighting condition, she had spent three months at the eastern end of the Med, patrolling the waters off Beirut and generally making the Americans very jumpy.

There were certain admirals in the Pentagon, and one in Chevy Chase, who thought she should have been sunk, forthwith, in deep water. There could, after all, be only one possible reason why the Islamic Republic of Iran should deploy one of her four diesel-electric inshore submarines in the Eastern Med. And that reason was all-purpose—to assist the terrorist organizations Iran had financed and supplied for so long.

According to U.S. Naval Intelligence, that could mean anything from supplying missiles to Hezbollah in Lebanon to opening fire on Israeli warships—the Russian Kilos carried 18 torpedoes—or perhaps even sinking a U.S. warship, since there is often an American fleet patrolling these volatile seas. This latter course of action would almost certainly turn into a suicide mission for the Iranians, but with Allah awaiting the crew in Paradise on the other side of the bridge, and sounding the three trumpets, this is not considered a bad fate for Muslim extremists. At least it's never deterred them before.

The Type 877 Kilo is a formidable opponent for even the most modern surface ship, because she bristles with state-of-the-art radar surface-search systems. Underwater, she is even more dangerous, equipped with the highly efficient Russian Shark's Teeth sonar.

She's silent under five knots and can dive to seven hundred feet. Her range is six thousand miles cruising at seven knots. However, her single shaft and 3,650-hp electronic engine can drive her through the depths of the ocean at greater speeds. If she struck hard, however, underwater against an opposing warship, she would be damn near impossible to find if the CO cut her speed.

The Russians have long gloried in the potential of this export-only submarine. Indeed, they have a big four-color trade advertisement which reads "THE KILO CLASS SUBMARINE—the only soundless creature in the sea." And when they wrote that ad, they had Hull 901 in mind. The address in St. Petersburg, complete with phone, fax, and E-mail, is that of RUBIN, Russia's central design bureau for marine engineering.

This is where the design refinements for the 240-foot-long underwater boat were perfected. The RUBIN scientists have worked for years trying to make the Kilo as quiet as the grave, every engine mounting, every working part, every vibration considered, improved, and eventually silenced. Running deep, Hull 901 would make no more noise than a modern computer.

All three thousand tons of her, superbly streamlined, can slip through the depths at six knots, betraying virtually nothing. She cuts her speed below five, she's vanished. Of all the underwater warriors, the Kilo is one of the most stealthy, partly because, unlike a big nuclear boat, she has no nuclear reactor requiring the support of God knows how many subsystems, all of them noisemakers.

There is but one flaw in this masterpiece of Russian design. And that happens when she needs to recharge the huge batteries that power her electric motors. The Kilo is vulnerable when snorkeling, because her generators are merely two big diesel internal-combustion engines, which, like a car, must have air.

And that requirement sends the submarine to periscope depth, where those generators can be heard, the air-intake mast can be picked up on radar, and the ions in the diesel exhaust can be "sniffed." If she's not careful, she can even be seen, and there is absolutely nothing she can do about it.

The *Kilo*-class submarine, moving swiftly, must snorkel and recharge her batteries every two hundred miles. Through the Mediterranean Sea, from one end to the other, she needs to complete this process twelve times before exiting into the Atlantic.

Of course, the U.S. Navy's detection systems are extremely advanced and the mighty *Los Angeles*–class nuclear boats are certainly a match for the covert Russian submarine. The chances of a Kilo getting close enough to hit an American ship are remote, just as long as no one takes their eye off the ball.

Nonetheless, the retired American admiral residing in Chevy Chase, Maryland, continued to believe Iran's Mediterranean submarine should be hit and sunk forthwith. President Bedford was inclined to agree, particularly since it was possible for a big U.S. nuclear boat to get rid of any foreign submarine and never be located.

In subsurface warfare, it has been ever thus. Because, contrary to popular perception, submarines cannot communicate with home base while they are underwater. Their only form of communication is via satellite, and for that they must have a mast, briefly, jutting above the surface.

Thus, all submarines have a daily call time, when they come to periscope depth, usually in the dead of night, and announce their course, speed, and position in a minisecond electronic burst to the satellite circling twenty-two thousand miles above the Earth. They then ask if there are any messages, scoop them up, and return immediately to the ocean depths. If the entire process takes more than fifteen seconds, then someone's been grotesquely inefficient.

The progression from this myriad of Naval Intelligence leads to one stark truth—if a submarine hits another with a torpedo, no one knows it's happened. The stricken ship will sink to the floor of the ocean, some-times without a trace. The first clue to its disappearance will be a missed call home via the satellite. And this might very easily be twenty hours after the hit.

And one missed call is not usually a five-alarmer, because the problem could have been electronic, or maybe even carelessness. Certainly one sin-gle missed call-in does not signify the ultimate horror of a submarine lost with all hands. And so to the second missed call, the following night. What does this mean? And what to do?

It might be forty-four hours since the submarine was sunk. And an en-emy could very easily have been traveling at twenty knots, speeding away from the scene of the crime. That's 880 nautical miles! *In any direction!*

Which leaves some hapless home base with a search area of thousands and thousands of square miles in waters perhaps one or two miles deep. Chances of crew survival: zero. Chances of location: close to zero. Situa-tion: hopeless. What to do: probably nothing.

The victim's navy will most certainly not admit what might have hap-pened. The perpetrator will, naturally, not know what anyone is talking about. And the entire incident may never be disclosed. By anyone. Has it ever happened? Of course. But the oceans guard their secrets darkly. Who knows how many iron coffins rest in the weird, lost canyons of the seven seas? All it takes is one well-aimed torpedo, with a big warhead, and no one will be any the wiser.

Which was why Admiral Arnold Morgan had, on several occasions, ad-vised President Bedford to hit that Iranian *Kilo*-class submarine—*before the sonofabitch hits us or the Israelis.* The submarine to which he referred was, of course, the very one that now carried General Rashood, com-mander in chief of Hamas, on his mission to assassinate Admiral Morgan himself—a poetic malevolence worthy of the Devil.

At 0400 on this Saturday morning, General Rashood was in the naviga-tion area, talking to the young officer who was plotting the course of Hull No. 901, Lt. Rudi Alaam, a career officer from the eastern Iranian prov-ince of Kerman. Both men were leaning over a circular computerized chart that highlighted the central part of the Mediterranean.

It showed the submarine, which was running hard, snorkeling at periscope depth, moving west through the channel north of the island of Malta and its tiny offspring Gozo, both of which lie in the broad waters that separate Sicily and Tunisia. The Med goes shallower through here, and it was the first time the navigation officer had had to attend to the depth of the water.

Almost immediately, running west away from the coast of Lebanon, the Kilo had run into vast ocean depths, nine thousand feet, lonely waters, the Greek island of Rhodes 240 miles off their starboard beam. The GPS read 34.00 North, 22.30 East when they were southwest of Crete.

Right here, 120 miles off the coast of Libya, the ocean floor shelved down even deeper, another three thousand feet. They passed well south of Sicily's Cape Passero with more than two miles of blue water under the keel. A land soldier rather than a sailor, General Rashood found the whole exercise somewhat creepy.

So far, they had not encountered any U.S. or Royal Navy warships. But headed for the narrow waterway where the tip of Italy's boot looks likely to kick Sicily straight into Tunis Harbor, the submarine needed to exercise inordinate care. This was an ancient throughway for the Royal Navy. The ocean was much shallower, less than two hundred feet in places, and the carrier battle groups of the U.S. Navy tended to treat the place like Chesapeake Bay.

Detection was something Captain Mohammed Abad wished to avoid, but not at the expense of his speed. If he thought he was being tracked by a U.S. nuclear boat, he would slow and dive. But he doubted the Americans would actually sink him right here in these busy shallows. He knew that once located by the hugely sophisticated U.S. sonars, they could track him with ease and put him on the bottom of the Atlantic as and when they wished, as soon as he ventured into deep ocean water.

But he had as much right to be here as they did, and, like all Iranian politicians and military leaders, he did not think they would dare.

Captain Abad kept going, transmitting as little as possible. He would sneak past the Sicilian port of Marsala, moving more slowly, and then accelerate through this stone-silent ocean, almost on the surface, in the dead of night, moving forward making course nor-nor-west, as swiftly as possible.

Neither he nor General Rashood realized that up ahead of them, a mere two hundred miles, ran the great, jet-black monster *Los Angeles*–class submarine USS *Cheyenne*, her captain already alerted to the possible presence of a rogue Iranian Kilo patrolling in the Med, doubtless up to no good.

No submarine in the world escapes the eagle eye of the United States Navy. The American admirals, without fail, know the whereabouts of every seaworthy underwater boat, nuclear or diesel-electric. Their attention is sharpened when a submarine goes missing from its home base, perhaps having ducked out between passes of the overhead U.S. satellites. Thereafter a swift, penetrating search from inner space is conducted, using secret technology that would make the Russians or the Chinese blink in amazement.

In the case of Iranian Hull No. 901, the Americans tracked her all the way to St. Petersburg as a matter of pure routine. Six months later, they observed her leaving the Russian shipyards, and tracked her easily through the Gulf of Finland, headed east around the coast of Estonia and through the Baltic. She went deep right there, and the U.S. observers merely switched their sights on the narrow Copenhagen Channel through which the Kilo must pass in order to make the open sea.

Captain Abad brought her through right on time, and the Americans watched her run past Norway's mountainous southern coast, and then into the North Sea opposite the Scottish city of Aberdeen.

It would have been a lot quicker to head down the North Sea and exit the Royal Navy's home turf through the English Channel. But the Americans knew the Kilo would never do that, and they saw her go deep and make a northern swing around Scotland, finally heading for the open Atlantic, running swiftly past the coast of Northern Ireland and out toward the granite ocean rise of Rockall.

The planners of the U.S. Navy's Atlantic Command guessed the Kilo would run through the Strait of Gibraltar into the Med and head directly for the northern entrance of the Suez Canal, the shortest route to the Gulf of Oman. They were correct. Almost. But the Kilo made a sudden swerve north, and the next time the Americans picked her up, she was directly off the coast of Lebanon, ten miles west of Beirut.

They had kept a weather eye on her ever since and watched with interest as the Syrian helicopter deposited a passenger on her casing on Tuesday afternoon, July 3. Captain Abad was already running west, and the Americans had, essentially, *no goddamned idea where the hell that submarine was going, and certainly no clues about the intentions of her commanding officer.*

They picked her up snorkeling, around midnight on Wednesday, July 4, and kept a loose fix on her all the way to Marsala. The ops room of the *Cheyenne* knew where Captain Abad was on the GPS, accurate to about thirty feet.

On this Saturday evening, the U.S. submarine was around fifty miles south of the Sardinian port of Cagliari. Her task was to locate the Kilo and then track her to the gateway to the Mediterranean, the Gibraltar Strait, and then let her head out into the Atlantic where another U.S. nuclear boat would follow her into really deep water.

It had not been definitely decided to sink the Kilo, but opinion in both the White House and the Pentagon was certainly swaying in that direction. There were a couple of firebrands among the Navy top brass who were perfectly happy to take her out in the deepest waters of the Med, but there was something irresistibly local about that area.

Ships from North Africa, Spain, France, Italy, and Great Britain, warships, freighters, tankers, and cruise liners ply their trade through here. And in general terms, the American Navy brass were more comfortable opening fire in the vast, bottomless anonymity of the Atlantic, where no prying eyes would ever catch a telltale sign of a submarine split asunder by a Mark 48 torpedo.

Captain Abad was oblivious of the mindset of his enemies, unaware that anyone even knew he had left Beirut, and he was certainly not contemplating the possibility of instant death and the destruction of his newly refurbished submarine.

The Iranian would be well past Marsala before he even found out that the *Cheyenne* was patrolling these waters. The Kilo would be at periscope depth, with its air intake above the surface, when Commander Hank Redford's sonars gained POSIDENT, and the *Cheyenne* could begin to move in closer.

0900 Saturday 7 July
Dublin, Ireland

Shakira Rashood waited in St. Stephen's Square for her hired chauffeur to arrive. She had been in the Shelbourne Hotel for three and a half days, which she considered to be quite long enough even for a girl as unobtrusive as Maureen Carson of Michigan, who had died several years previously in Bay City up on the shores of Lake Huron.

Shakira had been furnished with this information when she was given her second forged U.S. passport. God alone knew how the forgers had laid hands on the data, but somehow they had. And so far as the Shelbourne Hotel was concerned, Maureen Carson had just checked out, having scarcely left the premises during her entire stay.

Mrs. Rashood had made her own car-rental arrangements with the Iranian embassy, which had offices on Mount Merrion Avenue at Black-rock, on the south side of Dublin. The embassy overlooked the Irish Sea, beyond which lay the shores of England.

She had liked the Shelbourne, and indeed had dined there each night, once falling into conversation with a very cheerful sixtyish Irishman at the next table who told her he was in town for the Irish Derby, the million-dollar classic run each year in early July.

Shakira had wanted to know where, in a busy city like Dublin, did they have room to run a major horse race. The Irishman, whose name was Michael O'Donnell, explained it was run on the Curragh, a few miles out-side the city, in County Kildare, Ireland's most historic racecourse being set on a massive swath of grazing land that dates back to Roman times.

"And how far did you come to see this horse race?"

"More than a hundred miles," said Michael. "I'm up from County Tip-perary. I breed a few thoroughbreds down there."

"And is one of them running in the Irish Derby?"

"Not exactly. But a colt named Easter Rebel is. And I bred him. I still own the mare, Mighty Mary, and she has a filly foal at foot. I'll get a big price for her if the Rebel goes well."

Shakira, unsurprisingly, did not understand one single word of that. But she was one of those people who cannot bear just to say, "How inter-esting," and move on. Shakira Rashood had to know precisely what was happening.

Of course, she was so endearingly beautiful that she was, generally speaking, indulged, especially by men, and particularly by important men, from terrorist commanders to Irish stud farm owners. Women blessed with great beauty live by an entirely different set of rules.

"You mean a mare named Mighty Mary is the mother of Easter Rebel?"

"Precisely. I sold him as a yearling, but he won four races when he was two, and two more this past spring, one of them a group race over a mile and a quarter in England."

"Does that mean they all run together—a group race?"

And so on, until Shakira thoroughly understood that Mr. O'Donnell's broodmare Mighty Mary would be very valuable if Easter Rebel should win the Irish Derby, and that her foal, the filly, could go on to be an excellent racer if she could run half as fast as her brother.

"She's what's known as a full sister," said Mr. O'Donnell. "Same father, same mother."

"I assumed they all had the same father and same mother," said Shakira. "Is this like a marriage with horses?"

Michael O'Donnell laughed. "Hell, no!" he said. "We switch 'em around all the time, breeding the mares to any stallion who takes our fancy."

"What if she doesn't like him?"

"Oh, we tether 'em good and well so they can't escape, and then bring the stallion in at precisely the right moment in her cycle."

Shakira looked shocked. "But that's terrible," she said. "What if Mighty Mary hates every moment of it? That's rape."

"Ah, jaysus, Maureen," said Michael. "We're trying to breed winners, not run a dating agency. Tipperary is one of the most famous horse-breeding places in the entire world."

"Well, I'm not sure I like your attitude," she replied, "forcing those horrible stallions on the mares."

"I'll tell you one thing," said Michael. "The sire of Easter Rebel and the filly foal is not horrible. He's one of the best-looking stallions you'll ever see."

"Hmmmm," said Shakira. "What's his name?"

"Galileo."

"Could he run fast?"

"Maureen, there are three major twelve-furlong races run in England and Ireland in the high summer of the year—June and July. In 2001, Galileo won them all. And that does not happen very often."

"Is one of them the Irish Derby?"

"Sure it is."

"Then I hope Easter Rebel wins it, like his father."

"I hope he wins it for his little sister."

"Why is that important?"

"Well, today she is a very nice foal and may command £50,000 in the sale ring. If the Rebel wins this weekend, she'll be known as a full sister to an Irish Derby winner and may be worth £400,000."

"Who would pay that for a horse?"

"Probably the Arab sheiks, but in this case more likely the owners of the Coolmore Stud in Tipperary. She was born there, and they'd probably like her to come home eventually."

"Is it a beautiful place?"

"The best. Full of perfectly mown paddocks, horsemen who have looked after thoroughbreds for generations, and many of the finest stallions in the world. All of it right down there in the heart of Tipperary, so many foals and yearlings. That's the place, Maureen. Where the dreams begin."

"And sometimes end?" said Shakira.

"Ah, no, my girl," said the Irishman, somewhat mysteriously. "Nature never closes the book."

And with that, Michael O'Donnell took his leave, heading out of the dining room to meet his wife and daughter. As he went, he called, "There'll be some kind of a hooley at home on Sunday night if we win."

Her reply "What's a hooley?" was lost in the busy Shelbourne dining room.

And that, in a sense, was why Shakira was standing on the sidewalk in St. Stephen's Green, her forged passport in her bag, awaiting her driver. She had decided, pending the arrival of her husband in a few days, to visit Tipperary, somewhere near this Coolmore Stud, 110 miles south of Dublin.

0900 Saturday 7 July
Brockhurst, Virginia

Detective Joe Segel was becoming an expert on brick walls, dead ends, and roads leading nowhere. In the past five days, he had experienced all of them—in his fruitless search for the vanishing barmaid. In his own mind, he was as certain as an experienced detective ever could be that Miss Carla Martin had indeed stabbed Matt Barker to death. It also seemed certain that the big garage proprietor had launched some kind of sexual attack on her and paid for it with his life.

The only other certainty about Carla was that she had most definitely disappeared off the face of the earth. Just about every radio and television news station in the United States had carried the story. Not just the media in the local Virginia/Washington, D.C. area; the tantalizing mystery of the Barker Pecker had transported the murder story far and wide.

If Carla had been anywhere in the USA, and indeed been innocent of the crime, she would surely have called in to the 800 number at Joe Segel's police station to clear her name. But she had not done so, which meant one of two things: she had fled the country, possibly before the body was found, or she was hiding out somewhere in the States until the murder hunt died down.

It was now obvious that her passport was a forgery. The two establishments in London that she had submitted as references had never heard of her. Her apartment yielded absolutely nothing, and the film on the closed-circuit system at Chesapeake Heights was so indistinct and the exiting figure so awkwardly presented, not even Fred Mitchell could swear to God it was Jane Camaro.

The lady had covered her tracks with astounding efficiency. The fact was, Joe Segel did not even know her name. He did not even know her nationality. And he sure as hell did not know where she was. He'd even had the FBI and the CIA launch an international search looking for a port-of-entry clue in every major nation in the Middle East, not to mention London, Paris, Rome, Madrid, Amsterdam, Brussels, Geneva, Berlin, and Milan. Nothing.

Joe did not even have a car description or a license-plate number. There was nothing to go on. This particular murder hunt was headed for the "unsolved" file with near-record speed. There was only one suspect. And that suspect seemed not to exist.

Like Fred Mitchell five days ago, Detective Joe feared for his résumé.

1000 Sunday 8 July
National Security Agency, Maryland

Lt. Commander Ramshawe had to be at the Australian embassy for lunch. His time was thus limited, and he moved fast to make sure he caught Admiral Morgan before he went out.

And again he spelled out his fears to the great man, to no avail, even though he stressed the danger that must be prevalent since it was entirely possible that Emily Gallagher had revealed too much detail to the girl now wanted for murder.

"Arnie, is it not possible for you simply to change the dates?"

"Out of the question. After London, we're going up to Scotland to stay a couple of nights with Admiral Sir Iain MacLean, then we're all going to Edinburgh for the Festival and the Military Tattoo."

"I've been to that with Dad," said Jimmy. "It goes on for about a month. Can't you just go on a different night?"

"Jimmy, I'm taking the salute on a very carefully planned evening. The dates were only finalized on Friday. I have to go when I said I'd go. Anyway, it's a pretty big honor. A lot of very big-deal military men have taken the salute at Edinburgh Castle. Churchill did it. The prime minister of England is doing it the night after me. I wouldn't miss it."

"Hmmmmm," said Jimmy, reverting to his rich Aussie accent, as he normally did when under stress. "Basically, I'm wasting my time, right? Just trying to save your bloody life."

"Which is of course threatened by a barmaid. C'mon, kid. Let's stay real. I got plenty of protection, not to mention half the British Army."

"I'm not worried about the goddamned barmaid. I'm worried about her employers. That's all. You know there's some hotshot special operators in those jihadist groups. I'm just trying to keep you out of the crosshairs."

"Don't worry about me, kid. I'm fireproof. Gotta go."

Crash. Down phone.

"Stubborn old prick," muttered Jimmy.

1400 Sunday 8 July
Western Mediterranean

The *Kilo*-class submarine that bore General Rashood to his destination still ran fast at periscope depth, still snorkeling. Captain Abad was conning her through nine thousand feet of ocean depth, 150 miles south of Majorca in the Spanish Balearic Isles. That put her around fifty miles northwest of Algiers, 37.30 North, 02.30 East.

She ran just below the surface, making twelve knots. In this snorkeling mode, she was, by modern submarine standards, quite extraordinarily noisy, and she was picked up instantly by the sophisticated sonar carried by USS *Cheyenne*.

Right now, Commander Hank Redford had the big *LA*-class submarine patrolling slowly, approximately a hundred miles south of the island of Formentera, around 110 miles northwest of the oncoming Iranians. The American sonar operators were scanning the wide deep seas to the east, their long electronic towed array strung out astern of the ship like a giant black snake, catching and processing any electronic movement in the ocean. The sonar team, to a man, was watching, waiting for the distinctive engine lines of the Russian-built Kilo with its trademark five-bladed prop.

The bells of the watch came and went. The day finally gave way to night, and by now the Kilo was sixty-five miles closer. In waters this deep, there is no appreciable advantage to any ship, because it is not possible to "back up" against a "noisy" landmass and force your quarry to aim its sonars into the most confusing area. Out here, where the ocean is vast and empty, bereft of any land, all's fair. The hunter must stay quiet, and the hunted is supposed to stay even quieter, though in the case of Captain Abad this was impossible.

Generally speaking, a U.S. Navy underwater boat has it all over any perceived opponent, but the Kilo was only weeks out of refit, and in recent years the Russians had done a great deal of catching up.

Cheyenne, with that towed array, would certainly locate the Kilo first, but there was an excellent chance the Kilo would pick up the Americans in the end. Thereafter, it was a matter of Captain Abad holding his nerve and hoping to hell the U.S. commanding officer did not feel especially trigger-happy.

A bookmaker would almost certainly have made the Americans favorite to do anything they liked. And that would be logical, *if* it was just any old Kilo sliding through the water. But this particular Kilo was state-of-the-art, and there was a chance that some U.S. advantage might have been eliminated in the secretive laboratories of St. Petersburg's Admiralty Yards.

The watch changed at midnight. But no one left the sonar room. Everyone knew the Kilo must be approaching. Her course was plainly direct to the Gibraltar Strait, and, so far as the American navigators were concerned, she was already late.

The satellite pictures had recorded her leaving the coast of Lebanon, and she'd been snorkeling all the way at a steady twelve knots. In the hot still of this Mediterranean night, the Kilo kept going, oblivious of the presence of USS *Cheyenne*. Captain Abad was confident out here in the dark, in deep lonely waters, but he was instinctively concerned about the seascape further west in the busy shipping lanes which lead into, and out of, the Atlantic Ocean.

At 0034, still at periscope depth, with the air-intake mast up and the big diesel generators, deep within the submarine, running smoothly, the Kilo was picked up by the *Cheyenne* twenty miles away.

Chief Petty Officer Skip Gowans said quietly, "I might have something right here, just a faint rise in the level. It could be a rain shower, swishing on the surface—but I thought it was something . . . arrived kinda sudden . . . give me a few minutes."

Commander Redford was standing right at his shoulder. No one spoke, and the chief did not say anything more for at least four minutes. Then he said, "I have a definite rise in the level. I don't think it's weather—I'm getting something."

Again there was silence. Chief Gowans was a study in concentration. The entire operations center was hanging on his decision, and at 0044 he gave it: "Captain—sonar . . . I have faint engine lines coming up on the array. Relative eight-nine. Lines fit the sample, sir."

Commander Redford moved nearer to the "waterfall" screen, which now showed definite engine lines. The computer had already compared them with the Kilo engine sample built into the system.

Chief Gowans muttered, "They fit, sir. No doubt."

Hank Redford snapped, "Gimme the range."

"Not close, sir. I'm thinking first convergence. And the bearing hasn't moved. I'd say she's coming dead toward us. In my opinion, she's snorkeling right now. Those Russian Kilos are usually very quiet, but this guy's making one hell of a racket."

"We don't have orders to sink her," said the CO. "So long as she's coming straight at us, we'll hold this course and remain below ten knots."

"Sir," said Chief Gowans, "the solution looks good, she's still out to the east, maybe twenty miles, and still coming our way. She's not cavitating, which means she's making under nine knots."

Back in the Kilo, Captain Abad's team did not pick up the *Cheyenne*. He was now running close to the coast of Algiers, and he told himself for the umpteenth time on this journey that the stealth of the Kilo was always his ally. And he could, if necessary, vanish long before he was cornered. They kept running west-sou'west until dawn, making fifteen knots at periscope depth.

In *Cheyenne*'s ops room, the engine lines of the Kilo never vanished from the screens. But as her speed increased and the two boats closed to within ten miles of each other, the Americans altered course to one-nine-zero, steering almost due south to gain close contact. This was the most one-sided game of cat-and-mouse. Neither CO had orders to shoot, but the Americans essentially had the Kilo on toast.

1500 Saturday 7 July
County Tipperary, Ireland

Shakira Rashood made a leisurely journey across Ireland, driving out of Dublin and heading south across County Kildare and then on down through County Loais. She brought with her an ordnance map that marked the Coolmore Stud close to the little village of Fethard. So far as she could see, the nearest sizable town was Cashel.

She was not planning to buy a racehorse, but like many Arabs she had an inbuilt affinity with the thoroughbred, and she knew that most of the world's high-mettled racers traced their ancestry back to the desert sands of her forefathers. There was only one famous Arab horse of whom she had heard, and that was the Darley Arabian. And she wondered whether any of his descendants had ended up at Coolmore, which Michael O'Donnell had pronounced the greatest stud farm on earth.

She was not of course to know that every single flat-racing stallion on the Coolmore roster traced back to the Darley Arabian, through his direct descendant Eclipse. And she wished her husband had been with her, because he, somewhat surprisingly for a wanted terrorist hitman, was quite knowledgeable on the subject. General Rashood's own father, Iranian-born but London-domiciled, was a horse breeder of some note, having very nearly won the Ascot Gold Cup a few years back.

Shakira and Ravi often walked through Damascus to pick up the English newspapers, and she was accustomed to seeing him turn to the racing pages for the results, cards, and reports. He frequently said he missed going racing in England with his father, and that one day, if he could ever return, he would like to own a couple of decent runners. They both knew this was a distinctly unlikely possibility, mass murderers being generally discouraged from attending British and Irish racecourses.

Shakira had, of course, never even seen a thoroughbred in action, but it was a curious piece of unfulfilled ambition. She liked racehorses, liked being told about them, although it had been impossible for her to display anything but the most profound ignorance in the presence of Michael O'Donnell.

And now she was in the heartland of the thoroughbred, County Tipperary, where the great ones had either been born, been trained, or ended their days as stallions and broodmares. She stopped at the newspaper shop in Cashel and bought a small local history of the thoroughbred industry in and around the town.

The names were strange to her, the Derby winners, Nijinsky, Sir Ivor, Roberto, The Minstrel, Galileo, the world-famous sires, Sadlers Wells, Caerleon, Be My Guest, Danehill, Giant's Causeway. But the names rang with poetry, seeming to echo through the Golden Vale of Tipperary where she now stood.

Shakira signaled for her driver to park the car in a long drive in front of the hotel where her guidebook had suggested she stay. It was a grand pink-bricked eighteenth-century building, now converted into the Cashel Palace Hotel, a mecca for visiting horsemen from all over the world. There had been a mass exodus north from the town for Irish Derby weekend, and it was no trouble booking a single room for a few days. She just checked in, using a hitherto unused American Express card, issued to a British citizen, Margaret Adams. No one even asked to see her passport.

She took her suitcase up to her room, declining assistance from the doorman. She unpacked carefully, hung a few things in the gigantic old polished wardrobe, and stuffed her essentials into her regular leather handbag: forged passports, credit cards, wallet, several thousand euros in cash, her forged British driver's license with Margaret's address in Warwickshire, and her driving gloves.

She had one stop to make at the fishing tackle shop she had noticed in the main street. Shakira felt very vulnerable when she was unarmed, as she had been for several days, ever since she had left her principal weapon jutting out of Matt Barker's chest.

And now she went into the store and spent a few minutes looking at the fishermen's knife selection. Finally she chose one with a long straight blade with a serrated edge and leather-gripped handle. She asked the assistant to gift-wrap it, as it was a present for her younger brother.

Shakira did not for one moment expect to use the knife in any form of combat, but neither had she anticipated using her Syrian dagger. She very definitely felt a lot better for having the knife, and she ripped the paper off as soon as she exited the shop, tossed it in a trashcan, and placed the knife in her bag.

Thus rearmed, she climbed back into the car and asked her driver to take her out along the road to Fethard. She had no plans to visit any particular place. She just wanted to see the land where these amazing horses were raised. So far, the cool green landscape of southern Ireland had not reminded her even remotely of her desert homeland, where the Darley Arabian had once lived.

They drove east along the country road amid the endless green of the Irish pastures on either side of the road. In the distance, she could see mares and foals in lush paddocks, but none of them were close to the road.

She remembered that Michael O'Donnell had mentioned an enormous sum of money for his filly foal from Easter Rebel's dam, and imagined the security on these baby racehorses must be intensive. It did not seem possible that she could ever get close to them, and before long she suggested they turn around and return to the Cashel Palace.

When they arrived, Shakira said good-bye to her driver, who was returning to Dublin and promised he would have a local man at the hotel in the morning to transport her around the southwest of Ireland. No, he did not require payment. She could settle next week when he again came south to bring her back to Dublin.

This was not the first time she had really liked the Irish, and once more she made a mental note to forbid Ravi from killing any of them. So far as she was concerned, the Great Satan's European cohorts ended in England. The Irish were not to be included in any future attacks. They just weren't the kind of people to have anything to do with terrorists.

Back in her room, Shakira drew back the curtains on the tall windows for the first time, and she was utterly amazed at the sight that awaited her: high on a hill, directly above her room, were the stark ruins of the ancient Irish cathedral high on the Rock of Cashel, for seven centuries the seat of the Irish kings, St. Patrick's Rock. Great limestone walls, built in the twelfth century, were still standing. There were windows and a historic round tower. A Celtic high cross jutted into the evening sky, and all around the land fell away.

"The view must be breathtaking," she thought, flicking the pages of her local guidebook. "Tomorrow I will go and stand up there."

Shakira dined alone in her room, and later, restless for someone to talk to, she made her way down the wide staircase and asked the front desk if there was a coffee shop in the hotel. "No, we've no such thing," replied the desk clerk. "But if you go down those stone steps over there, you'll find the nicest bar you ever saw. Tell Dennis I said he's to make you an Irish coffee."

Shakira did exactly as she was told, and Dennis the barman delivered her an Irish coffee, its tall head of double cream obscuring a mighty measure of Jameson's finest whiskey. The bar was quite busy, and the former Carla Martin chose a corner seat with a small table and an empty chair next to hers.

She had no idea that she was sipping such a strong alcoholic drink, but it tasted so good, she never gave it a thought. After twenty minutes, she noticed a heavyset, rustic-looking local, aged around fifty, come down the stairs and order a pint of Guinness. Slightly to her surprise, he came and sat beside her, and she did not notice the look of concern on the barman's face.

The newcomer turned to her and said, "Good evenin' to yer, ma'am. I'm Pat Slater."

And almost before Shakira had nodded a greeting, Dennis came over and said quietly, "Now Patrick, this lady is staying in the hotel. And don't you be boring her to death with yer tales of bygone days."

Mr. Slater smiled and said he had no intention of boring anyone, and besides, he'd only come in for the one. He had a mare due to foal that night, and he wouldn't be far away from the barn now, would he?

Dennis retreated, and over the next ten minutes Pat Slater just asked politely what Shakira was doing in Ireland and how long was she staying.

But, unknowingly being bombarded with a pack of lies, he was good to his word and got up to leave. Just before he climbed the old familiar stairs, he leaned over and muttered to Shakira, "I wasn't always just a stockman. I used to have a very important career."

And with that he was gone. It was almost 9:30 P.M. now, and the bar was emptying out as residents left and went into the dining room. The place would get a "second wind" at around eleven o'clock, but in the meantime Shakira was almost alone.

She finished her Irish coffee and walked up to the bar to speak to Dennis. "That man told me he used to have an important career," she said, as always unable to resist getting right to the bottom of any unclear information.

And Dennis raised his eyebrows and said, "Miss Carson, that man is, secretly, a former freedom fighter with the Irish Republican Army, the fellers who shot and bombed the English into submission over Northern Ireland.

"Trouble is, he never got over it. Spends his entire life yearning for the good old days when he and a few others were out there causing mayhem. Most of 'em found it very hard to fall back into peaceful civilian life after those years when they were on the run, plotting and planning and killing. That kind of life was like a drug to some of 'em, and Pat Slater is one."

Shakira looked bemused. "Were these Irish Republican men terrorists, or did they fight like a national armed force?"

"No, they were never like that. They attacked the British along the borders, blew up train stations, and sometimes streets. They wore the badge of terrorists proudly, and said they were fighting a war to drive the British out of Ireland forever."

"And did they succeed?"

"As far as anyone could ever succeed in Northern Ireland, I suppose. But up there, the majority of the population wants to keep their British ties."

"But did the bombing and killing get results?" Shakira persisted.

"Oh, yes. No doubt about that. In the end, the Brits were really fed up with it, but so were the people of Northern Ireland. Everyone just grew tired of an endless conflict."

"Was it like the Muslim *Jihad?*"

"In some ways it was, but not on so large a scale. The IRA was a much smaller force, even though they had a few pretty ambitious targets. There was nothing like the Twin Towers in New York."

"Do you think their attacks proved that a great and worthwhile cause can be achieved by a sustained campaign of terror?"

"In a way, they did. The British government would never have given in so quickly if they hadn't been afraid of more bombs in London."

"Then it was good news for all terrorists," laughed Shakira.

"It wasn't that good," said Dennis. "Did you ever see a man so gloomy as Pat Slater? He's like all the rest. The glory for them was in the chase, not the objective . . . how about another Irish coffee? I'll have one with you before the late rush hour starts."

Shakira nodded cheerfully, and said, "I used to work behind a bar once, back in the USA."

CHAPTER *8*

0700 Monday 9 July
Western Mediterranean

Captain Abad's sonar room had finally located the U.S. submarine *Cheyenne,* currently steaming slowly on a southerly course, eight miles to the northwest. The total absence of any kind of aggressive move from the Americans, or even an increase in speed, gave him confidence that the Iranian Kilo was in no immediate danger.

Thus he made a decision to press on regardless, keeping up his speed and holding his course to the Strait of Gibraltar.

Cheyenne's sonar room kept watching. "She's headed straight to Gibraltar," said the CO.

"No doubt," responded the chief. "We never had one shred of intel that said anything about her destination. But this is obvious. She'll pass about seven thousand yards to starboard at her current speed, one hour from now."

"Keep tracking her."

"Aye, sir."

Back in the Kilo, Mohammed Abad kept the air intake raised and ordered the submarine to all-ahead, maximum speed. And the Kilo once more accelerated forward, the two masts leaving a slashing white wake above a turmoil of water being churned up by that big Russian five-bladed propeller only forty-five feet below the surface.

The wide ultrasensitive sweep of *Cheyenne*'s radar picked up the accelerating masts in a heartbeat. The Kilo was plainly making a run for it.

Commander Redford had little choice but to follow, since his orders were very definitely to stay in contact but also to stay in the Med. So the *Cheyenne* set off, making a southerly course at around twenty knots.

The Kilo out in front, moving fast, was still at periscope depth and making a major racket just below the surface of the water. The Americans could not fail to track her with consummate ease.

At 0900, high above, the American satellite photographed her wake, ensuring that U.S. military surveillance knew precisely where the Iranian submarine was located.

By 1115 that morning, the Kilo was a hundred miles southwest of Alicante, off Spain's Costa Blanca. To the south was the long hot coastline of Morocco. Progress was still fast, and no one had opened fire on her. By dark, the Kilo had progressed over a hundred miles, her speed was steady, and General Rashood, who was no stranger to submarines, estimated that he was more or less on time. He needed to be through the Gibraltar Strait tomorrow, Tuesday, and that could definitely happen at this speed.

His planned landing on the coast of southern Ireland on July 14 or 15 was still on, and suddenly the *Cheyenne* seemed to be losing interest, slipping back several miles astern.

At midnight, Monday, July 9, Captain Abad ordered an increase in speed as they headed directly to the Strait. She was now driving through the water at seventeen knots. And her CO would make several of these one-hour bursts, despite the stress it put on the battery.

1600 Tuesday 10 July
West Cork, Ireland

Shakira Rashood had left the Cashel Palace Hotel on Monday morning and asked her driver to take her to the wondrous Atlantic coastline of West Cork, upon which, sometime this week, her husband would land. The journey was a little over a hundred miles, and she had checked into a small hotel in the fishing village of Schull on the shores of Roaring Water Bay. She sent the chauffeur back to Cashel with instructions to collect her in Schull on Thursday afternoon.

Today she had taken a local taxi all the way down the long undulating road to the end of the Mizen Head Peninsula. And from there on this clear summer day she could see the distant lighthouse on the Fastnet Rock. The sea was very blue out here, and the deep Atlantic looked friendly, with two or three yachts sailing close-hauled into the soft on-shore breeze.

Shakira had grown to love Ireland in the short time of her stay. She liked the people and was truly astonished at the breathtaking beauty of the countryside. For someone brought up among the sands of the desert, the browns and the stony reds of the Arab landscape, she found Ireland, with its forty shades of green, to be almost beyond her imagination.

She felt as if she was standing in a giant oil painting on the cliff top of Mizen Head. Behind her stretched the switchback of hills that rise and fall among tiny stone-ringed fields that had been divided and divided again, down the centuries, as families had split, shared, and migrated, in the endless surge of Ireland's greatest export, her people.

All around her, she had sensed the history, the ancient myths, and the legends. Every time she spoke to anyone at any length, there was a story, because the past is never far away for the Irish. The entire landscape is dotted with reminders, the stone ring forts, the huge stone graves, the tall carved religious stones dating from 2000 B.C., the round towers, and the high crosses.

During her journey south from Dublin, Shakira had stopped whenever she saw something to which she could get close. On the great Rock of Cashel beyond her hotel room, she had spent three hours just wandering around the ancient fortifications, the roofless abbey, and the finest twelfth-century chapel in Ireland. She'd stopped on the road to gaze at ruins, checking her guidebook, perhaps because this sense of times long past was in her blood, this curiosity, this desire to imagine.

No race of people is more devoted than the Arabs to myth and history and far-lost stories of valor and achievement. Except perhaps the Irish. Nonetheless, Shakira Rashood was exceptional. If she had not been an Islamic terrorist, she might perhaps have been a scholar.

She climbed back into her taxi and told the driver to go slowly all along the road to Barleycove and Goleen. Because from those high cliffs she could see way down to the harbor of Crookhaven, the spot chosen by the

Hamas High Command, into which they would insert General Rashood after his long journey in the submarine.

Slowly they made their way back along the road to the West End Hotel in Schull, where she took a long bath and then walked downstairs into the bar for a glass of fruit juice before dinner. And as always, there was another legend being related, of how Bonzo, a local fisherman, had once drunk sixteen pints of draught Guinness in an hour and twelve minutes, which was considered to be an Irish free-standing record.

Shakira did not consider it to be in the same category as the legend of Brian Boru, who had stormed and captured the Rock of Cashel in the tenth century. But the bards of the Cashel Palace downstairs bar, on the subject of the great Irish king, were precisely the same as the seamen of Schull speaking of Bonzo. They all recounted the mighty deeds in the same reverential tones: all of them as if these pinnacles of Irish history had taken place yesterday.

Shakira was charmed by all of it, and wondered if it could ever be possible for her and Ravi one day to live here in peace and seclusion, half a world away from the flaming hatreds and death that would never leave the lands of her forefathers. But in her heart she knew that she and Ravi had gone too far, that they were both wanted in too many places, that there were too many people who would shoot them both on sight. The steely-eyed hitmen of the Mossad and the CIA would surely offer neither of them one shred of mercy.

0200 Wednesday 11 July
East of Gibraltar

Right above the Kilo, on the surface of the most westerly reaches of the Mediterranean Sea, the rain was lashing down. This was one of those great summer squalls known in the area as a levanter. Captain Abad welcomed it with all of his heart: the belting rain was sweeping across the dark water, giving him noise cover while the submarine ran at periscope depth, snorkeling. Despite the absence of danger, he still had those ingrained submariner's instincts—*the quieter we run, the better I like it.*

The majestic Rock of Gibraltar, looming above the narrow strait that separates Europe from Africa, was only about five miles to the west. The sea-lanes were quiet at this time of night, and it was no problem to keep the air-intake mast raised for the generators.

The Kilo was still running fast and making a mighty wake as she came powering through the water. Every twenty minutes, Captain Abad took a short all-around look at the surface picture and could see only a single oil tanker and a freighter, a big container ship, under the French tricolor, probably headed for the port of Marseilles.

There were, so far as he could see, no warships in the vicinity. And his radar sweep was detecting scarcely anything. The sea was surprisingly calm. And the huge generators purred with life, sending a mild shudder through the entire ship.

Captain Abad turned to General Rashood and told him first the good news, that no one was tracking them. And then the bad news, which was they would not arrive in southern Ireland until the small hours of Monday morning, July 16. "And that's only if we get a good fast run up the Atlantic," he added.

Ravi, who had been somewhat within himself for the past couple of days, nodded distractedly, as well he might. The terrorist commander had a lot on his mind, not least that sudden, unexpected signal from Shakira on July 3, the one that clearly indicated something had gone wrong—*evacuating immediately.*

For all he knew, his wife was under arrest. Anything could have happened. He did not even know what country she was in. He just hoped to hell she had made it to Ireland, that she would somehow be waiting for him in Dublin. Right now he could only be patient, trapped in this submarine, running slightly late but still more or less within his original schedule.

And Shakira was not his only problem. Because ahead of him was a journey to England, the country where he was still, probably, among the most wanted men, both by the police and the military. Wanted for three murders, that is, and the Brits did not know the half of it. The United Kingdom was by far the most dangerous place for Ravi, so many people knew him from the days, a lifetime ago, when he had been an SAS commander, a leader in Britain's most elite fighting force, Major Ray Kerman.

Encapsulated here, in this Iranian submarine, Ravi suddenly felt, for perhaps the first time, a pang of nostalgia, a mixed feeling of wistfulness, possibly even regret. He always tried to dispel memories of the old life, the camaraderie, the respect an SAS officer enjoys, and the lifelong friendships from his schooldays at Harrow. But he had rendered himself an outcast, estranged from his parents, estranged from the military, estranged from the country that had nurtured him.

He had "gone over the wall" in a moment of rash heroism, horrified by the deprivations being foisted upon the Palestinian people. But, in a sense, it had all been worthwhile. Terrorism had made him a wealthy man, but the greatest prize of all had been Shakira.

And now, in a sense, they were going once more into battle together, in the minefield that England would always be for him. But first they had to get into the country, through one of the most demanding security systems in the world. The mere thought of England sent a thousand more thoughts, all of them worries, charging through his mind—the passports, the immigration officers, the customs officials, the patrolling police in every airport and ferry terminal, the fear of recognition, and, perhaps above all, the target.

Admiral Morgan, he knew, would have ironclad security all around him; not as tight as in America, but sufficiently tight to allow Ravi only one shot, from a rifle not yet made. Beyond that was the gargantuan problem of getting away. Ravi understood with great clarity that he would need every possible moment in England to plan his strategy. He also knew that one mistake would almost certainly cost him his life. And then what would happen to Shakira? Of course, they might get her too, but that was more than he could bear even to think about.

He walked out of the control area and stood alone for a moment. "Sweet Jesus, keep her safe," he whispered, entirely forgetting about Allah and the Prophet. Ravi's prayer was to the God he had worshiped long ago at Harrow School.

The Kilo snorkeled in peace, right through the dawn that painted the eastern sky, far astern, the color of spent fire. At 1230, after a solid five hours running and charging the battery, Captain Abad ordered the generators to cease and the submarine to go deep, as they entered the Gibraltar Strait.

The channel is fourteen miles wide here, between the Two Pillars of Hercules, the Rock of Gibraltar to the north, and Mount Hacho on the Moroccan coast to the south. The Strait then runs for thirty-six miles west, narrowing to only eight miles, before widening once more and washing into the Atlantic.

On either side, the land is high—the Atlas Mountains of North Africa and the high plateau of Spain. You might consider this a colossal piece of irrelevance for a submarine journey. But that would be a misjudgment. From the high pinnacles of the Atlas to the Spanish plateau, the geological contours run underwater to form one gigantic continuous arc. Which is why the Gibraltar Strait is quite extraordinarily deep, *averaging* 1,200 feet.

For Captain Abad, this was hugely significant because it meant his ship could dive to six hundred feet and move quietly on her way, far from the prying eyes of the heavily fortified British naval base, which traditionally scours these waters night and day for signs of a rogue submarine—or anything else that might consider stepping out of line.

The Brits, of course, have irrevocable links with Gibraltar and, with their American allies, quietly control the only entrance to the Mediterranean from the Atlantic. Spain has never been very thrilled with this incontrovertible truth and has several times stamped its Iberian boot with anger. In fact, none of the Mediterranean countries—France, Italy, Greece, and the North African group—are crazy about this arrangement.

But the two heavyweights at the Atlantic entrance have never been inclined to listen to anything. Except for submarines. But there was a smile on the face of Captain Abad as he ordered the only soundless creature in the sea to go deep . . . *bow down ten—make your speed five, steer course two-seven-zero.*

Slowly the Kilo ran through the Strait, passing deep beneath the ferryboat from Gibraltar to Tangier and then accelerating steadily through the final miles, until the seaway widened to twenty-seven miles between Cape Trafalgar and Cape Spartel to the south. The Atlantic Ocean lies beyond that point on the navigator's chart.

Immediately after they crossed that unseen line on the ocean's surface, Captain Abad ordered a course change, forty degrees to three-one-zero. Ahead of them was a dead-straight 180-mile run across the Gulf of Cádiz to the southwestern tip of Portugal, Cape St. Vincent, and then north up the Atlantic to Ireland.

Ravi enjoyed spending time with the navigation officer, Lt. Alaam. They had each been born in the eastern Iranian province of Kerman, and the Hamas C-in-C liked to hear stories of the land of his birth. But today, when the hectic journey of the submarine had highlighted his concern over his wife, he felt curiously out of place.

Peering over the shoulder of the Iranian lieutenant, he could see on the computerized chart the two most famous capes on the Iberian Peninsula, each of them the scene of a titanic British naval victory two hundred years ago—Trafalgar, where Admiral Lord Nelson had destroyed the French and the Spanish in 1805, and St. Vincent, where Admiral John Jervis had crushed the huge Spanish fleet eight years earlier. General Rashood felt an instant connection with these names from a schoolboy past. It was an unspoken pride that nobody else in this submarine could possibly understand.

And, for the briefest of moments, he wondered what the hell he could possibly be doing, surrounded by renegade jihadists, on his way to assassinate one of America's most revered naval figures. It was, without question, the most mutinous thought that had ever crossed his mind since he had crossed the line and become a Holy Warrior in the cause of Islam, eight years before.

But, quickly, he pulled himself together, and he thought of Shakira and the merciless way her two very young children had been gunned down by a British Army sergeant in that hellhole of a battle in Hebron. And, of course, he knew there was no going back. Not now. It was too late. Much too late. All he could do was to hope his beautiful wife would be awaiting him in Ireland. Because, if she was not there, he now believed there was nothing left for him. Not in this life. Except for blood, sorrow, death, and tears, and a cause he believed might not be won.

They reached Cape St. Vincent at 1900 hours and made another turn to the north, heading out into deep Atlantic water, with three thousand feet below the keel. They ran at twelve knots now, at PD, which meant they would cover close to three hundred miles each day. It was Wednesday evening, July 11, and Shakira should be looking for Ravi on Monday, at the Great Mosque on the outskirts of Dublin.

It was thus essential that the Hamas military commander reach the shores of Ireland on Monday morning, because he would still be two hundred miles from Dublin. And he needed to make that journey unobtrusively, attracting no attention, revealing absolutely nothing about himself, leaving no imprint on anyone's memory.

One of the main drawbacks in being a terrorist was the necessity to eliminate your enemy completely. No trace could ever be left; no one could still be walking around with knowledge of you, however slight. Which was why, broadly, Matt Barker had perished.

Ravi understood his own situation as well as Shakira had understood hers. If, during his forthcoming journey across the Emerald Isle, any Irishman tried to get too close, or was too persistent, then Ravi would have no choice. The stakes were too high, the risks too great. It was costing $100,000 just to get him to West Cork. No one must interfere with his mission, however well-meaning.

And again, in this mood of self-examination, General Rashood wondered about his wife. Just what had gone wrong? And where was she? She had not tried to make contact again, but how could she? There was no cell-phone reception deep under the sea. Maybe she had tried. Maybe Shakira had cried out for help. Help that he could not provide. For all he knew, she could be in Guantánamo Bay, being interrogated by the servants of that evil bastard Admiral Morgan.

This particular thought sent that old familiar ramrod of steely resolve up his spine. If Shakira was in Cuba, he would make sure she was the last person Morgan ever sent there. And then, somehow, he and his warriors would get her out. "Can't this thing go any faster?" he asked Captain Abad.

"Sorry, General. This is top speed. We must be patient. The worst part is over."

1100 Thursday 12 July
National Security Agency

Lt. Commander Ramshawe called Detective Joe Segel down in Brockhurst every day. And both of them were growing increasingly depressed. The detective was heartily sick of chasing the impossible shadow of Carla Martin, and Jimmy was growing more and more concerned for the safety of Arnold Morgan.

He had alerted associates at the FBI and the CIA that the admiral would need more security during his trip to England. He had consulted with the Secret Service agents at the White House and requested extra vigilance at British ports of entry through which a would-be assassin might pass.

Jimmy had even had the FBI search through the airport records in Washington, Philadelphia, New York, and Boston for any passenger who had bought an expensive one-way transatlantic ticket on the night of the murder—either to London, Paris, or any of the big European terminals: Amsterdam, Bonn, Hamburg, Madrid, Rome, Milan, or Geneva. Nothing popped up.

Neither Jimmy nor the FBI gave one thought to Dublin, simply because it's not a big enough onward-journey airport. London probably has twenty international flights going anywhere you could name, anywhere in the world, to Dublin's one. Same with Paris and the rest. One call to Aer Lingus would almost certainly have revealed that last Tuesday morning, a woman named Maureen Carson had turned up at the airport and paid more than six thousand dollars with her American Express card to travel on the 10:30 A.M. flight to Dublin.

Such passengers are quite rare, people with no bookings or reservations, only going one way, plainly acting on a spur-of-the-moment decision. Even a bank robber would have found time for preliminary arrangements. Murder can of course be slightly less predictable.

And Carla had slipped through the net, with a lot of savvy and a bit of luck. Jimmy, armed with a lot of facts, but not enough certain knowledge, was unable to close in. There were too many gaps, especially the one in Dublin airport.

The other problem was that no one was very impressed with Jimmy's diagnosis of the situation. Like the admiral himself, it seemed no one could take seriously the vanishing barmaid as some kind of latter-day Mata Hari. Everyone was polite. But no one was convinced of the danger posed by the lady who had journeyed to Brockhurst with one mission in mind.

What really got to Jimmy was the fact that this Carla Martin had plainly succeeded in her mission. In a very few short days, she had moved in, befriended Arnold's mother-in-law, and found, almost to the hour, the time of their departure, their destination, and their hotel. The Australian lieutenant commander, on this unproductive morning, was mildly surprised that Carla, or whoever the hell she was, had not managed to come up with the room number or Arnie's breakfast order—*so some fucking terrorist can get in there and poison the bloody eggs and bacon.*

Those heavily connected facts and thoughts were quite sufficient for Jimmy's antennae to start vibrating. But the clincher was the antiseptic precision of "Carla's" departure. She had carefully erased every detail, sneaked around taking things out of the hotel files, signed for her apartment under a different name, handed over thousands of dollars. And left nothing behind. She had had no car, but there was obviously a 24-hour chauffeur to transport her everywhere: a chauffeur for whom someone was paying, with cash that had not come out of a barmaid's wages . . . *not to mention the bloody dagger, the one with "Syria" carved on the blade in Arabic.*

Jimmy's montage of facts sounded fine when he had them all together. It was simply one of those conundrums that did not play well to a third party. Too many little things, too much lack of one big overwhelming fact that could not be disputed. On the phone Jimmy could sense people growing more bored by the minute, thinking silently, "Shut up, Jim, the admiral's going to be fine. None of this adds up to an assassination attempt on Admiral Morgan."

Lt. Commander James Ramshawe knew better. Or at least he thought he did. He checked the airline schedules to London from Washington on Monday night, July 30. Arnie and Kathy would travel first-class on a U.S. airline, the trip arranged by the White House travel department. That would almost certainly be American Airlines, departing 2115, arriving Heathrow around 0830. They'd be at the Ritz by 1015 on Tuesday morning. In Jimmy's mind, thanks to "Carla," a Middle Eastern terrorist organization knew all that as well as he did.

He'd already had the Secret Service call the London embassy to ensure that the admiral always traveled in a bulletproof car. He'd asked for extra agents, he'd asked the FBI to alert Scotland Yard that there might be an attempt on Arnie's life, he'd had the CIA check in with the British secret services MI-5 and MI-6, just to keep everyone on high alert.

But he was still worried. He needed a bodyguard for Arnold Morgan, an experienced operator who would treat the subject as hair-trigger dangerous, as Jimmy himself did. And he did not know such a man, not one who would be available to drop everything and go to London with Arnie and Kathy. Everyone was so stretched these days, and the military would not have sufficient personnel to help out. Everyone was too busy chasing the goddamned insurgents in Iraq, Iran, or Afghanistan.

But he would not give up. He realized, alone above all other high-placed officials in government circles, that "Carla" had done her work. That something was going to happen.

2300 Friday 13 July
Tipperary, Ireland

Shakira was back in the Cashel Palace Hotel. She'd had a farewell Irish coffee with Dennis and retired to bed. The maids had drawn the curtains in her room and turned down the bed. But before she climbed between the spotless linen sheets, she drew back the curtains so she could see the illuminated outline of the Rock of Cashel, which was beginning to seem like an old friend.

Like most terrorists, Shakira Rashood slept only fitfully, awakening every two hours, alert for danger, her long fishing knife tucked under the pillow. She liked to see the ramparts of the Rock against the night sky, and she loved to contemplate its age and the centuries it had stood there, rising from a grassy plain, a place of kings and bishops, saints and choristers, Romans and Normans.

For a while she lay there, lost in the kind of peaceful speculation that so often eluded her because of the terrors of her calling. And then her mind moved on, back down to Mizen Head, where she had gazed upon great waters. And she pictured again those mighty acres of the Atlantic, dark now, flecked with whitecaps, nightcaps, far above the black submarine that was speeding through the depths, unseen, bringing her husband home to her.

Home? Could there ever be a home, like those of other people? Even the poorest of her people had homes, perhaps small, perhaps even squalid, but she and Ravi had nothing. The last home they had in Damascus had been bombed to smithereens by—she believed—the Israeli Mossad.

And it would always be the same. People trying to kill them. She and Ravi trying to survive, trying to live, and love, and do everything they could to destroy the West and all it stood for. All for the Muslim cause, everything for Allah and for the word of the Prophet. They were front-line warriors for the *Jihad*. But would Allah care for them in this life, as well as in the next? Shakira was not so sure about that.

And she turned once more to St. Patrick's Rock, wondering how many people down all the years had turned to the great patron saint of Ireland

and looked to him for guidance and protection, just as she and Ravi turned to Allah. And were the beliefs of those Irish people any less powerful than her own? She could not answer that, but she fervently wished that she did not need to leave this place tomorrow. And that she and Ravi could shelter here forever, in the shadow of St. Patrick, beneath the Rock.

But tomorrow she was leaving Cashel. Her driver was meeting her at nine in the morning, and she would return to Dublin. But not to the Shelbourne Hotel. She must move on, and she was booked into the Merrion, right around the corner from the Shelbourne, perhaps the top hotel in Dublin, an expensive little palace, exquisitely converted from five Georgian houses, one of which had been the birthplace of the Duke of Wellington, the Irishman who destroyed Napoleon at Waterloo.

She was leaving Cashel because she believed her place was in Dublin where Ravi was coming to find her. Perhaps he would be early; and if he was, she wanted to be with her cell phone in close proximity to their meeting point. When he did arrive, she guessed they would not linger. They would move directly to England, although she did not know how. And from there to the assassination of the man in the three newspaper cuttings she had seen in Gaza, her friend Emily's son-in-law.

It all seemed a long time ago. Irrationally she wondered how the ridiculous Charlie was getting along without her. That stupid, stupid Matt Barker. She would have liked to spend longer in Virginia, because she really liked Emily. Brockhurst had been another nice peaceful place, and it seemed the world was full of them. But not for her and Ravi, for whom every place was a battleground.

She drifted off to sleep, and the following morning she had a light breakfast in her room, packed her very few possessions, and said goodbye to St. Patrick's Rock. Her driver was waiting, and they headed northeast, back to the city. And once more Shakira sat back and admired the deep green landscape of Ireland and wondered if she would ever pass this way again.

1600 Saturday 14 July
The North Atlantic

The Kilo was still running hard, snorkeling as usual, a little over five hundred miles south of Mizen Head. The journey from the Gulf of Cádiz had been untroubled. If they had been detected by an Atlantic-patrolling U.S. submarine, no one seemed especially interested in these vast Atlantic waters. They never saw a warship, hardly ever saw any traffic except for an oil tanker the size of the Suez Canal, plowing north, laden with enough crude oil to fill the Dead Sea.

They were still making twelve knots average and would require only one more burst of speed before they landed Ravi, somewhere off Crookhaven Harbor. General Rashood's mood of despondency was still upon him. He was desperately worried about Shakira and was half expecting bad news every time they checked the satellite for signals from home base. These were of course unlikely in a "black" operation as secret as this one. And each time there was nothing, Ravi was quietly relieved. If Shakira had been captured or even arrested, he was certain the Hamas High Command would have been informed.

No news, he supposed, was good news, which meant Shakira had made it to Ireland. And thirty hours from now, he expected to join her in that country. Then all he needed to do was make it to Dublin. Ravi and Captain Abad, despite their tensions on board, had become good friends. Mohammed Abad was a dedicated Islamist, a native of the old Iranian medieval capital of Shiraz, south of the Zagros Mountains.

He had trained as a submariner for ten years and was today recognized as the best in the Iranian Navy. Subject to the inevitable regime changes and the ever-possible prospect of war with the West, his position was very strong, and he was widely mentioned as a future admiral. Ravi had not met him before he boarded, but he was deeply impressed with Mohammed's skillful awareness of the U.S. submarine that had been tracking them in the Mediterranean.

Like Ravi, Captain Abad, who was thirty-four years old, had a younger wife, who was, judging by the photographs he showed the Hamas military boss, just as beautiful as Shakira. Well, nearly. Mohammed himself was a tall—six-foot-two—somewhat imposing officer. He tended to speak quietly, and when he did, his staff listened. Mohammed had attended all of the long months of lectures and practical submarine craft in Russia.

He was the most experienced underwater operator in the Iranian Navy, an expert in navigation, hydrology, electronics, mechanics, and weaponry. Upon the slightest problem in the ship, the crew always called on the commanding officer, who understood the workings of his ship better than anyone else.

Mohammed Abad was a member of the new breed of Islamic jihadists, men who were almost as competent as the best of the Americans or the British. They were men who believed in their nation's right to total independence from the West and were quite prepared to fight to get it. Twenty-five years ago, such men had not existed. But the desert nations learned, and spent billions training the best of the best. And now the Middle East was bristling with these young, brilliant commanders, strategists both at sea and on land. There were two of them on Kilo 901.

The eight bells of the watch tolled out the midnight hour. Ravi and Mohammed sat companionably sipping sweet tea in the control room. The submarine captain knew better than to question the general about the forthcoming operation, but he could not miss the importance of the mission, the landing of the most renowned Hamas terrorist leader in a desolate civilian harbor in one of the most remote corners of the British Isles.

Whatever was going on was big. Mohammed understood that. And on this particular evening, as they neared the end of their long journey together, he risked a subtle probe. "Will you be working alone, sir?" he asked.

"I will," replied Ravi. "There is only one task for me, and no one can provide much help. Plus, it's quieter on your own. Less chance of attracting attention."

"Will I be picking you up, sir? I have no orders as yet. But no one's told me to go home."

Ravi smiled. "My exit from Ireland has not yet been established. I just have to see how things play out."

"Well, sir, I'll be here if you need me. And I think you might. Because it's unusual to be this late in the mission with no further instructions. I have a feeling they want me to wait around for your exit."

"I'd be grateful for that, Mohammed. You really know how to drive this thing."

"Give me a bit of deep water and a fully charged battery, and I can make this ship vanish if I have to," replied Mohammed. "And it would be my honor to pick you up and take you home."

"Those words will be a comfort to me in the few difficult days ahead. But I expect to come through it okay."

"Everyone has great faith in you, sir. Whatever it is, you get it done, and I'll be waiting for you."

General Rashood climbed to his feet, and he patted the captain on the shoulder. "You're a good man, Mohammed," he said. "I enjoyed the journey. And now I must get some sleep. Let's pray for calm seas when we reach Ireland."

The Kilo ran on, mostly making twelve knots. Captain Abad made no course change. He just continued running hard, snorkeling along the surface, on a course that would give the southwest coast of England a very wide berth. Right now, they were west of the Bay of Biscay, moving north through the Atlantic, straight up the ten-degree line of longitude, which passes ten miles west of Mizen Head.

Even with England and the west coast of Wales between two and three hundred miles off their starboard beam, Captain Abad was nervous about running into any patrolling Royal Navy submarines. These are deep waters, and all along the rocky shores of Great Britain's west there were, he knew, listening stations, usually operated in conjunction with the Americans.

He also knew that the two major Western sea powers would, by now, be aware that the Kilo had left the *Cheyenne* and was somehow out of their reach. Whether the Americans now knew the Iranian Kilo was heading into British and Irish waters was a difficult point. Captain Abad thought they must, and he also thought they would be much more likely to try to whack him out here than they would in the Med.

Right now Captain Abad did not wish to be detected, and he ordered the Kilo to two hundred feet, hammering his battery at ten knots and counting on the enormous area of the ocean to keep him out of harm's way. They ran all through the night, forced to snorkel every hour. By late afternoon, they were less than two hundred miles off the Irish coast.

As soon as night fell, they contacted the satellite and reported their course and position. There were no signals from home base, so once more Ravi dared to hope that Shakira was safe. Mohammed Abad expected them to run into their insert area sometime after 0400 on Monday, July 16.

General Rashood and the captain dined together for the last time on this journey shortly after 2100. The cooks prepared them Iranian *kebab-e makhsus,* the special kebab made of sliced tenderloin and served on a bed of *polo* rice, with *nun* bread. They drank fruit juice only, and Ravi retired once more to bed for a final rest before the insert.

And while he slept, the water began to grow more shallow as they headed for the hundred-meter line off the southwest Irish coast. The Kilo now ran 150 feet below the surface, and with every mile, the depth gauge recorded the upward slope of the seabed. They came inside the hundred-meter line at 0230, and almost immediately the water was a hundred feet more shallow.

Up ahead, two miles to starboard, was the great jutting crag of the Fastnet Rock lighthouse, guarding Long Island Bay, flashing its warning light every five seconds. Once more Captain Abad came to periscope depth, this time to take a look at one of the world's most famous maritime fixtures, a slashing white light across the water, a light that had been cautioning sailors for centuries.

The Kilo transmitted nothing except passive sonar, and on this clear moonlit night they again went to one hundred feet with the fifty-meter line only three miles ahead. Thereafter, the sea was only 120 feet deep, and the submarine would need to be very careful as she moved in toward Crookhaven. They needed at least ninety feet to stay out of sight, and this was a rocky seabed. Captain Abad would not dream of going too close to the bottom, and he intended to enter the outer roads into Crookhaven at periscope depth, and on tiptoes, slowly making his way forward.

The harbor at Crookhaven in mid-July is apt to be busy with moored yachts, and anyway the Iranian would not dream of making his entrance on the surface. The navigation planners in Gaza had specified that the submarine remain at PD one mile off Streek Head at the eastern end of the harbor, in approximately 120 feet of water. From there, General Rashood would make his own way inshore.

As they made their approach, the ship suddenly became full of activity. They were just a few feet below the surface now, and a small rubber Zodiac with a wooden deck was being prepared. A makeshift davit, which is a kind of small maritime crane, was being assembled. General Rashood had changed into street clothes: a pair of dark gray slacks, a black T-shirt, loafers, and his brown suede jacket.

His leather bag contained all of his documents, credit cards, and cash, thousands of euros and British pounds, a warm Shetland sweater, and driving gloves. His combat knife was tucked into his thick leather belt at the small of his back. The general carried no other weapons.

At twenty minutes after 4 A.M., Captain Abad ordered the Kilo to the surface, and the Iranian submarine came shouldering her way out of the ocean with a rush of dark water, phosphorescence, and spray. Eight crew members immediately climbed out onto the casing and assembled the davit. They hauled the Zodiac up and out into the air, where two crew members completed the inflation process.

By the time this was completed, a black Yamaha engine, fifty horsepower, was hauled out from the hatch and two ship's engineers bolted it onto the Zodiac's transom. Fuel and electric wires were connected, and crew members lowered it over the side into the calm summer sea. Next, they rolled out a net that ran down the casing into the water alongside the Zodiac.

Then General Rashood came onto the deck with the captain, and the two men shook hands. "Allah go with you," said Mohammed Abad.

"Thank you, Captain," said Ravi. And with that, he gripped the net and expertly climbed down into the Zodiac, tossing his bag in before jumping aboard himself. The engine was ticking over, and the crewman who had launched the boat now handed over the helm to Ravi and climbed back up the net.

The Hamas general was alone now, and he looked up ahead; the shape of the narrow land on the south side of the harbor made a dark line beyond the moonlit water. He looked along to the right, to the light on Streek Head, then quietly opened the throttle and began to run west, forward to the coast of County Cork.

And even as he pushed out through the first yards of his journey, the submarine moved gently forward and then slipped beneath the surface, heading back south. Ravi had no idea where she was going.

The night was cool now, and Ravi wished he had worn his sweater rather than stuffing it into his bag. The Zodiac ran easily through these inshore wavelets, but he did not want to wind her up and charge into the harbor at full speed, mostly for fear of awakening one of the yachtsmen and then being noticed.

Instead, he just chugged along, heading in toward Streek Head, making about six knots instead of the twenty this light, fast craft would undoubtedly achieve with the throttle open. For the first time in many days, he had no interest in the depth of the water. The Zodiac drew only about a foot and a half, and, as harbors go, Crookhaven has considerable depth. In the eighteenth century, mail boats from the United States, even clipper ships, had pulled in here. There were even dark mutterings during World War II that German U-boats had anchored here and been refueled, such was the widespread hatred of the English in this part of the world.

No one has ever admitted such a thing, but the rumors have persisted, and many people have stark memories of outbursts by mostly elderly Cork men, banging their fists on the table at the opening notes of "It's a Long Way to Tipperary"—"I'll not have it sung in this house. That's an English marching song."

It all dates back to the first quarter of the twentieth century and the English occupying army, the detested Black and Tans. Just thirty miles from Crookhaven, east along the coast, stands the village of Clonakilty, birthplace of the Big Fella, Michael Collins, commander in chief of the Army of the Irish Free State—the guerrilla warfare patriots who finally drove the English out forever.

Collins and General Rashood had much in common. Both men taught their eager but reckless troops to fight in a more orderly fashion, against an overwhelming force. Both men carried within them a burning hatred of the opposition, and both men took part in spectacular strikes against their enemy. The heartbreaking heroism of Michael Collins and his Cork-men in the Easter Rising in Dublin, 1916, facing English artillery with only pistols, is the very fabric of Irish legend, right up there with Brian Boru at Cashel.

There is still an annual memorial service down here in Cork on the anniversary of his death. There are books, there are films, there are songs.

> *Some they came from London,*
> *And some came from New York,*
> *But the boys that beat the Black and Tans*
> *Were the boys from the County Cork.*

Even now, it is still commonplace along this stretch of coastline to meet a perfectly normal young Irishman who, in the context of the Easter

Rising, will say, "Ah, yes. The boys fought very bravely that day." As if it had been yesterday. Always as if it had been yesterday.

That rugged coastline of West Cork, home to the boys who beat the Black and Tans, was a fitting place for the archterrorist leader to land that night—in the dark, after a long journey, with murder in his heart, the murder of an enemy to his people. The Big Fella would have been very proud of Ravi Rashood.

He rounded Streek Head at 0520. The flashing-light warning of a jagged rock on the right-hand side coming in was still effective. It was not yet daylight. But dawn was breaking in the eastern sky, behind Ravi.

Crookhaven Harbor is a mile long, and up ahead the Hamas general could see more big moored yachts than he would have ideally liked. There must have been twelve, at least, but none carried lights, and there was no sound from the sleeping crews. There was the occasional soft *clatter-clatter-clatter* of a loosely cleated halyard, but the yachts sat quietly on their lines in the light wind.

Ravi throttled back, cutting his speed to dead slow, chugging along with the Yamaha engine just idling behind him. So far as he could tell, there was no one on deck, no one looking, and no one on shore. Ireland is not famous for its early risers at the best of times, and Crookhaven Harbor would never have been confused with any seaport in the USA where, it always seems, everyone is up and shouting the moment dawn breaks, loading, unloading, weighing, casting off, revving up, selling, buying, drinking coffee, laughing, lying, doing deals.

Sleepy West Cork was the perfect spot for a mass murderer to slink into Europe's most westerly outpost. Ravi chugged on, sliding between the yachts, aiming for a little beach at the edge of the village. He knew there would be little shelving of the seabed in this deep harbor. So he just ran directly inshore, cut the engine, and planted the rubber bow of the Zodiac straight onto the sand.

He grabbed the painter, jumped forward onto dry land, and hauled the boat after him. Swiftly, he dropped his bag onto the sand, took off his shoes, socks, pants, T-shirt, and jacket, and stepped into the water in his boxer shorts. It was freezing, and he leaned over the gunwales to restart the motor. He dragged the boat around so that it faced back down the harbor, and then he leaned over some more and grabbed a tiny clock that had been lying on the deck, with several electric wires holding it in place.

Ravi turned the dial to the sixty-second mark, pressed a small button on the side of the clock, and then marginally opened the throttle of the Yamaha. Then he let it go, and the unmanned Zodiac chugged out into deep water, heading east, at around eight knots, down toward Streek Head. Ravi turned away and pulled on his T-shirt. He was only wet to his thighs, and he put on his pants and his socks and shoes.

But before he had time to pull on his jacket, there was a short dull thump in the water, the thud of explosives. And immediately the Zodiac began to sink, the bottom of its hull blown out with an expertly set hunk of TNT. Ravi had attended to this personally, inside the submarine. The hole in the Zodiac's bottom was perfect, four feet across. It took precisely fifteen more seconds to vanish completely, below the fifty-foot-deep outer harbor waters.

It was not yet six o'clock. And Ravi scanned the land around him. There was no sign of life. He looked out to the moored yachts and there was neither sight nor sound of anyone. *Excellent,* he thought, *I've landed in Ireland, and not one person knows I'm here.* But he was wrong. Someone did.

Up on the foredeck of the 54-foot American-built sloop *Yonder* was Bill Stannard, the skipper and helmsman. He had elected to sleep on deck after a four-hour alcoholic binge at the Crookhaven Inn, right next to the sailing club. Right now, in the early hours of the morning, he was very cold, and he was nursing the opening symptoms of a monumental hangover.

Bill, at thirty-eight, had sailed *Yonder* across the Atlantic from Rockport, Maine, with only two crew members. He was meeting the owner, a member of Boston's Cabot family, right here in Crookhaven two days from now. The previous evening's blowout at the inn was his last throw. He would not have another drink for a month, while the owner and guests were aboard. But this did not, of course, diminish his own plight right here on the foredeck, with a head that felt as if it had been hit by a guided missile.

The very slight chug-chug of Ravi's motor had awakened him. It was not so much the noise, but a change in the vibrations in the air. Bill was a former U.S. Navy submariner, a petty officer, stationed at New London, Connecticut. And like all submariners, listening was second nature to him: listening for the slightest change in the regular beat of the submarine's engines, for any alteration in the air pressure, for the merest vibration on the shaft, the distant rattle of a carelessly stowed toolbox.

Ravi's engine altered the air around the sleeping Bill Stannard, and in a flash his eyes opened and his senses came alert. It took a few more seconds for him to work out where he was, and indeed whether he was still genuinely alive. But he raised his throbbing head and looked out over the port bow, where he saw a slow-moving Zodiac making its way across the harbor.

At the helm was a heavyset man wearing a suede jacket, which was unusual in a seagoing community. Suede jackets belonged in London's Knightsbridge, Dublin's Grafton Street, or New York. Out here, seamen wore seamen's clothes, foul-weather jackets, not suede.

Bill was puzzled, but he was also feeling so acutely godawful that he closed his eyes again. And he debated whether he was sufficiently strong to raise himself up, go below for a cup of coffee, and then get into his bunk. He decided not, which was why the Hamas terrorist had seen no movement on the decks of any of the moored yachts in Crookhaven Harbor.

Ravi walked up to the village, holding his leather bag. He passed O'Sullivan's Bar and began to walk toward the road which he knew led to the main coast road, back to Goleen, Schull, Ballydehob at the head of Roaring Water Bay, and, finally, Skibbereen.

That was his direction, and the Hamas planners had made it clear that he should walk to Skibbereen, fourteen miles from Crookhaven, because there he could pick up a bus without attracting too much attention and without wasting much time waiting. They had pinpointed a bus from Schull to Skibbereen, but it ran only twice daily. Service from Skibbereen to the east was far more frequent.

Ravi would walk the fourteen miles at approximately four miles an hour, which was three and half hours. His schedule was to get on the bus and make for Waterford, using bus and train all the way, but not staying on any of them for long periods. He had accepted the fourteen-mile walk, but staring at the long uphill road to the top of the cliffs where a few days ago Shakira had stood was a fairly daunting sight, even for a man as fit and hard-trained as General Rashood had always been.

He set off resolutely, striding alone up the hill. In the half-light of the Irish dawn, he had seen no one, and now in broad daylight he still could see no one. Bill Stannard, far below on the foredeck, had not moved. And nothing stirred as Ravi reached the top of the hill, checked the signpost to Goleen, and set off along the high road, occasionally glancing out to his right, to the spectacular view out to the Fastnet lighthouse, Cape Clear, and Carbery's Hundred Isles.

Somewhere out there, the Iranian Kilo was moving away from the dropoff point. Ravi found himself thinking wistfully of those pleasant breakfast meetings with the captain and the navigation officer, the warm secure feeling, the hot coffee and pastries. Now he did not even have a bottle of water, and he needed to avoid all shops and stores. In rural areas like this, a stranger stands out, is remembered, and should accept human contact only with the greatest reluctance.

The ruggedness of the country was a surprise to him as he left Crookhaven behind. The hills rolled out before him, and the bends in the road came quickly, like a green-lined version of the Yellow Brick Road. Ravi did not think he was in Kansas any more, nor in Damascus, nor Tehran.

This Irish cliff top was like nowhere he had ever been. It could have been two centuries ago, for there was no sign of anything modern. So he just strode along, on his regular 4-mph pace, the same speed Napoleon's army made on flat ground, under full packs, on the march to Moscow.

In West Cork, there is a code about transportation. With no trains, hardly any buses, and, for a hundred years, a shortage of cars among the residents, it was customary to stop for anyone on the road and offer a ride to the nearest village.

City folk were always amused at the way local farmers tipped their hats and smiled, offering an unspoken *Top o' the mornin' to you,* as cars went by. None of this had yet happened to Ravi, until around 0630 when an old Ford truck, driven by Jerry O'Connell and laden with four large milk urns, came rattling around the corner and almost hit Ravi amidships. Jerry hit the brakes, skidded briefly, the milk urns clanged together, and no harm was done.

Jerry was an Irish farmer, fiftyish in years, and the ninth generation of his family to run a dairy farm down here on the Mizen Peninsula. Most of it was not perfect grazing land, but there were pockets of good grass, nurtured by a lot of rain and summer sunshine, with no frost or harsh weather. The warm air above the Gulf Stream washed around here, and men like Jerry knew precisely where cattle would thrive.

They were all from Catholic families, large Catholic families, with upwards of four or five children. Jerry himself was one of seven, and his younger wife, Katy, daughter of the harbormaster, had borne him five children of his own.

For basic survival money, Jerry made this three-mile journey with his fresh milk every day of his life to the dropoff point in Goleen, where the central milk trader picked it up, decanted it into the milk tanker, and drove it to the bottling plant. There would be four big empty milk urns, from yesterday's trip, awaiting him when he arrived in Goleen. There was no hanging around.

The near-miss with General Rashood shook Jerry to his foundations. He stopped the engine and jumped out to face the startled Ravi. "Mother of God, sir," he said. "I've nearly run you over, and sure that would have been a terrible thing to do. Can I offer you a ride somewhere? Because you'll not see a bus along here for nearly three hours. And that would be one hell of a lot of walking."

Ravi smiled. "Think nothing about it," he said, in the easy tones of a former British Army officer. "I was probably walking in the middle of the road anyway."

"Well, that would not have excused me for mowing you down, sir. Not at all. I'm trying to make reparations."

Ravi stared at the cheerful farmer. And Jerry stared back at the well-dressed stranger. He offered his hand, and said, "Jerry O'Connell. . . ."

Ravi accepted it, and offered, "Rupert Shefford . . . and thank you for the offer of a ride. Gladly accepted."

"Which way are you headed?" asked Jerry.

"Skibbereen," replied Ravi.

"Well, I'm not going that far meself, but I'll gladly take you along to Schull. There's a bus at eight o'clock—and wouldn't you admire the view from here, out to the lighthouse. My old grandpa always told me it was the finest view in Europe."

"Was he widely traveled?"

"Hell, no. He only once left here for more than three hours, when he went to Dublin for a family wedding. He was so homesick, they brought him home before the reception."

Ravi chuckled. "Well, I'll be happy to get aboard, Jerry, and thank you very much."

Mr. O'Connell did not seem to be in a hurry. "Ah, jaysus, Rupe," he said. "And what brings you to a tiny outpost like Crookhaven on a fine mornin' like this? You don't look like a sailor to me—and you sure as hell don't look like a farmer . . . did you stay in one of the hotels last night? I've an aunt who works at the Old Castle House."

Ravi's mind raced. "No," he replied. "I was staying down there with friends."

"On land?"

"Yes, on land. Couple of fellas from school."

"Ah, there's nothing like a reunion, Rupe, talking of old times with a couple of jars of Jameson's under your belt."

"We had a good time, Jerry," said Ravi. And even as he spoke, he realized the options were fast running out for the Irish dairy farmer, who pressed on with the conversation regardless.

"Now, who exactly are these fellows from school?" he asked. "My family have lived down here for three hundred years at least, and I'll be sure to know them. And their friend will be my friend. What's their names, Rupe?"

So far as Ravi was concerned, this was becoming lethal. His mind buzzed. Jerry O'Connell already knew far too much. He could identify him; everyone would know in a half-hour that there had been a complete stranger wearing a suede jacket walking along the cliff top at six o'clock in the morning. Lying about his origins. Claiming impossible friendships with people who did not exist.

Ravi could no more come up with names of Crookhaven residents than fly in the air. Whatever he said, the farmer would know he was lying. Ravi distractedly walked over to the farm truck and pretended to see a flat tire on the left rear wheel. Now half-hidden from sight, he delved into his bag and pulled on his leather driving gloves.

"I think you might be in a bit of trouble here, Jerry," he said. "There's no air in this tire."

"That rear one?" replied the Irishman. "Let me have a wee bit of a look."

He walked over to join Ravi just as the Hamas terrorist was reaching for his combat knife. Not to stab or slash, but to hold it the wrong way around, and to use the handle as a blunt instrument.

Ravi bent down to examine the tire, and as he did so, Jerry O'Connell joined him. "That tire looks pretty good to me," he said, uttering the last words he would ever utter. Because Ravi straightened up and struck like a cobra. He slammed the handle of the dagger hard into the area between Jerry's bushy eyebrows, and with the bone well and truly splintered, he dropped the dagger, drew back his hand, and slammed the heel of his palm hard into Jerry's nostrils, driving the bone known as the septum into the brain.

Ravi Rashood killed Jerry O'Connell instantly, with a classic SAS unarmed-combat blow. The Irish farmer was dead before he hit the roadside grass. His heart had stopped before he landed backward on the sparse grazing soil of West Cork. Wrong place, wrong time.

CHAPTER 9

With the body of the late Jerry O'Connell lying slumped at the roadside, General Rashood needed to move very quickly. On the right-hand side, the land fell away down the cliff toward the ocean, and Ravi elected to roll the corpse down there and hope to hell it jammed in the foliage but was hidden from view.

He checked that there was no further traffic from either direction and then dragged the dairy farmer to the edge of the cliff top and tipped him over. Jerry rolled down for about forty feet and came to a halt against a gorse bush that was still in flower. Ravi stared. Jerry was plainly visible.

Leaving his bag on the roadside next to the milk truck, he clambered down the cliff and dislodged Jerry, dragging the body around the gorse and jamming it into the far side. Now it would not be noticed from above, although it was still just visible if someone was really looking. Which, Ravi guessed, they would be before this day was done.

He climbed back up the cliff and considered his getaway options. Walk or ride? And then he boarded the milk truck, revved the engine, put it into gear, and took off, with the urns rattling in the rear. He considered that he was, more or less, safe for another half hour, before someone missed either Jerry or the truck.

There was only one way to drive, and that was straight along to Goleen, through the village, and on to Schull, Ballydehob, and Skibbereen. He kept his driving gloves on and kept going, passing the West End Hotel in Schull, where, unbeknownst to him, his wife had stayed last week.

Only one person in the entire fourteen-mile journey noticed him. Patrick O'Driscoll, the driver of the central milk tanker, was just coming out of Murphy's Breakfast Bar in Goleen when he saw O'Connell's truck with the usual four big urns of milk come fast through the village, drive straight past the dropoff point, and keep going out along the road to Schull. He found that puzzling, but guessed Jerry must have had an errand. *Still,* he thought, *he'd better get back here quickly, or I'll be gone, and then he'll have to drive to Skibbereen.*

Meanwhile, Ravi was approaching the market town of Skibbereen and preparing to ditch Jerry's truck. He slowed down a half mile out of town and turned onto a farm track that led to a house situated beyond a wood. Ravi swung into the trees and drove for about three hundred yards before coming to a halt in a dense clump of birch trees. He switched off the engine, grabbed his bag, and walked on to Skibbereen. It was 7:15 in the morning, and the town was more or less deserted.

Ravi had eaten nothing since the previous evening and had not had anything to drink for many hours. The lure of the Shamrock Café was too strong for him to resist, and he took off his jacket, which he knew made him very distinctive in these rural areas. He stuffed it into his bag and walked inside, where he ordered toast, orange juice, and coffee from a very sharp young Irishman, aged around twenty, who Ravi thought would probably end up mayor of Skibbereen one day. He asked about the bus to Cork City and was told it left daily at 8 A.M. from outside the Eldon Hotel on Main Street.

Ravi sat at a table with his back to the counter. The excesses of killing Jerry and climbing up and down the cliff had made him thirsty, and he hit the orange juice in one go, then ordered another. He was so thirsty, he ignored the terrorist's mantra never to do anything that would cause anyone to notice anything. The kid behind the counter might now remember.

The mistake was small, and Ravi cast it to the back of his mind. He ate his buttered toast and drank his coffee. He paid with his euros and made his way out to the Eldon Hotel for the bus to Cork. The journey was a little over forty miles, but it took General Rashood much longer.

Twice he left the bus, at Clonakilty and again at Inishannon on the Bandon River. Both times he waited for the next one, but at Clonakilty he caught sight of the Michael Collins Centre and spent a half hour standing at the back of a group of tourists, listening to the guide recounting the exploits of Ireland's great twentieth-century patriot.

Eventually he arrived in Cork just before 12:30, and, since he would shortly be wanted for murder, decided to take a circuitous route to Dublin rather than the regular direct rail link from Kent Train Station. He elected for a long train ride along the coast to Waterford, and then to take the three-hour ride on the railroad up to Dublin.

Every step of the way, Ravi did everything possible to cover his tracks. On the train to Waterford, he changed carriages every half hour. He spoke to no one, ate nothing, drank nothing, kept his head buried in a succession of newspapers. People may have seen him, but no one had time to take a lasting impression of him.

He arrived in Waterford late in the afternoon. It was Monday, July 16, the first day Shakira would be looking for him in Dublin, in the precincts of the Mosque at five in the afternoon. He was not going to make it. But the Mosque, in Ravi's mind, was only a "fail-safe." He had Shakira's cell-phone number, but intended to use it only in an emergency, perhaps just once, in the middle of Dublin where it would be untraceable.

And was this ever an emergency. In the following few hours, Ravi was aware, he would become an unknown but hunted man. He did not believe he had left many clues behind, but the Irish Garda would be very angry that a well-liked farmer from West Cork had been brutally murdered two miles from his home. And it would not take them long to deduce that the killer was a stranger.

1400 Same Day
Crookhaven, County Cork

There were two police cars outside Seaview Farm, where Mrs. Mary O'Connell was utterly distraught. Yes, Jerry had left with the milk at the usual time, and no, he had not been seen since. And no, he had never gone missing before.

Down on the waterfront, there were two more police cars, with Garda officers calling at every shop, business, and private home. There weren't many, but everyone who spoke to the Garda that morning knew Jerry, and had not seen him that day.

Detective Superintendent Ray McDwyer, who had taken over this re-latively routine missing-person case, was thoughtful. He sat alone in the police cruiser, waiting for his driver, Officer Joe Carey, who was busy talking to the girl who pumped gasoline at the waterfront garage.

When he returned, Ray suggested the most useful thing they could do would be to check out whether Jerry had indeed arrived at the dropoff point in Goleen with his four cans of milk. He made one quick phone call to the Central Milk Corporation and came up with the name of the tanker driver, Patrick O'Driscoll, who lived in Goleen.

Ten minutes later, they were at his front door, and Patrick quickly explained the unusual events of the early morning: "Sure, I saw Jerry's truck come speeding through the village around seven this morning. He drove straight past the collection point and kept on going."

"Did you see him come back?"

"I did not. And I noticed that his other four cans were still there when I packed up at two o'clock. I collected no milk from Jerry today."

"Was the truck going unusually fast?"

"Well, Jerry always did drive it pretty quickly, but this morning it was going real quick, even for him."

"Did he wave to you, or acknowledge you in any way?"

"He did not. Just went right by."

"Mr. O'Driscoll, I want you to think very carefully before you answer this question. Are you absolutely certain that Jerry was behind the wheel of that truck when you saw it drive straight through Goleen?"

Patrick O'Driscoll hesitated. "Well, I'd thought he was . . . when you see a fella like Jerry every day of your life, you get a kind of set impression. You know. Truck, milk, and Jerry."

Detective Ray McDwyer smiled. He was a well-dressed serious man of around forty and looked like the managing director of a bank. But he was a very good policeman, and there were those who thought he would climb even higher in his chosen profession.

"Patrick," he said, "I want you to swear to God you saw Jerry Driscoll in his truck driving through Goleen this morning."

Patrick was silent for a few moments. And then he said, "I'm trying to get the picture clear in my mind. And I can do no more. But I cannot swear Jerry was behind the wheel. That truck was past me in a flash, and to tell the truth, if I hadn't known it was Jerry's truck, I would not have known who the hell it was."

Detective McDwyer persisted. "Did you see his back, or his coat?"

"I did not. I was focused on the milk cans swaying around in the back. I just thought Jerry was off on some errand and that he'd be back. I didn't mean to mislead you, sir. You can trust me on that."

"I know you didn't," replied Detective Ray McDwyer. "The memory's a funny thing. It can trick you. And I'm grateful for your help."

Officer Joe Carey drove them back to the Crookhaven waterfront, where McDwyer called in the other cars. He asked all seven of his men to pay attention, and he told them, "It looks to me as if Jerry O'Connell was removed from his truck somewhere between the top road and Goleen, a distance of less than three miles.

"I want you to organize a search all along there with as many officers as you can find. This is getting more serious than I first thought. But Jerry's truck was seen driving fast through Goleen at around seven o'clock. You may assume he was not at the wheel."

There were many hours of daylight left, and another dozen policemen were drafted in from outlying districts. And for hour after hour they walked along the high road above the harbor, searching both sides of the road for signs of an injured man—or a dumped body.

At 4:30 P.M., Ray McDwyer himself was walking along the road, staring down in search of any clue as to where the milk truck had stopped. And he stopped at a short, maybe four-foot-long skid mark on the left-hand side of the road. To him, the rubber looked fresh and black, and he told Joe Carey to step up the search along this stretch of road, with six men on the left and eight on the right, along the cliff top.

At 5:25 that afternoon, they found the body of Jerry O'Connell, his septum crushed into his brain.

"Mother of God!" murmured Ray McDwyer.

1600
Atlantic Ocean off Southern Ireland
51.15 North, 08.29 West

The Royal Navy's 7,000-ton *Astute*-class hunter-killer submarine *Artful* was making a steady course southwest at twenty-two knots, bound for the Gibraltar Base. This part of the North Atlantic has been known for centuries as St. George's Channel, named of course by the English, possibly to let the hapless Irish know precisely who owned the great waters and who indeed might be expected to walk on them. *Cry God for Harry, England, and St. George.*

The ship was quiet. There were no U.S. submarines this far south, the French underwater boats were in their huge base at Brest on the Brittany coast, and the Russians right now had nothing beyond the confines of the Baltic. Everyone knew there was nothing around, and nothing was expected.

However, at four minutes past four o'clock, a short, sharp exclamation was uttered by one of the young sonar operators; uttered almost in disbelief, in language not normally associated with the formal idiom of a submarine on patrol.

"What the bloody hell's that?" snapped Able Seaman Jeff Cooper, staring at his screen. "I'm getting something, a rise, could be engine lines. I'd say it's a submarine."

A supervisor walked over and said, "Let me take a look."

AB Cooper just had time to say "Right here, sir," before the contact disappeared. And it did not return any time in the next five minutes. But then it did, and this time it was clearer, perhaps closer. Jeff Cooper coordinated the data quickly.

"Level of certainty they were engine lines?"

"One hundred percent, sir."

"You thought it was a submarine?"

"I'm sure it was."

"Well, that's very peculiar. We have no notification that there is any submarine within two hundred miles of our track. What does the computer conclude?"

"Single shaft. Five blades. Compressed cavitation. Fits Russian diesel-electric *Kilo*-class boat."

Five minutes later, the commanding officer was informed. Immediately, he ordered *Artful* to periscope depth and sent a signal to the satellite.

Noon Same Day
National Security Agency
Fort Meade, Maryland

Lt. Commander Jimmy Ramshawe stared at the signal in front of him, which had arrived direct from Naval Intelligence. It was not couched in alarming tones, nor was it regarded as urgent. It just stated: *RN HMS* Artful *51.15N 08.29W picked up short transient contact on very quiet vessel at 161604JULY12. Insufficient hard copy for firm classification—aural, compressed cavitation, one shaft, five blades, probably non-nuclear. No information on friendly transits relates.*

"That, old mate," said Jimmy decisively, to the entirely empty room, "is a bloke who was bloody sure he just heard a submarine."

He pulled up his computer chart for the northeastern Atlantic and checked the precise whereabouts of *Artful* when the transient contact was detected. *About twenty-four miles south of Kinsale in County Cork . . . now, what in the name of Christ is an unknown submarine doing there? Unless the crew wants a decent round of golf—my dad played Old Head, Kinsale, last year—shot a 98!*

He hit the secure link to COMSUBLANT and spoke to a lieutenant he knew well, questioning the likelihood of a submarine patrolling the coast of Ireland.

"Jack, I think it might have been Russian," he said. "Five blades, that's Russian for sure, and non-nuclear. The Brits obviously think it's a Kilo, but they haven't said so in as many words."

Jim, we do have something on the boards. Only one, an Iranian Kilo, recently out of refit in the Baltic. We were tracking it in the western end of the Med, then tracked it north maybe a week ago. That's probably her.

"Well, the Brits are damn reliable and wouldn't make a mistake like this. Were you guys tracking it subsurface?"

Sure. We had Cheyenne *in there.*

Jimmy closed down the link and phoned the Big Man, who was, for once in his life, not betraying outright impatience.

"Listen, kid. You are sure the only submarine that has gone off the boards is that Iranian Kilo, right?"

"I am sure. COMSUBLANT has every other underwater boat on earth under observation."

"And now a submarine, which fits the pattern, is located by the Brits twenty-four miles south of Kinsale in Ireland, right? Maybe 1,500 miles from its last known."

"Correct."

"Well, that Kilo can probably cover three hundred miles in a day, snorkeling. I guess that's gotta be it. Hull 901 on the loose, way south in the Irish Sea."

"That's how I figured it, boss."

"And what do you want me to do about it? Fire a torpedo?"

"Nossir. But I just had a few thoughts."

"Don't tell me. You think the Kilo is being driven by a barmaid from Brockhurst?"

"Close. I'll talk to you later."

As he said good-bye, the lieutenant commander could hear Arnold Morgan chuckling . . . *heh–heh–heh,* the knowing laugh of an ex–nuclear submarine commander who still thinks he's one jump ahead.

Which was precisely the opposite of what Jimmy Ramshawe thought. For the first time in his life, he considered the Big Man to be several steps behind. And if he didn't shape up, he'd be several steps dead. And now Jim pulled his biggest computerized chart into zoom-out mode, showing the ocean from Gibraltar to Kinsale.

He studied it, measured it, and deduced that the distance was almost 1,500 miles—that was five days, maybe less if she was in a major hurry. And since there was no likelihood that it was proposing to open fire on someone, Jimmy considered it most likely that the submarine was either picking someone up or depositing a person or persons on the shores of Ireland. Probably yesterday.

Intelligence officers of his caliber often act on a hunch. And right now Jimmy did so. He called a regular contact at the FBI and asked him to check whether anyone, repeat anyone, had purchased an unbooked ticket, either first-class or business-class, on a flight to Shannon or Dublin on the morning of July 3. "Almost certainly Aer Lingus," he added. "They have a virtual monopoly on flights into southern Ireland from the USA. Try Washington, New York, and Boston."

One hour later, he had an answer. A Miss Maureen Carson of an address in Michigan had purchased a first-class ticket from Boston to Dublin on the Aer Lingus flight that left at 10:30 A.M. on Tuesday, July 3. "Better yet, Jimmy. Aer Lingus booked her into the Shelbourne Hotel in Dublin that night."

"Have we checked that out?"

"Sure. She was there for three days, then checked out, paying with her American Express card."

"Did you check that out?"

"Sure. It was originally issued to the Jordanian embassy in Paris. Miss Carson is an extra signatory."

Jimmy's heart stopped beating. In his mind, he'd just found Carla Martin. And he'd made the Islamic connection. She was a Middle Eastern agent. And she'd gone to Brockhurst to check out when Arnold and Kathy were leaving the country. She'd killed big stupid Matt Barker, driven to Boston, and bought a ticket to Dublin.

And, if he was not absolutely mistaken, she'd just been joined by at least one other Middle Eastern agent who'd been landed on the Irish coast by Kilo Hull 901. Carla was either Syrian or Jordanian. The new one was an Iranian.

No one could string together a long group of unconnected facts like Jimmy. And now he was off and running, his mind in a turmoil. First he called back his pal, Lieutenant Jack Williams at COMSUBLANT, and advised him to keep a watch on the Gibraltar Strait for the return of the Kilo.

"She left through there, and she'll return through there," he said. "Either to restation off Lebanon, like she was before, or to go through the Suez Canal and then home to the Gulf."

Jack wanted to know what the Kilo was doing skulking around the Irish coast. Jimmy filled him in. "She dropped someone off, someone who was up to no bloody good whatsoever."

Then he called the FBI back and asked if they could make some kind of a search on Maureen Carson, either in Ireland or in Great Britain, where he believed she was headed. This was not going to be a problem, and they would also instigate a check on the Maureen Carson passport.

Jimmy called the Big Man, yet again. And he was not as cooperative as COMSUBLANT or the FBI. He listened carefully, and then said, rather coldly, "Kid, you have no goddamn idea what the submarine was doing off the coast of Ireland. She could have been on a training exercise. You need better facts. Your imagination will lead you nowhere."

"It led me to Maureen Carson," he said bluntly.

"Congratulations. Some nice rich lady on a shopping expedition. Not one single shred of evidence against her. Lemme know when they find her, willya?"

Christ, Arnie could be infuriating.

1830 Monday 16 July
Plunkett Train Station

Ravi pulled into the Waterford station after his long, meandering journey from Cork, tired, hungry, and very thirsty. He went into the little bar and asked for a large glass of water and a cup of coffee. He also bought a couple of fresh-looking ham-and-cheese rolls. He gulped down the water and took the rest to a passenger bench in the station to wait for the 7:00 train to Dublin.

He finished his picnic and then went to the ticket office to purchase a single fare to Dublin. There were two people in front of him, and the clerk was slow. The young woman in front of him turned and said, "You'd think we were going to China, eh?"

Ravi smiled. She was a pretty girl. But Ravi tried to avoid her gaze. By tomorrow morning, he'd be the most wanted man in Ireland, and he did not want her telling the police she'd traveled to Dublin with the murderer on the train.

He pretended not to speak the language, and replied in Arabic, which was probably an even bigger mistake. But it discouraged her, and she turned away, bought her ticket, and walked off. At the counter, he bought his ticket, but then the phone rang and the clerk turned away to answer it before he gave Ravi his change.

The Hamas general hadn't been thinking about the amount, twenty-eight euros, and had handed over a fifty-euro bill. And now, to get his change, he was going to have to stand here facing the office, where a secretary was still working. So he just took the ticket and retreated to his passenger bench.

Three minutes later, the clerk came in search of him and handed him the twenty-two euros in change. Ravi thanked him and tried not to look at him, but he was now probably firmly in the memory of the clerk.

The train ride up through beautiful Kilkenny and County Carlow was picturesque all the way. The track followed the River Barrow for several miles and then swerved right across Kildare before following the Grand Canal into Dublin. Ravi arrived in Heuston Station, just south of the River Liffey along the quays, at 10:15 P.M.

He stepped out of the station and into a dark shop entrance and dialed Shakira's number. She was sitting in her room at the Merrion, watching television, and she answered immediately.

"Be quick, Shakira," he said. "I'm in Dublin. Meet me at the Mosque, tomorrow morning at 11 A.M. Where are you?"

"I'm in the Merrion Hotel, around the corner from St. Stephen's Green."

"Good girl. Don't be late."

Shakira almost went into shock. All these weeks waiting to see him, and now he just said "Good girl" and vanished into the night. What was that all about? She was on the verge of stamping her foot in temper when the phone rang again.

She answered it immediately, and a voice just said, "I love you," before the line went dead.

She was not quite sure whether to laugh or cry. And she chose the latter. With happiness. That he was safe, and he loved her, and tomorrow they would be together.

Ravi too was discontented with the fifteen-second duration of their call. But he had to adhere to that rule, because that rule meant the call could not be heard, traced, or recorded. Ravi was keenly aware that the National Security Agency in Maryland had tapped into Osama bin Laden's phone calls and often listened in on the terrorist mastermind talking from his cave to his mother in Saudi Arabia. If they could eavesdrop on the great Osama, they could locate him. Fifteen seconds only.

He had the name of a Dublin hotel, and he flagged down a cab before it drove into the station and told the driver to take him to the Paramount Hotel, corner of Parliament Street and Essex Gate. The place had a Victorian façade, but inside it was all 1930s, very comfortable, and Ravi thankfully checked in. Last time he had slept had been in the submarine, and dearly as he would have liked to join Shakira in the Merrion, he thought he might get more sleep this way, and anyway he did not wish to be seen publicly with her in a place where staff might recall them.

Tomorrow morning he would risk watching the television news.

0900 Tuesday 17 July
Skibbereen Garda Station

Detective Superintendent Ray McDwyer decided he needed help. The wound to Jerry O'Connell's forehead was something he had never seen before. The bone was completely splintered between the eyes, and the nose bone had been driven upward and into the brain with tremendous force. The crushing blow to the forehead could have been delivered by a blunt instrument, but there was no sign that any implement whatsoever had been used on the nose.

Ray had spoken to the police pathologist, and he too was mystified. And together they decided that there was something all too precise about this killing. The murder had been carried out by an expert, someone who knew precisely what he was doing. There were no signs of a struggle, no other bruises, no abrasions. The killer had taken out Jerry O'Connell instantly, with the minimum of fuss.

At twelve minutes after nine o'clock, Ray McDwyer phoned London and requested help from New Scotland Yard, Special Branch.

At first Scotland Yard wondered what all the fuss was about, the murder of a dairy farmer in a remote spot on the Irish coast. But Ray was persuasive. He told them he thought they were dealing with a highly dangerous character, who might have come in from the sea and might have bigger things on his mind than knocking over a dairy farmer. And after about ten minutes, the duty officer at the Yard was inclined to agree. "We'll send someone over," he said, "direct to Bantry. This morning."

Twenty minutes after Ray put down the phone, a local farmer, Colm McCoy, walking his dog, found Jerry's truck hidden in the birch trees. He'd already seen the *Cork Examiner* and knew about the murder and that the truck was missing. The newspaper had specified there were four large milk urns in the back, and Colm knew what he'd found.

He called in to the Garda Station, and ten minutes later two police cars turned up, with four officers including Ray McDwyer himself. Behind them came a tow truck to haul Jerry's vehicle out.

"Touch nothing," said Detective McDwyer. "Take it away and have them check for fingerprints. Then tell the Milk Corporation to pick up the cans, dispose of the milk, and return them to the O'Connell family."

Meanwhile, back at Crookhaven, officers in a Coast Guard launch were calling on every yacht and fishing boat in the harbor, asking everyone aboard if they had seen any strangers, either afloat or on land.

The operation had been going on since 8 A.M., and they had drawn a complete blank until they reached *Yonder*. And there Captain Bill Stannard told them about the little boat that had chugged past him just before six o'clock the previous morning.

"It was a Zodiac," he said. "Maybe twelve-foot. Yamaha engine. We got one just like it riding off the stern."

"Did you see who was driving?"

"Sure, I did. Just one guy. There was no one else aboard."

"Did you see his face?"

"Not really. He was going past, real slow, when I woke up. He was not an old guy, and he looked kinda broad and tough, short, dark curly hair."

"What was he wearing?"

"Now that's what I do remember. It was a brown jacket. Could have been leather, but I think it was suede. Looked smart, kinda out of place out here on the water."

"Collar and tie?"

"No. He had on a dark T-shirt. I think it was black."

"Did you see which way he went?"

Bill Stannard pointed to the shore, farther into the harbor. "He was headed that way, but I was real tired, never saw him land. I guess the boat's over there somewhere, because I definitely never saw him leave."

"Any idea where he came from?"

"Hell, no. I never caught sight of him until he was more or less alongside. But there's nothing much down toward the harbor entrance. The guy just showed up, out of nowhere."

In the following twenty minutes, the police and Coast Guard searched the harbor from end to end for a twelve-foot Zodiac with a Yamaha engine. Nothing. And no one else had seen it, either. Which presented the investigation with a blank wall, the main trouble being that everything, including the murder, had taken place too early, when hardly anyone was awake.

Back in Skibbereen, Detective Ray McDwyer decided to concentrate on the killer's getaway. It was clear that he had driven away from the crime scene in Jerry's truck and had come as far as Skibbereen at the wheel. But what then?

The Crookhaven team called in to report the mystery man in the Zodiac, arriving in the harbor wearing a brown suede jacket and a black T-shirt. Both he and, more surprisingly, the boat had vanished.

Ray assessed that the man had somehow left the area from Skibbereen, and since there was no car dealer open at that early hour, he must have either gone on the bus, taken a taxi, walked, or stolen a car. There had been no report of anything stolen, so Ray dispatched an officer to check the taxi company. He and Joe Carey made calls to any business that might have been operational at seven in the morning.

The choice was limited. In fact, it didn't stretch much beyond the Shamrock. Joe Carey went in first and beckoned for the youth behind the counter to come over for a quick word. The two had known each other all their lives, and Joe was friendly.

"Hello, young Mick," he said. "Right now we're looking for a fella who may have come in here yesterday morning, a little after seven."

"Anything to do with that murder in Crookhaven yesterday?"

"Mind your business."

"Sure, it is my business," replied Mick, quick as a flash. "Any time there's a bloody killer out there threatenin' the lives of me and my fellow citizens, right there you're talking my business. Anyway, I already read your boss is in charge, so it must be about the murder."

Mick Barton proceeded to fall about laughing, despite the seriousness of the situation. He was only two years out of school, where he had been the class wit, and now he was the café wit. Joe Carey punched him cheerfully on the arm.

"Come on, now, the boss will be in here in a minute. Just let me know if there was a fella in here yesterday, early, wearing a brown suede jacket. A complete stranger."

"No jacket," said Mick. "But there was a fella, a stranger who came in. He drunk two big glasses of orange juice down in about twenty seconds. Then he had toast and coffee."

"What was he wearing, Mick?"

"I think it was a black T-shirt, and he was carrying a leather bag."

"Anything else you recall about him?"

"He could have been foreign. He was dark, short curly hair, heavyset. But he spoke English, naturally, or I wouldn't have known what he was talking about."

"Any idea where he went afterward?"

"Sure. He asked me about the bus to Cork, and I sent him up to the Eldon Hotel for the eight o'clock."

Outside the Shamrock, Ray McDwyer put three men on the bus route to check with the drivers where the man in the black T-shirt had gone. They made contact with the Bus Eireann office and had their drivers check into the Skibbereen police station as soon as they pulled into town.

At midday, Ray and Joe left for Bantry, twenty-four miles away. Two detective inspectors from Scotland Yard's Special Branch had flown direct from London to Cork and been transported by a Garda helicopter to the town of Bantry, where the body of Jerry O'Connell was in the morgue beneath the new Catholic Hospital.

Joe and Ray met them at the little airport, which had been constructed mainly to service Bantry's major oil and gas terminal. All four went immediately to the hospital, and the two men from London expertly examined the body.

The chief inspector touched it only once. He gently pressed the area in the central forehead with the flat of his thumb. Then he stepped back and said immediately, "Ray, this farmer of yours was killed by an expert in unarmed combat. Death was caused by something smashing into and weakening the big forehead bone, which allows the combatant to slam the septum into the brain much easier.

"I've seen it before. But not often. When you're looking at a murder like this, you instantly think of the SAS or one of the other Special Forces. But I can tell you, this cat really knew what he was doing. The farmer died in under five seconds. This was a lethal blow."

Ray McDwyer nodded thoughtfully. "I wonder who the hell he was," he said.

"That's always the question, right? But this was a very local man, I imagine, no business far beyond West Cork?"

"West Cork!" said Ray. "Jerry O'Connell didn't have any business beyond Crookhaven."

The inspector chuckled. "And that means he probably died by accident. I mean, the killer had no intention of harming him when he arrived in the area. Jerry just somehow got in the way."

"I've assumed that from the start. At least I assume it on the basis that the murder could not have been committed by wandering Irish scoundrels."

"Absolutely not," declared the inspector. "This was committed by a professional. The issue is, why was he here, and what's he doing now?"

"I've got half the force trying to trace him. But we're having only limited luck. I'll know more when we get back to Skibbereen. Are you fellas willing to stay a little longer?"

"Well, we had planned to return to London right away, but this is very brutal, and very bewildering. Do you have any ideas yet where this character came from?"

"Not really. First sighting was from a yacht captain in Crookhaven Harbor. He saw a man, who answered the rough description, cross the harbor in a Zodiac at the right time. Needless to say, the boat's missing, but the yacht guy said it came in from the outer harbor."

"Could he have been dropped at sea?"

"It's hard to imagine how the hell he got there before six o'clock in the morning if he hadn't been." Joe McDwyer was visibly uneasy. But, as the Irish host, he stayed cool.

"Okay," he said. "I'll get you a couple of rooms at the Eldon and we can have a strategy meeting this afternoon. I'm grateful you could come, but your diagnosis has made a grim situation somewhat worse."

0800 Same Day
The Paramount Hotel
Dublin

General Rashood awakened reasonably early, showered, shaved, and had breakfast in his room. He opened the door and found the *Irish Times* on the carpet. He picked it up and nearly jumped out of his skin when he saw the lead story, straight across all eight columns of the front page:

WEST CORK SEAPORT STUNNED AT BRUTAL MURDER
Dairy Farmer Found Battered to Death
Garda Baffled at Senseless Slaying.

There followed a lurid account of how the longtime Crookhaven resident had gone missing and then been found dead on the cliff top, his truck and 160 gallons of milk missing. The newspaper speculated that it might have been just a milk thief, but later quotes from Detective Superintendent Raymond McDwyer suggested something much more sinister.

Extra police were due to be drafted into the area, and a nationwide search for the killer was launched last night. D-Sup. McDwyer was still in his office at 3 A.M. trying to piece together the many separate parts of his investigation.

Who might want to kill Jerry O'Connell? Did they mean to kill him? Was it mistaken identity? Or was this a homicidal maniac who might strike again? Either way, the pressure is on McDwyer to come up with something.

Ravi put down his newspaper and turned to the television news, which was making an even bigger meal of it. There was a camera crew in Crookhaven, reporting "direct from this heartbroken community." There was a crew in Skibbereen awaiting news from "the murder inquiry head-quarters." There were pictures of the harbor, pictures of the cliffs, pictures of Seaview Farm, interviews with Mary O'Connell, wedding photographs of the couple, an interview with Mary's aging father.

Ravi pulled some clean clothes out of his bag and began to dress. His new T-shirt was white. He skipped through the remainder of the newspaper, pausing only to look at a story which told of a gigantic bomb blast that had knocked out all the windows in the American embassy in Tel Aviv.

"Well done, Ahmed," he muttered.

He stuffed a pile of euros into his pocket, picked up his bag, and went downstairs to check out. He paid the 190-euro bill with four fifties. Outside, he jumped into a cab and asked for the Mosque at Clonskeagh, which stands on the south side, next to University College Dublin.

The Mosque, which was opened by President Mary Robinson in 1996 and backed by the great Dubai statesman and racehorse breeder Sheik Hamdan al Maktoum, is one of the finest buildings in Dublin, a massive brick-and-steel edifice with a minaret tower and a breathtaking metallic dome. It is built within a giant square, a total of nine buildings including a prayer hall of majestic beauty. The Mosque is surrounded by perfectly kept lawns. It is the Mecca of the Emerald Isle.

Ravi had heard much about it and had been wanting to visit for several years. Now, however, it was an irrelevance, for within its precincts today was the only reason Ravi had to live, his beloved Shakira, the Palestinian girl for whom he had laid down his life and career.

The taxi swung into the wide entrance to the Mosque and headed for the main building. He could see Shakira leaning on the wall, dressed in jeans, sandals, and a white blouse. There she was, waiting for him, longing for him, and entirely oblivious of the fact that he had left behind in County Cork a manhunt as big as the one she had left behind in Virginia.

Should he tell her? Perhaps not. She had quite enough to worry about, without burdening her with yet another preoccupation. Still, she would have to be aware of the need for the utmost caution, even if he did not quite tell her the full details of the murder of Jerry O'Connell.

Ravi permitted the driver to stop about fifty yards from where Shakira stood. He paid, climbed out, and walked slowly back toward her. She was looking the other way, and he put his arms around her from behind; without seeing, she knew it was him. She twisted and flung her arms around him as if she would never let go, and he held her close and told her over and over that he loved her above all else.

But then he broke away from her embrace and said sternly, "Nothing in public that would ever attract attention. Not in our business."

"I know, I know," she said, a shade petulantly. "But it's been so long and I miss you every day. Where are we going now?"

"We are leaving Ireland as fast as we can," he said. "This was just a port of entry for us. We have to get to London as fast as we can."

"How do we do that?"

"We get a taxi to a place called Dun Laoghaire. It's right on the coast, and it's not far from here. That's the ferry port to England."

"I can't see any taxis."

"No, I'm going to call for one. I arranged it this morning. I have the number."

Ravi dialed a number on his cell. Shakira heard him say, "Hello, Robert Bamford here. Taxi to pick me up at the Mosque. I ordered it this morning. Yes, that's correct. I'm right at the main entrance ... to Dun Laoghaire, cash. Okay, five minutes."

0700 Same Day
National Security Agency
Maryland

Jimmy Ramshawe was fielding a succession of catastrophically depressing E-mails, all of them confirming that Carla Martin had most definitely vanished. The Maureen Carson lead came to nothing. The passport was forged; the only Maureen Carson of Michigan with correlating numbers was dead. The Jordanian embassy in Paris said they had never heard of Miss Carson, which was, Jimmy guessed, unsurprising since she did not appear to exist.

The Jordanian attaché had told the FBI that since Miss Carson appeared to have a forged passport, she probably had forged her American Express application as well. Worse yet, the Shelbourne Hotel had not the slightest idea where she had gone after leaving them.

The Kilo had not shown up anywhere along the route from Ireland to Gibraltar. And yet the Ireland connection continued to bother Jimmy. He still believed Maureen Carson was Carla Martin. *Who the hell else buys a pricey one-way first-class ticket to Dublin at an hour's notice, unless they're on the bloody run?*

And all the bloody documents are forged, for Christ's sake. Something's going on, and I can't understand for the life of me why nobody can see it except for me. And what in the name of Christ are the fucking Iranians doing frigging around in a submarine, a drive and a nine iron from Kinsale Golf Club? Tell me that. Jimmy, all alone in his office, was working himself into a lather about Ireland.

So much so that he opened his computer and Googled the *Irish Times* just to see what the hell was going on over there. And what greeted him was that whacking great front-page headline announcing the brutal murder of the Irish dairy farmer Jerry O'Connell.

Jimmy wrote down *Crookhaven* and checked the distance along the coast to Kinsale Old Head—forty-two miles along the shore. He then compared the GPS numbers; not the numbers that separated Kinsale from Crookhaven, but the ones that separated Crookhaven from the submarine when the Brits detected her. The latitudes were submarine 51.15, Crookhaven 51.32, about seventeen miles different. Longitude, submarine 08.29, Crookhaven 09.34. About the same forty-odd miles, with the submarine running predictably south.

She'd been running all day. It was 4 o'clock in the bloody afternoon. I don't know what happened to the Irish farmer. But something's really weird here. Bloody great headlines, murder, Maureen Carson, towelhead submarines. All concerning Ireland. Give me a break. They've got to be connected.

And this is where Jimmy Ramshawe parted company, mentally, with Admiral Morgan, who told him bluntly, "Kid, you still lack the one truth that might bind all this together. Right now they're all floating coincidences.

"Nothing's connected to anything else. Nothing puts Carla or Maureen on the submarine. Nothing connects either woman with the other. Nothing suggests the submarine was doing anything except a training exercise.

As for this murder, no one knows who committed it, and there is not one shred of evidence to indicate that one of the Iranians got off and then kicked an Irish pig farmer to death."

"Dairy."

"What?"

"Dairy farmer, not pig."

"Oh, thank God. That makes all the difference."

"Arnie, I agree nothing quite adds up. But something's going on, and I don't think you should go to England. . . ."

"Bullshit."

1400 Tuesday 17 July
Dun Laoghaire, Dublin

General Rashood bought two first-class passenger tickets for the two o'clock ferry to Holyhead in North Wales, a journey of sixty-five miles across the Irish Sea. This was unusual, because the Stena Line fast ferry is essentially for cars and trucks, roll on, roll off. The vast majority of passengers were planning to drive through Wales, England, or Scotland, either vacationing or going home. There were some passengers without cars, but mostly students, backpackers, and hitchhikers. Ravi and Shakira did not fit the pattern.

Nonetheless, they found their way up to the first-class lounge, and ordered hot sandwiches for lunch. The stewardess would bring them complimentary coffee throughout the journey.

The summer sea was calm, and the ferry, a giant hovercraft, charged toward the United Kingdom in a blizzard of howling spray, ripping past a regular shaft-driven ferryboat as if it had stopped.

Holyhead, their destination, sits on Holy Isle, the northwest point of Wales, jutting out into the Irish Sea. This in turn is joined to the ancient twenty-mile-long Isle of Anglesey where the A-5, the main road into England, begins. Or ends, depending on your direction.

Ravi and Shakira had to wait for the cars and trucks to leave the ship before foot passengers were permitted to walk off. They joined a busy line of mostly young people going through the passport control area, and twenty minutes later, with only the most cursory glance at one of

Shakira's four passports, the British one for Margaret Adams, they waved her through.

Ravi, the former British Army officer, said "good afternoon" crisply in that unmistakable tone the British use to intimidate the lower orders, and was waved through immediately. The official paid hardly any attention to this well-dressed Charles Larkman, in his expensive brown suede jacket and white T-shirt.

However, the closed-circuit camera behind him was more observant, and there was a photographic record that Miss Adams and Mr. Larkman had indeed entered the United Kingdom, off the two o'clock ferry from Dublin, on July 17.

From the immigration area, they walked to the car-rental desks, and Shakira hired an Audi A6 for a month, using her new American Express Gold Card, originally issued to a staff member at the Syrian embassy in London. She offered one of her three driver's licenses, the one in the name of Margaret Adams, and Ravi booked himself in as an extra driver using Mr. Larkman's clean British license.

Thankfully, they stowed their two bags in the trunk and set off on the long 300-mile journey to London, Ravi at the wheel.

The regular route for most drivers is to cross the Menai Strait onto the mainland and then travel all along the North Wales coast until it reaches the fast motorway system south of Liverpool. Ravi would do it differently, driving through the mountains of North Wales, southeast to Shrewsbury, and then south into Hereford, home of the British Army's elite SAS, his old stomping ground. It was perhaps the irresistible urge of the outlaw to return, in the broadest possible sense, to the scene of the crime.

1700 Tuesday 17 July
Skibbereen Garda Station

Shortly after 5 P.M., the two officers from New Scotland Yard agreed to consult with MI-6, Britain's overseas intelligence agency. It was clear to both of them that the man who killed Jerry O'Connell was no passing villain: this was a man who had almost certainly made illegal entry into Ireland, and if challenged in any way would kill ruthlessly and without compunction.

Both men had previous experience with such operators, mostly in the field of counterterrorism. The IRA had men like that, and the various jihadist organizations were full of them. Fanatics.

At the heart of the O'Connell killing was the fact that the murderer had been trained militarily. No one can kill like that, not without expert instruction. MI-6 listened attentively and promised to make immediate inquiries, find out if there was a rogue Special Forces operator on the loose.

One hour later, it was clear that MI-6 had raised a serious hue and cry. They'd talked to the CO at Stirling Lines, headquarters of the SAS; they'd touched base with military intelligence in all three branches of the service. They even heard about the suspect Iranian submarine, and it seemed everyone in the entire intelligence community understood there was something very strange about the death of the Irish farmer.

Same Day
In the USA

At 7 P.M. in England, 2 P.M. on the East Coast of the United States, the FBI was put in the picture. This was no longer an Irish-country-murder inquiry; this was now a preliminary examination of a possible terrorist on the loose in the British Isles. Jimmy Ramshawe, who was no longer in the office, was informed by a young duty officer that his buddy in the FBI had called and wanted to talk urgently.

Jimmy was in his apartment at the Watergate with Jane when the message came through. He called back and listened as the agent explained that the Special Branch had flown into Ireland from Scotland Yard and all hell seemed to be breaking loose over the death of the Irish farmer.

"Any idea why?" asked Jimmy innocently, hardly able to contain his excitement.

"Yeah. He was apparently killed by an unarmed combat blow which could only have been delivered by a Special Forces guy, you know, a Navy SEAL or an SAS man."

"I KNEW IT!" yelled Jimmy.

"Knew what?"

"I knew there was something going on in connection with southern Ireland."

"Not to mention southern Virginia. Christ, Jimmy, we've made more calls for you than we have for ourselves. Carla Martin, Maureen Whatsername, Aer Lingus, Shelbourne Hotel, passports, embassies. I gotta tell you, buddy, it looks like there might be some connection here—"

"NO SHIT!" yelled Jimmy, ungraciously. He thanked his buddy for the call, pressed the cutoff button, and dialed Admiral Morgan.

And once more he related the myriad of "disconnected facts" that suggested to him that someone was going to make an attempt on the life of the president's most trusted adviser, scourge of the Middle Eastern terrorists.

But this time he was leading up to a payoff line. And with something of a flourish, he revealed the priceless information to the admiral: that the Irish farmer had been killed by a blow which could only have been delivered by a member, or at least a former member, of the U.S. or British Special Forces.

"You're telling me, Jimmy, that someone hopped off that Iranian submarine, right out there in the Irish Sea, and killed the farmer on his way to killing me?"

"Well, not exactly. But I do know that an agent, wielding a Syrian dagger, befriended your mother-in-law very deliberately and then vanished from the face of the earth, in the full knowledge of your arrival time and hotel reservation in London on Tuesday, July 31.

"And that female agent, in my opinion, went to Ireland. Where the submarine was, and where another agent, a colleague and Special Forces guy, has just committed a murder on the way to his final destination, which might just be the Ritz Hotel."

"Steady, kid. There's too many gaps. Too few real links. Although I recognize the death of the Irish farmer is significant, and according to your story it does look as if the killer might have got off that submarine."

"Arnie, will you cancel London?"

"Hell, no. I got a lot of security around me. I'll be fine. You can't let 'em rule you, kid, otherwise they've won. And we're not gonna let that happen, right?"

Jimmy ended the phone call, and contemplated the sheer futility of trying to convince Admiral Morgan that he might be in danger. And he racked his brains to think of a link, or even a terror suspect who might have killed Jerry O'Connell.

He pulled up his most-wanted list of Middle Eastern hard men, guys suspected of heinous crimes against humanity, guys who'd killed and maimed in Israel, murdered in Jordan, committed atrocities in Iraq and Afghanistan and at various U.S. embassies in Africa.

Had one of them traveled to Ireland in the missing Kilo? And why Ireland? Arnie wasn't going there. He tried to put himself in the shoes of the terrorist, and went through a process he had perfected years ago:

Right, guys, here I go. I'm gonna kill the Big Man at the Ritz Hotel. Shoot him stone dead. Question: what with. Answer: a rifle, telescopic sights, no bullshit. Where do I get it: London, because I cannot possibly get such a weapon into the country, too much security at the airports and seaports. You get caught with a weapon like that, trying to smuggle it into Great Britain, they'll put you in the slammer and throw away the key.

Jimmy leaned back reflectively as Jane reentered the room. "Could I ask why you're talking to yourself?" she said brightly. "Aside from the fact that you might be losing your mind through overwork."

"I'm not talking to myself," he replied. "I'm processing information. Forming strategy."

"Okay. It just sounded to me a lot like you were talking to yourself."

"Perception, Jane, perception. Try to look beyond the obvious."

"Well, I did. And you were obviously talking to yourself."

"Jane, I was strategizing. And I still am. And I want to ask you a question. You are a terrorist, and you're trying to get into England, unarmed, and with a passport. How do you do it?"

"Me? I get a flight to Heathrow, and walk through with my passport."

"That's what you won't do. They make a record of that. Computerized. The security is unbelievable, and remember you've got to get out after you murder your target."

"Okay, I'll come in by car, off a ferry, from a different country. I know they're not nearly as strict at the ferry ports."

"Okay. Which country are you coming from? France? Holland? Spain?"

"Yes. I suppose so."

"And how do you get in there?"

"I fly in."

"Wrong. Then you run into that heavy European security again."

"Okay. Well, how do I get in?"

"Ireland, by sea, Jane. It's always been the soft option. For years they did not even have passports between the two countries. And it's not much different now, even in England, not if you're holding a European Union passport. Ireland's the way into England."

"How about flying into Ireland from a foreign country?" asked Jane.

"That's much more difficult. The Irish adhere to the European rules as best they can. They want to know who you are, how long you're staying, and the rest."

"Well, how the heck do you get in then?" said Jane, tiring of the conversation.

"You get in by sea. There's miles and miles of coastline, and the Irish have hardly any Coast Guard protection. You could land from deep water just about anywhere. You'd never try the same thing in England. Because they'd catch you. They arrest people all the time."

"So the method for a killer is into Ireland by boat, then a ferry to England, and no one would know you were in the UK."

"Precisely."

"And you think Carla did that?"

"No. Carla's not an assassin, though I doubt Matt Barker would agree. But her mate is. The one who killed Jerry O'Connell."

2300 Tuesday 17 July
Belgrave Square, London

Shakira's fast Audi A6 came swiftly into London's grandest square after their long journey halfway across England. They had made it in seven hours, which was superb driving considering that the general had elected to duck and dive through country roads and never to stick to a predictable route down the high-speed British motorways.

His reason was clear. If anyone had managed to identify them, or somehow get on their trail, it was ten times easier for the police to patrol the freeways than to organize a search through the highways and byways of the rural heart of England.

He'd stuck to the A-5 all the way to the historic river town of Shrewsbury, then cut to the M-5 freeway south of Birmingham, through Herefordshire, on roads he had once known like the palm of his hand. He exited at number 10, picked up the A-40, and in the twilight of this fine July evening raced through some of the loveliest country in England, to the wonderful steep Cotswold town of Burford, and then fast around the Oxford Ring Road onto the M-40.

From there it was a straight shot at London, past his old school, Harrow, and then off the freeway into the Holland Park area. He knew these roads better than he knew Damascus, and he cut through to Knightsbridge, swung right just before Harrods, and made Belgrave Square right on time.

He pulled up outside No. 8 and immediately two staff members from the Syrian embassy ran down the steps to greet him. One said, "General, please take your wife inside immediately. We will take care of everything."

Ravi and Shakira ran inside, while one Syrian grabbed their bags from the trunk and the other slipped behind the wheel and drove the Audi around the square and into the underground Motcombe Street garage, where the embassy had many reserved spaces. The two runaway terrorists had spent exactly seven seconds on the sidewalk.

The ambassador was there to meet the Hamas C-in-C, with his wife and the military attaché. One of the cultural attachés was also there, but he knew roughly as much about culture as Genghis Khan. Ahmed was a terrorist and a spy, fresh from slamming a bomb at the U.S. embassy in Tel Aviv.

Dinner was set for the six of them, and the ambassador requested that Ravi and Shakira not take time to change, which both of them thought was very thoughtful since neither had much to change into, their bags containing mostly a pile of laundry.

His Excellency understood entirely and poured everyone a glass of Château-bottled French Bordeaux, 2002, never mind Muslim disapproval of alcohol, and led them to their allotted places for dinner. The ambassador sat at the head, with Ravi and Shakira on either side. Lannie, his wife, sat next to Shakira, and Ahmed was next to the general, with the military attaché at the foot.

As dinner-table place settings go, with four men and two ladies, it was thus all over the place, but this was a military strategy meeting, not a social gathering. Lannie was only there as a politeness to Shakira.

The conversation was grim and extremely serious. The Syrians understood entirely the purpose of the visit. For they too had little reason to thank the USA for its attitude to them. And they were frankly furious at the recent bombing of the street near Bab Touma in Damascus.

Everyone at the table knew that Admiral Arnold Morgan was behind all of the carnage, and they were honored indeed to have been selected by the Hamas High Command to provide a headquarters for the legendary Palestinian terrorist general, who planned, finally, to dispose of the American Prince of Darkness.

"You have accurate dates and times?" asked the ambassador, who was a very smooth-looking Arabian diplomat, medium height, slim, perfectly dressed in a light suit cut for him by Prince Charles's tailor, Huntsman, on Savile Row.

"Thanks to Shakira, I do," replied Ravi. "I must visit the gunsmith tomorrow; we have only two weeks to plan everything and organize my exit, first from Piccadilly, then from England."

"We've done the documents and arranged the transportation," replied the ambassador. "In the end, timing will be everything."

"It usually is," said Ravi.

The ambassador smiled. "Don't miss," he whispered theatrically.

"I never miss," replied the Hamas general sternly.

0900 Wednesday 18 July
Garda Headquarters, Dublin

Detective Superintendent Ray McDwyer was combing through the evidence that had been gathered from the bus and train companies. Despite all of Ravi's shenanigans, jumping on and off various buses and changing railroad carriages, the Irish police had traced his route all the way to Dublin. Ray had thus made his new headquarters in the city, where they now believed the killer was.

So far as the investigation was concerned, there were only two people who had come face-to-face with the murderer. There were others who claimed to have seen him, bus and train staff who might have seen him. But only two who had both seen and spoken to him.

One was the ticket clerk at Waterford Station, who could not swear it was the right man because he could not remember the facial makeup of the passenger on the bench who had left behind his change from a fifty-euro bill.

The other was Mick Barton from the Shamrock Café, who had served the stranger, recalled what he was wearing, and directed him to the bus stop outside the Eldon Hotel. Officer Joe Carey had called in and asked if he would be prepared to come to Dublin and spend a day looking through closed-circuit television footage, to try to identify the man to whom he had served two large glasses of orange juice.

"Forget it," said Mick. "I'm too busy trying to earn a living, not pouncing around all day on wild-goose chases like yourself."

Joe put him in a cheerful headlock, and told him this was a serious matter. Mick said his neck was probably broken and he'd be suing for a million.

Joe asked how he'd feel about a private helicopter ride up to Dublin, and they would award him two days' full pay for his time.

"Done," said Mick. "What time?"

"Tomorrow morning. Eight o'clock. Right here in the square."

"Where's the helicopter gonna be?"

"Right over here in that field."

"Oh, jaysus, Joe . . . I can't . . . I forgot . . . I have a dentist's appointment."

Joe sighed the sigh of the profoundly suspicious.

"Of course you have," he said. "All right, three days."

"Done," said Mick. "Final offer?"

"Final offer."

"I'll be there."

0900 Thursday 19 July
Dublin

Mick Barton arrived at the Garda Station in style, in the back of an unmarked police car. He was led into a private room, where Ray McDwyer met him with a cheerful "Morning to you, Michael."

At the back of the room were a projector and an operator. At the front was a large white screen.

"Okay, lad, you know what you're doing. We are going to show you a steady line of people going through security at Dublin airport getting onto international flights only. We just want you to stop us and identify the man you served the orange juice to on Monday morning."

"Do I get a bonus if I find him?"

"Absolutely not," said Ray. "You might make something up, just to get the bonus!"

"Who, me?"

"I've only known you since you were three years old. Yes, you."

Mick laughed, half flattered. He saw himself, after all, as a hard-driving businessman. But suddenly he was dead serious. "Roll 'em," he said. "If he's there, I'll find him. Black T-shirt, right?"

And slowly the projectionist began to run the film, and Mick sat quietly, sometimes leaning forward asking for a pause or a rewind. He worked solidly for three and a half hours, drinking just one cup of coffee, which obliged him to ask, formally, whether it had been percolated in Dachau. Everyone laughed, which Mick expected, being Skibbereen's established breakfast-bar wit and everything.

He had looked carefully at hundreds of air travelers, and found a couple of marginal candidates, but in the end he always said the same thing, "No, that's not him."

They gave him a ham sandwich and an ice cream for lunch, and then settled down to show him the much shorter lines of people disembarking the Irish Sea ferries in England. As expected, they were mostly backpackers and hitchhikers. "Bloody rabble," observed Mick, but he kept going, checking every person who had sailed from Dun Laoghaire or the Dublin Port Terminal over a two-day period.

He found nothing, not until three o'clock in the afternoon. They were rolling the seventh tape from Holyhead, when Mick asked first for a rewind. Then for a pause. Then he stood up and stepped closer.

And he shoved out his finger, pointing directly at a passenger wearing a jacket and a T-shirt, accompanied by a very good-looking lady who was standing slightly aside.

"You want me to zoom in, Mick?" asked the projectionist.

"Good idea," he replied. "On the guy in the jacket."

The image came up bigger. Mick pointed again at the man in the jacket, which was now obviously made of suede or some other kind of soft leather.

"That's him," said Mick. "That's definitely him."

"One thing, Mick," interjected Ray McDwyer. "That T-shirt he's wearing is white, not black."

"Personally," replied the kid from the Shamrock Café, "I don't give a rat's ass if it's pink. That's still him, the thirsty bastard who couldn't find his own way to Cork City."

Ray McDwyer chuckled. And Mick added, "I'll tell you something else, and there's no charge for this—that's a very fair piece of crumpet he's got with him."

CHAPTER *10*

Ray McDwyer looked hard at the image of the man who might have killed Jerry O'Connell for reasons unknown. And he also looked hard at Mick Barton, the local Flash Harry, upon whose memory this entire case rested. Could Mick be trusted? Maybe. Did he have any doubts about this identification? Apparently not.

Ray suddenly viewed the entire scenario with mixed feelings. If Mick was correct, the murderer was no longer in Ireland: he'd gone to England on the two o'clock ferry from Dublin to Holyhead. Right now he could be anywhere. And there were only sixty million people in England.

So far as Ray was concerned, his task was more or less over. The killer had gone, and the most the Irish detective could do was to circulate the picture to all the relevant agencies and see if anyone recognized the man in the brown suede jacket.

This could, of course, be achieved extremely fast with modern E-mail, and Ray instructed a young Garda officer to have the photograph digitally enhanced to the highest possible standard and then transmit it to New Scotland Yard, MI-5 and MI-6, Interpol, the CIA, the FBI, and the Mossad. Each of those agencies would forward the picture on to various military intelligence operations, and within a couple of hours every branch of every secret service in the Western world would be staring at the apparent killer who had come into Crookhaven from the deep rough water that pounds the Fastnet Rock.

Ray McDwyer, though nominally the officer of record on the case, was essentially finished with it, unless someone arrested the suspect and he was brought back to County Cork to face trial. Meanwhile, he would return to Skibbereen, and politely he asked Mick Barton if he would mind sharing the helicopter.

"Yes, I think I can put up with that," replied Mick. "Although it's not something I'm used to."

Two hours later, Mick was walking down Main Street on his way to his home on the outskirts of Skibbereen, and Ray McDwyer was back in his office. So far as he could tell, nothing had broken loose. But he was wrong. Because it had, two and a half thousand miles and two time zones away, in Tel Aviv.

2100 Thursday 19 July
Mossad Headquarters
Tel Aviv

Colonel Ben Joel, leader of the Mossad team that had somewhat spectacularly blown up Bab Touma Street in Damascus the previous February, was sitting with two of his most trusted officers, Major Itzaak Sherman and Lt. Colonel John Rabin. It was a hot, quiet night in the city, and the three of them were planning to go out for a glass of wine somewhere off Dizengoff Square.

Right now, they were just examining the last of a pile of photographs of people on the Mossad "wanted" list. They checked the latest photographs every night before leaving, just in case there had been a sighting, somewhere definite, of someone they really wanted to find.

Tonight there was nothing. Until, staring at the last two or three pictures, Colonel Joel suddenly exclaimed, "Jesus Christ . . . look who we have here. . . ."

He was holding an eight-by-ten printout of the closed-circuit picture of General Rashood and Shakira at the English ferry port of Holyhead. The E-mail transmission had just arrived from MI-6 in London, with a request for identification if possible.

And had that photograph ever landed in the right place. These three Mossad hitmen had been charged with eliminating Ravi and Shakira in that highly expensive and well-planned operation only five months ago. They had been beaten in the mission mostly because of sheer bad luck. The couple had returned to their house separately, accompanied by different people, and it had been too dark to see the discrepancy. The bomb went off in the main room while Shakira was in the basement-level kitchen and Ravi was not even in the house.

But no one knew what Ravi looked like better than Colonel Joel, who had photographed the Hamas commander through a telescopic lens, from right across the street, had observed him in daylight, would recognize him anywhere.

The other two also knew precisely what Ravi looked like, and there was no doubt in any of their minds. The man in the English ferry port was General Ravi Rashood, and the lady with him was his Palestinian wife, Shakira.

For one final check, the colonel called for comparable pictures of the general, and Itzaak pulled them up on the big computer screen set into the wall like a plasma television. The group consisted of three pictures taken on a cliff top in the Canary Isles and the expansive set of photographs the colonel himself had snapped from across Bab Touma Street in Damascus.

No doubt. This was General Rashood and his wife, arriving in England, and now identified by no lesser figures than the Mossad's top assassination squad, and Mr. Mick Barton, of the Shamrock Café in faraway Skibbereen.

Colonel Joel called for the MI-6 report, which mostly contained an assessment by Detective Superintendent McDwyer of the murder of Jerry O'Connell in County Cork, and the likelihood that the man in the picture had committed the murder. The report also mentioned the possibility that the murderer had been landed from an Iranian submarine patrolling off the coast of southern Ireland.

The Mossad men knew all about that submarine. They too had been tracking it, not with another underwater boat like the Americans, but via the satellites. And they too had been aware that the damn thing had vanished somewhere in the deep water off the eastern coast of Majorca. Like the Americans, the Israelis had not regained contact, and were more or less certain the Iranian submarine was no longer in the Mediterranean. Somehow, the Israeli Navy believed, it had broken out through the Gibraltar Strait into the Atlantic Ocean.

Colonel Joel sent a POSIDENT signal to all the appropriate departments in the King Saul Boulevard headquarters. He put it on the nets to the Navy and all branches of Israeli Military Intelligence, particularly Shin Bet, the interior intelligence operation, equivalent of London's MI-5. No one wanted Ravi Rashood's head as badly as Ben Joel.

Back in England, MI-6 E-mailed the picture to Military Intelligence, with a special copy to SAS headquarters in Stirling Lines, Hereford, where once Major Ray Kerman had served with honor and courage. By the time the photograph arrived, it was mid-evening, and it would not be examined in the normal course of business until the following morning. However, an urgent communication was picked up from the Israelis at around 10 P.M., and the duty officer instantly summoned the commanding officer.

The communiqué from Tel Aviv read: *POSIDENT photograph English ferry port Holyhead. The man is General Ravi Rashood, commander in chief Hamas, formerly known as Major Ray Kerman, 22 SAS Regt. The woman with him is Shakira Rashood, his Palestinian wife, last known address Bab Touma Street, Damascus.*

Rashood wanted for murder in County Cork, Ireland. Local farmer Mr. Jerry O'Connell, killed by obvious Special Forces method—smashed central forehead, nose bone rammed into the brain. Looks like Rashood back in England. We stand by to help if required. Joel, Israeli Intelligence.

Lieutenant Colonel David Carter, CO 22 SAS, walked through steady rain to his office, accompanied by Major Douglas Jarvis. Neither of them had been in Hereford when Major Kerman had jumped ship back in 2004, but both of them knew the seriousness of his crimes. It was common knowledge nowadays that Kerman had murdered two highly regarded SAS NCOs and had then wreaked havoc on behalf of the well-funded Hamas terrorists. The name Ray Kerman represented the most inflammatory utterance in SAS history.

The two Special Forces officers shook off their rain smocks and made their way quickly to the CO's office. Lt. Colonel Carter had served with Ray Kerman in Sierre Leone a dozen years ago, knew him well. The duty officer had put the photograph up on a wall screen, and David Carter took one look at it and said, "That's Ray. Not a single doubt."

Douglas Jarvis picked up a hard copy of the report from Tel Aviv, and said, "Christ! He's here."

Lt. Colonel Carter replied, "Well, he was when that ferry came into Holyhead. Who knows if he's still here?"

"What do we do now?"

"Well, I suppose we better confirm our positive identification of Kerman to all of the interested parties, looks like Israeli Intelligence, MI-5, MI-6, CIA, FBI, and the Irish. We'll send our confirmation direct to MI-6 and they'll take care of the rest."

"Did you read that bit about he's supposed to have killed the Irish farmer, sir?"

"Not yet. What did it say?"

"Well, he used our regular unarmed combat blow. You know, smashed forehead bone and upward drive on the nose. I seem to remember from the report, he used that very same method to kill Sergeant Fred O'Hara in Hebron."

"After eight years with the enemy, he's probably getting careless. Thinks he's safe. Looks like he's getting so confident, he thinks he can move in and out of England any time he wants to."

"Do you think we'll ever catch him, sir?"

"Possibly. But we'd need a hell of a bit of luck."

1600 Thursday 19 July
National Security Agency
Maryland

The Mossad communiqué, via the CIA, landed in Lt. Commander Ramshawe's computer at 4 P.M. It was accompanied by an urgent phone call from his pal at the CIA, and then another call from Army Intelligence. General Rashood and his wife had been photographed at the English ferry port.

And at that moment, a thousand questions that had been swirling in Jimmy's mind were answered. In fact, *all* the questions that had been swirling in his mind were answered. Except for one. Was the woman in the picture with Ravi none other than Carla Martin?

There were only a very few people in the world who could tell him. One of them was Emily Gallagher; another was Jim Caborn, manager of the Estuary Hotel; and, of course, there were Matt Barker's buddies.

In Jimmy's judgment, this required a further visit to Brockhurst. But the game had now changed drastically from a very local murder hunt to a hunt for an international terrorist with the most serious implications.

Jimmy seized the picture, and the reports from the Mossad and the Irish police, and proceeded in a major hurry to the office of the director, Admiral George Morris. The somewhat lugubrious ex–battle group commander was studying a copy of *Jane's International* magazine when his deputy came through the door without knocking.

Big George knew urgency when he saw it. He looked up and said quietly, "Steady, Jimmy. What's going on?"

"Every damn thing in the world, if you ask me," he replied. "You know all that business I was telling you about a terrorist group trying to locate and then assassinate Admiral Morgan?"

"Of course I do."

"Well, it's happening. Everything just sprang into place. And you'll never guess who's at the back of it."

"Lay it on me."

"Hamas. General Ravi Rashood. And his wife. Take a look at this picture."

He handed it to Admiral Morris, who said, "From what I remember, that's him. I've never seen a picture of her. Tell you what, run me through it quickly, will you? Refresh my memory."

Jimmy did so, fast, recounting the chain of circumstances that led to Carla's sudden vanishing, in full possession of the admiral's ETA and hotel in London. Then he reconstructed Ravi's trip to Ireland, the murder of the farmer, and the police hunt for the master terrorist, which apparently had ended in the ferry port.

"And here they are," he said, waving the photograph, "after their rendezvous in Dublin, arriving in England, where Ravi will attempt to blow Arnie's brains out without getting caught."

Admiral Morris nodded thoughtfully. "One thing, Jim," he said. "Why Ireland? Why did they not just go to England?"

"Even with forged passports, that would be very risky. There's nowhere hotter than London for a terrorist to make port of entry. My guess is that Ravi went to Ireland, landed on one of the loneliest coasts in the world, probably from that missing Iranian submarine, and then tried to sneak into England through the back door, the Irish ferry."

Admiral Morris was thoughtful. "And what do you need to find out? What brought you in here with such obvious urgency?"

"Sir, I need to know whether that girl in the photograph is definitely Carla Martin from the Estuary Hotel."

"Well, is that difficult?"

"No. Not as soon as I can get down to Brockhurst. And I was wondering if I could take a helicopter, right now."

"You may. And then we better meet right here in the morning to plan some kind of strategy, stop Arnie from going to England. At least stop him from sticking to his original schedule."

"Okay, I'll get going. And be warned—Arnie is not going to take kindly to this interference with his plans."

One hour later, Lieutenant Commander Ramshawe came in to land on the grassy banks of the Rappahannock River, at the north end of the township of Brockhurst.

Still just in his shirtsleeves and still holding the picture, he walked up to the main road and turned left toward the house owned by Mrs. Emily Gallagher. If she was not in, he would make straight for the hotel. If she was at home, he might not need to bother with a further personal call, because he could probably get Jim Caborn to walk up the street to Emily's house.

Which was how it turned out. Emily welcomed Jimmy warmly and immediately went to make some tea. Then she took the photograph, placed her spectacles at the end of her nose, and stared at the images.

"My goodness, yes," she said. "That is very definitely my friend Carla. Where on earth was this photograph taken? She's never bothered to contact me, you know. So disappointing, so very disappointing."

She then telephoned the Estuary, and Jim Caborn said he was on his way. Ten minutes later, he arrived and confirmed precisely what Mrs. Gallagher had said. Yes, that was Carla Martin, and no, she had never been in touch.

The three of them sat quietly sipping tea, and Jimmy told them that Carla was almost certainly married to General Rashood, perhaps the most wanted terrorist in the world. Emily and Jim were astounded but seemed grateful for the knowledge, as if a dark cloud had been removed from their lives, some final clarification as to the identity of the girl they had both befriended and whose mysterious disappearance now seemed to make more sense.

Emily remained puzzled why Carla had found it necessary actually to murder Matt Barker, rather than just fight him off. And Jimmy tried to explain to her the mantra of the international terrorist. How, in their minds, there can be nothing to draw attention from anyone.

No matter who gets too close, they must be eliminated. They cannot be allowed to live. And there was no question of just stabbing Matt Barker somewhere on his body where death would not result. Carla could not risk Matt Barker, dripping blood, chasing her down the street like a bull elephant, with all the attendant publicity and questions that would cause. Stealth was her watchword. Matt must die.

Emily seemed to accept this. And it was soon time for Jimmy to leave. Since Detective Joe Segel had never met Carla, he was out of the loop so far as Lt. Commander Ramshawe was concerned. He decided to chat with him on the telephone tomorrow. Meanwhile he said his good-byes to Emily and Jim, and walked back up the street, to board the U.S. Marine helicopter for the ride back to Fort Meade.

All his suspicions were now confirmed. Yes, Carla Martin had journeyed to Brockhurst specifically to find out when the admiral and Kathy would be leaving for a vacation. Yes, the murder of Matt Barker had been a somewhat unforeseen circumstance. Yes, Carla had fled to Ireland carrying a different passport to meet the landed terrorist Rashood in Dublin. And here they both were, entering England to murder Arnie.

And what now? So far as Jimmy was concerned, the Brits could begin a nationwide search for Ravi and Shakira, but they probably would not find them. So far as Jimmy could tell, the only way to snuff out the danger was to persuade Arnold not to go to London under any circumstances whatsoever. And he still had no hopes of that, despite this blazing new evidence which was, in his mind at least, decisive. Hamas had decided that Arnie must go.

He came in to land at Fort Meade and was driven to the parking lot. There he boarded his Jaguar and headed downtown to the Watergate, where Jane awaited him. She poured him a beer and told him she had successfully launched a raid on the Australian embassy kitchens and left with a couple of prime-cut New York sirloins, which she would grill on the balcony while he had another row with Arnold Morgan.

The steaks were perfect, and the row was predictable. Arnold would not hear of canceling his trip, Ravi Rashood or no Ravi Rashood. "You can't run your life around these bastards, kid," he said. "If this character wants to have a shot at me, he'll have to get past the best security agents in the world. I'll brief them, and they'll be waiting for anyone who thinks they can carry out an assassination."

He added that he was not worried, and that he would keep a sharp lookout all through his forthcoming trip. Cancellation? Out of the question.

The search for the general, Jimmy knew, would now turn out to be a rare marriage between local civil authorities and military personnel. Shakira was wanted for murder in Brockhurst, Virginia, and that was Joe Segel's territory, and Ravi was wanted for murder in West Cork, which was where Ray McDwyer was still in charge. Concurrently, both Ravi and his wife were wanted by the Mossad for murder, treason, and God knows what else; Ravi was wanted by the SAS for murder and desertion; and the British government wanted him for murder and treason against the state.

After dinner, Jimmy and Jane sat and watched the television news, sipping glasses of his father's vintage port. Finally Jane asked, "Do you really think someone is going to try and kill Arnold?"

"I know they're going to try, babe. It's only a matter of whether they can shoot straight."

0930 Friday 20 July
Central London

They brought Shakira's car around to the front of the Syrian embassy shortly after breakfast. Ravi and his wife ran down the steps into the car, and the general drove them around Belgrave Square and out along Pont Street to Knightsbridge, just below Harrods.

Here they turned left and headed out, against the morning traffic, along the tree-lined Cromwell Road toward the western suburbs of the capital city of the United Kingdom. The road followed the River Thames for two miles and then veered upward onto the long, perpetually busy M-4 motorway to South Wales. Ravi, however, did not veer upward. He ducked off, expertly, and drove along the gloomy old road beneath the freeway, running left of the massive gray stone pillars that support the Chiswick flyover.

When the motorway swung slightly north, Ravi headed due west, turning onto the Great West Road for another couple of miles before the Heston junction. And there he turned north, through an area that often looks like a suburb of Calcutta rather than London. Out here, in the colorful suburb of Southall, migrating Asians have built an entire community.

There are three-generation families living here, all tracing their blood roots back to the Subcontinent, to the Punjab, Bombay, Karachi, Jaipur, Bengal, and Bangalore, many of them hardworking families who resolutely faced the hundred-year struggle to fit in, to be accepted, to be British.

And a high percentage prospered as natural businessmen. The entire area is redolent with shops and stores, open all the hours God made. Southall is a thousand light-years from Belgrave Square and London's West End—but it lives and it thrives, an Indian and Pakistani enclave—a modern reminder of the price of empire.

Ravi headed straight along Merrick Road, crossed the railroad near Southall Station, and plunged into a labyrinth of side streets full of rowhouses. Finally, he turned onto a quiet residential avenue. He checked a piece of paper that Shakira handed him and headed for number 16.

They pulled into the wide driveway and parked close to the front door of a big double-fronted Victorian house. Ravi noticed a new BMW parked around the far side of the property. But that measure of opulence did not extend to the garden, which was heavily overgrown. The grass needed a lawnmower, the bushes were too tall and overhanging the drive, there was not a flower planted, and the general effect was an unkempt section of wild woodland.

The house, however, was immaculately painted, with white window frames and trim and a shiny, jet-black double front door. Ravi left Shakira in the car and knocked.

It was answered by an elderly man of Indian appearance. He was wearing a turban and the kind of short gray work jacket a butler might use for cleaning the silver.

"Good morning, sir. Mr. Spencer?"

Ravi nodded.

"Please come this way."

Ravi followed him down the hall to a small padded leather door, which opened softly when the Indian inserted a credit card–shaped key into the lock. A green light flashed, and Ravi was faced with a well-lit staircase going downward, with deep steps carpeted in dark green pile.

From below came a voice with an Indian inflection. "Please come down, Mr. Spencer. I am of course expecting you."

Ravi descended and shook hands with his host, Mr. Prenjit Kumar, whom he understood to be one of the best private gunsmiths in England. There was no one else in the basement workroom, but there were three definite work areas, each one illuminated by a bright overhead light, slung low over a surface that looked like dark red baize. The place was much more like a jeweler's than an armament factory.

Mr. Kumar was a tall, slender Indian from Bengal. He wore dark blue pants and a white shirt beneath a dark blue sweater. Almost covering his entire wardrobe was a large green apron, like that of a freemason. He wore no turban and stared evenly at Ravi through slim wire spectacles. His eyes were almost black, and his expression was wary.

"You come highly recommended as a client," he said. "And I understand you require a custom-made piece, a one-off, tailored to your precise requirements."

"Correct," replied Ravi. "A sniper rifle, which you'll probably reconstruct from the Austrian SSG 69."

Mr. Kumar smiled. "You like that old design?"

"I have never really used anything else."

"No need, Mr. Spencer. It is a superb piece of engineering. No one has ever built a better rifle—and a lot of people have tried."

Ravi nodded. And Mr. Kumar smiled. "I know better than to ask," he said. "But perhaps you were in the SAS in another life."

"Perhaps I was. But now I must be more careful. And I think our biggest problem may be that I need to dismantle the weapon and carry it in a briefcase, no larger than, say, twelve inches by eighteen. About four wide, maximum."

"You are not thinking of trying to transport it through an airport, are you?"

"Absolutely not."

"You understand that I must be very guarded, Mr. Spencer. In certain quarters, my work is well-known, even though I would not engrave this rifle with a serial number. It would not be in either of our interests for you to be . . . er . . . apprehended."

"I understand that, of course," replied Ravi. "You have my assurance that the rifle will never leave the UK."

"You understand the SSG 69 fires only one single highly accurate shot, although it has a five-round feed magazine?"

"I do, and despite the rather laborious reloading process, it can still achieve a shot-grouping of less than forty centimeters from eight hundred meters."

"It's nice to speak to someone who understands the excellence of the rifle. Do you have precise measurements written down for me?"

"I do. And I will require a silencer and a telescopic sight, 6 x 24 ZFM."

"That will not be a problem, but I do anticipate, given the restrictions on storage and carrying, that your barrel cannot realistically be longer than, say, thirteen inches. Naturally, you have no choice but to go to a bolt action. You have no room for a gas chamber, or anything else to give you a repeater."

"I anticipate firing only once."

"Range?"

"No more than a hundred yards. And I must ask you, can you purchase a brand-new SSG 69 and then make the adjustments?"

"People in my trade, Mr. Spencer, can purchase anything."

"Are you confident about a removable stock?"

"Yes. I am sure of that. But you will not want the regular Cycolac stock, which is rounded and firm and will take up too much room. I will cut and remove it and build you a slim screw-in stock made of aluminum that will fit into your case."

"Speaking of which, I was hoping you would also make the case."

"Of course. I will build the rifle first and then build the case around it. And I must ask you now, will you be firing from a moving position? Or will you be still? I ask because it is important to know whether you anticipate reloading and firing once more."

"I'll be still. But I do not think there will be time. One single head shot is probably all I will get. I prefer the head because it may be several seconds before anyone locates the bullet hole in the skull. A chest shot always tends to be messy and very obvious."

"Yes, and under such circumstances, the silencer needs to be effective. That way nobody hears, nobody can trace the direction, and you may get one more try if you miss, eh?"

"Mr. Kumar, we are both in a precision business. If the rifle is perfectly constructed, I will only need one shot."

"Very well, Mr. Spencer. You would like me to build you one bolt-action sniper rifle, reconstructed on the lines of the SSG 69 Austrian masterpiece of the 1980s. Barrel hardened under the regular cold-forging method. A 7.62mm bullet, muzzle velocity 860 meters per second. Lightweight. Short barrel. Malfunction risk: zero."

"Correct. With case."

"And, Mr. Spencer, the payment method? After I tell you the cost."

"Tell me."

"Including everything. The purchase of the original. The hours of highly skilled work. The new materials, the practice bullets, the specialized target bullets. I would not touch it for under twenty thousand pounds."

"Cash," said Ravi. "Ten thousand now. Ten more when I pick it up. How long?"

"Three weeks."

"Too long. I need it by Saturday morning next week."

Prenjit Kumar was silent. "Mr. Spencer, I would have to work on that rifle night and day, to the exclusion of all else. There may be some adjustment in the cost."

Ravi, however, knew one thing for absolute certain: he knew the hawk-faced Indian before him understood that there were ten thousand pounds in his pocket. Ten thousand pounds that he did not get offered every day.

"There will be no adjustment," he said. "The time you work is not relevant. You know what I want. You have stated a price and I have agreed. It matters not whether it takes you one week or one year. The price is the same."

"And what if you should arrive and the weapon is not completed?"

"In that case, I would have to make other arrangements and use a different rifle. One that might expose me to greater risk. And you would be very disappointed, and perhaps even resentful, and then I would have to kill you."

Kumar was well used to dealing with the thugs of the international arms-dealing world, the occasional terrorist, and regular mercenaries. But the man standing before him was like no one he had ever met. To his dark eyes, Ravi was calm but menacing, confident but careful, and there was a coldness about him that had alarm bells ringing in the Indian gun-smith's head.

"Your rifle will be ready, Mr. Spencer," he said.

"Twenty thousand?"

"Twenty thousand," he repeated. "And I am assuming you will want bullets that will explode on impact, making survival from a head shot impossible."

"Yes," said Ravi. "Those will do very well." He reached into the right in-side pocket of his jacket and pulled out an envelope which contained two hundred £50 notes. He handed it to Kumar, who acknowledged the down payment with a smile and a respectful nod of his head. He did not count the banknotes.

Kumar escorted him to the front door, the two men shook hands, but before he left, Ravi had one last request.

"Kumar," he said, "I would also like you to provide me with a pistol. Standard issue, but lightweight and terminally deadly with one shot."

"That will not be a problem," the Indian replied. "I'll find you some-thing, and there will be no further charge."

The Hamas C-in-C smiled at this confirmation that £20,000 had in-deed proved ample payment. And he climbed behind the wheel of the Audi and headed out of the driveway. Hardly glancing to the left or right, he and Shakira drove straight back to the Syrian embassy, from which he would scarcely venture during the coming week.

Meanwhile, news of General Rashood's sudden appearance in Holy-head flashed through the intelligence networks. New Scotland Yard in London, while anxious not to make a public manhunt out of it, pressed all the buttons to ensure that the archterrorist would not find it easy to leave the country.

The photograph was circulated to all seaports and airports. Serving officers and men from 22 SAS who had known Major Ray Kerman were seconded in teams of six to check passengers at every port of entry or exit in the country. They were detailed to find him at any cost, and not to al-low him to slip through the net.

The police, customs officials, and security guards had their leaves can-celed in the areas where General Rashood might show up. Heathrow, Gatwick, Luton, and Manchester airports looked like military strongholds. The English Channel seaports were steel-ringed with military personnel and armed police who boarded the ferries, searched the freighters, and checked out private yachts.

Even the smaller airports, Bristol, Bournemouth, Southampton, Newcastle, Edinburgh, Glasgow, and Prestwick, were inundated with police and antiterrorist officers. Most of the airport and seaport staff had no idea why there was this sudden red alert. But the atmosphere was so serious, everyone was happy to cooperate. Flights were delayed, ships were held up, and no one even caught a sniff of General and Mrs. Rashood.

This was mostly because they never again left the Syrian embassy for the first five days of their visit. They were officially on Syrian soil, even though it was in Belgrave Square, and all of those usual diplomatic taboos were strictly observed at the Court of St. James. The London police did not harass the embassies, because retaliation was too easy: give the Syrians a hard time in London, and the next thing would be some kind of a witchhunt at the British embassy in north Damascus.

Back in the USA, Lt. Commander Ramshawe was helpless. There was nothing the Americans could do except offer assistance if required. The Hamas military boss and his wife were in hiding somewhere in the UK, and no one knew any more. And with each passing day, Arnold and Kathy were one step closer to the assassination attempt Jimmy Ramshawe was certain would happen.

All week there was only one break. At 0630 (local) on Tuesday morning, July 24, the Royal Navy ops room at the Gibraltar Station detected the Iranian Kilo moving slowly through the Strait, a hundred feet below the surface. They picked her up again several hours later, snorkeling in the narrow seaway, and reported it back to COMSUBLANT.

Again there was nothing anyone could do. The Iranians, despite some hefty breaches of international law, were still entitled to send their navy anywhere they wished on the high seas, just so long as the Kilo did not open fire on anyone. In turn, for a Western power to attempt to sink the Iranians would have been a flagrant act of war, which no one felt like committing. At least not in the Mediterranean.

Jimmy Ramshawe, in receipt of the signal that pinpointed the Kilo, felt nothing but a sense of total frustration. The submarine had turned up where he said it would turn up, a bit late, but it was a long voyage from the south coast of Ireland. He was frankly astounded that his early diagnosis of the plot to kill the admiral was not now universally accepted. Of course the Kilo had dropped off General Rashood in County Cork, and of course Rashood was now in England with Carla Martin, awaiting the arrival of Arnold and Kathy.

He accepted the difficulty of arresting the terrorist couple, of finding them, and, with mounting anxiety, he once more called the admiral. And Arnold, for the first time, seemed to accept that Jimmy might very well be on to something. But he was not being ruled by a goddamned towelhead, nossir. Not even one as lethally dangerous as Ravi Rashood.

"When you have outstanding security, provided by the President of the United States of America, you gotta trust your guys," he growled.

Jimmy, slipping into a broad Australian outback accent, retorted, "Kinda like JFK and Ronald Reagan."

"No, not like them. They were both on public duty; JFK was in a motorcade, Ronnie was outside a hotel with a crowd of people waiting. I'm an unknown former U.S. Naval officer on a private visit with my wife. Hardly anyone will know I'm there."

"I can think of at least two bastards who will know: that bloody barmaid, and her reptile husband who went missing from 22 SAS. For Christ's sake be careful. That's all I can say."

0915 Wednesday 25 July
Piccadilly, London

The wide thoroughfare of Piccadilly was gridlocked, all the way from the Wellington Arch at the western end of Green Park to Piccadilly Circus. The morning rush hour was under way, and it was quicker to walk than to take a bus or a taxi.

General Rashood stood among the fast-moving crowd on the corner of Dover Street, diagonally across from the Ritz Hotel. Mick Barton would not have recognized him. He was wearing a slim blond wig, a trimmed moustache and goatee beard, and heavy spectacles, with jeans, a white T-shirt, and sneakers. No jacket. He carried a briefcase.

Right now he was trying to get his bearings, assessing the distance across the yellow-painted lines of the junction into Arlington Street, to the entrance of the hotel. He stood there for only three minutes and then turned and walked through glass-paneled swing doors into the glum reception area of a London office block.

The entrance was sited amid a line of shops that curled around the south side of the block, from the Post Office on Dover Street, briefly along Piccadilly itself, and then around into Albemarle Street. The offices were situated on all six floors above the shops. Ever since the recent property collapse in London, there had been vacancies not only in this building, but in most others.

Ravi had stumbled into a buyers' market. He wished only to rent, but if necessary he would purchase a leasehold. In this financial climate, however, a leasehold would most certainly not be necessary. Renting would be just fine, at a price way too high for a small space, but not ruinous.

He walked up to the doorman and requested the office manager. "I did call this morning," he said. "Haakon Fretheim, Finland Farms Marketing Board."

"Certainly, sir."

Ravi was led up to a second-floor office fronting on Piccadilly. The rental agent was a bespectacled thirtyish lady wearing a blue suit and a Sotheby's International name tag—Judith Birchell.

She confirmed to Ravi that there were seven available suites of offices at present, but the one she had mentioned on the phone, the single room with reception annex, was probably sufficient for one accountant and a secretary.

"It's on the fourth floor, right above here," she said. "Views directly across to the Ritz and St. James's Street . . . let's go up and take a look."

Ravi followed her out to the hall, and they took the elevator two floors higher. There were several doors off the central area, two of which were open with sounds of activity from within. Two others had lights on, and the last one required a key to gain entry.

Judith showed Ravi into a carpeted office with a bright south-facing window. Ravi checked the catch and decided not to request permission to open it. There was a Venetian blind, which obviously could be lowered, and a desk and chair, which the agent said came with the rental, the last tenants having left the furniture and a rent debt for several hundred pounds.

"They left in a bit of a hurry," she said. "They'd been gone more than a week before we realized they weren't coming back."

Ravi chuckled. "What rent were they paying?"

"A little over three thousand a month," she replied. "But there's been a rate cut since then. This is yours for twenty-two hundred, first and last deposit, on the six-month lease you mentioned."

"Can I have it right away?"

"Oh, certainly. This building has a resident cleaning staff. The whole place has been vacuumed, carpets steam-cleaned, and the desk cleared out. The phones are connected, there's central Internet, and the bathroom is right across the hall. Right next to it is the incinerator. You may dump the dry contents of your wastebasket down there, just paper and unwanted documents, not kitchen waste.

"If you leave the deposit, I'll give you two keys, and one for the front door. The doormen are on duty from 7 A.M. until 10 P.M. Don and Reggie. You'll find them extremely helpful."

"That will be excellent," said Ravi, taking one more look through the window, straight at the curved dark blue- and gold-trimmed awning above the main entrance to the Ritz Hotel. "This will do very nicely indeed."

"It's a standard rental agreement, same for everyone. You can sign it in my office, subject to the references I mentioned, plus a bank statement, and a passport if you're not a British national."

They returned to the second floor and Ravi produced a nicely forged reference from the Egyptian embassy confirming that they had dealt many times with Mr. Fretheim concerning Finnish trade agreements, and they knew him to be trustworthy and aboveboard. Judith photocopied his equally well-forged Finnish passport, and glanced at the bank account of the Syrian ambassador, upon which the name had been changed and copied to read *Haakon Fretheim, of 23 Ennismore Gardens, London SW7.*

It showed a current balance of £18,346 in credit, and Ravi, with a remarkable display of affluence, paid Judith a total of three months' rent with an American Express card issued originally to the military attaché in the Jordanian embassy in Paris.

The agent handed over two office keys and told him to collect frontdoor keys from Reggie, who was working the morning shift today. "I'll call him before you get down there," she said. "I expect I'll see you around."

Ravi shook hands with Judith Birchell and made his way downstairs. He stopped for a chat with Reggie the doorman and exited through the glass-paneled doors, back to the corner of Dover Street. He stepped forward and looked up to the window of his new office. He moved to stand directly below it and then looked at the angle diagonally across to the main entrance of the Ritz.

When the traffic light at the top of Arlington Street turned red, he moved swiftly across the central no-parking zone, corner to corner, pacing the precise distance from the outer wall of his office to the six white stone steps that led up to the polished mahogany revolving door of the hotel.

The traffic light had halted the one-way line of vehicles heading directly out of Arlington Street, across Piccadilly and north up Dover Street. But the onrushing line of cars and taxis running toward central London was up and moving faster than Ravi was walking, and he was hustled along by a couple of loud blasts on the horn from cab drivers. He did not look up.

Instead, he kept walking, and kept counting, until he reached the hotel steps: fifty-four yards, add six for the height of his office building, and he was looking at a shot, from sixty yards out, at an angle of fifteen degrees from the horizontal of his office outer wall. That, he considered, would be a breeze for the powerful Austrian sniper rifle with its proven needle-point accuracy from almost a half mile.

Quickly he took stock of the Ritz entrance—the curved brass rails down either side of the steps, the two curly, potted evergreens, like sentries left and right of the steps, the rounded archway of the awning. And directly in the front of the hotel, the no-waiting area, entirely controlled by the top-hatted doormen, moving the guests along, arrivals and departures, with the authority of Metropolitan policemen.

Ravi did not catch the eye of either doorman. Instead, he walked quickly past and kept going for another hundred yards until he reached the pub on the corner of Bennet and Arlington, the Blue Posts, with its cheerful line of small outside tables, none of them occupied.

Ravi sat down and waited for a few minutes until a waiter came out and agreed to bring him orange juice and coffee. And there England's most wanted man, heavily disguised as a native of Finland, sat and quietly watched the comings and goings at the Ritz Hotel, acquainting himself with the patterns of the traffic and the people. He was already concerned that this was not a huge area, but one that could easily be swamped by security men.

Even more irritating was the little traffic queue that formed at the top of Arlington Street right outside the main door into the Ritz. A tall vehicle waiting in there could obscure his shot, although he imagined the U.S. embassy car, which would undoubtedly be awaiting the admiral, would already be ensconced in the prime spot at the base of the six white steps.

After an hour, he paid and walked back across Piccadilly to Dover Street and into his new quarters.

"Hello, sir. Back already?" said Reggie.

"Just delivering some of my stationery," replied Ravi. "I'll take the elevator."

Inside his office, Ravi moved the chair to the front of the window. Then he dropped the Venetian blind, bent one of the lower laths downward, and peered across to the Ritz entrance. Five times in the next fifteen minutes, he made notes of a high-sided vehicle driving past the hotel. Two of them parked outside in traffic for between thirty-three and thirty-nine seconds, two drove straight past without coming to a halt, and one was so far over to the right that it made no difference whether it stopped or not.

Only one of the five would have caused him a problem, which the Hamas general decided was a risk with which he would have to live. Once more he exited his new office building, and this time he turned right, walking the length of Picadilly, then crossing, via the Hyde Park Corner tube station, the gigantic road junction at the end of Grosvenor Place.

He strolled into Belgrave Square on an easy stride, pleased with his morning's work, but full of regret that he dare not take Shakira out this evening to some of his old London haunts—the ones that had decorated his young life, a thousand years ago, when he had never even heard of Hamas, nor the pious self-righteous philosophies which accompany that glowering terrorist organization.

He thought of the Grenadier, just around the corner in Grosvenor Crescent Mews; he thought of the Bunch of Grapes in Knightsbridge, where almost every wealthy young Catholic girl in London could be found after Sunday morning Mass at Brompton Oratory; and he thought of the Scarsdale Arms, and the Windsor Castle, and the Italian restaurants in Fulham Road and King's Road. So many places where he had once been made welcome, with a credit card provided by his father. But these places would now be like a minefield, still populated, no doubt, by people who might very well recognize him.

With the most profound regret, Ravi finally realized that he was an outlaw in a once-friendly city, an outcast in his own land, an enemy of the people. And at that moment, if he could have turned the clock back and been allowed to do things differently, he would most certainly have done so. Except for Shakira. Always Shakira. Surely, he thought, no man had ever lived with a greater, more perplexing conundrum.

Greater love hath no man than this, muttered Ravi, adjusting the Gospel of Saint John, *that he would lay down his country for his wife.*

Grinning at the dexterity of his own words, he walked calmly up the steps to the Syrian embassy and rang the bell, as arranged. He was ever the visitor, never a resident. And the lady for whom he had laid down his country welcomed him as if he had been away for six months rather than four hours.

For Shakira, the presence of her husband was the only solace for the long lonely hours she spent in the gilded splendor of the embassy. Occasionally she would be offered lunch or perhaps tea with a visiting Arab sheik, and they would speak politely about the political situation in the Middle East. But on each of the next two days, Ravi would leave in the morning and go to his office, always acquainting himself with fellow tenants if possible, and especially with Don and Reggie the doormen.

He normally lunched at the embassy, but in the afternoons he made another visit to Dover Street, and on Friday evening he was there yet again at 8 P.M., leaving at 9:30, carrying his briefcase, still dressed in jeans, T-shirt, and sneakers, still wearing his blond wig, moustache, and goatee. Still speaking in what he guessed, wrongly, was a Finnish accent, but in truth sounded more like Trinidad than Helsinki.

Nonetheless, the farm marketing executive from Northern Europe, Haakon Fretheim, quickly became a familiar figure in the building, perceived as a busy, industrious, and courteous gentleman who worked erratic hours for an accountant.

0900 Saturday 28 July
Southall, West London

Ravi drove out to the workshops of Prenjit Kumar alone. He parked the car in the same spot and was led down to the basement by the gunsmith himself. And there, lying open on the red baize beneath the light, was a hand-tooled brown leather case containing all the parts of an Austrian SSG 69 sniper rifle, each one set into precision grooves carved into a black velvet interior.

The barrel rested in its own groove, above the main firing section, which contained the bolt and the magazine, plus the trigger and guard. The silencer also had its own section, around which were set the light metal components which would form the newly designed stock, made specifically to fit General Rashood's shoulder and arm length. Along the bottom part of the interior were spaces for six of the exploding bullets, and the gunsights.

"Problems?" asked Ravi.

"None," replied Kumar, "except that I have had no sleep for a week."

"Then you have earned your money," he said. "Perhaps you would assemble the rifle and then I'll dismantle it and put it together myself."

"Of course," replied the Bengali gunsmith. "And I hope you agree, this is the most beautiful object, a work of art. Very light and very deadly."

He removed the main firing section from the case and picked up the barrel carefully, as if he were handling precious gems. Expertly he screwed the barrel into place, and then clipped in the sights.

He took out the metal plate that screwed into the neck behind the trigger guard, and then took two silver struts for the stock and screwed each one into place, using just his fingers. The top one went out straight, perpendicular. The second was set at more of an angle, but finished level at the end. Then he took the cast-bronze base of the stock, made to fit Ravi's shoulder precisely, and clipped it onto the struts, forming the outline shape of a rifle stock, but without the bulk. Ravi looked on approvingly.

Above the magazine there were two clips, set five inches apart. To these Kumar attached the telescopic sight, sliding it into place and locking it securely. Finally he screwed the silencer into the barrel. And then he held the rifle at arm's length and said, admiringly, "Magnificent, hah?"

Ravi took it from him and held it against his shoulder, staring into the telescopic sight, straight at the crosshairs. Then he relaxed and held the rifle in the palms of both hands, away from his body, as if weighing it, balancing it. During his years in the SAS, this weapon, or one precisely like it, had been like an old friend—super accurate, super quiet, and super reliable, all the qualities a professional sniper requires.

This SSG looked different now. But it felt the same, a little lighter, but with the same familiar well-balanced deadliness about it.

"Can we try it?" he asked.

"Certainly," said Kumar. "Follow me. I'll bring a half dozen practice bullets." He walked to a door set halfway along the exterior wall, opened it, and beckoned Ravi through. The corridor was well lit, and they walked maybe twenty yards to an indoor shooting range—a long dark tunnel, lit only at the far end, where a large target had been set on an easel. There were wires attached to the target, which was a twelve-inch-wide bull's-eye. In front of Ravi just below shoulder level was a countertop on which to lean.

"You have five bullets," said Kumar. "Let's see how the rifle suits you."

Ravi leaned forward and, pushing the specially designed safety catch, freed up the rifle to fire. He aimed carefully, placing the crosshairs right across the red heart of the target. He squeezed the trigger, but the target was fifty yards away and it was difficult to see the result of his marksmanship.

In fact, Ravi took no notice of his success or failure. He just fired all five, and then signaled for Mr. Kumar to pull up the target for inspection. The Indian wound it in with a small wheel, exactly the same as in a fairground, but he raised his eyebrows when he checked the piece of cardboard.

All five bullets had gone through virtually the same hole. To the left, there was a very slight bulge, maybe an eighth of an inch, and at the bottom there was another minuscule variance. None of the five shots had strayed beyond the basic red circle of the bull.

"Very nice, Mr. Spencer. Very nice indeed. It's a privilege to be in the company of a master."

"Sentiments I share," replied Ravi. "This is an outstanding rifle, and I thank you."

Together they walked back into the main workshop, and Ravi carefully dismantled the weapon, placing each piece into its allotted slot in the new case. He took his time and then clipped the case shut. He handed over a large brown envelope that contained the balance of the money, again two hundred £50 notes. And again, Prenjit Kumar did not count it.

This omission was noted by Ravi, who perfectly understood that there had been no necessity to check the cash for the down payment last week, since he was scheduled to return. This, however, was different. After today, Ravi would probably never see the gunsmith again, and he looked up and said, "You don't want to count it?"

The Bengali smiled. "Of course not," he replied. "I know when I am in the presence of a gentleman."

And then he presented Ravi with a heavy cardboard box, around five inches square and three deep. "There's thirty practice bullets in here," he said. "You will want to adjust the sights for perfect vision from the precise distance of your target. It may take a while, of trial and error, so I have given you plenty of ammunition. Here also are three targets that may be useful."

General Rashood smiled and thanked him. He offered his hand and said quietly, "Mr. Kumar, there are only five people in the world who know that you have made this rifle for me. Two of them you know, and all of them I know. Should anyone discover our secret, all four of us will know that you have been indiscreet. I am sure you understand what the penalty would be."

"Mr. Spencer," he replied, "my own risk is equally great. There will be no indiscretions, I assure you."

Before he led Ravi up the green-carpeted stairs to the front door, he presented him with one further item, wrapped in a black velvet bag. "This is the pistol you requested. It's a new Austrian Glock 17 9mm. The safety catch comes off when the trigger is pressed. It will not discharge if you drop it. And it will not let you down."

Once more they shook hands, and the master terrorist softly said good-bye to the gunsmith from Bengal.

He drove back to the embassy in a thoughtful mood, aware that this was Saturday and of how much he longed to take Shakira out for the evening, perhaps the theatre, and then dinner at the Ivy where the "stars" are apt to gather after a show. Ravi did not have a shred of time for self-obsessed play-actors or any other kind of celebrities, but Shakira would have loved it. Anyway, he doubted that he could have secured a table.

And a much bigger "anyway" was that the entire thing was out of the question. One recognition, by anyone from his former life, and he'd either have to kill them or flee the country. So once more he faced up to a long waiting day at the embassy. Aside from the boredom, he was, however, eternally grateful for the perfection of the cover he enjoyed behind the ramparts of No. 8 Belgrave Square.

Up in their bedroom, he presented Shakira with the pistol, which Kumar had thoughtfully loaded, and Shakira did precisely as she was told and placed it in her large handbag. "You will carry that wherever you go," he told her. "We have many enemies."

They had lunch at the embassy, where the cooks were under orders always to produce food that reminded the ambassador of the desert and the culture of the northern end of the Arabian Peninsula. Thus lunch when it arrived was chicken kebabs, rice, houmus, and salad.

They sipped fruit juice and then sat in the opulent rear drawing room. They read the newspapers, and Ravi watched the King George VI and Queen Elizabeth Stakes at Ascot, won for the umpteenth time by the Irish with a superb dark bay colt sired by the Coolmore-based champion stallion, Galileo.

Shakira, who had been paying scant attention, suddenly heard the word "Coolmore" and almost jumped out of her chair. "I've been there!" she exclaimed.

"Where? Ascot?" asked Ravi.

"No, Coolmore," she said. "I visited it while I was waiting for you in Ireland."

"Did you see the great Galileo? That horse who just won was his son."

"Well, I didn't actually go in, but I saw the big iron gates, and I saw all the green countryside where the horses live. It's in Tipperary."

Ravi, of course, like anyone with the remotest knowledge of horse racing, knew all about Coolmore. He grinned at Shakira and asked, "How on earth did you find your way down there?"

"I met a man in the hotel in Dublin who owned a filly foal. I think she was born there," she replied, accurately. "And it was very important to him that her brother, called Easter Rebel, would win the Irish Stakes or something."

"The what?"

"The Irish something. I can't remember. But it mattered to him."

"That would have been the first week in July. It was probably the Irish Derby."

"Derby, that's it. He wanted Easter Rebel to win the Irish Derby."

"And did he?"

"I forgot to find out."

Ravi laughed. "I'm not sure you've mastered an in-depth appreciation of horse racing," he said. "Otherwise, you'd have remembered to find out what happened to Easter Rebel."

"I'll tell you what I do remember," she retorted. "Easter Rebel was also the son of that telescope man—what's his name, Galileo."

"Was he? Well, you ought to know whether the Rebel won and made your new friend rich."

"How can I find out?"

"I'll do that for you. If I can use that laptop computer over there on the sideboard."

Ravi walked over and opened it. He searched with Google and found a site for the *Racing Post*. Then he tapped in the name "Easter Rebel" and, nine seconds later, learned that the colt had not won the Irish Derby, but had been beaten by a head in a photo finish.

"Just lost," he told Shakira. And he made a signal with his right hand, placing his index finger about a quarter of an inch above his thumb. "That much," he added.

"Poor Mr. O'Donnell will be very sad," she said.

"I assure you he won't," said Ravi. "I expect he's going to sell his filly, and most breeders would be happy going through the ring with a sister to a colt beaten by a head in the Irish Derby. Don't feel sorry for him."

"Okay, I won't."

"Was his filly also by Galileo?"

"Can't remember," she said absently, leafing through her fashion magazine.

Life and death for Mr. O'Donnell, total lack of interest by Shakira. Ravi smiled and thought of his father, the man the newspapers always referred to as the *"shipping tycoon and racehorse breeder."*

He missed seeing his family but was certain that they now knew what he had done and what disgrace he had brought upon them all. Treason, mutiny, murder. My God! He hardly dared to think about it.

Toward the end of the afternoon, Ravi retired to his embassy suite, leaving Shakira to watch a sitcom on the television. He opened the leather case and started counting. Carefully he took out the sections of the rifle, assembling them into the finely engineered finished product.

Then he started his count again, disassembled the weapon, and placed the pieces back in the case. It had taken him twenty-eight seconds to put it together and twenty-four seconds to take it apart. The twenty-eight did not matter, but the twenty-four was critical and it was too long. From the moment he fired that lethal 7.62mm shell at the admiral's unprotected head, every second counted. Because right then he would be in the critical part of the operation, the getaway.

Twenty-four seconds was almost a half minute. There would be, he knew, American Secret Service agents, London police security, and possibly military personnel swarming outside the Ritz. If they had even an inkling of where the bullet had come from, they would be across Piccadilly in fifteen seconds and into the building where his office was situated. If they were through those glass doors before he was out, he'd be trapped, overwhelmed, and headed for the gallows on charges of murder and high treason against Her Majesty's forces.

That twenty-four seconds had to be reduced, and if it couldn't, he might have to abort the mission. But Ravi knew it could. Over and over, he assembled the rifle and then disassembled it. For almost two hours he practiced, finally realizing that the principal solutions to the operation were the swift removal of the telescopic sight and the level of tightness on the wide silver-plated finger screw which attached the stock to the neck.

After another hour, he could disassemble that sniper rifle in eighteen seconds. Within two hours, he had it down to twelve, and those twelve seconds would be all he could afford while packing the rifle away and bolting down the stairs to the freedom of Dover Street.

Early that evening, before dinner with the ambassador, Ravi went shopping alone. He walked through to Knightsbridge and wandered into Harrods, to the busy ground-floor men's department where once he had shopped with his mother, purchasing a new tweed jacket for school. Today he wanted a new dark gray suit, a blazer, a few shirts, a couple of ties, boxer shorts, socks, and shoes.

It took him forty-five minutes to punch a serious hole in £2,500, and he paid with his Amex card, which would eventually be billed to the government of Jordan via the Paris embassy. He then made his way to men's sporting goods and purchased a loose-fitting tracksuit and a medium-sized athlete's duffel bag.

Casting aside the green Harrods plastic shopping bags, he folded his purchases neatly into the sports bag and walked back to the embassy via Sloane Street and Cadogan Place. He and Shakira dined with the ambassador that evening, in company with two visiting Saudi sheiks.

The following morning, Sunday, July 29, the day before Admiral and Mrs. Morgan were due to board the London flight from Washington, D.C., Ravi summoned the Audi from the Motcombe Street garage and asked one of the embassy staff to fill the tank, because he and Shakira were going on a journey of almost 150 miles.

They left at around 11 A.M., both dressed casually in jeans and sneakers, Shakira wearing a blue shirt and denim jacket, Ravi in his black T-shirt and suede jacket. This was his Irish killing gear, although he did not anticipate murdering anyone today. Indeed, he did not expect to meet, or speak to, one other member of the human race all day.

They once more drove west, but not on the gloomy old A-4 under the Chiswick flyover. This time they sped straight over the top and out onto the wide, fast M-4 motorway. They drove past Heathrow and proceeded for almost an hour to where the landscape begins to rise into the foothills of the Berkshire Downs.

They left the M-4 at Junction 13 and headed north up the A-34 toward Oxford, finally branching left to the switchback road that leads to the village of West Ilsley. This is land where all villages seem to lie in the folds in the Downs, invisible until you are actually in them.

Ravi remembered this country well. He had been out here many times with his father, to look at racehorses being worked, to visit his father's two trainers. In his mind, he recalled the majestic sweep of the Berkshire and Oxfordshire "prairies," miles and miles of undulating land where wheat and barley are grown, the endless fields split only by narrow roads and the horse-training gallops.

But most of all, he remembered the long woods, big but narrow growths of trees set high on the summits. In particular, he recalled those above the horse-racing village of Lambourn. He had seen nothing like it, anywhere in the world, these stark stands of high trees, sometimes four hundred yards long and rarely more than a hundred yards deep, like great, dark Medieval castles ranged along the heights.

Ravi did not know precisely where he was going, but he would know it when he saw it. And he drove through West Ilsley and on through the prairies, through literally square miles of ripening wheat and barley, up through the high village of Farnborough, and then fast down the three-mile-long hill to the town of Wantage, birthplace of King Alfred the Great and the largest town in the fabled Vale of the White Horse.

From here, he drove along the road that leads to the 374-foot chalk carving of the white horse, which has peered across the valley at Uffington for more than two thousand years. Ravi, however, swerved off up the hill to the sensational view of the Lambourn Downs, right across the rolling land, to the castles he had come for, the long woods. And there they were, ranged before him, forbidding, even in the bright summer sunlight. The one closest to him stood high above one of the most important jump-racing stables in the world, that of the maestro Nicky Henderson, godson of the late Field Marshal Viscount Montgomery of Alamein.

Like all of the other five long woods, this one was shadowed, several hundred yards in length, and only a hundred yards wide maximum. It did, however, unlike the others, lack privacy, because the road down to Lambourn village ran hard beside it.

Ravi stopped the car and stared out toward the west. High on the Downs to the left, there was the wood that runs close to the gallops used by many trainers. Directly in front, maybe a mile away, were two high woods situated way up on the land above Kingston Warren. But down below, at the far end of the hundreds of acres belonging to Henry Candy and his family, there was a long wood set in a shallow valley, completely out of view of the trainer's house.

This was a very lonely spot, on the edge of the border country between Henderson and Candy, neither of whom was in any way acquainted with the Hamas commander in chief. It was absolutely perfect for a quiet spell of fine-tuning for a planned assassination.

Ravi drove down from the hills and parked the Audi. He took out the brown leather case and left Shakira in the passenger seat. He walked to the end of the wood, studied the landscape for a few minutes, then climbed the gate and entered the deserted wood. It was just one o'clock on this Sunday, lunchtime. Ravi remembered quite enough about England to know that this was a sacred time for men who work seven days a week throughout the racing season. He did not expect to be disturbed.

First he walked into the center of the trees, and then chose his "range." He used a small drawing pin to fix one of Mr. Kumar's targets to the tall trunk of an ancient oak, two feet off the ground, giving him a downward angle. Then he walked back for sixty paces.

He assembled his rifle, fitted the silencer, and slid a practice bullet into the breech. He stared through the telescopic sight and then made two small adjustments on the screws that varied the crosshairs. There was nowhere to rest the weapon, which there would be in his office, so he leaned on a tree to steady his aim, and squeezed the trigger. The sound was hardly discernible, and, still holding the rifle, Ravi walked the hundred paces to the target and saw that the bullet had smashed into it around three inches to the left of center.

He walked back and once more adjusted the crosshairs. Then he fired again, and again, and again. When he walked back to the target, he could see that he was still slightly left. Once more he made the slight adjustment. Too far. Three more bullets hit home a fraction to the right. They were well grouped, but right.

The operation took another twenty minutes of painstaking correcting and recorrecting, back and forth in this gloomy private firing range, undisturbed, unseen, and all alone.

Finally he had the range and the accuracy. He took down the two battered targets and fixed his last new one to the tree. Again he walked back, reached his firing mark, leaned on the tree, aimed, and fired. This time he required only one shot.

He walked back to the target, which was pristine save for one small round hole, 7.62mm across, straight through the dead center of the bull's-eye. The next time he fired the SSG, the bullet would smash straight through Arnold Morgan's skull, metal splitting the bone, and then blowing the great man's brains out. Instant death. Ravi was certain that he could not miss.

Slowly he dismantled the rifle and, with the utmost care, placed it back in its case and clipped it shut. That, he decided, was a good day's work. The long wood at the end of Henry Candy's one-mile gallop would keep the secret well, and he sincerely hoped Mr. Kumar would do the same.

CHAPTER *11*

Monday 30 July
London

General Rashood had been curiously out of touch with the outside world for almost the entire month of July. In particular, he had been out of touch with the United States of America. And since the death of Matt Barker, Shakira too had little or no idea what America was thinking with regard to her crime, and whether anyone had connected her activities with Admiral Morgan.

No one from the Hamas organization had dared to put in a cell-phone call to either of them, and E-mail was impossible since neither Ravi nor Shakira was traveling with a computer. The general's regular contact in the United States, Ahmed, the cultural attaché at the Jordanian embassy in Washington, was aware of the furor Shakira had left behind in Brockhurst, but had been able only to inform the Hamas High Command in Gaza.

And since, at the time, General Rashood was deep underwater in the Mediterranean Sea, it was a) nearly impossible, b) unwise, and c) totally unnecessary to risk satellite detection, so they sent not a screed of information about his wife's antics on the other side of the world.

Thus Ravi was operating totally in the dark. He had no idea whether anyone in the USA understood that Admiral Morgan might be in danger. Shakira had, of course, told him precisely what had happened, but she had been far away from Brockhurst even before they discovered Matt Barker's body. She was on the other side of the world before the Washington press corps finally switched on to her absence.

The questions haunted the general. What level of security was being employed for the admiral's trip? How many agents from the USA would accompany him? What did the Brits think? Had they been requested to provide extra security? Would Admiral Morgan be surrounded by CIA hard men? Did Scotland Yard have their typical shoot-on-sight team awaiting his arrival?

And, perhaps above all, how long was the admiral staying at the Ritz? How long did Ravi have? If there was a foul-up, where would he and Shakira next locate Admiral and Kathy Morgan?

Ravi could only find answers in the broadest possible sense. In his opinion, Shakira would most certainly have been found out. The FBI would have interviewed anyone in Brockhurst who knew her, and that would most certainly include Mrs. Gallagher. Yes, there would be heavy security surrounding the admiral. And yes, the CIA would almost certainly have been in touch with the British authorities concerning the protection of President Bedford's closest personal adviser, the man who had put him in power.

In Ravi's mind, the worst possible time to attempt the assassination would be the moment of the admiral's arrival. If the security was anything like as ironclad as he thought, it would be impossible to strike and then get away. There would be police everywhere, probably outriders on motorcycles, and it would be early morning, the streets of London not yet busy. Ravi did not relish the thought of being pursued across a near-deserted Berkeley Square by mounted officers, sirens wailing.

Arnold's arrival was important, but only as an observation point. He knew roughly what the admiral looked like from newspaper photographs, and he knew what Kathy looked like from newspapers and magazines. But he anticipated some kind of a mob scene when the party arrived at the Ritz, and there would be confusion and jostling, with a lot of people on high alert.

It would be fatal to attempt a shot, miss, hit someone else, and instantly find every building surrounded by London's tough and efficient police force. There would also be no question of a second shot.

For a visit like this, Ravi considered it likely that the police would insist on searching and inspecting all office buildings that overlooked the Ritz.

The fact was, he knew, nothing would be too much trouble, because if anything happened to Arnold Morgan in London, the police and security services would most definitely get the blame.

ARNOLD MORGAN ASSASSINATED
Why, oh why, was security so lax?

Ravi could imagine the bleating of the media. And he thus anticipated heavy police activity all around the Ritz Hotel both today, Monday, and in the early morning tomorrow, when the admiral was due to show up. Those were the times he must hold his nerve, and if necessary allow himself to be interviewed as the Finnish marketing accountant going quietly about his business.

They were not, however, times for a head shot at Arnold Morgan. That would wait. Ravi would hit the admiral the first time he and Kathy left the hotel. Because then, if they were just going shopping or sightseeing, there would be a far more relaxed atmosphere. On a scale of one to ten, security would be at ten for the arrival, maybe only six for future excursions from the hotel.

It was, however, critical that Ravi be in close attendance when that motorcade pulled in at 7:30 in the morning. He needed to see the admiral through a telescopic sight, and he needed to identify Kathy and assess the weight of the security detail.

And right here, Ravi did have a further problem. He did not wish to arrive at his office soon after 7 A.M. and be noted by Reggie as the first man into the building. That would draw attention. Besides, Arnold's flight might be early, as transatlantic planes often were when coming from west to east with a tailwind.

He would need to be in position the previous night, which would mean evacuating the embassy this afternoon and bringing everything he needed with him, all crammed into his new sports bag. Shakira would stay one more night with the Syrians and then meet him. It did not occur to the Hamas general that he might be captured.

The doormen at the Dover Street office worked two separate shifts. This week, Reggie was 7 A.M. to 2 P.M. Don came in from 2 P.M. 'til ten. They did not keep personal records of each tenant's comings and goings, because in this central area people were always going out and coming back.

But like most good city-center doormen, they usually knew who was in and who was out, especially in a relatively small building like this with only thirty tenants maximum. This meant Ravi would need to be on station at 1 P.M. Reggie would see him come in, but Don would not know Ravi was in the building unless he emerged from his office.

At noon, he and Shakira had a light lunch at the embassy, just salad and fillet of sole with fruit juice. Ravi had packed his duffel bag, taking only what he needed. There was little in it. Shakira would have the embassy dispose of the clothes he was not taking with him. The cooks had prepared him a pack of sandwiches wrapped in tin foil, plus a flask of coffee and a couple of bananas. Finally, he put on his loose dark blue tracksuit and sneakers from Harrods, and fitted on his blond wig, trimmed moustache, goatee, and heavy spectacles. Then he slipped his brown leather case into the duffel bag.

He and Shakira prayed together in the bedroom before he left, facing to the east, toward Piccadilly Circus. They intoned the words together . . . *I have turned my face only toward the Supreme Being who has created the skies and the earth . . . to You be glory, and with this praise I begin this prayer. Allah is the most auspicious name. You are exalted and none other than you is worthy of worship—*

> *Guide us on the straight path*
> *The path of those on whom is thy favor*
> *. . . Light upon Light*
> *God guides whom He will, to His Light . . .*

Ravi said good-bye to Shakira and boarded an embassy car, which took him on the short journey to Dover Street. The driver dropped him right on Piccadilly, and Ravi walked the last two hundred yards. He pushed open the doors and said hello to Reggie, who looked up and said: "'Afternoon, Mr. Fretheim. Been out jogging?"

Ravi smiled and replied, "Not yet. But I might give it a go later."

"That's the spirit, sir. Keep the old heart pumping."

Ravi took the elevator up to his office, let himself in, locked the door, and settled down for a long wait. He drew down the Venetian blinds but set the angle of the laths to allow him to see the street. At 2 P.M., he was in position and watched Reggie cross the main road at the traffic light and head for Green Park Underground station. The new doorman, Don, did not know Ravi was in the building.

The afternoon passed slowly. Ravi sat in his chair and had a brief nap. He did not use his cell phone and he did not turn on a light. No one phoned him and no one came to the office door. The evening was light, and every half hour Ravi spent time watching the main steps of the Ritz Hotel. By 7 P.M., he realized there was one action he did not want Admiral Morgan to take, and that was to walk down against the right-hand rail, because if anyone walked with him, on his left, that would obscure the view, obscure the opportunity for a clean shot to the head.

As he sat alone up on the fourth floor, Ravi bolstered his own psyche by revisiting the evil that Admiral Morgan had perpetrated upon the jihadists just this year. He sat and pondered the known brutality of Guantánamo Bay. And he wondered about his friends, in particular about Ramon Salman, the Hamas lieutenant who had made the fateful phone call to the house in Bab Touma Street on the night of the Boston airport bombing last January.

Was Ramon in Guantánamo? And how about Reza Aghani, the ambitious young Hamas hitman who had carried the bomb into the airport? Ravi knew he had been shot and captured by a Boston cop, and he also knew of the arrest of Mohammed Rahman, the Palm Beach baggage handler. Were they all in Guantánamo Bay? And had one of them, under torture, handed over his own address in Damascus to the Americans?

The image of Shakira, sobbing, covered in blood, terrified, in the backyard of the house stood stark before him. And his hatred of the West welled up in his mind. What right had they to bomb a street in Syria just because they disliked the occupant of a house? Who did they think they were, trampling over the rights of Middle Eastern citizens? All the trouble had been caused by the West and by the Americans' insatiable demand for oil.

And at the heart of every problem the freedom fighters of Islam had suffered in the past few years stood the malevolent figure of Admiral Arnold Morgan. Even his own people were enraged by him. He, Ravi, had read the American newspaper cuttings that proved it.

His mission had the blessing of Allah. General Rashood believed that. He also believed that if he should be killed in action, he too would join the martyrs who walked across the bridge to the sound of the three trumpets, into the open arms of God.

Ravi believed he was a Holy Warrior, on a holy mission to rid his people of their greatest enemy. He must not fail: the eyes of Allah were upon him. The Prophet Mohammed was gazing down, willing him forward, as Mohammed himself had gone forward, fourteen centuries previously. For Ravi, failure was unthinkable. He was the Chosen One, the highly trained warrior for whom this mission was nothing less than destiny.

He stood before the window and ate one of his bananas. The light in London was fading now, just before 9 P.M. One hour hence, Don would leave and lock the building behind him. Neither doorman ever bothered to check if anyone was still working; and on the rare occasion when anyone was still there, the tenants had keys and knew to lock the door behind them.

Midnight came, and Ravi was dozing quietly in his chair, slumped on the desk, his head cradled in his arms. The building was eerily quiet, and the Hamas C-in-C sensed there was no one else in residence. In the quiet of the city, he heard Big Ben chime in the distance. He unlocked the door and tiptoed across to the bathroom. In his pocket he carried a glass paperweight, because if he did encounter anyone in these offices in the dead of night, he would have no alternative but to kill them instantly and haul the body into the safety of his office. Kill them, just as he had killed Jerry O'Connell in County Cork.

Ravi, with his Middle Eastern heritage, had a very dark beard, and he had decided to shave. He locked the bathroom door, took off his tracksuit top and placed it along the base of the door, and switched on the light. The bathroom had no window or outside wall, and he ran the hot water for as little time as possible. Then he peeled off his moustache and beard, shaved, and carefully placed them back on at the conclusion of the operation.

Back in his office, he once more sat in the dark, facing up calmly to the long wait through the small hours of the morning. It was 7 P.M. in Washington, D.C.

1800 Monday 30 July
Dulles Airport, Washington, D.C.

Ahmed, the cultural attaché at the Jordanian embassy, sat quietly in a rear seat in the airport lounge, watching the first-class passengers board American Airlines Flight 163 for London. He kept his head down, buried in the *Washington Post*, but over the top of the newspaper he could see Admiral Arnold Morgan and Mrs. Kathy Morgan, surrounded by four obvious Secret Service men, walking toward the door to the jetway.

They were in a separate group from the regular first-class passengers, boarding first. Ahmed noted that two of the Secret Service men went with the admiral and his wife, one at the front, one at the rear. The other two remained behind, standing with the ticket girls, glancing over their shoulders at certain passports. Not until the flight was completely boarded did these two heavyweights walk through and take their seats across the aisle from Arnold and Kathy.

Ahmed had no idea of the seating arrangements on the plane, and that was not his business. He waited until the doors were closed, and then moved away to a viewing area from where he could see, from behind glass, the aircraft take off. He watched the American Boeing 747 back away from the jetway, and then saw it taxi away to the end of the runway.

Ten minutes passed before he saw it again, racing forward and then lifting off into the evening skies. He took out his cell phone and punched in a number in London. When the military attaché at the Syrian embassy answered, he just said: *AA163 took off 1846. Four bruisers with seadog.*

0100 Tuesday 31 July
Dover Street, London

Ravi's cell phone vibrated in his tracksuit pocket. He pulled it out and answered. A voice just said, "They've taken off, sir, 1846, four agents with them. ETA London Heathrow 0626." The line went dead and the Hamas commander decided to have his dinner, since at last he was feeling hungry rather than churned up with the tension of not knowing where the admiral and Kathy were.

As it happened, things had gone precisely to plan. Kathy Morgan had delivered Kipper as promised to her mother's house in Brockhurst, and the robust King Charles spaniel had lived up to Arnold's description of him to the letter. He came charging through the front door, fell joyfully upon his old buddy Charlie, and capsized Emily's perfectly laid tray—cups, saucers, milk, sugar, boiling-hot coffeepot, and cookies—all over the living-room floor. As Arnold had observed, *that dog's as silly as a goddamned sheep.*

Eventually Kathy got away and met the admiral right on time at the airport. All Ravi had to do was wait for their arrival, and then for their first shopping expedition into the West End of London. Then it would be over swiftly.

Feeling much less frustrated, Ravi pulled on his driving gloves so as not to leave fingerprints, because he would not be taking the coffee flask with him. He ate his chicken sandwiches thoughtfully and sipped the coffee from the wide lid of the flask. He saved enough for one more cup, and also saved a couple of sandwiches.

And the hours slipped away. In the still of the night, Ravi heard Big Ben chime every fifteen minutes, with the massive main bell resonating on the hour. Two o'clock, three o'clock, four o'clock—and then at a quarter to five there was a minor commotion.

Ravi was half asleep, but he heard the sudden, short, sharp wail of a police siren, two police sirens. He peered out through his closed Venetian blinds and could see the spinning blue lights reflecting in the street-level shop windows. So far as he could see, there was a police cruiser parked on either side of Dover Street, Piccadilly end, right outside the front door to his building.

He had never heard, or even sensed it, before, but he somehow knew people were entering the building. He packed into his duffel bag the remains of his dinner, the two small sandwiches, and the flask. He slipped his briefcase into the wide central drawer of his desk and moved to a position behind his office door, which was locked.

The police were obviously in the building, and he heard, or certainly felt, the dull thud down below as the main front door, between the glass swing doors and the street, was slammed shut. He must have heard it before, but this morning it sounded amazingly loud. He could hear a succession of loud thumps from the lower floors, voices, shouting, growing nearer all the time.

Then he heard Reggie's voice from almost outside his office. "There's no one here, boys, you can trust me on that." Then he added, "Don would have checked the building before he left." This was of course palpably untrue. Neither doorman had ever checked the building before leaving.

The banging continued, and Ravi guessed the police were knocking hard on every office door. There were intermittent shouts of *POLICE! ANYONE*

THERE? Occasionally Reggie could be heard calling someone's name—"*Mr. Marks—it's Reggie here, just checking the building—no worries.*"

The footsteps grew closer, and finally, shortly after five o'clock, there were three sharp, loud bangs on Ravi's door. The terrorist chief froze against the wall.

ANYONE THERE? POLICE!

Ravi knew he could have made a different choice, left the door open, lights on, and been sitting at his desk working. But that would have meant he'd been there all night. Bad idea. Ravi had decided to throw the dice and gamble on the police checking, but not opening, every door in the building.

He heard them banging on the office next door. He heard them go into the bathroom where four hours earlier he had shaved. Then he heard them climbing the stairs to the next floor, and he checked his watch. It was 0516, and he thought about the admiral for the millionth time this night. Seventy minutes from landing. That would put him somewhere over Ireland right now.

He could still hear the footsteps above him, and finally he heard them coming back down the stairs. He heard Reggie say, "Well, I did tell you the place would be empty. Anyway, it's good you've got your blokes in position."

As the footsteps continued below him, he caught one of the policemen saying "Thanks for coming in, Reggie."

And he heard the Cockney doorman's reply: "You can pick me up in a squad car any morning you like, old mate. 'Cept the bloody neighbors'll think I've been nicked!"

The footsteps died away. And there was but one thought in the ex–SAS major's mind: there were fewer people going downstairs than there had been going up. Somewhere, up above him, the police had left two or three men behind. Ravi stayed absolutely still, waiting for more footsteps descending the stairs. Nothing.

He tried to dismiss it from his mind. But he could not. In Ravi's opinion, there were at least two, maybe three, London policemen, probably marksmen, stationed on the roof of this building, watching the main entrance of the Ritz Hotel, watching for the sudden appearance of an assassin, a man who might burst out of the crowd and fire a shot at Admiral Morgan, just as that crazed kid John Hinckley had done to President Reagan outside the Hilton Hotel in Washington in 1981.

Ravi's assessment was accurate. Scotland Yard had marksmen on the roof of every building that overlooked the main entrance to the Ritz. They were not exactly SWAT teams, with heavy machine guns and missile launchers, ready to repel attack from the air. But they were top-class police snipers who would be unlikely to miss, firing directly down at a would-be assassin.

Lt. Commander Ramshawe had put just enough of a scare into the security authorities for them to install a very serious steel ring of protection around the admiral. But, in Jimmy's opinion, it was not nearly enough to take care of a top international assassin, the kind of high-level, trained terrorist who he believed would imminently strike at the best friend of the President of the United States of America.

The Dover Street office block again went quiet. Big Ben chimed six times. Ravi went to his leather briefcase and took out the telescopic sight to his rifle, training it on the deserted front steps of the Ritz, staring through the crosshairs, imagining the dimension of his task later this day.

The transatlantic passenger jets were beginning to come in now; staring south through the window, Ravi could easily discern the flight pattern as they came in, banking steeply over East London and the city and then tracking the River Thames along the south bank, out past Hammersmith, Chiswick, and into Heathrow, directly into the prevailing southwest wind.

The sun, just rising now, glinted on the fuselages as one by one they dropped down toward the world's busiest airport. Northwest Airlines, Air Canada, British Airways, Delta, Virgin, American, line astern at the end of their Atlantic crossing. Ravi tried to spot incoming AA163, and at 0615 he thought he saw the sunrise lighting up the entire length of a Boeing 747. He guessed that was the reflection on the familiar bright silver surface of American Airlines.

He may or may not have been correct, but his phone signaled an incoming call that relayed to him only two words: *"American landed."*

Just thirty minutes later, at 0645, the phone rang again and a voice said: "Seadog plus bruisers. Two U.S. embassy cars plus two police cars left Terminal 3."

What the man from the Syrian embassy did not know was that four police outriders, on motorcycles, had joined the four-car motorcade along the slip road to the M-4.

The order of the convoy was now two motorcycles, side by side, riding shotgun in the lead; then one police car, containing four armed Metropolitan police officers; then the first U.S. embassy car, containing the admiral and Kathy, plus two armed CIA men in the front seats; then the second embassy car, containing Arnold's regular three armed Secret Service agents and the new man, George Kallan; then the second police car, with four more armed policemen; then the final two outriders bringing up the rear. No sirens sounded, and the only flashing lights were on the leading motorcycles.

The convoy ran swiftly into West London. They were in moderate traffic, which was not yet into the eight o'clock gridlock. And there were no holdups whatsoever until they reached the big junction where Cromwell Road meets the Earls Court Road. Then everything slowed down.

But as soon as they crossed that junction, the outriders opened up their sirens, just short sharp *whoops* that caused the very savvy British drivers to ease over to the left, giving the convoy an almost free run into Knightsbridge.

They swung right down Beauchamp Place and ran straight through to Belgrave Square. Shakira, looking through her bedroom window, saw the motorcycles and cars come streaming past and guessed immediately who was in the black one with the darkened windows. But she thought not of the archterrorist-buster Arnold Morgan, but of his wife, her friend Emily's daughter, the very beautiful Washington socialite, who only the previous day must have delivered Kipper to Brockhurst.

Shakira was unaccountably overwhelmed by a feeling of sadness, not so much for the mayhem and murder her husband was about to inflict on that family, but for her own lost life, the absence of normality, of calm and happiness. Perhaps Ravi would gun down Arnold Morgan later today. But Shakira was assailed by the fear that wherever the admiral fell, Ravi too must lie someday.

As she turned away from the disappearing convoy, tears trickled down the exquisite face of Shakira Rashood.

. . . *Light upon Light,*
God guides whom he will to His Light . . .

The convoy ran south out of Belgrave Square and then turned east, toward the endless high wall of Buckingham Palace. They sped past the

Royal Mews and the Queen's Picture Gallery, and then swerved around onto the Mall, still at a fast speed.

They passed Clarence House, where Prince Charles lives, and at the next traffic light made a left, past St. James's Palace, and then straight up St. James's Street heading north.

Just before the Piccadilly traffic light, the outriders opened up their sirens again and made a sudden left turn along Bennett Street. With the convoy past, two London policemen, each with a submachine gun slung across his shoulder, stepped off the sidewalk and dragged three traffic cones across the entrance to the street.

At the Blue Posts pub, desolate at this time in the morning, the convoy swung right onto narrow Arlington Street and came to a halt right outside the Ritz. The two lead motorbike cops drove several yards beyond the main door, as did the first police car, which left Arnold Morgan's armed embassy chauffeur to pull up directly at the flight of six white stone steps.

The American security guards were out and on the sidewalk in a split second. The outriders deployed strategically, still on their bikes, engines running. Right now, it was impossible to gain entrance to the street from either end. Arnold's four guards went immediately to the left rear door and clustered around as the great man disembarked.

Two of them mustered to his right, the other two to the left. Four Metropolitan policemen made the same formation around Kathy as she exited the right rear door and made her way around the front of the car to join the admiral. Thus, eight guards formed a kind of armed rugby scrum around the couple as they walked up the steps into the hotel.

High in his office, General Rashood held his finely tuned telescopic sight to his left eye. He could see everything with immense clarity. A head shot on the admiral would have been as near to impossible as making no difference. There were just so many people. Aside from the eight-man scrum that surrounded the American visitors, there were also two doormen. At one point, Ravi counted twelve people on the steps. The two guards who walked closely on the admiral's right side almost obscured him. Which was, of course, the general idea.

Ravi estimated that there had been two "windows," of perhaps two seconds each, when he might have risked a shot. But this was very, very tight. The greatest marksman in the world might have missed and hit someone else.

Ravi Rashood might very well have been the greatest marksman in the world, but from the scene playing out below him, he would not have dared to pull the trigger. It was too difficult a target, there were too many police and security officers, and the odds against success were just too great. There would be better times.

He did have some kind of a view of the admiral, who was not a tall man but was powerfully built, immaculately tailored in a suit from nearby Sa-vile Row and an Annapolis tie. Ravi could see his steel-gray hair, and for the briefest moment had the side of his head in the telescopic sight. He had no wish to kill Kathy, and merely noted her alongside her husband. She was wearing a dark blue suit, and her red hair was loose on her shoulders.

Even from his fourth-floor redoubt, Ravi could see that she was a very beautiful woman, and he wished her no harm. He did not give one single thought to the fact that he was about to break her heart and wreck her life, all with one of Mr. Kumar's exploding 7.62mm bullets.

Within moments, the entire crowd had dispersed through the revolving doors. The police hung around for a while, and then the outriders pulled off into Piccadilly and turned left toward Hyde Park Corner. Both police cars pulled away and headed east to Piccadilly. The embassy cars remained in place outside the hotel, engines running, drivers at the wheel.

Inside the hotel, two security guards accompanied the admiral and Kathy to their suite. Both men remained on duty outside in the corridor. There were two doors from the corridor, one of which led into the small drawing room, with the bedroom off to the left. The other led directly into the bedroom and had not been opened for about forty years. This was a suite much in demand, and it had never been necessary to turn the bedroom into a single room.

Admiral Morgan outlined his plan of battle to his wife. "Right now I'm going to sleep for two and a half hours. Then we will have a lavish break-fast delivered right here to the room—English bacon, eggs, and toast. My favorite, reminds me of the old days in the submarines, Holy Loch.

"Then we will venture out and take a stroll along Piccadilly to my fa-vorite bookstore in all the world, Hatchards. We will browse in there, buy some books that we would not see in the USA, and have Hatchards send them all directly to Chevy Chase.

"I will then accompany you to Jermyn Street, where we will shop for a while at Fortnum and Mason's and request that our food selections also be forwarded on to Chevy Chase, by courier, to arrive the day we get home.

"And then we will wander among the greatest shirtmakers in the world and place some orders for both of us, and likewise have them sent directly to the USA. Thereafter, we will cross to the north side of Piccadilly and I will permit you the freedom of the Burlington Arcade while I wander up to my longtime tailor, Gieves and Hawkes at the corner of Savile Row, to be measured for a couple of new suits. How's that?"

"Not bad," said Kathy. "What about lunch?"

"Forget that," said the admiral. "I intend to eat such a gargantuan breakfast, it will not be necessary."

"What about me?" asked Kathy. "How would it be if I didn't want to feast like Henry VIII at ten o'clock in the morning? Imagine that I wanted only some fruit and coffee, and then a light lunch, perhaps a small fillet of Dover sole and some salad?"

"Then it would be my very great pleasure to provide it for you at Green's restaurant, corner of Duke of York Street."

"And what will you do while I eat my lunch?"

"Me? Oh, I'll probably have the same."

Kathy could not help laughing. She had never been able to resist laughing at this irascible titan of American foreign policy—his ups, his downs, his fury, his brilliance, and his wit; the way he answered to no man, the way he loved food and wine, his natural assumption that nothing short of the absolute best could possibly be good enough for him. And indeed for his wife.

Kathy smiled at him and asked if he intended to get right into bed, pajamas and all, or whether he was just going to lie on top of the spread.

"Christ, women!" he exclaimed. "These sheets are costing us about fifty bucks a square inch, and I'm taking total advantage."

"You mean straight in?" said Kathy.

"Straight in," he replied. "Coming?"

"Probably," she laughed, somewhat sassily.

Across the street, Ravi was trying to commit to memory the images still clear in his mind of the four bodyguards who had surrounded the admiral as he entered the hotel. They were all six-footers, taller than Morgan, and the one certainty of the morning was that at least one of them would step outside before Arnold and Kathy.

Like the admiral himself, all four agents had their hair cut closely. One of them was virtually bald, one of them was black, and the other two were fair-skinned with light-colored hair. From this distance, Ravi could not tell if either of them was gray. From the shape of their jackets, the Hamas chief was sure they all wore shoulder holsters, and likely knew how to shoot straight.

He could no longer see the U.S. embassy cars, but there was a police car down Arlington Street beyond the Blue Posts. At the bottom of the steps, on the sidewalk, the doorman was speaking to a uniformed London cop.

The traffic was still light, but it was now flowing along Bennett Street, through Arlington to the Piccadilly throughway. Ravi permitted himself three guesses—a luxury in which he rarely indulged. The first was that the police snipers were still on duty on the roof of the building; the second was that Reggie was at his desk in the foyer. The third was that Admiral Morgan's car would be summoned by phone when he left the Ritz, and that the security detail would make certain that he and his wife were quickly into the vehicle. His fourth thought was an assumption, not a guess: that his "window" of opportunity would again be very short-lived, but less crowded.

It was only just 8 A.M., but people were beginning to arrive. Ravi could hear the elevator creaking as it went up, but it made no noise as it descended. If the two cops, the ones he assumed were still on the roof, left via the elevator, he would not know they had gone.

Equally, Reggie did not know Ravi was in the building. No one did, and the last image Reggie had in his mind, concerning Mr. Fretheim, was from yesterday, of a man in a loose-fitting dark blue tracksuit, wearing sneakers and carrying a sports bag. Images were critical in operations like this, because they affected the memory, shaded the truth, and distorted the reality.

Ravi poured himself the last of his coffee and ate the remaining two chicken sandwiches. He did so in front of the window, from an area to which he had shifted his chair. When he stood up, he slipped the window catch and pushed upward. The old-fashioned lower section rose, and Ravi kept pushing until it was open all the way.

If the security men were scanning the front of this building, they would not notice the lower open window, because it was fully open. He adjusted the Venetian blind so the light breeze from the southwest would not cause the laths to rattle.

While Arnold and Kathy slept, Ravi made his final preparations. He realized the Americans might not leave the hotel until after lunch, maybe not until tomorrow, and during this time he would be a virtual prisoner in this office. He resolved to change clothes at 10:30 A.M. and take up his position at the window immediately afterward. He would not move again.

And now he peeled off his tracksuit and sneakers. He pulled a dark gray suit out of his bag, plus a new shirt, tie, and shiny black loafers. He dressed carefully and slung the suit jacket over the back of his chair. Everything else, except for the briefcase, he crammed into the duffel bag, which he left behind the office door.

Inside the suit pockets he had crammed cash, an English driver's license in the name of Michael Barden, and a British passport to match. It stated his birthplace as Maidstone, Kent. In the wallet was an American Express card under the same name, on an account registered, if anyone was looking, to the attaché at the Jordanian embassy in Paris. Credit limit: 100,000 euros.

Ravi would need only to dispose of the duffel bag, and now he went to the briefcase, released the catch, and opened it wide on the desk. He took out the barrel of the SSG 69 and carefully began to assemble the rifle. He handled it lovingly, the instrument of his holy mission. The pieces slotted and screwed together perfectly.

When it was completed, he loaded the six silver-headed bullets, five into the breech, one into the firing position in front of the bolt. His last actions were to clip on the telescopic sight and the silencer, which he did with practiced expertise. He balanced the weapon in his hands and smiled at the memory of the final shots in the Long Wood out in Oxfordshire. If he could get a clear view, with this rifle he could not miss.

Eleven o'clock came and went, and still Ravi stood motionless before the window, staring at the Ritz entrance, watching hotel guests come and go, up those six steps. Taxis came. Taxis went. Chauffeurs pulled up, helped people with baggage, and departed.

At 11:30, Admiral Morgan's bald bodyguard stepped out of the hotel. He said one quick word to the doorman, who immediately stepped out into the street, raised his arm, and signaled for a car. Ravi heard him blow hard on a whistle.

From way down Arlington Street, the embassy car with the darkened windows came sliding along to the Ritz. Four police outriders led the way. Inside the lobby, Admiral Morgan was telling his other three agents that it was such a beautiful morning, he and Kathy would prefer to stroll along to Hatchards. All three of them objected, telling him that with a terrorist alert in progress, it would make everyone much happier if he were given safe passage in the big bulletproof embassy car.

"Goddamned Ramshawe still causing trouble," said Arnold ruefully. "He's been waiting for this moment for a month, trying to curtail my simplest pleasures."

"Darling, don't talk about him like that," scolded Kathy. "He cares about you more than anyone in the world, except for me. He is genuinely worried, as you well know."

"I know all that, but he's still a goddamned nuisance," replied her husband. And he turned to Big George, his new bodyguard, and demanded, "And where the hell do you think you're going to park that thing while I'm in the bookstore? In the biography section?"

"Don't worry about that, sir. The car will be right there when you come out. I'm only following orders. The president insists you play everything by the book while we have this terror threat."

Admiral Morgan scowled. But did as he was told. George checked outside. "Car's here, Admiral," he said. "Let's go."

Kathy took Arnold's right arm, and the five of them walked across the carpeted lobby. George went through the revolving doors first, followed by the other two guards, then Kathy, last of all the admiral.

From high above, Ravi leveled the Austrian precision rifle at the Ritz entrance. One by one he watched them emerge, gravitating to the right-hand brass rail. The doorman, however, was standing on the left, and when the admiral himself came out, he stood next to the doorman as Kathy took his right arm. They started down the steps, and the moment Arnold moved forward, Ravi had his clear head shot, for less than one second.

But Big George, sensing the admiral's unprotected left flank, suddenly swung around on the fourth step down and took a giant stride back up to Arnold's left.

Ravi tensed, kept the rifle steady, the crosshairs on the admiral's head, and pressed the trigger. The sound was a soft *phutt*. The 7.62-millimeter shell ripped out of the barrel just as George reached for Arnold's arm, stepped across, and completely blocked him from the left.

The bullet caught the big bodyguard full in the temple, splitting the skull right in front of the hairline, penetrating the brain, exploding on impact inside his head. George died while he was still holding on to the left-hand brass rail.

He pitched forward, pushing Arnold and Kathy to the right and falling into the top step, his neck twisted. The small wound to his left temple was obscured. And for at least five seconds, no one had the slightest idea what had happened. Then the blood began to trickle down the steps.

All three remaining agents formed a cordon around the admiral, one of them shouting, *"Police! Right here we have a shooting! One of our guys is dying!"*

The doorman blew his whistle and the agents hustled Arnold down the steps and almost hurled him into the embassy car. The police outriders swung around and drove the motorbikes into tight formation around the vehicle. With Arnold now onboard, the American agents raced up the steps to collect Kathy, who was standing next to the doorman.

George's immediate boss, the black Secret Service man Al Thompson from the White House, was on the phone while he was helping to half-carry Kathy down the steps and into the vehicle with Arnold. A police cruiser came howling around the corner from Bennett Street. Everyone knew the drill as far as an attempt on the admiral's life was concerned—and that was to get him as far away from the datum as possible, immediately.

Right now, Ravi had shut the window and was dismantling his rifle. He'd missed. He knew that. Missed because of a million-to-one fluke, when the late Big George suddenly swung onto the admiral's left side and blocked the path of the bullet. The seconds ticked away, and Ravi clipped the case shut. He then applied the finishing touch to his disguise—a thick but neatly trimmed black wig.

He now wore no blond moustache or goatee. He was clean-shaven, of dark complexion, and in his gray suit and tie he looked like an elegant businessman, a persona he had never assumed before. Neither doorman had ever seen him in anything but jeans, T-shirt, and sneakers, or a track-suit. Twenty-four seconds had elapsed since he pulled the trigger. And now he picked up the duffel bag and briefcase, peered out of the office door, and stepped out, locking the empty room behind him.

There was no one on the landing, nor on the one above. He crossed the floor and softly rammed the duffel bag down the incinerator. Then he moved swiftly down the stairs, and, without even a sideways look at Reggie, walked across the foyer and pushed open the swing doors.

He was a totally different person from the fair-haired Finn Haakon Fretheim. No one would have guessed the transformation. Reggie glanced up and saw the departing figure. Not the face, just the dark hair, suit, and leather briefcase. The man could have been visiting anywhere in the building, and Reggie did not remotely recognize him. He turned back to the sports pages of *The Sun.*

Ravi turned right and headed straight up Dover Street, walking steadily but in no great rush. Behind him, across Piccadilly, pandemonium had broken out. At least three police cruisers were howling toward the scene of the shooting, one of them swerving right in front of the colonnaded north portico of the Ritz, blocking the westbound route along to Hyde Park Corner. They also blocked Bennett Street and directed traffic north up Albemarle Street into Mayfair.

A detective superintendent was already on the scene, talking to the admiral's bodyguards, trying to get an idea of the direction from which the bullet had been fired. All three of the Americans had seen Big George go down, and all three confirmed that the shot he took to the left temple must have been fired from a building across the street.

Arlington Street itself was under strict scrutiny by the security forces and the police. No one had fired from ground level, or someone would have seen them. The shot most definitely had come from one of the two buildings on the south corners of Dover Street, most probably the one on the southeast.

The superintendent looked up and could see the police marksmen on top of the building. He turned to the sergeant who was supervising the deployment of his men as they arrived, and asked, "Did we search that building this morning?"

"Certainly did, sir. Just before 0500 this morning. I was in there myself. We checked every office, top to bottom. The place was deserted. It never opens 'til 7 A.M."

"Did you go inside the offices?"

"No, sir. They were all locked up for the night. But we tried every door, checked there were no lights on."

"Who's the doorman?"

"Reggie Milton, sir. We picked him up at home in Putney just after four this morning, sir. He took us through, swore to God no one was left in the building last night, swore to God no one was there when we entered this morning."

By this time, the car bearing Arnold and Kathy had swooped through the Hyde Park underpass and then swung into Belgravia. Two police outriders led the way and came to a stop in Lowndes Square. One of them dismounted and walked back to talk to the chauffeur from the U.S. embassy.

"We're evacuating Admiral and Mrs. Morgan," he said. "Out of London immediately. By helicopter. Somewhere to the west, avoiding flying over the city. Ask the admiral if there's anywhere he'd especially like to go. Otherwise we were thinking of somewhere like Henley-on-Thames, actually anywhere that's quiet and secret. I imagine you know that that bullet was meant for him, not Big George."

"I think we all know that," replied the chauffeur. "I'll just follow you to the takeoff point."

"No problem," said the outrider. He remounted and headed south, back down to Eaton Square, and then turned left toward Buckingham Palace. And from there he turned into Birdcage Walk and accelerated down to Horse Guards, the giant military parade ground that stands in the shadow of Great Britain's Admiralty at the end of St. James's Park.

He rode to the north corner and signaled the embassy car to park. Then he told the two CIA men in the admiral's car their transportation would arrive any moment.

In the backseat, Kathy Morgan was terrified. She clung to the admiral's arm and kept saying, over and over, "They could have killed you, my darling, they could have killed you."

Arnold himself was strangely philosophical. "In my line of business, kid, this kind of thing can happen. For us, the main thing was they missed. For Big George's family it's tragedy. I guess I've cheated death a few times, but I agree with you, this one was close."

Kathy wanted to know what their new plan was, and Arnold was, as usual, resolute. "Well, we're going up to Scotland in a couple of days to see Iain MacLean. And I wanted to spend the spare time in London. But, hell, we can have a nice time in the English countryside, and I'm pretty damn certain we can stay at a little place up the Thames River. Iain stays there when he comes south, says it's his favorite restaurant."

Arnold pulled out his cell phone, dialed a number, and asked to be put through to the U.S. ambassador's office in Grosvenor Square. When his old pal Sandra King, ex–White House, answered, he asked her to somehow trace the restaurant for him and see if he could get rooms there for a couple of nights.

As one might expect from the secretary to one of America's most important ambassadors, Sandra called back within ten minutes and told him the place was called the Leather Bottle, downstream from Wallingford on the Goring Reach. She'd booked him and Kathy in for two nights, in the new bridal suite.

"Attagirl," said Arnie.

Meanwhile, the police were swarming into Ravi's office block. They told Reggie to lock the door. "No one leaves until we're done," said the Metropolitan Police detective sergeant. "We need to speak to every tenant, every staff member of every corporation with space in here."

They started on the ground floor and questioned everyone. On the second floor, they found three offices locked, but spoke to everyone else. On the fourth floor, they found Ravi's office locked. By the time they reached the top floor, they had interviewed all the tenants except for seven where the offices were locked and no one was in.

The detective sergeant asked Reggie if they could enter the locked premises, and Reggie said he was sure that would be fine and he would get the keys. When he unlocked the door to Mr. Fretheim's room, he was quite surprised at how thoroughly empty the place looked.

He had never been in there when the accountant with the Finland Farms Marketing Board was working, but still he imagined there would be the usual office paraphernalia, computers, writing pads, pens, books, ledgers, maybe a couple of cups or a coffeepot. But this place was desolate.

The detective looked quizzical. "How long's this character been here?" he asked.

"'Bout a week, I suppose," replied Reggie. "Seemed a nice sort of bloke. I saw him yesterday lunchtime. He was in his tracksuit, said he was going jogging later. I expect in the park."

"What did he look like?"

"Youngish. About thirty. Fair hair. Moustache and goatee beard. Spectacles. Not very tall—less than six feet. Spoke with a Finnish accent."

"Do you know what a Finnish accent sounds like?" asked the policeman.

"'Course not," said Reggie. "Never spoke to one of 'em, have I? 'Cept for Santa Claus—and Mr. Fretheim."

"What I mean, Reggie, is, was that a Finnish accent, or could it have been French, or German, or Arabian?"

"Beats me, guv'nor. Could have been anything. I just assumed it was Finnish, because he said that's where he was from."

The detective smiled. "Anything else about him?"

"Not really. But I had the impression he was an athletic sort of bloke. I mean he was always dressed very casual, jeans, T-shirt, and sneakers."

The detective nodded. "Did he keep regular hours?"

"Well, I can't rightly say about that. Our shifts change at 2 P.M., so we don't really know if people are in or out when we come on afternoon duty."

"Did he ever come in at unusual times, like evenings or anything?"

"I don't think so. I never saw him here in the evening. Matter of fact I haven't seen him since yesterday lunchtime."

"And you never saw him leave?"

"No. But I wouldn't, would I? Don did the afternoon shift and locked up last night."

"Could Fretheim have been in the building overnight?"

"No. Don would have known that. You always know if someone's here in the evening. Tell you the truth, we usually nip out for a pint around nine o'clock, and the first thing you'd notice would be a light on at the front of the building."

"Perhaps Mr. Fretheim was sitting in the dark," said the detective. "Thank you, Reggie. Tell Don we'd like a word this afternoon."

"Righto, sir."

At that moment, the two police marksmen were making their way down from the roof. When they reached the detective sergeant, one of them said, "We just heard, on the phone, sir. But neither of us saw a thing, and we never heard anything either. Me and Brian here were watching the area around the hotel all the time. Whoever fired must have done it from somewhere in here. But it was a damn quiet gun, I'll say that."

In the meantime, General Rashood had completed his walk up Dover Street and had turned left down Hay Hill and into Berkeley Street. He crossed and strolled into the narrow walkway of Lansdowne Row, where he was when the police began their search of his office building.

He knew Lansdowne Row mostly because it contained one of the best newspaper shops in London. Ravi used to go there with his father occasionally to pick up Middle Eastern publications.

He bought the London *Daily Telegraph* and *Daily Mail* and then walked into the café next door and ordered some coffee and buttered toast. He took off his jacket and placed it over the back of his chair, and put down his briefcase. He'd been here before, in another life, and it looked much the same, but better. It seemed bigger, and Ravi thought they must have purchased the flower shop next door.

Anyway, it felt like a haven right now, and happily he did not recognize the proprietor. Calmly he sipped his coffee and read the newspapers. It was a busy place, filled with shirtsleeved young advertising and financial executives. Ravi fitted right in, and outside, to the south, he heard the constant wail of police sirens. And the distant clatter of a helicopter swooping low over the city.

It was a little after 12:30 when he left. He put on his jacket and walked into Berkeley Square, which was lunchtime busy. He made his way up the west side of the square, past the distinctive awning of Annabel's, the world's most exclusive nightclub, and then turned left into Mount Street.

Up ahead he could see the Audi, Shakira at the wheel. He watched her step out and walk around to the front passenger seat. Casually, he made his way to the driver's side, tossed his jacket and briefcase in the back, and positioned himself behind the wheel. Without a word, he drove down the north side of Berkeley Square and then swung left, heading up the one-way system in fast-moving traffic. He neither stopped nor spoke for fifteen minutes. Shakira knew everything had gone wrong, but at least he had not been shot, and in a sense she felt an overwhelming feeling of relief.

The helicopter he had heard was currently standing on the Horse Guards parade ground. Arnold and Kathy were aboard, along with two of the secret agents. They were just waiting for the luggage to arrive from the now-besieged Ritz Hotel, which currently contained more policemen than guests.

The body of Big George had been removed by ambulance to St. Mary's Hospital. And before it left, the police pathologist had confirmed that the bullet had been fired from a height and had hit George at a shallow angle to the horizontal.

The westbound lanes of Piccadilly were still blocked, and the hotel staff car containing the Americans' luggage was forced to take a circuitous route to Horse Guards. When it arrived, the loadmaster packed the suitcases into the hold, and the helicopter from the Queen's Flight took off, heading west. Destination: classified.

The Royal Air Force pilot followed the River Thames all the way, flying at around ten thousand feet. Putney Bridge, Hammersmith Bridge, Barnes Bridge, and Chiswick all passed beneath them. They continued on to the Berkshire town of Maidenhead, then Henley-on-Thames, where Arnold could still see the famous blue-and-white tents at the end of the Royal Regatta course.

This had once been familiar territory for the Big Man. He'd rowed here in an Annapolis crew more than forty years before, got beat by the Harvard lightweights. "Bastards," muttered Arnold.

"Sorry?" said Kathy.

"Bastards," repeated Arnold wistfully. "They got a half length at the start, beat the umpire's call. We never pegged 'em back. Finished only a canvas down."

"Who did?"

"Oh, sorry," he said. "I was just reliving one of my early disasters, when the Naval Academy got beat down there at the Henley Regatta. See those blue-and-white tents? Where the river runs straight? Right there."

"Were you rowing?"

"Stroke. But I can't talk about it. It's too painful."

"You mean you can talk about some lunatic almost blowing your head off, but you can't speak about a boat race?"

"Correct. The lunatic missed, so it's just a fantasy. But the boat race was real. Oh boy, was it ever real."

Kathy shook her head, and the helicopter kept going west until it swung right just before the market town of Wallingford, with its thirteenth-century bridge over the Thames. And now the pilot began to lose height, dropping down and flying a hundred feet above the river, following it downstream.

To the left were the Chiltern Hills, to the right the Berkshire Downs, and along the lonely river valley, clattering noisily in the soft summer air, came the helo from the Queen's Flight, bearing the admiral to a place of safety. You could search for a hundred years and never find him here.

The GPS numbers in the cockpit finally signaled their arrival, and the pilot slewed the helicopter in the air, making it almost stationary forty feet above the water. And there before them, on the banks of the river, was the picturesque Leather Bottle, except it was spelled differently—The Leatherne Bottel.

"Jesus," said Arnold, staring at the lettering on the sign. "These guys can't even spell, never mind cook!"

"Olde English," yelled the loadmaster. "This place has been here for centuries."

The pilot dropped down almost to water level and then edged forward, landing on the concrete parking lot, with the tail jutting out over the river. The admiral and Kathy disembarked with the two agents, who unloaded the baggage, and the four of them walked across the stone terrace and into the bright, low-ceilinged restaurant with its stunning views across the river to the Downs. Way along the summit, it was just possible to see one of the fabled Long Woods.

"Beautiful place," said Admiral Morgan to James, the young man who was supervising the luggage.

"One of the best views in England," he said. "Shall I take your bags up to your room? We're not really a regular hotel, just two suites for VIPs, which I imagine you must be."

"Not us," said Arnold. "We're just a couple of strays with no other hotel room, looking for a place to stay for two or three days."

"Absolutely," chuckled James. "Nearly everyone who comes here arrives in a Royal Air Force private helicopter from the Queen's Flight."

At this moment, a police car came swiftly down the steep, winding approach to the Leatherne Bottel to check that all was well. The sergeant asked to see the manager, to stress the importance of privacy and secrecy for the guests. He told her that a limousine from the U.S. embassy would be arriving shortly, with two more security men, and that the four agents would share the second suite.

James led the admiral and Kathy back out to the terrace and seated them at a table right on the riverbank beneath a pergola. It was just one o'clock and the sun was high. Only an hour and forty minutes had elapsed since the Hamas general had tried to assassinate Arnold Morgan.

"I'll bring you some lunch, if you wish," said James. "How about some fillets of plaice and spinach? Chef's just cooking it now."

"Perfect," said Kathy.

"How about a roast beef sandwich with mayonnaise and mustard?" asked the admiral.

"Shut up, darling," said Kathy, and then, turning back to James, "Two plaice and spinach. Ignore him."

Arnold chuckled. He was always amused at being bullied by the only person in the world who even interrupted him, never mind argued.

James hesitated, but Arnold confirmed, "She's the boss. Well . . . mostly. And would you give the guys whatever they want? Everything's on my tab."

"I don't think so, sir," he replied. "We were told specifically that every last charge would be handled by the U.S. ambassador's office in London."

"Guess I'm more popular than I thought," said Arnold.

Meanwhile, Ravi and Shakira were still driving north and had reached the Hertfordshire town of Baldock, where he pulled into the parking lot of the King's Arms Hotel. Ravi took out his cell phone and tapped in the numbers for the Ritz Hotel.

"Would it be possible to speak to Admiral Arnold Morgan?" he said.

The operator was silent for a few seconds, and then said, "I'm sorry, sir. The admiral and Mrs. Morgan checked out more than an hour ago."

"Did they leave a forwarding number or address?"

"I'm sorry, sir. We have no further information on that."

Ravi, who had been timing the call on his watch, clicked off his phone. It had taken twenty-five seconds, and Ravi knew full well it would have taken the police around fifteen seconds to log into the call, and perhaps trace geographically the cell phone's position.

He knew it had run too long, but he needed to know the admiral had left the hotel. The police, who he guessed correctly were already tapped into the Ritz switchboard, probably now knew someone had called the admiral from the Hertfordshire area.

This meant he had to get out of the area, and he backed out onto the main road, and headed up to Cambridge, to a city he knew slightly, and to an anonymous hotel. They had to go somewhere, and he had to find out the whereabouts of the admiral. Otherwise everything would have been for nothing.

The journey took around an hour, and they located the Sheraton out on the edge of the city, checked in for the night under the name of Mr. and Mrs. Michael Barden. Ravi's impeccable English accent eliminated the need for passports. They ordered coffee and biscuits in their room, and sat down to work out a plan to locate Admiral Morgan.

After a half hour, there was only one name that had not been discarded. It was that of Emily Gallagher, who a) obviously knew where the Morgans were going and b) might tell a friend of the admiral's. She would most definitely not tell Carla Martin, who had let her down so badly over Charlie and Kipper and who might have murdered the owner of the Brockhurst garage.

So far as Ravi could tell, either he located the admiral and his wife, or the entire mission, with its vast expense and three murders, was on the verge of being aborted. Arnold Morgan could be anywhere. Maybe even at another hotel in London. But wherever he was, security would surround him. In Ravi's opinion, there was not much difference from trying to take him out in England or in the USA. The risks were huge, there was an American security presence, and everyone involved was taking the matter extremely seriously. Especially the British police.

Ravi wrote off the possibility of using official channels. Anyone making any inquiries whatsoever would immediately come under suspicion by those hard-eyed London cops. The only chance was family, and that meant Emily Gallagher.

He told Shakira he would make one call only, since he was confident that Emily's phone would now be tapped by the FBI. He had no idea how long he would have before they located his cell phone, and there was no point trying to make the call on a land line from the hotel. They'd pinpoint that in under ten minutes.

Somehow he had to make the call from out in the open and see if he could outfox the old lady. Shakira said she didn't much like the idea of involving Emily again, of forcing her to play a part in the smashing of her own daughter's happiness.

But Ravi was becoming fixated by the thought of Arnold Morgan. It was as if there was nothing beyond the American admiral. Shakira thought he was possessed by some kind of obsession about Arnold Morgan, and she was afraid that obsession would lead to his own death.

She noticed how withdrawn he had become, how reluctant he was to talk to her. And now, in the teeth of the gravest danger, he wanted to make a personal phone call to Emily. In Shakira's opinion, they had both done their very best and should now retreat, back to Gaza where it was relatively safe. It was time to let someone else try their luck. This was becoming, in her opinion, ominously beyond the reasonable call of duty.

Ravi paced the room. He checked his watch. It was almost five o'clock, noon in Virginia. They were on the top floor of the Sheraton Hotel, and he had noticed a sign for the roof terrace. He told Shakira somewhat curtly to "wait here." Then he left the room, walked along the corridor, and stepped out onto the deserted terrace.

He tapped in the numbers—zero-zero-one. Then area code 703, then the number. It rang three times, and then a voice said, "Hello, this is Emily Gallagher speaking."

"Oh, good morning, Mrs. Gallagher. This is Commander Toby Trenham, of the Royal Navy in London. I'm a very old friend of Admiral Morgan's from our days in Holy Loch. And he gave me this number to call if I missed him while he was staying in the Ritz."

"Well, I'm very sorry, Commander. I only know about the Ritz and I thought he was there today. If they aren't, I really have no idea where they've gone."

"Oh, gosh. How disappointing. I was going to give them dinner at Admiralty House. You have no clues where I might pick up their trail?"

"Commander, I really don't. Except Arnold did say something about going to Scotland for a few days."

"No idea where, I suppose?"

"Not really. It's a very big place, you know, all those Highlands, and Lowlands, and Western Isles, and Loch Lomond, and Loch Ness where that frightful underwater creature lives."

"It doesn't sound promising, Mrs. Gallagher, I agree. I think I'd better abandon it. If you do hear from the admiral, you might just tell him I called. Trenham, Commander Toby Trenham."

"I'll be sure to. Good-bye, Commander."

CHAPTER *12*

Ravi walked back into the room and instructed Shakira to pack and be prepared to leave.

"But we only just arrived," she said. "Aren't you tired? You haven't been to bed for two days."

"I am tired. But we are both on a mission for our people."

"I know that. But where are we going?"

"Scotland," he replied.

"Where's that?" asked Shakira.

"About four hundred miles north of here. It's the top part of England."

"Why are we going there?"

"Because Emily Gallagher just told me that's where Admiral Morgan is headed, and we don't have one single other clue about his whereabouts."

"But Scotland's a whole country, right? With towns and everything?"

"It sure is. And we don't have any idea which part he's visiting."

"Well, where do we start?"

"I don't know. All I do know is we either go there and try to find him, or go home—wherever that is."

"But how do we get to Scotland?"

"Drive. Airports are out of bounds for us."

"How about a train?"

"Same. And anyway we'll need a car, and I don't want to risk renting again. In case it slipped your mind, darling Shakira, I am wanted in the British Isles for two murders."

1930 Tuesday 31 July
Goring-on-Thames

Arnold and Kathy sat on the banks of the Thames in the warm embrace of the Leatherne Bottel and its staff. The admiral had ordered dinner for 8:30, and now he and Kathy were sipping a superb white Burgundy, a 2004 Corton-Charlemagne made by the maestro, Franck Grux, for Olivier Leflaive Frères. This bottle is widely regarded as one of the longest-lived, most delicious wines in the world.

Arnold considered it perfect for the first evening of their vacation, the best kind of soothing elixir to steady the nerves after someone has just made a bold attempt to blow your head off.

The Thames is wide along this reach, and the occasional boat chugs by on its way down to the lock at Goring. Ducks meander along the riverbank, and the views are always wondrous with the changing light of a summer evening.

Kathy had rarely seen the admiral in a more mellow mood, and she decided to mention the strictest taboo in their lives.

"Jimmy was right, wasn't he?" she said.

The admiral sipped luxuriously. "Yes," he replied. "Jimmy was right. Clever little sonofabitch." Even in defeat, Arnold still needed to take one last swing.

"What about his whole thought process—you know, the girl in Brockhurst, the murder in Ireland, the submarine? Do you think they were all correct, all connected?"

"Of course they were," the admiral harrumphed. "Every one of 'em. His conclusions were too quick, but the outcome was correct." At which point, he took another good solid gulp of Corton-Charlemagne and added, "Beginner's luck, in a way."

"Arnold!"

"Well, he's never worked on a case like that before. Half civilian, half military. And he'd solved it before it started."

"Very clever," said Kathy.

"Very goddamned fluky," said the admiral. "He didn't have anything like the evidence you need to leap to wild conclusions like that."

"Do you think he might be a genius?"

"Probably," growled Arnold. "But just remember, I invented the little sonofabitch. But for me, he'd still be working in the mailroom."

"There are times, Arnold, when you are a disgrace. Jimmy is the son of an admiral and a very senior diplomat. He came to the NSA as a highly recommended intelligence lieutenant. And he's one of the youngest lieutenant commanders in the history of the United States Navy. He did not graduate from the mailroom."

"I meant that metaphorically, of course," said Arnold, adding, pompously for him, "I have always been wary of precocity."

"Jesus!" said Kathy. "You're the most precocious person I ever met. And I bet you always were."

Arnold laughed. "All right, all right. Jimmy out-thought me. I'm too old; I've lost my edge. This is Socrates and Plato all over again. The pupil overtakes the master."

"Oh, don't be too hard on yourself, darling," she replied. "What I really want to know is, do you think the London assassin might try again?"

"Well, he won't know where we are any longer, will he? Your mom told Carla about the Ritz, and that's where he showed up. Even we aren't certain where we're going to be in the next few days. So I doubt he'll ever locate us in time to take another shot."

"Arnold? Are you sure we shouldn't head home, right now?"

"Not 'til we've finished dinner," he chuckled. "Remember, no one has the slightest idea where we are and where we're going. Not even you."

The admiral signaled for James to take the white Burgundy in, to the table, and to serve him a glass of the 1998 Château de Carles, which had been opened an hour previously. This particular deep red Bordeaux, made on the right bank of the Gironde River, has a pedigree dating back to the eighth century when Emperor Charlemagne camped in the area.

Château de Carles itself dates back to the fifteenth century, and all that history, plus the distant presence of the great warrior Charlemagne, tipped the balance for Arnold, away from his favorite Château Lynch-Bages to the earthy black fruit aromas of the wine from Fronsac.

"Always remember, my boy," he said to James. "Ninety-eight. St. Emilion and Pomerol, right bank of the river. That's where they made the top vintage."

"I did know that, sir. But I've never really known why."

"Because it rained like hell on the left bank," snapped the admiral.

"Really? Well, how wide's the river, sir?"

"About a hundred times wider than the one outside the front door," chuckled Arnold, as he led the way to the table, hugely looking forward to the forthcoming house specialty of honey-glazed duck with pickled plum.

At 10 P.M., British television announced details of the fatal shooting that had taken place on the front steps of the Ritz Hotel that morning. They named the dead man as George Kallan, an American national employed by the U.S. embassy in London and believed to be on the staff of the U.S. admiral Arnold Morgan, who was staying at the hotel. There had been no arrests, and, as yet, there were no suspects. The shot was believed to have been fired from a building on the opposite side of Piccadilly.

From the newscast, it was plain that the police had been very reticent about the nature of the crime. Scotland Yard did not have a representative supplying any extra information, and it was almost impossible for journalists to speculate, given the paucity of information.

Behind the scenes, however, there was pandemonium. Scotland Yard called in MI-5 and MI-6. The long-anticipated attempt on Admiral Morgan's life had indeed happened. The attack, which had been flagged by the FBI, the CIA, and even the National Security Agency, had been carried out by persons almost certainly connected with the Middle Eastern *Jihad* against the West.

One way or another, one of the Holy Warriors had tracked down the admiral, the first time he had left the United States in six months. According to all known intelligence, gathered internationally in the last few weeks, the culprit was General Ravi Rashood, the former SAS major, who appeared to be on the loose somewhere in Great Britain. Right now, he was wanted for the murders of Jerry O'Connell and George Kallan.

The news reached Jimmy Ramshawe at 5 P.M. (local) at Fort Meade. It came in the form of a private signal from one of his buddies in the CIA: *Jim, someone tried to assassinate Admiral Arnold Morgan at the front door of the Ritz Hotel in London today. The bullet missed, but hit one of the admiral's bodyguards, George Kallan, killed him instantly.*

Lt. Commander Ramshawe went white. He felt no sense of triumph, no feeling of exoneration for all the grief he had been given by the admiral. He actually felt scared, for Arnold and for Kathy. This represented all his dreads. And it was not the stray rifle shot across Piccadilly that bothered him. It was the fact that this organization, to which General Rashood belonged, had very obviously decided the time had come to eliminate the Big Man.

They had, Jimmy was certain, gone to the most enormous amount of trouble and expense to mount this operation, and it had plainly gone wrong. He, Jimmy, had been on to them from the start, and in his opinion they were not the kind of guys to quit. They would regroup and start again, searching for the man who had been their bête noire for so long.

He touched base with the CIA's London desk, and they informed him that the admiral and Kathy were quite safe and in hiding somewhere west of London, under heavy CIA and police protection. There were two Flying Squad cars on permanent station outside the small hotel where the Morgans were staying. That was a total of seven armed British officers. There was Arnold's regular Secret Service detail, and an armed boat from the London River Police was on its way up through the locks and expected to arrive before midnight. If Hamas, or whoever, was planning to try again, this would not be an ideal time.

Nonetheless, Jimmy was extremely worried. Despite all the warnings and alerts received by the security authorities, this character Rashood had slipped through the net and had actually managed to park himself in a building opposite the admiral's hotel and open fire on him the first time Arnie set foot outside the door. And then get away!

This was no ordinary assassin, Jimmy decided. This was a top-of-the-line professional, Rashood, the former SAS commander, a man once headed for the very top in Britain's most elite branch of Special Forces.

If Admiral Morgan was to be protected, he would need at his side a man of comparable talents, not some half-trained London bobby. And Jimmy did not know what to do about that. He called Admiral Morris, his boss, who told him to come along to the director's office immediately. George had not yet heard the news.

And when Jimmy arrived, Morris listened wide-eyed while his assistant recounted the events in London earlier that day.

"Sir," said Jimmy, "we got to get him a bodyguard. Not a cop, or an agent, a Special Forces guy, someone like an ex–Navy SEAL or a Green Beret. Someone who can shoot, fight, or kill if necessary."

Admiral Morris nodded sagely, and wondered if it had occurred to Jimmy that such a man might not be allowed to operate with impunity in a foreign country.

"There are such things as laws, Jimmy," he said. "Particularly in a socialist country like England. And those laws prevent ex–Navy SEALs from opening fire on wandering terrorists, whatever their crimes. The Brits have been neurotic about the human rights of criminals ever since that cream-puff Blair and his lawyer wife smooth-talked their way into 10 Downing Street."

"Couldn't we fix something with the Brits?"

"I think that's very possible, if we can get the president on our side. Arnold obviously needs specialized protection, and the Brits won't relish getting the blame if anything should happen to him while he's in their country."

"Can you talk to President Bedford?"

"Well, not right now. He's fishing up in Kennebunkport with George Bush. But he's coming back in the morning. I'll catch him then."

"Okay, sir. Let's assume something can be arranged. You want me to talk to John Bergstrom, see if he can suggest anyone?"

"Good idea, Jimmy. We don't want anything to happen to our guy, right? Let's start things moving right away."

Jimmy returned to his office, checked his watch—2:30 P.M. in California—and punched in the numbers for SPECWARCOM in Coronado, San Diego. It took the assistant to the director of the National Security Agency approximately three minutes to be put through to Vice Admiral John Bergstrom, who was in the final weeks of his tenure as head of Special War Command.

He and Lt. Commander Ramshawe had met previously and shared in common a profound admiration for Admiral Morgan. It took Jimmy only two or three minutes to outline the events in London that morning, and the potential danger to Arnold, for the king SEAL to offer his undivided attention.

Finally Jimmy came to the point. Both he and Admiral George Morris were convinced that Arnold now required a very special bodyguard. Jimmy pointed out the skill and devilish determination of the assassin who everyone now assessed as the C-in-C of Hamas in person.

"He's a highly trained SAS commander, Admiral," said Jimmy. "And the truth is, he's been a couple of jumps in front of us ever since we first suspected there was a Middle Eastern agent who'd been tracking down Kathy's mom."

"Did he actually get inside a building opposite the Ritz Hotel and then open fire on Arnold?" asked Admiral Bergstrom.

"He sure did," said Jimmy. "We're working with the London police to try to identify and then locate him. But I'm highly unhopeful."

"You mean this bastard is still on the loose?"

"Correct. And, so far, the best we've been able to do is surround Arnie with a group of London bobbies. And that's not anything like good enough. Not with a trained Special Forces assassin like this guy on his trail."

"What do you need, Jimmy?"

"Ideally I'd like one of your top guys. Maybe a recently retired SEAL. Someone who's fit, hard-trained, and savvy, a guy who's worked in the hot-spots, who knows what to watch for, who can spot danger before it arrives."

"Uh-huh," said the admiral. "We got guys like that. But let me ask you one thing—will the Brits allow us to move in an armed warrior to protect one of our own?"

"Admiral Morris says yes. Mainly because they will not want to get the blame if anything happens to the Big Man."

"Who's asking them? That's important."

"George says President Bedford will do it."

"That's good, because if he asks, they'll say yes. It's one of those perfect situations. You ask for that kind of favor, and they say no, then you've got 'em by the ears, because if something goes wrong it's obviously their fault. I should think they'd be delighted to hand Arnie's security over to us."

"Then," said Jimmy, "if it all goes wrong, it's totally *our* fault, right?"

"You got it. Trouble is, I'm real stretched at the minute. We got guys all over the place, Iraq, Iran, Burma, Afghanistan, Saudi Arabia, Bahrain. And you want a top guy, like a full SEAL commander. And we don't have that many. But I do have a guy in mind."

"Who's that?"

"I'm considering our old friend Commander Rick Hunter. And I'm considering him for several reasons, the first and main one being he's probably the best we ever had. Secondly, he is a great fan of Arnold Morgan's. And thirdly, he's retired and could easily take the time."

"Has he stayed fit?"

"Hell, yes. He has a private gym at his home, and he runs around that darned great farm of his every day."

"Is that SEAL-fit, combat-fit?"

"That's Hunter-fit, which is almost certainly better."

"Where does he live?"

"Kentucky."

"Oh, yes; I remember now. His family runs a thoroughbred horse-breeding farm, right?"

"That's him. And quite honestly, I don't think his wife—Diana—would allow him to go into combat again. But this is not combat, is it? He's just got to go with the admiral and make sure no one tries to kill him. It's nothing like the danger level he's used to."

"Who should ask him, sir? You, I hope."

"You, I'm afraid," said the admiral. "I asked him once before to undertake a special mission, and he got shot in the thigh. I think Diana might hang up on me if I called."

Jimmy laughed. "Well, I can't just phone him and suggest that he load his machine gun, can I?"

"Certainly not. You need to go and see him, and you'll find it harder getting Diana to agree. She's very protective and senses, but does not know, just how important a warrior her husband is."

"Sir, will you call him and tell him I'm on my way to see him, and I should be treated with consideration?"

"Not me. But I'll send him an E-mail and tell him he should at least see you."

"Tomorrow, sir. This is urgent. None of us wants Arnie to get killed."

"You got it, Jimmy. I'll send it now. By the way, Rick's address is Hunter Valley Farms, Lexington, Kentucky. Better get out there."

0930 Wednesday 1 August
The White House

President Bedford already had an E-mail requesting that he speak to Admiral Morris at the National Security Agency at 9:45. Even presidents tend to hop to it when Crypto City comes calling. Because Crypto City does not usually bother the president unless it's a five-alarmer.

When the admiral came on the direct line, Paul Bedford was both polite and extremely curious. When George Morris began to explain the situation and the clear and present danger to Arnold, Bedford was appalled.

"We have to bring him home," he said. "These people are killers. And we cannot mount proper security in another country—not even with our friends in Great Britain."

"That's half the trouble, sir," replied George. "We've been trying to curtail this trip for several weeks. He won't give it up. And he always says the same thing, about giving in to the goddamned terrorists. You know what he's like."

"But surely he feels differently now, with George Kallan being murdered."

"I'm afraid not, sir. You see, Arnold hardly knew George. Met him for the first time at Dulles Airport and never really spoke to him again. George was not on his regular Secret Service detail. This was his first assignment with Arnold."

"Yes, but what about bringing him home, the funeral and everything?"

"According to Al, his chief bodyguard who's spoken to Lt. Commander Ramshawe, the admiral said the one place in all the world he would never go would be to Kallan's funeral. He thinks that's where the killer is most likely to strike again."

"Where's Kallan from?"

"Peru, Indiana."

"Birthplace of Cole Porter," replied the president.

"If you don't mind my saying, sir, that's a truly remarkable piece of information. I thought he was from Long Island, New York."

"So do most people," said the president, grinning down the phone. "Guess that's why I'm . . . er . . . sitting in this chair, et cetera, et cetera."

Admiral Morris laughed. He really liked Paul Bedford. "Anyway, sir, the purpose of my call is to request your help in protecting Arnold from further attempts on his life. We're trying to recruit a Navy SEAL, a combat veteran, to fly to England and take up position beside Arnold at all times."

The president instantly approved of that. "Great idea, George. We got John Bergstrom on the case?"

"Yes, sir. We'll get the best man we can. But he's got to be armed, and able to shoot if necessary. That's probably against the law in England, and we need you to get special permission for our man to be permitted to do everything in his power to protect Arnold."

"No problem," said the president. "I'll call the British PM right away. He'll fix it at the highest level, not because he wants to, but because it'll take the heat off them if anything else happens."

"My assessment precisely, sir. But we are in a bit of a hurry—could you help get our man there in the fastest possible time?"

"Let me know when he can leave. I'll take care of it."

1130 Same Day
Blue Grass Airport
Lexington, Kentucky

The U.S. Navy's Lockheed Airies came swiftly in over Bourbon County, high above some of the most renowned racehorse farms in the world. Blue Grass Field was out on the west of the town, and the Navy pilot, who had made it in just over seventy-five minutes from Andrews Air Force Base, could see the runway up ahead.

He banked around to the south of Lexington, flared out, and landed the Airies immaculately in Kentucky. There was one passenger only in the aircraft, and the navigator walked back to let him out.

The uniformed Lt. Commander Ramshawe thanked him and climbed down the steps to a waiting farm truck, which had the words HUNTER VALLEY inscribed on the door, above a picture of a mare and foal. Jimmy Ramshawe had no luggage, and the truck driver just held the door open and let him in.

He introduced himself as Olin and revealed that he worked in the coverin' barn all winter and spring, then took care of the farm vehicles all summer and autumn.

"Is Hunter Valley a big place?" asked Jimmy.

"Hell, yes," said Olin. "Hundreds of acres. Around seventy mares and foals in residence. A lot of 'em born here."

"That's a big operation, right? Does Mr. Hunter run the whole thing himself?"

"Well, he's the boss. But a lot of the staff here worked for his father. That makes a big difference. The department heads know as much about the place as he does. But Mr. Rick is the main man. And he's got his daddy's touch with a breeding stallion."

Lt. Commander Ramshawe was not exactly certain what that last part meant. But it sounded important, and for a moment it crossed his mind that Commander Hunter might be altogether too busy to save Arnold's life. However, he understood that, somehow, breeding race-horses was a seasonal business; and he asked if August was a busy time of the year.

"Not really. Thoroughbred stallions cover mares between February and July at the very latest," he said. "Their foals gotta be born in the new year, up through May. No one wants what we call a June foal."

"How long are the mares pregnant for?" asked Jimmy.

"Eleven months. And that means we don't really want them going in foal too late."

"Why don't people want a June foal?" said Jimmy.

"Well, all racehorses have their birthday on January 1. On that day, any foal born two years previously becomes two. They are young and imma-ture, still growing; but the horse who was born in January really is two, where the one born in June is only nineteen months. And that makes a difference when they get on the track. The older ones are stronger and bigger, and usually faster. No June foals, sir. No June foals."

"So there's no action in August. The stallions are resting."

"Correct, sir. We have the usual anxiety about mares in foal. But it's not like the spring, when everyone's giving birth. And the stallions are work-ing day and night. And the staff are often up all night."

"Including Mr. Hunter?"

"Oh, sure. He's a real hands-on kind of guy."

"So I've heard."

Olin drove the truck through big stone gates, in front of which was a two-ton rock with HUNTER VALLEY carved smoothly on its surface. The drive was long, lined with lime trees and carefully trimmed grass.

At the end was another pair of stone pillars, set to the left. And beyond there was the main house, standing back across a wide lawn. There were Doric columns on either side of the front door, and to the left was a three-acre paddock in which there were three mares, two of them with foals at foot.

Diana Hunter saw the truck arrive and came out to meet the naval offi-cer from Fort Meade. She was dressed in riding boots, jodhpurs, and a white shirt, and her accent was English. She was a great-looking horse-woman, slender, with swept-back blonde hair, light blue eyes.

"Lieutenant Commander Ramshawe?" she said. "Hello, I'm Diana, Rick's wife. He'll be here in a few minutes. Come on in and have some coffee."

"Pleased to meet you, ma'am," said Jimmy. "This is a very beautiful place you have here. Olin's been trying to educate me about racehorses."

"He'll be pretty good at that," she laughed. "His family's been in the business for five generations, like mine. He's our head stallion man—and he's the great-great-grandson of the man who looked after Black Toney."

"Black Tony!" exclaimed Jimmy. "We had a Black Tony back home in Australia."

"Was he a thoroughbred?"

"Not likely. He was a bank robber."

Diana Hunter laughed, already taking to the intelligence officer who sounded like the Man from Snowy River. "Out here, Black Toney was a great Kentucky stallion," she said. "Sired two winners of the Kentucky Derby in the 1920s and '30s. Probably not as interesting as your Black Tony."

"Probably not," agreed Jimmy, earnestly. "Our Black Tony was Tony McGarry, knocked over the Sydney National Bank for a million dollars and shot four cashiers dead. They hanged him about sixty years ago. He was no relation."

Diana Hunter laughed loudly this time. "I didn't think he was," she said. "Your name's not McGarry."

"No, but my grandma's was. I forgot to mention that."

Just then, Commander Rick Hunter came in. "Okay, you guys," he grinned, "what's so funny? I could do with a joke."

"Oh, nothing," said his wife. "Lieutenant Commander Ramshawe just thought Black Toney was a bank robber who was hanged for murder."

Rick Hunter walked over with his right hand outstretched. "Hi," he said. "Lieutenant Commander Ramshawe? Admiral Bergstrom refused to tell me what you wanted, so I'll get a cup of this coffee and you can fill me in."

The ex–Navy SEAL commander stood a little over six feet, five inches tall. He was built like a stud bull, carried not one ounce of fat, and looked as if he could pick up a thoroughbred stallion with his bare hands.

Jimmy Ramshawe knew all about him, having checked out the commander's biography on the Navy networks. Rick had served on SEAL teams all over the world—Burma, Iran, Russia, Iraq, Afghanistan, and Argentina. He'd been in sole command six times, fought, been wounded, and always come out on top. He would have received the Congressional Medal of Honor for valor but for a sudden and premature retirement from the Navy after his best friend and colleague was unjustly brought before a court-martial six years previously.

There were still very senior officers in the United States Navy who would have moved mountains to get Rick back into the SEALs. But he was a rather unusual member of the armed forces. His family was long-established Bluegrass horse breeders, and the young Rick Hunter had wanted more excitement in his life than waiting months on end for thoroughbred mares to produce expensive foals.

However, when the Navy disgraced Commander Dan Headley by finding him guilty of mutiny, despite overpowering mitigating evidence, Rick never felt the same. He resigned with his buddy, and the two of them retired to Kentucky to run the farm. Both of them were married within two years, Rick to one of the daughters of the revered Jarvis horse-training family in Newmarket, England. It was a dazzling match. Diana's younger brother was a major in Great Britain's SAS.

And now the towering former SEAL stood before Lt. Commander Ramshawe, wondering what on earth the National Security Agency could want from him. Jimmy took a sip of coffee. Diana motioned for everyone to sit down and made it perfectly clear that she was not going anywhere at this particular moment.

"Rick," said Jimmy, "you are, I believe, acquainted with the president's closest friend, Admiral Arnold Morgan?"

Commander Hunter nodded.

"Well," said Jimmy, "he is in England right now, and for some weeks we have been concerned there would be an attempt on his life. And then yesterday morning, outside the Ritz Hotel in London, someone tried to kill him. It was a high-powered rifle shot to the head, and it killed one of his bodyguards instead of him. But it was close."

"Was the shot from street level?" asked the ex–SEAL team leader.

Jimmy shook his head. "So far as we can tell, the killer fired from high up, from a building on the other side of the street."

And from there Jimmy took the story through from the beginning, from the barmaid-agent in Brockhurst, to the submarine, the subsequent murder of the Irish farmer who got in the way, and finally the sighting of the Hamas chief, in the ferry terminal in Holyhead, with the barmaid.

"Jesus," replied Rick, "that does not sound in any way good. Because you're not dealing with some nutcase, you're dealing with a professional operation from the Middle East. If they can knock down the Towers, I guess they can knock down Arnold."

"Not if we can help it," said Jimmy. "And it has now been agreed that we will call in either a U.S. Navy SEAL, or a Green Beret, or a Ranger, to stand personal guard over the admiral. Obviously we want a real combat veteran, preferably a man who has fought with our Special Forces not only in a remote and rural environment, but also in an urban theater."

Rick got it. And he raised his eyebrows. "And that's why you're here? To ask me to rejoin the Navy and fly to Europe to protect Arnold Morgan?"

"Yes, I suppose I am."

"Out of the question," said Diana.

"I guess you heard the lady," added Rick. "I couldn't possibly do that. I have vast responsibilities here, I couldn't just up and leave."

"Not even for two or three weeks?" said Jimmy. "I know August is your least busy month. Now the covering season is over."

"How can a man who thinks Black Toney is a bank robber possibly know that?" asked Diana, smiling.

"Olin told me," said Jimmy, simply. "But I don't think I have explained very well how important this is. As you doubtless know, Admiral Morgan is closer to the president than anyone else in the country except for his wife. Paul Bedford relies on Arnold for all advice on global problems and threats to the United States.

"He is well acquainted with the grave danger this General Rashood poses. And he immediately suggested that Admiral John Bergstrom be brought into the equation. You are Admiral Bergstrom's choice. And by now the president knows full well, and approves, that you should be the chosen man."

"Hmmmm," said Rick, his mind racing. "Under no circumstances can I undertake this, but no one likes to personally turn down the President of the United States."

"Rick, this thing is going higher than even I know. President Bedford is speaking to the British prime minister today, requesting special permission for an armed American bodyguard to have free choice in the matter of Arnold's safety . . . to legally open fire if necessary."

"Guess the guy'll need that," said Rick. "These things are always split-second. You spot something and act instantly. If you don't, the target's dead."

"And of course," said Jimmy, smoothly, "you would not be the target."

"Neither," said Diana, sweetly, "was this George Kallan. But he's still dead."

"Rick, if you were to accept this assignment, you would look back in years to come. And you won't remember the inconvenience. Only the honor of being chosen by the U.S. president to carry out a mission that close to his heart.

"Right now, you are hearing it from this lowly lieutenant commander from the National Security Agency. If I go back and say you've refused, you'll be in the Oval Office tomorrow, trust me."

"Well, even the president can't force us to agree, can he?" said Diana.

But Rick added, "He probably couldn't force you, Diana. But you're not an American, and sometimes I think you don't quite understand what that office means to all of us. Especially if you've served in the military."

And Rick turned to Jimmy and said, "I have to admit, I would find it very difficult to tell the President of the United States that I would not answer his call to protect his closest friend, who just happens to be one of America's finest strategists and greatest patriots."

Jimmy nodded, unsmiling. "I can't stress this too much, Rick—the highest powers in this country want you to go to Great Britain, on behalf of the president, and do everything you can to prevent this terrorist from killing Arnold Morgan."

"It's so unfair," interjected Diana. "Rick's not even in the Navy any more. Why should he have to step in when there are so many young guys who would be honored to go on a mission like that?"

"Mostly because Rick is the best Navy SEAL there's ever been," said Jimmy. "At least that's what the Navy high command thinks. And that's what the president believes. That's why I'm here. And you can turn me down. But that won't be the end of it. The president will want to see you."

"And what will Rick get out of it, apart from the honor?"

"I'd guess anything he asks for," replied Jimmy. "But if there was an incident, and he managed to save the admiral, I'd guess you'd be looking at the Congressional Medal of Honor. Since Rick would officially be in the Navy for the three-week length of the mission."

"You mean the president could deem that Rick was a serving Navy officer and facing an enemy?" asked Diana.

"The president can deem anything he darn well pleases," said Jimmy. "He's the commander in chief. No one can argue."

"Including me," said Rick. "You are making this very difficult."

He turned to his wife and added, "I do understand, Diana, that as a civilian you cannot quite tune in to . . . well . . . a warrior's call to the flag. It's not easy."

"And it would be even less easy if you managed to get killed," she retorted.

"Diana, that's the one thing I'm not too worried about. An assassin usually has to spend a lot of time lining up his position and his shot. The best sniper rifles don't have automatic loading, which means he only gets one shot, if he intends to escape.

"And the guy involved in this case is not some kid high on opium and happy to commit suicide. At least it doesn't look that way. From what Jimmy says, this assassination will be carried out by the top commander in Hamas or Hezbollah, a guy we've never arrested or even gotten a chance to kill. We know he's ex-SAS, so he'll be damn good at his job.

"Jimmy, my biggest hesitation is that I might fail. And then have to live with the blame."

"Rick, that's not going to happen. Everyone agrees: if you can't do it, it can't be done. There will be no announcements, no one will ever know you were there. This mission is just about as classified as anything can get. You will travel in secret, operate in secret, and return home in secret. If you should fail, no one will ever know."

"I'll know," said Commander Hunter. "And that's why I can't allow anything to happen."

Jimmy, recognizing the superior rank, asked flatly, "Sir, does that mean you'll except the assignment?"

"Affirmative," replied the SEAL.

Diana stood up. "I know when I'm beaten," she smiled. "And I'm comforted by only one thing—this assassin's not firing at Rick, is he?"

"He won't have time," replied Jimmy. "Not if he hopes to get away."

"When do you guys need me on station?" asked Rick.

"Certainly in the next few days," said Jimmy. "The trouble is, no one quite knows where Arnold is going. Since he left the White House, he's been pretty secretive. My boss, Admiral Morris, has spoken to the CIA, and they think he's going to Scotland."

"I have met him, you know," said Rick. "A couple of times. Only briefly, but he's a damned impressive guy. He was talking to me about the Middle East, and Jesus, he really knows his stuff. In just a few minutes he let me know why he can't stand Arabs or Russians. Doesn't trust 'em, any of 'em."

Jimmy then told Rick that he could expect a call from Admiral Bergstrom, and probably from the president, before he left. "You'll fly direct to Andrews Air Force Base from here in a Navy jet. And from there you'll fly private to either Edinburgh or Glasgow, if Arnie's in Scotland, or RAF Lyneham in Wiltshire, England. All your gear will be preloaded. Do you have a weapon you prefer?"

"I'll need a short-barreled CAR-15 automatic rifle. I'm used to it, and it's the best I've ever used, probably the best military weapon ever made—fires a .223-caliber cartridge at high velocity. It has a thirty-round magazine. It's very powerful, hits with enormous force. Just a small bullet, but it would stop a mountain lion dead in its tracks."

"Anything else?"

"Yes, tell 'em I'll also take a Sig Sauer 9mm pistol. That's standard issue for SEALs. And let me have a couple of extra fifteen-round magazines. If I'm on duty, I'd feel half-dressed without it."

Jimmy made a note in his small brown leather book. "I don't think you'll take combat clothing, Rick. George Morris told me this morning you'd be operating disguised as a London policeman."

"Good idea," said Rick. "It'll make me a lot less conspicuous."

"You just need your regular street clothes," said Jimmy. "Anything else, the Brits will take care of it. They, by the way, are going to be thrilled you're coming. Because your presence means they don't have to take the blame for anything."

Rick chuckled. "You staying for lunch?"

"Not this time. I need to get back."

"Okay, I'll whistle up Olin. He'll take you to the airport."

"Thanks, Commander. I appreciate that. Sorry to disrupt your life like this."

"The whole operation sounds like a real challenge. Tell the truth, I'm quite looking forward to it." The big Navy SEAL was grinning. "And, as you know, August is the least busy month."

0930 Thursday 2 August
Goring-on-Thames
England

The admiral and Kathy slept late and decided to stay another day at the Leatherne Bottel. And, in the meantime, Ravi and Shakira continued to head north to Scotland.

The general had allowed himself to be persuaded to spend Tuesday night in the Cambridge Sheraton. And they had begun the long drive on Wednesday morning, cutting west across to the A-1 motorway just north of Huntingdon, and then running due north all the way to Yorkshire.

Ravi had decided to make for the more westerly city of Glasgow rather than the Scottish capital, Edinburgh, and that meant leaving the motorways that run up the eastern side of England and driving right across the Pennines, the range of mountains that runs down the backbone of the country.

The Hamas general had made the journey before, and decided to take the spectacular A-66 for fifty-five miles straight over the wild and glorious Yorkshire moors, across Stainmore Forest and into Cumbria.

They arrived in the town of Penrith, the gateway to the Lake District, shortly before 5 P.M. and pulled into the Claymore, a pleasant-looking inn situated in the historic town center.

Shakira, who had been very withdrawn throughout the entire journey, finally elected to engage in conversation, asking why her husband had elected to leave the fast, direct freeways on the east side in favor of a beautiful but time-wasting drive over the mountains.

Ravi, who was tired of her endless silences, explained carefully that Admiral Morgan's biography had pointed out that he had served in the U.S.

submarines in Holy Loch. "The whole area along the Firth of Clyde is full of ex-submariners," he said. "And there's a chance that Admiral Morgan might want to visit his old stomping ground. If he's in the area, there might be a reference in the local paper. He's a very influential person, former national security adviser to the president. He's too big a man to get lost entirely."

"Will you try to kill him again?"

"Certainly," replied her husband. "That's why we're here, and in particular that's why we switched to the east side of the country, where he's most likely to be."

They checked into the Claymore, and Ravi slept for two hours. Shakira went out and bought some magazines, which she came back and read. It was obvious to anyone, at least anyone who was awake, that she was sick and tired of this relentless chase to assassinate the American.

Shakira had a foreboding that it would end in tears. In her opinion, everything had gone wrong, right from the start—the ludicrous Matt Barker, the unlucky Jerry O'Connell, the equally unlucky George Kallan. They were all dead, and in Shakira's mind she and Ravi would soon be dead if they didn't call the whole thing off and leave for the Middle East forthwith.

Even Ravi had admitted that the amount of security surrounding the admiral was very intense. But as her determination waned, so Ravi's had increased. And Shakira was afraid he might be losing the cold-blooded streak of realism that had always kept him on the straight and narrow, no matter what the mission.

In Shakira's opinion, this was all connected to that terrible night in Damascus when their house had been flattened by a bomb and she had been so lucky to get out. She'd never really gotten to the bottom of that, but she had asked Ravi, and he had been very vague except to say that he suspected the Israelis, under American guidance. Especially under Arnold Morgan's guidance.

But it had all taken so long. They had journeyed so far. And now they were off on some wild-goose chase to find the admiral, and they did not even know his address. They did not even know what town he was in, never mind what country. And there was an unreasonable determination about her husband. He was a man possessed. Nothing else mattered to him. Shakira had never seen him like this before.

She sat disconsolately in an armchair in their room at the Claymore. For a while she read *Vogue,* then she switched to the more gossipy *Marie Claire.* But she could find nothing of interest in either of them. She walked across the room and picked up a brochure about the town of Penrith and noted there was a castle on the outskirts that had been built in the fourteenth century.

Against all Muslim teaching, she felt like a glass of wine; she phoned down, asking someone to bring up two glasses and to reserve a table for two in the dining room for 7:30 this evening.

Ravi awakened at seven and without a word went into the bathroom to take a shower. He was totally preoccupied and was becoming almost distant. Shakira did not for one moment believe he was losing interest in her, but she was beginning to worry about this obsession that had taken over his life. Because it was an obsession to kill not an opposing force, but one single man whom he had never even met.

Generally speaking, Shakira did not believe this was a healthy situation. And she did not believe commanders of serious military organizations should behave in that way. It seemed both unnatural and unnecessary.

But Ravi maintained a passionate hatred for the American admiral, and when he came out of the bathroom, as if reading her mind, he said, "I'm not giving up, Shakira. If I have to pursue him to the ends of the earth, I will do so."

Dinner that evening was thus fraught, and the tension between them seemed to grow, as Shakira harbored more and more doubts about this very personal vendetta in which her husband was involved.

Ravi, for his part, was more determined than ever to end the admiral's life, but he sensed that his wife did not wish to hear any more about it. Shakira wished only to tell her husband yet again that she wanted to call the entire thing off, but did not dare to do so. As silent dinners go, this one was right up there.

They were only around thirty miles short of the Scottish border, but it was another ninety miles to Glasgow, which was their vague destination. The truth was, Ravi did not know where the hell he was going. All he knew was that Great Britain's submarine roads were out to the west of Scotland's second city, and that was where Admiral Morgan had served as captain of a nuclear boat out of the American base at Holy Loch.

Emily Gallagher had confirmed that her daughter was going to Scotland, but the rest was pure guesswork on Ravi's part. His game plan was to check into a hotel in Glasgow, one with access to the Internet, and start searching for any shred of evidence that a former NSA to the American president was expected in the area.

He and Shakira once more drove with hardly a word spoken. They reached the outskirts of Glasgow around noon and moved fast around the city on the freeway. Ravi followed the signs to the city center, crossed the River Clyde, and pulled up outside the Millennium Hotel in George Square, Glasgow's focal point.

Ravi had not been here for many years, but he remembered Scotland's last great shipbuilding city, and he smiled for the first time this week when the receptionist told him there was a large double room which he and Mrs. Barden could have for two nights. And yes, there was a communications room for visiting businessmen who wanted access to the Internet. There were four desktop Apple Macintosh computers in there, and it was open twenty-four hours.

Ravi and Shakira checked in, and immediately his mood began to lighten. He took Shakira down to the hotel's conservatory, which looks out onto the square, and ordered coffee and chicken sandwiches for lunch.

He apologized for his melancholy demeanor and tried to explain that he had taken a sacred oath, among his peers in the Hamas High Command, that he would rid the *Jihad* of its most sinister enemy. For him, it would be the most terrible loss of face to fail. And there was no turning back. He must assassinate the admiral or die in the attempt.

"But what about me?" asked Shakira, plaintively. "I won't let you die alone. But I still don't understand why this cannot be like any other military operation. You try, you fail, then you retreat, regroup, and perhaps someone else takes over as leader. Great victories are sometimes won at the second or third try. It does not have to be all or nothing, every time."

"This one does, Shakira. This one is to the death."

"Do you have any real hope of finding him here? This Glasgow is a very big place."

"I know," said Ravi. "It's a kind of surprise after driving all through that amazing lonely country—the Yorkshire moors, then the Lake District, then the border country, and suddenly there's this giant metropolis right on the banks of the Clyde."

"And those freeways, it was like being back in London."

"A long time ago," said Ravi, "Glasgow was described as the Second City of Empire. After London, that is. And there were a lot of cities in the British Empire. Half the bloody world. It was a very important place."

"You still haven't told me what happens to me if you manage to get yourself killed. What am I supposed to do? Where could I go?"

Ravi was once more silent. "You are right in your thoughts. There would be nowhere else for you to go. Because they'd hunt you down and charge you with the murder of Matt Barker. Plus God knows how many other crimes. Shakira, I am pretty hard to kill, and I'm not even considering that possibility. But if we have to die, we die together, like Holy Warriors."

"Well, I'm sick of this dying business," she replied. "I'm sick of blowing things up and hating everyone. I've been in the West for a long time now, and I can't think of any reasons why we should go around trying to kill people. I've liked nearly everyone I've met. I'm not even sure this Admiral Morgan is all that bad."

Despite the seriousness of Shakira's mindset, Ravi laughed. He had another bite of his chicken sandwich, principally to give himself time to think up a reply, and then he said, "Sometimes there is a far bigger picture than the little corner we occupy."

"I'm not in a picture," she said. "I'm right here in Glasgow eating chicken sandwiches, and I don't want you to go off and blow this admiral's head apart with your special bullets, and then get shot by the police. That's all."

"Sssssshhhh!" he hissed. "Someone will hear you."

"And I don't want to go around being told to *ssshhhh* for the rest of my life. Why can't we go back to Ireland? I liked it there. And we could live peacefully, miles away from all this terrorist stuff."

"Because I'm wanted for murder in County Cork," replied Ravi. "And there would never be any peace for us. We have just one choice. I have to complete my mission, and then we go back to Gaza or Damascus where we will be protected. We must live in an Arab country, because that's where we will be looked after for the rest of our lives."

Shakira made no reply for a full minute. And then she said, "I just have a bad feeling about this mission. And I have not experienced anything like it before. The Americans must know that a Middle Eastern group tried to kill the admiral. And if he stays here, they will have extra security all over the place.

"I think our task will be harder now than it's ever been. And those Americans will be armed with machine guns. And we know they can shoot straight. I think we should call the whole thing off and Hamas can try again next year. Let someone else take the risk."

Ravi gazed at her sternly. "Shakira," he said, "this one is to the death."

"Even though you might be committing suicide? I mean, how the hell do you think we'll get away? All those assassins in the past were caught. I read the other day, they got the man who shot President Lincoln, they got that Oswald guy who shot JFK. President Reagan and John Lennon were both shot, and the police got both gunmen. Same with Martin Luther King, and Bobby Kennedy."

"Hey," said Ravi, "how come you know so much about assassinations?"

"I read a magazine article about them in the hotel last night. I've been saving the knowledge to hit you with it. All those men who pulled the trigger on famous people were caught and tried in a court of law."

"They didn't catch me," replied Ravi. "I walked away scot-free. And I'm still walking."

"Well, you might be a bit cleverer, that's all," she replied. "But your luck may not hold out forever."

"I assure you," said Ravi, momentarily stunned by his wife's insolence, "luck had absolutely nothing to do with it. I walked away because I planned it better."

"I accept that," said Shakira, retreating. "But I just wish we could give it up and try to get on with our lives. We've both done enough in the cause of Islam. No one could deny that."

"I can only repeat what I said before. I have too much to lose in terms of reputation, and in case you had forgotten, I am still an English national, and that will always cast a shadow over me among some Muslims. There would be suspicions about my commitment. You make me say it again. This one is to the death."

They finished their lunch, and Shakira went up to their room. Ravi kissed her and said he treasured her above all else, and then he walked into the communications room.

He sat in front of one of the computers and, after a quick Google search, connected to the Web site of Glasgow's excellent newspaper *The*

Herald. And there he typed the words *Admiral Arnold Morgan,* waiting patiently while a search was carried out for any mention of the American during the past few weeks. In the end there was nothing.

He tried Web sites for *the submarine service,* for *Holy Loch,* the old U.S. base. And for *Royal Navy reunions.* All in the vain hope that somewhere, somehow, Admiral Morgan's name would pop up. It didn't. But then Ravi decided there needed to be a change of tack, since he was working on the pure assumption that Arnold was returning to his old stomping ground in the west, around the Clyde estuary.

But perhaps he wasn't. Perhaps he was coming to Scotland for entirely different reasons. Maybe Glasgow was a waste of time. Perhaps Admiral Morgan was going to the capital city, Edinburgh. And perhaps it would be better to search through Scotland's other national newspaper, *The Scotsman,* which was based in Edinburgh.

Ravi switched Web sites and tapped in the name *Admiral Arnold Morgan* and waited. Nothing came up. He decided to scroll through some recent editions and see if he could find some inspiration. His luck turned with last Monday's newspaper, which had an entire page on the forthcoming Edinburgh International Festival, an annual August event, to which 500,000 people were expected.

The chairman of the Festival was someone called Lady MacLean, married to a retired Royal Navy admiral, Sir Iain MacLean. Her name was Annie, and there was a substantial interview with her about the wide-ranging aspects of the Festival, the films, the plays, the ballet, the chorale, and finally the Military Tattoo, which began on Saturday.

Lady MacLean had revealed a list of high dignitaries who would sit in the Royal Box at Edinburgh Castle and take the salute. The fourth one down, in extremely small type, was Admiral Arnold Morgan, U.S. Navy (ret.).

The reporter who compiled the page must have been struck by the unusual nature of a U.S. admiral showing up for this very British event. And he had plainly pressed her on the subject. Lady MacLean had rewarded his persistence by explaining that this former presidential staff member was a very old friend of her husband's, and would be staying with them at their home in Inveraray before attending the Festival. Both Sir Iain and Admiral Morgan had commanded nuclear submarines.

Each night, a different person takes the salute at the Tattoo, and Admiral Morgan would have the honor on Tuesday, August 7. Ravi could hardly believe his luck. He felt so relieved, he did not even take into consideration that Admiral Morgan, during his tenure on the Castle Esplanade, would be surrounded by heavy personal security plus half the British Army.

His initial thought was to attempt to shoot Arnold Morgan while he was at the house in Inveraray. If that proved impossible, he would have another chance at the Tattoo. Five minutes ago, he had had no chances whatsoever, and now he had two. Ravi sensed that his luck had turned around.

He made two short notes in his leather book and then took the elevator to the sixth floor, where Shakira was asleep. He woke her gently and told her that he was attending afternoon prayers at the Central Mosque of Glasgow, which stands on four acres right by the river. He did not tell his wife, but he was feeling in urgent need of spiritual reinforcement, so cutting had her words been earlier in the day.

The flat brand of logic that was Shakira's specialty had, in a sense, gotten to him. Because there was of course much truth in her argument. Why should he and this beautiful Palestinian girl continue to risk their lives, or at best face life imprisonment, when no one else seemed to be doing anything?

He needed encouragement, and although Muslims do not communicate directly with God—not even the ayatollahs do that—Ravi usually felt an affinity with Allah inside the mosque, and, as the Chosen One, he lived in hope that one day he would hear the voice of the Great One.

He was not losing his new faith. But he was most certainly questioning it. And that was something no one could help. Ravi knew, above all else, that he needed to stand alongside the Prophet Mohammed in order to carry out His work on the planet Earth. The Muslim dream of a vast kingdom stretching from the Horn of Africa to Morocco was well within the grasp of the oil-rich sheiks of the Middle East. But only if men like himself, General Rashood, could pave the way by eliminating the more troublesome warriors of the West.

Just to hear the mullah call the faithful to prayer, to sense those rhythms of the ancient desert religion. That was his need, his requirement, here in this strange Scottish city where he was struggling to regain an impassioned belief in his God, the same belief that forced him every day to turn to the east, toward the holy shrine of Mecca in Saudi Arabia, and prostrate himself before Allah.

Ravi took a cab to the Mosque, which turned out to be a hugely impressive building, bigger than the Regents Park Mosque in London, with a massive, geometric steel-and-glass dome and a separate minaret. When Ravi heard the call of the mullah, he once again felt the old familiar lure of the desert.

This was a call to the faithful, and now he was back among that vast throng of faithful Islamists. He belonged there with these people, many of whom wore Arab dress. And he joined them in removing his shoes, and he walked inside to the great hall of prayer, and once more he prostrated himself before his God, and the recent words of Shakira faded away into the darkness of the unbelievers.

When he returned to the hotel, Shakira was awake and changed for the evening, and he explained that he was taking a long drive out to the small town of Inveraray, which stands at the top of Loch Fyne, a 55-mile journey from Glasgow.

He did not wish her to join him, and he hoped to be back by 10 P.M. Shakira accepted the news with equanimity and said she would have dinner by herself. She seemed, once more, both distant and disinterested. But she noticed that he did take his briefcase with him when he left, and distractedly wondered if she would ever see him again.

1500 Same Day
Goring-on-Thames

Arnold and Kathy were finally ready to leave the Leatherne Bottel. The Royal Air Force helicopter was once more down in the parking lot, rotors spinning, luggage loaded. There were two police cars stationed top and bottom of the entrance drive, which winds down a steep hill. Two CIA hard men were positioned either side of the entrance door to the helo, and two other guards, Al Thompson and a new man from the U.S. embassy in London, were outside the restaurant's main entrance, ready to walk close quarters across the terrace with the admiral and his wife.

With everyone on board, strapped in, doors locked, the pilot took off, rising and backing at the same time, until the screaming military aircraft was stationary over the middle of the River Thames. At which point it tilted forward and rocketed upstream, gaining height, rising up to a thousand feet, before it clattered over the thirteenth-century bridge that guards the ancient town of Wallingford.

The pilot headed north, leaving Oxford to his port side, then Birmingham, then Leicester, Nottingham, and York. At this point he changed to a slightly more westerly course, across north Yorkshire, before coming in to land at RAF Leeming for his refuel. The first two hundred miles of the journey had taken a little over an hour.

The ground crew was awaiting the helicopter's arrival, and they were on their way again after twenty minutes, flying high, directly over the A-66 where Ravi and Shakira had driven the previous day.

They flew right across the north Yorkshire moors, and then over Durham and Northumberland, before crossing the Scottish border just east of the city of Carlisle. Their route to the estuary of the Clyde took them almost identically over the route Ravi and Shakira had taken into Glasgow.

They left Loch Lomond to starboard and flew across the Forest of Argyll, coming out of the east to Loch Fyne, where, under guidance from Arnold Morgan, the pilot swept across the water and put down on the wide flat lawn of a beautiful white Georgian house on the west bank of the loch.

Standing there to meet them was the still-commanding figure of Admiral Sir Iain MacLean, now almost seventy years old. He was accompanied by three rambunctious black Labradors who all charged into the water to meet the helicopter, and then charged straight back out again when the pilot elected to come down on dry land.

Barking and shaking water all over everyone, they hurled themselves at their old friend Arnold Morgan, who greeted them like lost brothers, roughing them up the way Labradors expect to be treated. The American admiral introduced his staff to Sir Iain, and the helicopter's loadmaster helped with the luggage.

In moments, the helicopter was gone, flying back south, trying to make it before dark. It was exactly 5:30. Fifty-five miles away, Ravi Rashood was just driving away from the Millennium Hotel in Glasgow, heading for Inveraray with his briefcase.

Sir Iain hugged Kathy and shook hands with Arnold. They were all old friends, and the tall Scotsman was delighted to see them both. But as they walked up the lawn, Arnold could see three Navy staff cars and two police cruisers from the Argyll force.

"The chaps have been telling me about that trouble in London," he said. "I read about it, of course, and I guessed it might have been connected with you. Although no one seemed very sure. I had the distinct impression that the police were not releasing any information they could reasonably keep secret."

"That's about right, Iain," said Arnold. "They never caught the killer, of course. He was up and out of there before they realized George Kallan had been shot. It was a very professional operation."

"A bit too professional for my taste," said Kathy. "Arnold could have been killed. Those Middle Eastern hitmen are damned dangerous, don't you think?"

"Most certainly they are," replied the Scotsman. "But you have enough security here to keep you very safe. The police chief, chap standing over there, told me they plan to surround you until you leave."

Arnold laughed. And Kathy added, "Of course, he flatly refused to go home. And we had a message from the president this morning that he's sending a Special Forces team leader, ex–Navy SEAL, to take personal charge of the situation. He's arriving on Air Force One, if you can believe it. Tomorrow morning. Just one passenger."

By this time, they had reached the house, and the American bodyguards dispersed to make their arrangements. The Navy had taken rooms in the local hotel in Inveraray and provided cars for them to drive to and from the house. Sir Iain MacLean ushered Arnold and Kathy inside and had his butler/chauffeur Angus take the baggage up to their usual room. "Let's go and have a cup of tea, and then you two can have a rest before dinner. Annie will be home in a few minutes. She's been playing golf. God knows how she does it. I've retired from the bloody game, bad back and a slice that frequently borders on the grotesque."

1830 Same Day
Forest of Argyll

Ravi gunned the Audi fast along the mountainous, curving A-83 road through the forest and crossed the river at the top of Loch Fyne, four miles from Inveraray. He did not know the precise location of Admiral MacLean's house, but he had a feeling it might be obvious.

He drove fast through the village and, still on the main road, suddenly saw up ahead a parked police car, blue lights spinning, right across the main gates of a big white house. He steadied his speed and drove sedately past, noticing another cruiser in the drive. Ravi did not need to inquire precisely whose residence this was.

A short distance beyond the house, he noticed a wide track leading up into the woods, and he swung right, driving for a half mile until he had a clear view straight down to the loch. The house was largely obscured from his view by tall trees, but through his telescopic gunsight he could see enough.

Positioned on the roof were two plain and obvious police marksmen, along with what looked like a machine gun but might have been a guided missile system designed to repel air attack.

He could see two more police officers standing by the lake, speaking to two very obvious armed bodyguards. The gateway to the house was jammed by the cruiser. There were dogs all over the place, big Labradors whose sunny nature, he knew, could quickly be replaced by fearless, snarling aggression in the presence of an enemy, which he most certainly was.

Ravi pulled out his cell phone and dialed the Millennium Hotel, room 622, and told Shakira he'd be back for dinner after all.

Then he drove back down the mountain track and turned left onto the main road, back the way he had come.

Option One was shot. Not the admiral, just the option. And Ravi looked crestfallen. He glanced into his rearview mirror and could still see the revolving blue lights on the police cruiser outside the gates.

"That," he muttered, "was no place for me. It's Edinburgh or nothing."

CHAPTER *13*

No aircraft had landed for a full twenty minutes. The runways were clear, especially the longest one designed for the world's biggest passenger jets. And flying east across Renfrewshire came SAM 38000, the huge presidential Boeing 747, losing height, bearing Commander Rick Hunter to Scotland with full landing privileges. This was Air Force One, and, as always, the world practically stopped dead for its arrival.

Airline officials fumed, as flights were made late, landings delayed; but the request had come direct from the White House for SAM 38000 to be treated as if Paul Bedford himself was on board. The fact that it was designated SAM 38000 meant he absolutely was not on board, because that is the code name for Air Force One if anyone else is using the aircraft—Special Air Mission 38000.

Dead astern, around five miles distant, flew a smaller Boeing owned and operated by the National Security Agency. This is not an unusual occurrence, because America's super-secret intelligence system wishes to know every last vestige of information that might be transmitted anywhere near the President of the United States.

It was not the cheapest operation in the world, since Air Force One alone knocks down around $60,000 an hour in costs. But this Admiral

Morgan scenario was way beyond mundane matters like expense. President Bedford wanted him kept safe, and he wanted ironclad security. Dollars were not a consideration.

All the way across the Atlantic from Andrews Air Force Base, east of Washington, the operators inside the NSA jet had swept the skies for sign of a tracking device. And Rick Hunter had slept in peace, dining like a king on New York sirloin and apple pie with ice cream.

There were no other passengers on board, and Rick, who had left Lexington at 4 A.M. (local), had been attended by just two stewardesses. The No. 2 crew, who would fly the aircraft home tonight after the refuel, were at the rear of the cabin, as opposed to the presidential suite in which Rick was ensconced.

The ex–Navy SEAL had been told specifically by Lt. Commander Ramshawe that President Bedford would take care of the transportation, and he sure as hell had done that.

SAM 38000 swooped low over the town of Paisley and touched down at three minutes after 6 P.M. The pilot taxied up to an open, designated place outside the international terminal, and a mobile set of stairs was instantly put into place. Rick exited the aircraft and came down the stairs carrying his CAR-15 light machine gun in an olive-drab–colored holder as if it was a group of salmon-fishing rods.

A customs officer was awaiting him, in company with a Royal Navy lieutenant commander, and both men saluted him. The customs officer put a small discreet chalk marking on both the machine gun case and the duffel bag that Rick carried with him.

Just beyond the group was a red Royal Navy helicopter—the high-speed Dauphin 2 which can, if required, fire Sidewinder AIM-9M air-to-air guided missiles. Rick carried his bag and sniper rifle on board and strapped himself in, and the helicopter immediately took off, heading northwest, straight over Loch Lomond to Loch Fyne and Inveraray.

The Dauphin 2, in battle conditions, is capable of flying at almost 200 mph, and this evening it flew very fast, coming in to land on the lawn of the MacLean residence only thirty minutes after takeoff. Rick arrived at precisely the same time as Lady MacLean, who did not have the slightest idea who he was.

She stood outside the house with three policemen and watched the Dauphin take off, heading back to the Navy base of Faslane on the Gare Loch.

"We assume he's on our side?" Lady MacLean asked the policemen as Rick walked toward them.

"Oh, yes, m'lady," replied the young constable in a rich Argyll accent. "We've been expecting him. He just landed in Glasgow from America on Air Force One, the president's private aircraft."

Annie MacLean's eyebrows rose. "Good Lord," she said. "Who is he?"

There was no time to answer that, since Rick had very much arrived. He walked directly toward her and surveyed the slim, blonde-haired, sixtyish Scottish aristocrat who stood before him and said, "Ma'am, I'm Commander Rick Hunter, United States Navy. I believe Admiral MacLean is expecting me."

"Yes, yes, of course," said Lady MacLean, hurriedly. "You just took me slightly by surprise. I've only just returned myself."

"Ma'am, in my trade I'm real used to surprising people," replied Rick.

"Aha," said Lady MacLean. "Are you the Navy SEAL my husband told me about?"

"Yes, ma'am," he said. "I'm actually retired. I'm on special assignment."

"You look a lot too young to be retired," she smiled, with the practiced grace of the wife of a very senior Navy commander, a wife who had spent a lifetime trying to put young officers at their ease while knowing perfectly well they were terrified of her husband.

"Oh, I had a lot of family commitments," he offered. "My dad runs a pretty big thoroughbred breeding farm out in Kentucky, and he kinda needed me."

"Oh, you must tell me all about it," she said. "But we'd better get inside. I'm already an hour late, and I expect you would like to get rid of your luggage."

Rick followed her in, through the open French windows and into a large sunlit room that contained a highly relaxed Admiral Sir Iain MacLean, Admiral Arnold Morgan, and Kathy Morgan, old and trusted friends in comfortable surroundings.

Arnold Morgan stood up immediately and walked across the room. "Hello, Rick," he said. "It's been a long time. I'm glad to see you."

Lady MacLean made the introductions, checked her watch, and said, "Well, it's almost seven o'clock, shouldn't we be having a drink? Has no one offered you anything, Arnie? Honestly, Iain, sometimes I think you were too long in the Navy being waited on hand and foot—and here's poor Rick, flown thousands of miles from the middle of the United States. He's probably dying of thirst."

Angus appeared magically and took everyone's order, white burgundy, except for Rick, who would accept only mineral water, "Just in case we come under attack. . . ."

Arnold Morgan laughed wryly. "The way things are going, that might not be too far from the truth," he said. He did not of course realize that at this precise time General Ravi Rashood was high in the woods behind the house, staring through the telescopic sight from his long-range sniper rifle.

Five minutes later, when the drinks arrived, Ravi was gone, slightly unnerved by the sheer strength of the security that surrounded the admiral. Had he waited around much longer, up there in the woods, he would have been even more unnerved, as another Navy helicopter swept the area with infrared radar, searching for the slightest sign of unauthorized human presence among the pine and spruce trees of the Argyll Forest.

There was no doubt that the police and military on both sides of the Atlantic had been seriously spooked by that wayward silver-headed bullet that had ripped into the skull of agent George Kallan. Especially since the National Security Agency had been predicting something like it for several weeks. Security services hate being made to appear even remotely slow-witted.

Annie MacLean showed Rick up to his room and pointed out where Arnie and Kathy would be sleeping. "I don't suppose you need to sit outside their door, armed to the teeth, do you?" she said.

"Not with those beautiful dogs of yours in the house," he said. "But I probably will not shut my own door. I need to pay attention if they bark."

"If you leave your door open, they'll all be on your bed," she said.

"Ma'am. There's two things I'm real good at: that's dogs and horses. They won't bother me."

"Well, I noticed they all clustered around your feet downstairs . . . funny thing about Labradors, they always know who likes them."

"I got a couple back home in Kentucky," said Rick. "Black like yours. They wander in and out of the stallion boxes, and I'm amazed they never get kicked."

"Well, you have full permission to kick them off if they invade your bed," she replied. "Come down for dinner at around eight-fifteen. It's a warm evening; Iain and Arnie will both wear polo shirts, no jackets."

Rick stared through his bedroom window at the long view down the lawn and across to the far shore of the loch. He knew Admiral Morgan was also sleeping on this side of the house, and with the all-night guard posted outside, he doubted any would-be assassin could get anywhere near him, not from this side.

At dinner, he was questioned about his forthcoming role as head of Arnold's security and told them frankly, from what he had seen, it would be just about impossible to hit the admiral within the confines of the house.

"So far as I can tell, this is likely to be an urban operation, where your gun is not the priority. In big cities like Edinburgh, you need your brain, you need to be quick, observant, on top of your game.

"I've read the Scotland Yard report on the Ritz Hotel murder, and I'm left with one thought—someone fired that rifle from that building across the street, so the window to the room must have been open.

"The sniper would have been leaning on the window ledge, and the rifle barrel would have been jutting out when it was fired. Nobody saw it. All I can say is, a Navy SEAL, on guard duty, would have seen it and blown the guy's head off, no questions asked. I would have seen it, because I would have known what I was looking for."

"You may find it's rather more difficult to react like that in England than it is in the back streets of Baghdad or Kabul," said Admiral MacLean.

"Sir," replied Rick, "I am reliably briefed that in this case, the British police, the military, and the government are in agreement with the President of the United States. There will be no questions asked. If an assassin tries his luck, my task is to capture or kill him, whichever is the most expedient."

"I presume you are an expert in unarmed combat?" asked Annie MacLean.

"Every Navy SEAL is," answered Rick. "And usually, if your assailant has managed to get close enough to aim a gun at his target, there is no time to fire accurately at him. You need a swift physical response, which may be deadly, but is usually not too late."

"You lead an exciting life, Commander," said Lady MacLean.

"This is kid's stuff to him," interjected Arnie. "I'll deny ever saying this, but Commander Hunter and his men once blew up an entire oil refinery in Iran. Now that was exciting."

Rick chuckled. "Can't live on past glories, sir. Right now I have to make certain that Admiral and Mrs. Morgan come to no harm in the city of Edinburgh. I understand you will be returning to the United States immediately after the Military Tattoo?"

"Guess they forced that on me," replied Arnold. "Wrecked my vacation, worried Kathy to death, and ordered me home immediately. It's amazing what I have to put up with."

"I hear you're taking the salute at the Tattoo on Tuesday night, sir?" said Rick. "And that's where we need to be very careful. Two things I did want to ask: How dark is it in there? And how many people are expected?"

"There are around ten thousand each night for three weeks," said Lady MacLean. "And mostly it takes place on the main Castle Esplanade. Sometimes it is quite dark with spotlights on the performers, like a theatre. But for the main event, the demonstration by the Marine Commandoes, almost all the lights will be lowered."

"What's it like in the Royal Box where Admiral Morgan will be?"

"The lights are always on there," Lady MacLean continued. "Subdued lights from the rear, but brighter than the other seating areas."

"So we have a darkened stadium where no one can see anything except the Royal Box and the people in it?" said Rick. "Hmmmmm."

"Well, not exactly. The spotlights constantly illuminate various parts of the performance, all over the castle, especially down on the Esplanade where the massed military bands will be playing."

"Is access to the Royal Box easy? I mean, can anyone get in?"

"Absolutely not," said Sir Iain. "There are armed guards at both entrances and all around. You need a VIP ticket to get anywhere near."

"I'd like to scout the place out for a while tomorrow, if that would be okay," said Rick.

"No problem. The helicopter will pick you up here in the morning."

900 Sunday 5 August
Glasgow

Ravi and Shakira checked out of the Millennium Hotel early, drove out to the M-8 motorway through West Lothian, and set off for Edinburgh, a distance of forty-six miles. They arrived before 10 A.M., and Ravi, who had read every word written about the Edinburgh International Festival in the past week, drove straight to the Caledonian Hilton at the end of Princes Street behind the castle.

Brimming with confidence, he parked outside, asked the doorman to keep a watch on the car for a few minutes, and walked inside to speak to the receptionist.

"Good morning," he said politely. "I'm very sorry to trouble you, but I'm Captain Martin, ADC to the CO of 42 Marine Commando. Could you possibly tell me, are the head honchos of the Military Tattoo staying here this week? I appear to have lost the boss."

The girl behind the desk laughed, and replied, "Sadly not this year, sir, though they often do. But I believe they are all in the new Cavendish Hotel, right on Princes Street and closer to the castle than we are."

"I'm grateful," said Ravi. "You've probably saved my career."

Back outside, Ravi once more settled behind the wheel and drove into Princes Street, moving slowly along Edinburgh's main thoroughfare until he saw the high rise of the Cavendish on the left-hand side. He pulled over around a hundred yards from the main entrance, and Shakira jumped out, wearing an inexpensive black dress and carrying a large too-expensive handbag which she hoped no one would notice.

She walked up to the doorman and asked him who to see about a job. "Go straight to reception, young lady," he said, "and ask to see Mrs. Robertson. She's the undermanager."

Shakira did as she was told, and five minutes later was sitting in a small first-floor office with a stern, neatly dressed Scottish lady of around fifty, Janet Robertson, gray-haired, currently at her wits' end with staff shortages in the busiest month of the year.

She was polite but businesslike. "Have you experience?" she asked. And, seeing Shakira nod, proceeded to ask her in which department she would like to work.

"We have vacancies in housekeeping and room service, and we need two waitresses in the restaurant, and in the residents' lounge. But we do need references."

"I can do anything, and I have references," said Shakira. "I've worked in several hotels, in Ireland, London, and the United States."

"Do you mind shift work? That's evenings and early mornings."

"Not at all."

"Do you require room and board?"

"No. I'm living locally with my sister."

Mrs. Robertson had already noted Shakira's neat appearance and respectful manner, and she scarcely looked at her Irish passport in the name of Colleen Lannigan, nor at the reference from a central London bar in Covent Garden.

"Very well, let's give it a try, shall we?" said Mrs. Robertson. "I'd like you to start as a maid on the twelfth floor, where we are very short of help. And this evening, if possible, I'd like you to assist in room service.

"As a nonresident, we'll pay you £10 an hour, plus time-and-a-half for anything over seven hours' work a day, not including a lunch break. We of course provide whatever meals you require while you are on duty. There's a staff canteen on the basement level."

"Thank you very much, Mrs. Robertson," said Shakira. "Will I require a uniform?"

"Absolutely," said the Mother Superior of the Cavendish Hotel. "I'll call the housekeeper and she'll arrange everything. Just take the service elevator to the twelfth floor, and someone will meet you."

A half hour passed, and, as arranged, Ravi drove away. He took a spin around the enormous castle, set on its mighty black volcanic rock, and stopped to make a phone call, direct to the Cavendish Hotel.

He managed to book one of the last rooms, on the third floor of the hotel, thanks to a Sunday-morning cancellation. Then he found a parking lot and walked through Edinburgh's Old Town into the precincts of the castle, across the Esplanade to the public entrance. There were two armed military guards on duty, watching carefully as members of the public paid to see the huge assemblage of historic buildings inside the ramparts of the twelfth-century fortress.

The castle has in its time been a royal palace, a military garrison, and a state prison. The Crown of Scotland is on display in the palace building, where, in the sixteenth century, Mary Queen of Scots gave birth to James, the future king of both Scotland and England.

Ravi, however, was not remotely interested in Scottish history, however rich and turbulent it may have been. Ravi was here to scout out the security that surrounded the Military Tattoo, because herein rested his last chance to kill Arnold Morgan, before the United States government would surely compel the admiral to return to Washington.

He paid £10 for his ticket and walked through onto the roadway that climbs right through the castle, way up to the high ramparts, from which there is the most spectacular view over the city. Ravi trudged all the way up to the One O'clock Gun, which is fired with a thunderous report every day except Sunday, frightening tourists to death.

Ravi walked the ramparts, past ancient St. Margaret's Chapel, along the Argyle Battery, past the Governor's House and the prison and the Great Hall. He stared down over the great curved front of the Half-Moon Battery where, in the sixteenth century, artillery was ranged to defend the eastern wing of the castle. It was steep. Everywhere was steep. The castle rose up, constructed layer after layer onto its towering black crags, until it dominated the city. And this week, at least, it was as heavily patrolled as a U.S. Army garrison in Baghdad five years ago.

Everywhere Ravi walked, there were young soldiers, on duty, sometimes in groups, sometimes just in pairs. And all of them carried the standard weapon of the British Army, the SA80 semi-automatic short-barreled rifle, with its 25-round magazine, 5.56mm caliber.

As a pure precaution, Ravi stopped as he walked by and attempted, with only marginal success, to affect the wide-eyed blank stare of the truly ignorant.

"Excuse me," he said to the Scots Guards corporal. "Is that gun loaded with real bullets?"

"Aye, sir, it is."

"Well, that's very dangerous," replied Ravi.

"That's the general idea," said the corporal.

Ravi shook his head in mock exasperation, and continued his walk, going down now, back to the public entrance. And as he did so, a red Royal

Navy helicopter circled briefly above the castle and slowly dropped down to land on the wide concourse behind the barracks, the biggest building in the ancient stone complex.

The area had been temporarily cleared by the military for the arrival of the American Navy commander, Rick Hunter, in company with Lady MacLean, the all-powerful chair of the entire Festival and Rick's personal guide for the next hour.

Annie MacLean had made the decision to land on the higher level in order to point out to Rick the precise layout of the Tattoo. She showed him a view of the Esplanade from the heights, the temporary grandstands, and in particular the Royal Box where they would all be seated on Tuesday evening.

She showed him the huge sloping walls of the Half-Moon Battery, down which the warriors of 42 Marine Commando would abseil, before making a final descent to the Esplanade for their formation and finale.

Rick did not love it. "The whole place will be in darkness during this time?" he asked.

"Everywhere. Except for the Royal Box," she told him. "The military will spotlight the Marines as they climb down the walls to the lower levels. Their display is designed to show how they capture a fortified garrison."

Rick still did not love it, mainly because there was so much he would not be able to see. And Arnold, so far as he could tell, would be floodlit as he took the salute, and silhouetted in his seat for the rest of the time. The only aspect of the entire exercise that gave him any confidence was the heavy presence of armed guards, all highly trained military personnel.

The Navy SEAL had worked with the Brits before, and he knew how outstanding they were. Whichever way he looked at it, it would be damn near impossible to get at Admiral Morgan without getting apprehended or shot. Arnold would be accompanied at all times by five personal guards, including himself, and a phalanx of armed police.

Rick stood thoughtfully on the ramparts of the Half-Moon Battery, assessing the precise distance Arnold would be from the base of the wall and from the stands that had been erected along the flanks of the Esplanade.

He noted also that the gradient of the amphitheatre was a slight slope and the surface was uneven. He considered the possibility of an assassin running across the ground toward the admiral and dismissed it. Because, he decided, you could not do this with a pistol, you'd need a rifle, and if you produced one of those here, there was a good chance the guards would hit you with a hundred bullets before you hit the ground.

Anyone could sense the place was on high alert. And it seemed to Rick that Arnold would be safe here tomorrow night. But he still did not love it.

He and Lady MacLean walked back up to the helicopter, which immediately took off and headed west, back to Inveraray. Ravi Rashood, driving back to the Cavendish Hotel, saw it leave, climbing up over the city and accelerating away. He wondered, as any ex–SAS officer might, who was in it and why they had paid such a fleeting visit to Edinburgh Castle.

He checked into his room, knowing it was impossible to find Shakira. This place was as big as the Kremlin, and he would have to wait until she located him. She knew either he was checked in here under the name of Captain Harry Martin, or he would leave her a note, addressed to Miss Colleen Lannigan (Cavendish staff).

There was a local map of Edinburgh and its environs, which Ravi studied carefully. He was looking north, along the great expanse of the wide estuary of the River Forth, known locally as the Firth of Forth. He checked the locations of Musselburgh and Port Seton, communities that were on the water, and as he did so, his bedside phone rang. Shakira said eleven words: *"They'll be on the top floor, all rooms overlooking Princes Street."* The line went dead.

Then he checked the Yellow Pages, found what he was seeking, and went downstairs out onto the sidewalk. Ravi crossed the street and stared up at the flat roof of the hotel, assessing the distance between the top of the wall that surrounded the roof to the line of windows on the sixteenth floor. Right now, Ravi was into a possible Plan B, because he was having doubts about his capacity to successfully hit Admiral Morgan and then make a getaway, in the face of that hard-trained security force in the castle.

And with this in mind, he took a half-hour drive out to the coast. He pulled into Port Seton, hoping the marine store was open, assuming it would be on a busy boating Sunday in August.

It was not only open, it was crowded with yachtsmen and power boaters buying all kinds of equipment: dock lines, cleats, lifejackets, winch handles, halyards, and varnish. After a twenty-minute wait, Ravi reached the counter, behind which were large reels of line of varying thickness, all made of modern white nylon, soft to the touch but very strong, with a pattern in either red or blue.

He ordered two 35-foot lengths of the second largest gauge, and asked for a shackle to be spliced onto one end of each line. The marine store assistant called out "*Splice, Jock!*" and a young seaman came over and slowly formed an unbreakable join, working in front of a small flame, into which he held the rough end of the line and watched the nylon melt into a mass, which he bound with white tape.

"Don't forget, sir," said the assistant, "if you need to cut this stuff, you need a flame to weld the end like that."

Ravi nodded, and also purchased a safety harness, the kind seamen wear in bad weather with the shackle clipped onto the boat to avoid being swept overboard and lost. He also bought a half dozen of the metal rope clips that climbers use to pay out the line in short takes.

Expertly, the assistant slung each line into a three-foot-long coil and then wrapped the end tight around the "throat," and handed them to Ravi holding just the shackles. Ravi bought a small inexpensive seaman's bag and paid in cash. His equipment had cost him the thick end of £150.

He returned to the city center and parked the Audi in the open-air lot, close to the castle. He walked back to the Cavendish and waited for Shakira to find him in his room.

Two hours later, she arrived and flopped down on the bed, exhausted. "I was told they were short of staff on the twelfth floor," she said. "But I didn't know they were *that* short. I've made about a thousand beds, with only one other girl. I didn't even get a turn on the vacuum cleaner."

Ravi laughed and kissed her. And then he said, with great seriousness, "Shakira, time may be running out for us. I have two plans, both of them highly dangerous. Right now I need to attend to the details, and then try to formulate an escape route. There are several tasks you must complete."

And then, somewhat darkly, he added, "In the end, it may be up to you."

It was 4:30 P.M. now, and Shakira had to report to room service. "I won't see you until ten o'clock," she said. "Where will you go now?"

"I'm going to the Mosque for evening prayers," he said. "These are difficult days, and I need a guiding light. And there is only one light."

1600 Monday 6 August
Inveraray

A third police car pulled into the MacLeans' drive, and a detective sergeant disembarked, holding what looked like dry cleaning, three plastic-covered hangers containing police clothing—dark blue trousers, royal blue sweater with insignia, two white shirts, blue tie, and a bright yellow rain jacket. In his left hand, the sergeant carried a white plastic bag containing shoes, leather belt, and peaked uniform cap with its badge and familiar black-and-white checked headband.

He walked to the door and told Angus they were for Commander Rick Hunter. Ten minutes later, the U.S. Naval officer walked out disguised as a Lothian and Borders police constable.

He carried with him his rifle, in the holder that made it look like fishing rods, and his traveling bag. He waved a brief good-bye to everyone in the household and climbed into the police car. Sir Iain stepped out to see him off and called, "See you tomorrow, Rick."

The police driver pulled out onto the main road and set off on the hundred-mile drive to Edinburgh. The helicopter was considered too ostentatious for an operation as clandestine as this.

They arrived at the Cavendish Hotel a little after 7 P.M., and Rick spoke briefly to the receptionist, who summoned a porter to escort him to the sixteenth floor. The police car waited right outside the main door.

Rick checked his watch, and walked with the porter along to room 168, a large double bedroom that had an open connecting door to the biggest suite in the hotel. This was situated on the corner of the building and was composed of two large bedrooms with bathrooms, and a substantial drawing room suitable for entertaining sixteen people. This was the room that led into Commander Hunter's bedroom. It formed what could be, at any time, a three-bedroom suite, suitable for visiting royalty and heads of state, with personal staff and protection.

The porter asked Rick if he would be needing him further, but Edinburgh's newest policeman declined and handed over a £10 tip, which the porter thought was not too bad, for a policeman.

Rick wandered through the rooms, wondering which bedroom he should allocate to Arnold and Kathy, and which to Sir Iain and Annie.

TO THE DEATH 367

The five of them were very much on first-name terms by now, the Scottish aristocrats having long accepted Rick as one of their own—educated, multimillionaire horse breeder, and perfectly mannered naval officer.

It had been agreed that he alone would decide who slept where, since he alone carried the ultimate responsibility to ensure that no one murdered Arnold Morgan. On this, his initial recce, he checked that the windows were fastened, checked the door locks, and checked that the phone lines were all working.

Then he called down to inform the desk that no staff was allowed anywhere near the big suite without his express permission and his personal attendance. That included maids, the housekeeper, room service, and anyone else who might wish to attend the two admirals and their wives when they arrived the following day.

He put his rifle in the wardrobe, hung up his jacket and civilian trousers, and placed the DO NOT DISTURB sign on the door handles out in the corridor. Then he placed his Sig Sauer service revolver in his belt, took the elevator down, and climbed into the back of the police car.

"Over to the castle, sir?" asked the driver.

"Thank you," said Rick. "Main entrance."

The opening ceremony at 9 P.M. was still an hour away when Rick arrived, but the crowds were already gathering to watch the stirring massed pipers and drummers of the most revered Scottish regiments march down the Esplanade. Rick was rather looking forward to it.

But right now he was very preoccupied. He walked around to the Royal Box and sat down in the center of the front row, staring out at the grandstands, trying to assess where an assassin might position himself for a long-range shot at the admiral.

He established there would be either a police or military presence on duty at both ends of the rows of seats. It would plainly be impossible for anyone to smuggle in a rifle, not under the eyes of these trained security men.

Privately Rick thought a shot from the higher battlements would somehow be too far in the dark, however well the Royal Box was lit. And, anyway, the entire place was crawling with military guards, every fifty yards on the ramparts, all around the castle. Christ, he could see them from here.

He walked the length of the left-hand grandstand to check whether it went right to the end wall of the Esplanade. It didn't, and there was a throughway between the last line of seats and the wall with two military policemen on duty, demanding to see people's seating tickets.

He found it almost impossible to find a spot from which to fire a high-powered rifle anywhere beyond the Esplanade and the grandstands. He was finding it difficult to find anywhere in the entire castle environs where anyone could produce a rifle without being arrested in a matter of moments.

Rick went back to the Royal Box and sat down in one of the empty seats along the front row. He watched the huge crowd growing as they took their places around the arena. The VIPs were arriving now, among them two high-ranking generals, plus the Royal Navy's First Sea Lord, who would take the salute tonight.

The Tattoo began with a rousing piece of music played by the band of the Royal Navy, "Fanfare for the First Sea Lord." And then the massed pipes and drums of the Scottish regiments led the huge parade through the entrance onto the Esplanade. The Guards, the Highlanders, the Borderers were followed by the bands of the Irish Guards, the Royal Gurkha Rifles, and the Rats of Tobruk.

The ancient sounds of the Scottish marching songs split the night sky above the capital city. The haunting strains of "The Campbells Are Coming" evoked proud reminders of the Siege of Lucknow in 1857, when General Sir Colin Campbell, at the head of 4,500 Scottish troops, marched across the Punjab to defeat 60,000 Indian rebels besieging the British residency.

It was a superb military pageant, and Rick ignored the unease he felt at the end of the performance when the First Sea Lord stood up in his seat to take the salute. Rick too stood up with the crowd and joined the applause, understanding that every Scotsman in the arena felt an age-old rising of pride in a warlike past.

The U.S. Navy commander thought it was terrific, and he was almost relaxed when the Royal Marines of 42 Commando began their display, dozens of them abseiling down the castle walls, then forming up and firing their rifles into the air to signify a successful assault on a fortified stronghold. Rick had already checked. Blank rounds.

He stayed until the end, watching and applauding the Russian Cossack State Dance Company, the massed bands of the Royal Marines with their

"Celebration of Trafalgar," and the 600-strong massed military bands, with pipes and drums, playing their world-famous Edinburgh Tattoo specialties "Mull of Kintyre" and "Caledonia."

For the finale, before a Royal Navy Guard of Honor, the entire thousand-strong cast of musicians played "Auld Lang Syne," and, as the sacred Scottish notes died away, the Lone Scots Guards Piper appeared high on the battlements of the castle, and played a pibroch lament, the slow melancholy classical music of the bagpipes.

This effectively brought the house down, and Rick stood up and cheered as it ended. And then he stood transfixed as a mighty roll on the drums signified the moment when the great throng of musicians and serving soldiers began the March Out, in strict formation, kilts swirling, to the drums and bagpipes playing "Scotland the Brave."

Commander Richard Hunter, a career U.S. Navy officer, had never before seen anything so perfect, so moving, and so inordinately impressive. He'd almost forgotten why he was there, forgotten about the policeman's uniform he wore, forgotten about the grave threat to the life of the great American he was sworn to protect.

He stood and surveyed the happy crowd leaving the area, and then he walked down among them, back down the Esplanade to the main entrance and through the gap between the left grandstand and the end wall. He found himself thinking, "If I'd just shot Admiral Morgan, I'd bolt straight through here and make for the street in this big crowd . . . that would mean I'd need to wait until the very end. . . ."

He found his police car and was driven back to the Cavendish. He returned to his room and stripped off his yellow police raincoat and the dark blue sweater. He put on his regular sportcoat and returned downstairs to the busy second-floor grill room and ordered himself an Aberdeen steak and a Jack Daniel's on the rocks.

Rick did not notice another lone diner sitting close by, a man in a black T-shirt and a brown suede jacket, sipping a Scotch whisky and eating a chicken sandwich. He too had been to the Military Tattoo, but had spent his time high in the upper regions of the castle, just checking guard movements and watching the Marines form line of battle before their mock assault on the great Scottish fortress.

Both men, on this night, would sleep uneasily. And the issue for both of them was timing.

1500 Tuesday 7 August

The MacLeans and the Morgans drove away from Inveraray in convoy. A police car led the way, followed by Sir Iain's Range Rover, and then Arnold's four personal bodyguards in a Royal Navy staff car, with a second police car bringing up the rear.

They drove around the lochs and finally picked up the M-8 motorway, which took them all the way into Edinburgh, approaching from the southwest. The police did not use lights or sirens, preferring to make the journey as unobtrusively as possible. They covered the hundred miles in three hours and arrived at the Cavendish Hotel a little after six in the evening.

Two police officers escorted Sir Iain and Annie, Arnold and Kathy, and the four bodyguards to the sixteenth floor of the hotel, where there was just one maid on duty, using a noisy vacuum cleaner at the beginning of their corridor.

She looked up as the party approached and said quietly, "I'm sorry about this—we were running very late today. I'll be finished in two minutes."

One of the policemen replied, "Okay, lassie. No problem." Shakira, in the middle of her dinner break, carried on cleaning the carpet diligently.

They reached the door of the big suite, marked 170–172, and the four bodyguards entered first, moving swiftly between the rooms, checking cupboards and bathrooms. When they went through the open connecting door to Rick's room, they found the big SEAL commander with his feet up, reading the racing pages of *The Scotsman*.

"Hello, sir," said Al Thompson. "Taking it easy for a while?"

"Trying to," said Rick. "Everyone here?"

"Yup," replied Al. "We're just checking out the area. We'll have two men outside the door at all times. We're all staying on this floor."

"Sounds good," said Rick. "How about tonight, when the admiral takes the salute at the Tattoo?"

"We'll all be over there, sir. I was going to ask you about deployment. I'll station the guys wherever you want."

"Okay, let's get everyone settled, and then you and I can take a look at this map of the castle. I guess you'll want the guys on station by around 8 P.M. Admiral Morgan wants to be there at ten minutes before nine, just before the start."

"I'll leave one man with him permanently, and there'll be six cops, plus a military escort, to walk him and Mrs. Morgan to their seats."

"That ought to do it," said Rick. "But I'll tell you something, Al. That darned castle's a big place, and most of it's going to be in darkness. The security's red-hot, as you'd expect, but the place gives me the goddamned creeps."

Al Thompson laughed. "We'll be all right, sir. I'll see you in a minute."

Rick could hear the two admirals and their wives moving in. He heard the luggage arrive on a trolley outside in the corridor. Then Arnold popped his head around the corner and said, "Hi, Rick. How was it last night? Good display?"

Rick stood up. "Admiral," he said, "it was fantastic. So much tradition, and marvelously well-done."

"Was it mostly music?"

"I guess it was. But there were fabulous displays by the troops, and Russian Cossacks dancing, and God knows what else. The military bands were great, pipes, drums, and bagpipes. I'm really looking forward to seeing it again."

"Don't forget about me, for chrissakes!" chuckled Arnold, before he disappeared next door. "I'd sure hate to get shot while you're dancing the fucking Highland fling or whatever the hell they call it."

"No chance of that, sir. I'm all over it."

"See you later, pal," said Arnie as he left.

At 7:30, a general evacuation of the sixteenth floor began. Al Thompson left for the castle with two of his men, all three of them armed, by special permission of MI-5 and the Lothian Police Force. They were accompanied by four police officers, men who had been on duty at the Inveraray house.

Forty-five minutes later, the MacLeans and the Morgans left with one bodyguard and Rick Hunter, who was now in his full police uniform, his CAR-15 automatic rifle loaded with a thirty-round magazine and slung over his shoulder. Four police officers met them at the elevator, and they all stepped on board.

The doors slid silently shut and the elevator began its descent. Thus no one saw the same maid, carrying a small inexpensive seaman's bag, use a master key to open the door up to the roof. Sixteen floors below, the maintenance chief had not yet missed his key.

Meanwhile, over at the castle, high on the west side, General Ravi Rashood was in hiding. He had been there since mid-afternoon, sitting quietly behind a low wall, out of sight of the security team responsible for moving out the paying visitors before 6:30 in preparation for the evening.

He was situated in one of the loneliest parts of the battlements, and had no intention of moving until the light began to fail. When it did, at around 8:15, he reached for his combat knife, which, as ever, was tucked into his belt in the small of his back. He waited until the guards had passed, and then moved quickly to the high wall of what he now regarded as his operational center.

Way above him was a powerful light, a temporary fixture, designed to illuminate the entire area. Tonight it would not function. The electric wire that fed it was fixed loosely to the stonework, and Ravi severed it swiftly. Then he slipped unobtrusively back to his hideout, unseen and unobserved. It was growing darker now, especially in this area on the high west side, where there was no light.

For their short journey to the castle, Lady MacLean and her party traveled in a big black Royal Navy staff car. There was a police car in the lead, and another right behind, in which the bodyguard and Rick were traveling.

They turned right off Princes Street, into the side streets of Old Town, and arrived at the castle on time at ten minutes before nine. The military escort from the Scots Guards was in place as the car drew up, and Admiral Morgan and Kathy were led up to the Royal Box with Sir Iain and Annie walking right behind them.

Rick Hunter, his rifle still slung over his shoulder, walked between the two couples, and four Scottish policemen followed. Arnold's four personal bodyguards now closed in and positioned themselves strategically close to the front row as the two admirals took their seats in the center of the VIP line.

By now, the Royal Box was filling up. The provost of Edinburgh University and his wife sat directly behind the admirals, flanked by the chief superintendent of the Lothian Police and the commanding officer of 42 Commando, which would again present their display. Another ten city and military dignitaries filled the remainder of the seats.

At this time, just before the Tattoo began, Ravi was just above the new barracks, standing back, out of sight in the shadows. He was still there when the massed bands opened the evening's proceedings with, in Admiral Morgan's honor, "The Fanfare to the United States Navy," specially composed by the conductor of the Royal Marine Bands for the occasion.

Ravi was not, however, interested in the music. He was concerned only with the guards who were in position along the walls, on this night of the Tattoo's most rigorous security alert ever.

He was unarmed, except for his knife and a small but weighty glass paperweight, which he carried in his jacket pocket. He was dressed as a perfectly normal tourist, except for his shoes . . . well, boots, which were black and laced high beneath his dark gray trousers.

Ravi was waiting for the guards to send for tea, a procedure he had watched four times on the previous night. The complete guard detail was four men, but every half hour they met, high up on the western ramparts. And that was when one of them walked down to fetch four cups of tea from the military canteen, set up temporarily next to the old hospital buildings.

And now he waited, watching for the single soldier to break away and begin the walk down to the canteen. The Tattoo had been running for exactly fifteen minutes when the four guards came together. They chatted for two or three minutes, and then one of them turned around and began to stride down the hill, into the now-darkest area of the castle.

The soldier was humming along with the music when Ravi burst out of the shadows like a panther, running toward his prey, coming in from the left, but from the back. He swung back his right arm and, with a stupendous display of strength, smashed the paperweight into the guard's head—right into the brain's critical nerve center behind the ear.

The heavy glass weight obliterated the protective skull bone, and the young man, who had only yesterday informed the Hamas chief that his rifle was indeed loaded with live bullets, crumbled to the ground. Stone dead.

Ravi, working in almost complete darkness thanks to the missing light, ripped off the man's combat jacket, undid the belt, and tore off the loose trousers. He grabbed the man's rifle and his woolly hat. Then he lifted the guard under the armpits and heaved him straight over the wall. It was a fifty-foot drop to the rocks and undergrowth that would surely obscure the body until well into the morning. Ravi heard the twigs snap as the Scots guardsman thudded into bushes.

Ravi raced back into the shadows with his new combat kit, and pulled it on over his street clothes, making certain that his combat boots, purchased in a local army surplus store, could now be plainly seen.

He pulled on his leather driving gloves and set off on the twenty-minute walk down to the Half-Moon Battery where the Marine commandoes were setting up their abseil ropes for their daredevil descent to the Esplanade. Ravi did not join them. Instead he hung back, with his rifle slung over his shoulder like a backwoodsman, or indeed an SAS officer going into combat.

The minutes passed and the military displays continued to rousing applause. And then over the loudspeaker came the words—*There will now be a demonstration by the commandos of 42 Royal Marine, who will display their versatile skills and efficiency in the capture of a fortified enemy stronghold—Ladies and Gentlemen—the Marines in action!*

The lights in the stadium were dulled, and lancing spotlights lit up the high walls above the west end of the Esplanade. Every eye in the grandstand was on the rampart that circled the Half-Moon Battery. It was just possible to see, in the spotlights, the ropes snaking out over the battlements, down the first sixty-foot-high sheer stone wall to the flat rocky promontory. Then there were more ropes over the lower wall, dropping down over the buildings onto the Esplanade.

Ravi stayed back in the shadows, when suddenly there was movement. The first four commandoes ran for the battlements, and, on the word of the commander, grabbed the ropes with their gloved hands, swung backward over the wall, and dug in with their boots. Then they leaned back and pushed out, dropping down, down, down with each kick off the stone surface, the rope sliding expertly through their grips.

It was a breathtaking example of high-caliber soldiering as, four by four, the men bounced down the wall, crossed the rocks at top speed, then abseiled down the last section to the ground. Back at the top, Ravi waited. The formations were slightly more ragged now, simply because some of the troops had been faster than others, and the ropes supported uneven numbers across the battery wall as each man descended.

There were only six men left up there in the darkness, and Ravi suddenly emerged from the shadows and ran in toward the battlements with the others. He had selected his rope and arrived simultaneously with two others.

"Righto, mate, after you," one of them snapped, barely looking at the Hamas chief.

And Ravi grabbed the rope. He'd done this a hundred times in the SAS and, perhaps more expert than all these young commandoes, he swung over the battlements and bounced his way down, backward, the way a trained Special Forces officer is expected to complete this discipline.

Seconds later, he was on the rocks, running over to the last descent and abseiling onto the Esplanade. In front of him, the troops were lining up on the ground. Ravi moved back against the wall. There were essentially two differences between him and the rest. He was not lying flat on the ground, and his standard issue SA80 semi-automatic rifle was loaded with live ammunition, as opposed to the blanks the demonstration team would fire.

The last two men were down, and the subdued backlighting up ahead on the Royal Box was still silhouetting Admiral Morgan, sitting in the front row, four seats from the left. The VIPs were standing now, applauding the breathtaking display. Ravi could see Admiral Morgan, with Sir Iain to his right and Kathy in her green linen suit to his left.

Commander Rick Hunter was standing away to the right, on the end of the front row, when the first line of Marines opened fire into the air, demonstrating their opening assault on the enemy.

Rick's mind raced. He had always hated this darkened castle, with his man plainly visible out in front. A thousand instincts honed on the battlefield with his brave and beloved SEALs crowded into his thoughts. He braced himself for the attack, thinking only that this stadium was right now in darkness, and men were firing rifles and he could not see them, and he had no idea who was shooting at what.

Ravi Rashood, two hundred yards away, steadied himself on the wall, and, from out of the night, he aimed his SA80 directly at Admiral Arnold Morgan's chest.

He held his breath and pressed the trigger. But Rick was about a hundredth of a second faster. He bounded two strides forward and launched himself sideways across the front of the Royal Box. He hit Arnold Morgan with a full-blooded rugby tackle that flattened the great man to the floor. They hit Kathy on the way down and flattened her too. Rick tried desperately to protect the admiral, raising himself and instinctively covering Morgan's body with his own.

Women screamed. The gunfire continued. The police ran in to break up what looked like a fight between two Americans. And as the guns were finally silenced, everyone stood up and dusted themselves off.

No one spoke, but Arnold and Rick could see a line of 5.56mm bullets studded into the back of Arnold's seat. Directly behind, the provost of Edinburgh University, covered in blood, was slumped dead in his chair.

Rick helped Kathy to her feet. Neither she nor Arnold was hurt, but they were both very shaken. Arnold stared in disbelief at the bullets lodged in his chair. The police called for an ambulance, and the main lights came on. An announcement was made that owing to an unfortunate incident, the remainder of the Tattoo had been called off because of the suspected murder of the provost of Edinburgh University.

The 10,000-strong crowd was told to leave in an orderly manner and that either their tickets would be renewed or their money refunded.

And down behind the left-hand grandstand, in the dark, under the seats, Ravi was tearing off his army clothes and returning to civilian life. As suspected by Commander Hunter, he had bolted through that gap between the grandstand and the back wall. And now he dumped the trousers, jacket, and hat into a trashcan and walked out with everyone else, taking a circuitous route around to Princes Street. For the moment, he abandoned the Audi and walked back to the Cavendish, wearing his suede jacket, with the short-barreled rifle tucked underneath, half down his trousers, out of sight.

He had missed for the second time, and he knew it. He had seen the schemozzle in the front row of the Royal Box, seen the admiral go down just as he had fired. For a split second he'd thought the bullet had hit home, but Special Forces commanders have an instinct about these things. And in his heart he knew he'd missed the admiral.

The important thing, however, was that he was still free, on the loose and able to fight another day. Except that, in this particular case, it would be this day. He said hello to the doorman and headed straight up to his room, hoping to hell Shakira would contact him and finalize their arrangements.

It was after 10:30 now, and Shakira took half an hour to call. Ravi answered the phone and she just said, "They are all arriving. I'll be down."

Two minutes later she let herself into the room, having just seen Admiral Morgan and his wife, and having ascertained that, again, her husband had missed the target for which they had both strived for so long.

"Darling," she said, "can we go home now? Let's just get away. We have the car, we can make it."

Ravi shook his head. "This is not a military mission," he said. "This is the sacred work of Allah. I cannot abandon it. I would burn in hell if I did that. We must complete what we began."

"But why? We've both tried so hard. Maybe this is not meant to be. Why can't we just go?"

Again, Ravi shook his head. "Is everything ready on the roof?" he asked.

"Yes, but I don't want you to go."

"Can't you see that I must?" And Ravi's voice began to rise. *"I have to kill him. He is the enemy of my people, the attack dog of the West, the sworn foe of the Prophet, the scourge of our armies. The admiral must die by my hand. . . ."*

Ravi was shouting now, and Shakira was frightened someone would hear. Worse yet, she was afraid of Ravi now, afraid he had lost all sense of reason.

"Go," he commanded her. "GO! And do the bidding of Allah, as I must. Now GO!"

He watched her walk through the door, and minutes later he followed her along the corridor to the fire escape. He took with him a balaclava and goggles he had bought in the same army surplus store where he purchased his boots.

He climbed the stone steps, fourteen floors, to the stairwell of the sixteenth. He was standing inside the door Shakira had opened earlier that evening. The last short flight of stone steps led to the roof. Ravi checked his watch; three minutes later, Shakira came in.

Ravi told her they were each precious messengers of Allah, and that this task tonight might be the last time they would see each other on this earth. They would, however, be united in the arms of Allah, who would surely welcome two of his finest Holy Warriors into everlasting paradise.

"Besides," he added in conclusion, "there is nothing here for us any more. Nowhere to go, to live. We'd be hiding for all the days of our lives. Tonight Allah will decide for us."

He put his arms around her and held her close. Together they'd risked everything for the *Jihad,* and now there seemed to be nothing left. For a while, Ravi had considered that Admiral Morgan was the one trapped in a corner. And that may have been true, but the corner he and Shakira were in was slower and more deadly.

He kissed her good-bye and said quietly, "Shakira, you know what to do. And if I can make this work tonight, we will still have a chance to escape. If I can't, we've had many wonderful years together, and Allah will unite us soon."

And with that, General Rashood climbed the stone steps to the roof, and there, standing hidden in the shadow of the air-conditioning unit, was the seaman's bag containing the dock lines and the harness. He fixed the ends around a thick water pipe which was cemented into the wall, and ran them both through their shackles.

He slipped the safety harness on and fastened it tightly, attaching it to the second line with the rock-climbers' clips which he could adjust on the way down, playing out the line. And then he waited for Shakira's call.

In the meantime, over at the castle, the police were trying to make up for lost time. They sent a detail to the Marine commando headquarters and checked every man who had gone over the wall. Everyone was present, every man still had his rifle, and every rifle was empty, having fired only blanks. The police stationed officers at every door, and they began to search people as they left the Tattoo.

Finally they had the CO summon the guard and conduct a roll call of the men who had been on duty. There was, of course, one missing, a 23-year-old Scots guardsman who had been armed with an SA80 semi-automatic, loaded.

This was a rifle with the precise same bullets that had been fired at the U.S. admiral and killed the provost. At 11:30 P.M., the police decided they had a suspect—a missing suspect, but still a suspect.

They posted a further guard detail on the Cavendish Hotel, with men again on duty on the sixteenth floor. Arnold's four-man bodyguard team was still working, and Rick elected to stay close to the admirals and their wives.

Right now they were having supper in the hotel grill, and no one felt like going to bed after the narrow escape from death Arnold had suffered.

"Jesus, Rick, you saved my life," he said. "Guess I owe you and Ramshawe together."

"You don't owe me anything, sir," replied the ex-SEAL. "It was an honor to carry out my duty."

"I guess I'm getting too old for these front-line politics," said the admiral. "And I think I might be getting stupid as well."

"I'd find that very hard to accept," said Sir Iain.

"Even if you took into consideration the very obvious truth, that young Jimmy Ramshawe has been trying to warn me for more than a month that this trip was a truly godawful idea?"

"But, Arnie," protested Annie MacLean, "you can't react to every wild theory that someone comes up with."

"No. I guess that's why I insisted on coming. It was as if I thought I could outsmart whoever these goddamned assassins were, no matter what the facts were telling me. Or at least were telling Ramshawe. I wasn't listening."

"It's often the way with very clever people," said Sir Iain. "They get so accustomed to being right, when everyone else is barking up the wrong tree, they end up thinking they can shape events just by their own intellect."

"I think it's sometimes called megalomania," interjected Kathy, smiling for the first time in several hours. "Right now, I think I'm having a nervous breakdown. Because whoever opened fire on Arnie is still out there."

Rick Hunter looked grim. He had shed his yellow police jacket, and it was currently lying on the banquette next to Kathy, covering up his CAR-15 rifle.

"He is still out there," agreed the former SEAL. "And I'm assuming he's still armed. We need to be very careful. I've called home, and the president has sent the 747 to pick us up at Edinburgh airport first thing tomorrow . . . we're out of here, sir, no ifs, ands, or buts. Pushing your luck is one thing—but this is crazy."

He glanced at his watch. It was thirty-five minutes after midnight. "It's around 7:30 in Washington," he said. "The boss said they'd be in the air from Andrews a half hour ago."

"What time do we cast off tomorrow morning?" asked Admiral Morgan.

"They expect to refuel Air Force One at 7 A.M.," replied Rick. "I guess we'll get on board around 7:30. Leave here at 6:30."

"Better get the hotel to give us a shout around five," said Arnie.

"No need, sir. I won't be sleeping," said Rick. "Not until they shut the door of that aircraft and take off for the U.S. of A."

"Well, I'm going to try to sleep," murmured Kathy. "But I'm so tired, and so on edge, I expect it will be impossible. It's not every day someone tries to blow your husband's head off. But I'm kinda getting used to it."

Everyone laughed. Nervously. And Rick summoned the two policemen standing inside the grill room doorway to step forward. Arnold's four bodyguards, sitting at the next table, were also on their feet.

Flanked by his protectors, Admiral Morgan made his way out to the lobby, with Rick leading the way, his rifle now openly in the firing position. Sir Iain, Annie, and Kathy walked behind Arnold, with the two policemen bringing up the rear, weapons drawn.

All eleven of them stepped into the elevator, and all eleven stepped out at the sixteenth floor. They walked in convoy down to room 168, where two more policemen were on duty. The security men went in first, swept the rooms for intruders, pronounced them "clean," and signaled for everyone to come in at last.

Rick announced that he would be on permanent duty and would like two of the bodyguards with him at all times. Al Thompson volunteered to share the first watch, and Rick detailed two policemen to stand guard in the corridor throughout the night.

Admiral MacLean, who had been subconsciously concerned that all this was giving Scotland one hell of a bad name, suggested that everyone gather for a farewell nightcap in the drawing room. "Who knows when we will all be together again?" he smiled.

Two of the policemen now went off duty and left the suite, walking along the corridor to the elevator. Neither of them was concerned by a maid pushing a trolley, about forty feet ahead of them. And neither of them saw her put a cell phone to her ear, which caused a soft ringtone high on the roof of the hotel.

Ravi was ready. His lines were clipped, harness tight, rifle loaded and ready. His balaclava was pulled down. He wore goggles, and he edged his way to the 180-foot precipice of the hotel roof.

Carefully he tested the lines, pulling on them hard, ensuring that they could take the strain; and then, for the second time this night, he leaned back and prepared to descend. He began slowly to abseil down the wall, until he was right above the line of windows on the sixteenth floor.

Right here he adjusted his clips, giving himself another six feet on both lines. Now poised high above Princes Street, he released the safety catch on the SA80, and said a final prayer to his God.

Admiral MacLean was just pouring four glasses of Scotland's finest, when Ravi, with a massive double-footed kick, launched himself, temporarily, into space, backward, until his lines stretched tight to the horizontal. At which point, gravity took over, and Ravi plummeted downward and inward.

He hit the windowpane with the soles of both boots and obliterated the glass. The huge force of his body weight carried him through to the window ledge, and his rifle was already spitting bullets.

Ravi could see Admiral Morgan, and he had eyes for no other. He rammed down his finger on the trigger, aiming straight at Arnold. The first bullet ripped into the admiral's shoulder, and a stain of blood seeped through his shirt.

And in that split second, Commander Rick Hunter swiveled and opened fire, pumping a line of 5.56-millimeter shells straight into the head of General Ravi Rashood, killing him instantly. Slowly he dropped his rifle and flopped backward through the window from whence he had come. His lines held fast, and the body of the Hamas C-in-C swung theatrically above Princes Street, steadily dripping blood on anyone who happened to be passing sixteen floors below.

The two policemen on duty outside the suite had now rushed inside, and Arnold's wound was being wrapped in towels from the bathroom. Rick insisted that Arnie rest on the bed while he, so often the medic on his SEAL teams, took a look at it, mostly to make sure the bullet was not still in the admiral's shoulder.

Arnold hung tough. "It's bullshit," he confirmed. "Stupid fucker couldn't even shoot straight. No wonder he kept missing. Anyway, who the hell is he?"

At which point there was a gentle tap on the door, and a voice said "Room service."

"Come in," snapped the policeman, who at the time was fetching more towels. But Rick Hunter, suddenly remembering his instructions to the front desk, looked up just in time to see a service cart, laden with food covered with a white tablecloth, being pushed through the door.

"STOP!" he yelled. "GET OUT—RIGHT OUT! RIGHT NOW!"

But the service cart kept coming, and the good-looking, dark-haired maid from along the corridor kept pushing. She made it into the room, and then slid her right hand under the tablecloth, and when it emerged it was gripping the deadly Austrian revolver provided by Prenjit Kumar.

No one noticed, except Rick Hunter. And Shakira never had time to take aim at Admiral Morgan. Rick blew her away, studding her perfect face with a line of bullets that knocked her backward into the corridor, blood pumping from her head.

"*JESUS CHRIST!*" bellowed Arnold Morgan. "*THIS IS LIKE THE FUCKING WILD WEST!*"

By now there were about twenty more policemen thundering along the corridor. Squad cars, blue lights flashing, sirens howling, were pulling up outside the hotel's main entrance. Lady MacLean had almost fainted with terror, and Kathy Morgan, as white as the tablecloth, was holding Arnold's hand while her husband griped and moaned about too much fuss being made about a small incident.

It was after two o'clock when the room was restored almost to normal. The body of Ravi was hauled back onto the roof, and once more his lines held fast. They wheeled Shakira out on a hospital gurney, and the police summoned a doctor and three nurses from nearby Edinburgh Royal Infirmary to tend Arnold's mercifully superficial wound.

"I'd prefer you to be treated in the hotel," the chief superintendent told America's former national security adviser. "I just have a feeling that if you step outside the door, another bloody gun battle might break out."

Admiral Morgan chuckled and said, gruffly, "Words of appreciation don't come naturally to me. But I would like to say 'thank you' for everything you all have done for me. I've been a very stubborn old man, and I've put a lot of good people in great danger."

"For the last time," responded Kathy. "Because you, Arnold Morgan, are retired—no more advising, no more telling presidents what to do. Your service to your country is over. That's if you want to stay married."

EPILOGUE

0730 Wednesday 8 August
Edinburgh Airport

Air Force One was refueled. The stairway was in place, and the Royal Navy staff car pulled up twenty yards away. Admiral Morgan, with his arm around Kathy, stepped out and climbed the steps to the giant presidential aircraft, right behind Commander Hunter. The four American agents were already on board.

The huge door was immediately closed and the Boeing 747 that bore the Presidential Seal of the United States of America began to push back, ready to taxi down to the end of the runway.

Little was yet known about the identity of the two would-be assassins, but the communications officer was instructed to stand by for information from the Lothian and Border Police in Edinburgh.

Somewhat poignantly, they were thirty thousand feet above West Cork at around 9 A.M. when the coded communiqué came through:

Dead assassin identified as Major Ray Kerman, deserted from Great Britain's Special Air Service eight years ago. Dead hotel maid believed to be his Palestinian wife, Shakira Rashood. Search of her luggage, in Kerman's room, revealed five different passports, one of them American in the name of Carla Martin. Both the deceased are believed to have been Islamic extremists operating on behalf of the terrorist organization, Hamas."

"Goddamned towelheads," growled Arnold Morgan.